Anne Douglas, after a varied life spent elsewhere, has made her home in Edinburgh, a city she has known for many years. She very much enjoys life in the modern capital, and finds its ever-present history fascinating.

She has written a number of novels, including *Catherine's Land*, *As The Years Go By*, *Bridge of Hope*, *The Butterfly Girls*, *Ginger Street*, *A Highland Engagement* and *The Road to the Sands*, all published by Piatkus.

D1391941

Author's Note

I should like to thank all those who helped me with my researches for this book, especially the City Library staff in the Edinburgh Room and the Scottish and Reference Libraries. Of the many books and papers consulted, I found the following particularly useful:

DORAN, Wendy & DARGIE, Richard
Change in Scotland, 1880-1980

JEFFREY, Andrew
This Present Emergency, 1992

McSHANE, Harry
Three Days That Shook Edinburgh, 1994. (1933)

NIMMO, Ian
Scotland At War, 1989

PINKERTON, Roy & WINDRAM, William J.
Mylne's Court, 1983

The files of *The Scotsman* newspaper.

A Land – a building of several storeys of separate
dwellings, communicating by a common stair

Sir Daniel Wilson,
Memorials of Edinburgh in the Olden Times

Beginnings

A merchant built it in 1701. A fine six-storeyed tenement on the site of an older house in Edinburgh's Lawnmarket. Not so tall as some of its neighbours, but spacious and grand. There were twelve apartments, two to each floor, all opening off a common stair, and Matthew Kerr, with an eye to the tenants he hoped to attract, had seen to it that everything was of the best quality. Woodwork, plasterwork, glazed windows – no expense had been spared.

Edinburgh at that time was small and overcrowded. Because of attacks in the past, mainly from the English, building had never extended beyond the old city walls. People of all classes – titled ladies, lawyers, doctors, wigmakers, milliners, lamp-lighters, grocers – all lived together in the 'lands', the tenements built high, though naturally the quality took the best rooms. The Lawnmarket, where Matthew had fitted in his new house, was at the top of the Royal Mile, below the Castle. Cloth had been sold there in the old days, and maybe country wares, but it was now considered a desirable place to live and Matthew had no trouble letting his apartments. The middle floors went to the gentry so that they might avoid the noise and smells of the street, while the remaining flats went to the less well-to-do and the ground floor was let to shops. Matthew himself lived on the second floor with his wife and family. So pleased was he with the success of his property venture, he decided to give his house a name.

'Now, madam, what do you think I should call it?' he asked his wife, a proud lady who had borne him seven children, all living.

'Why, Master Kerr, I should think it obvious!' she retorted, 'am I not named Catherine and is that not the finest name you could find?'

'Catherine's Land it shall be, then,' declared Matthew. And so it was.

In due course, Catherine's Land passed to Matthew's eldest son, then to his grandson, then to strangers. As landlord followed landlord, the house changed, as Edinburgh itself changed. Scotland had formed a union with England, the fear of attack had faded, the city was free to expand. All the land beyond the Castle became available, the Nor' Loch was drained, the New Town laid out. Down the Mound created by the excavations flitted the gentry and the middle classes to the fine new streets and crescents below, while the Old Town above was left to the poor. Decline was inevitable. Like its neighbours, Catherine's Land became a slum.

So it remained throughout the nineteenth century, until in 1905 new owners carried out a programme of restoration and modernisation. The roof was repaired, the windows replaced, kitchens, lavatories, gas and water systems were installed. By 1907, when a widow named Jean Ritchie rented one of the upper rooms, Catherine's Land had once again become a respectable place to live.

'Mind, there's still fights, there's still noise, and nobody cleans the stair,' Jean Ritchie wrote to her only son and his wife in Southampton, but she was happy enough. Until Will Ritchie, a merchant navy man, was killed in an accident on the docks.

After the funeral, Jean sat with her daughter-in-law, a sweet-faced girl named Madge, in the parlour of the little house Madge could no longer afford. Jean spoke of Catherine's Land.

'It'd no' be what you're used to,' she declared. 'But it's no' so bad, it's no' like some o' the places in the Old Town. And it'd be somewhere for you to live, somewhere to bring up Will's girls.'

The two women in their mourning looked at the three little girls in their black frocks and pinafores, Abby, nine, Jennie,

4

five and Rachel, four. Madge, picking up a piece of sewing, sighed and said nothing.

'Now, Madge, you've no kin and no money,' Jean went on, 'you tell me how you're going to manage!'

'I've my dressmaking,' Madge said after a pause.

'Aye, but what you need is family. You need support, you ken that's true. Now, if you came up to Catherine's Land, you'd have me. You could have two nice big rooms with your own WC and all your own things. The rent's no' much and I've a bit put by, I could help you till you settle.' Jean's dark eyes were steady. 'Come on, now, what do you say?'

Madge looked again at her girls, who sat quite still, watching.

'I don't know, Gramma Ritchie, I don't know.'

Jean let out a long sigh and sat back, folding her arms across her narrow chest. 'Och, I'll say no more,' she muttered. 'Come if you've a mind, Madge, I'll leave it to you.'

Madge threaded her needle. 'I've a mind,' she said, quietly, 'thank you, Gramma Ritchie.'

The three little girls looked down at their button boots.

That was in 1912. By 1920, after so many years in Catherine's Land, Madge could imagine no other life. Two of her daughters, though, dreamed of something very different.

Part One
1920

Chapter One

Dusk had come early to the city that October afternoon. Standing at the darkening windows, Madge Ritchie said, 'Seems like it'll be night before we've had our tea. Let's close the curtains, Abby.'

Now seventeen and tall, Abby had the Ritchies' dark good looks and a quick intelligent gaze. She was in service in Edinburgh's West End. This was her afternoon off, but she could never leave her place before two and had to be back by seven; it wasn't long. Joining her mother, she looked down from their third floor flat to the Lawnmarket below. The shops closed for Sunday were in darkness. Only the streetlamps, newly lit, shone through the gloom.

'Yes, let's shut out the night,' Abby agreed and drew the curtains.

Someone on the stair outside stumbled and fell against Madge's door. A voice swore, another laughed. The footsteps thundered on.

'Oh, dear, the Kemp boys coming home,' Madge murmured, 'or else the Rossies.'

'What a racket!' Abby said crossly. She had always hated the noise of Catherine's Land.

'You should hear them on Saturday nights,' called twelve-year-old Rachel from the table where she was covering grocer's paper with drawings of squares and triangles. She lifted a delicately pretty face to her sister. 'You don't know how lucky you are, Abby, to be away.'

'I don't know that I'd call it lucky to be in service,' Abby retorted.

'No indeed!' cried Madge. She was still sweet-faced, with wide blue eyes and fair hair worn in a loose knot. At thirty-six, she looked younger, at least when she was happy, as she always was on Sundays when Abby came home. Only Jennie her second daughter was like her. As Jennie came in now and began to argue with Rachel about clearing the table for tea, Madge quietly touched Abby's arm.

'You know I never wanted you to be a housemaid, Abby. It was only Gramma who was so keen. I mean, knowing Mrs Moffat, saying it was such a good place.'

'Oh, I know.' Abby gave a wry smile. 'Two print frocks and two black, all my food and twenty-nine pounds a year. What more could I want?'

'Oh, Abby!' Madge's face crumpled. 'I blame myself, I do. You were worth something better. Always so clever at school, such lovely reports!'

'Ma, please don't go on. It doesn't matter now.'

'But you know how it was – Gramma'd been so good . . .'

They were both silent, remembering.

'What we'd have done without her, I don't know,' Madge murmured. 'I'll never forget what she did for us when your dad died. But she's gone now, and you don't have to stay on at Glenluce Place, Abby, you could find something else.'

'Not what I want, though. I'm not ready to move yet.'

'Not ready? What do you mean?'

'Well, I'm studying, Ma. When I can. I'm teaching myself book-keeping.'

Madge's face lightened. 'Book-keeping? Why, Abby, that's wonderful! You'll be able to get an office job!'

Abby shrugged. 'Maybe. I'll get something better than housework, anyway.' She moved purposefully towards her sisters. 'Rachel, come on now, let Jennie have the table. And you might help to set it yourself. I'd like some tea before I go.'

'Oh, Abby, I wish you didn't have to go at all!' cried Jennie. 'Only one afternoon a week, it's not much to spend with us.'

'Why, Rachel here thinks I'm lucky to be away,' Abby said, lightly. 'Isn't that right, Rachel?'

Rachel, moving her drawing papers and pencils with bad grace, threw back her dark ringlets and said over her shoulder, 'I only meant you were lucky to be out of Catherine's Land.'

As Madge bit her lip and went out to fill the kettle at the sink in the passage, Abby shook Rachel's shoulder hard.

'Rachel, don't upset Ma! It's not her fault we have to live here.'

'I know it's not.' Rachel squirmed out of Abby's grasp. 'But I don't have to like it, do I?'

'I like it,' Jennie put in, 'I've always liked it. Why are you two always complaining?'

'I'm not,' Abby replied. 'At least, not to Ma.'

Everything was ready now for Sunday tea – the table set with one of Madge's good cloths, the bread and butter cut, the jam in a dish, the teacakes and currant cake sliced. On the black-leaded range, the kettle sang and sputtered and Jennie called, 'Ma, shall I make the tea?'

'Yes, please,' Madge answered. As they took their places at the table, she gave a contented sigh. This was what she liked, this was all she wanted, for them to be together. But how quickly the time was going by! The hands of the old cottage clock over the range seemed to be whizzing round and then tea was over and cleared away, and Abby was putting on her hat in the bedroom she had once shared with her sisters but which was now theirs alone. Madge hung her clothes there but slept in a curtained recess off the living room, which was not ideal but quite common practice in the tenements.

One of these days, thought Abby, studying herself in the spotted mirror over the chest of drawers, I'll get Ma a house again, where she can have her own room and somewhere to put her things, and a garden with an apple tree, like we used to have. And that's a promise! she told the dark-eyed girl in the mirror, but the girl did not smile.

'Who's coming with me to the tram?' Abby cried, when she was ready.

They all came, clattering down the twisting stair and out into the Lawnmarket, a name which had intrigued them until they realised it was just another street, even if it was part of the Royal Mile. But the Royal Mile was certainly something special. There weren't many streets that stretched from a castle at one end to a royal palace at the other. 'With a' the history of Scotland in between,' Gramma Ritchie had told

11

them, 'no to mention a' the troubles.' By which she meant not only the drinking in the pubs and alehouses of the High Street and Canongate, but the long cavalcade of fights and hangings and riots that belonged to the old stones. Nothing had fascinated the girls so much in their early days in Edinburgh as Gramma's stories. Of Mary, Queen of Scots and the Palace of Holyroodhouse, of John Knox and Bonnie Prince Charlie, of the old Tolbooth prison, now marked only by stones in the road in the shape of the Heart of Midlothian, where, believe it or not, Gramma said they might spit! 'As if we would!' they had cried, but Gramma said you did it for luck and never got fined.

'Aye, you've got no history like this in England,' Gramma once remarked with satisfaction. To tease her, Madge had said, 'Yes, but we're all one nation now.'

Gramma had given her an astounded look and cried, 'Niver in this world!'

Sometimes they talked of the Catherine who had given her name to Catherine's Land, and wondered what she would think if she could come back and see her husband's house still standing after so many years.

'Gramma,' Jennie once asked, 'do you think Catherine's Land will always be here?'

'Aye, I do,' Gramma said firmly.

Sighing, Abby and Rachel thought she was probably right.

'Goodnight, Frankie!' Abby called now to a young man with curly dark hair, who was standing at the door of one of the ground-floor shops as they left the house.

'Goodnight!' he called eagerly, then melted away into the darkness.

'I think Frankie was waiting for you, Abby,' Rachel said, with a mischievous look. 'Maybe he'd like to walk you to the tram,'

'Frankie?' Abby only laughed.

'Well, didn't he used to walk you to school?'

'That was a long time ago.' But Abby remembered holding Frankie's hand all the way down the Canongate, and the humbugs and toffees he used to bring her from his mother's sweetie shop. When she went into service he had moved to Glasgow to find work, but now he was back, playing the piano in pubs and cinemas. And still watching out for her on the stairs.

'Here comes my tram,' Abby murmured as they reached the stop on the Mound. 'Bye, everybody, see you next week!'

They watched and waited as she climbed into the swaying, lighted vehicle, then waved as she waved and saw her borne away.

'Come on, Ma,' Jennie whispered, taking Madge's arm, 'she'll only be gone a week, you know!'

'I know, I'm foolish.' Madge shook her head and smiled. 'It's just that I look forward so much to Sunday afternoons and they're always over so quickly.'

'And Sunday evenings are awful,' Rachel muttered. 'Nothing to look forward to but Monday and school. Jennie, don't you dare say you like school!'

'You know I don't. I can't wait for next year when I leave.'

They hesitated for a moment, looking out over the lights of the city lying below the dark outline of the Castle. Then they turned and walked back up the Mound to Catherine's Land.

Chapter Two

Young Annie Lossie was putting on lipstick (strictly forbidden during working hours) in Mackenzie's Bakery, and Madge was putting on her hat. It was after six on Monday evening. They had had a long day on their feet and were late away as usual, because of the city clerks crowding in at the last moment to buy up unsold buns and bread. You could hardly turn them away, said Miss Dow, the manageress, but, och, they got on her nerves, holding everybody back, and she with the cash to do as well! But Annie liked to laugh with them and so did Madge, even if they did tease the Hampshire accent she had never lost.

'One or two of they clerks is sweet on you, Madge,' Annie said, keeping her voice down, 'd'you ken that? I mean the older ones, of course.'

'Of course,' Madge answered, smiling. She buttoned up her coat and checked to see she had put her Mackenzie's loaf and a teacake in her shopping bag, where she already had a packet of sausages bought in her dinner hour.

'I'll bet if you gave 'em half a chance, they'd ask you out.' Annie combed her short red hair and pulled on a beret. 'And I think you ought to go.'

'They have asked me out,' said Madge.

'No!' Annie's round eyes sparkled. 'Madge, what did you say?'

'I said I'd rather not, if they didn't mind.'

'Oh, Madge, why? Your Will's been gone for years. Is it no' time you were thinking about someone else?'

Madge glanced at Miss Dow, busy with the cash. She said in a low voice, 'If I met the right one, maybe.'

'Might wait for ever for him! You should just go out, Madge, have a bit of fun.'

'I've got my girls, they're all I want.'

Annie shook her head. 'They'll grow up, you ken. They'll no' always be with you.'

Madge said quietly, 'I know that.'

'Have you two no homes to go to?' cried Miss Dow, rattling coins on the counter. 'Come away, now – I'll lock up.'

'Poor old Miss Dow,' Annie whispered, as she and Madge faced the mist of Thistle Street together. 'She's forty-two, you ken. No' much hope for her, eh?'

By the time they reached Princes Street, the mist had thickened into fog. They could scarcely make out the street lights or the Castle on its rock, and Annie's tram was almost at the stop before she could read the number.

'That's me!' she cried, moving forward with the queue. 'Goodnight, Madge. Will you be all right, walking? At least, it's no' far.'

That was true. Catherine's Land wasn't far from Princes Street. Just up the Mound, through Lady Stair's Close and into the Lawnmarket. But it was another country.

The lights of the little ground-floor shops were shimmering through the fog as Madge emerged from the short cut of Lady Stair's Close and turned towards home. Frankie's mother, Mrs Baxter, a dour widow in her forties, was reading the evening paper in her sweetie shop, while Mr Kay the grocer was still at work weighing out sugar, and Archie Shields the tailor was still cutting cloth.

Archie, a small, dapper man, had been keen at one time for Madge to do stitching for him, but his airless premises that smelled of sweat and scorched pressing cloths did not appeal. She had made the excuse that she only wanted to sew for ladies, which was true, even if no ladies seemed to be requiring her services. Though she had her machine all set up, no one came in answer to her little cards in the stationer's and she had ended up serving in Mackenzie's. It wasn't too bad, she got on well with Miss Dow and Annie and could buy bread and cakes at reduced prices. She supposed she should consider herself lucky to have a job at all, with so much unemployment about.

15

Peace, it seemed, was not as profitable as war. But sometimes, she didn't feel so lucky.

She sighed, looking up at the house Matthew Kerr had built so long ago, or as much as she could see of its six storeys through the wreaths of smoking fog. He had built well. It still seemed solid enough in spite of its years, the stonework crumbling in places but on the whole strong, the carvings over the windows still in place, the rescued roof intact. Below the shops were basement rooms for storage, a wash house with a copper to heat the water, a massive mangle, and pulleys for drying.

My turn to wash tonight, thought Madge, drearily, for she could have done with putting her feet up, but she must take her turn or miss it. How she hated Mondays! Rachel was right about Sunday evenings. Nothing to look forward to but work for her followed by a struggle with wet sheets. If it had been summer, she might have hung them on the lines on the green at the back of the house, but they'd never dry there this weather. Or even at the high windows of the tenement, where washing sometimes flew like tattered banners in the wind.

Madge's eyes found her own window and saw there were no faces looking out to catch sight of her coming home. The girls must have drawn the curtains against the fog. But they would be up there, waiting. Putting aside the barefoot Irish children playing in the passageway, waving to Mrs Finnegan, standing with the latest baby at her door, Madge ran up the stairs to the third floor, ready to cry, 'Girls, I'm home!'

In Madge's eyes, her flat was pleasant enough. She had two large rooms, off which were cupboards for coals and storage, a sink and a lavatory. Gramma Ritchie always used to say she'd been lucky to have one of the middle floors for they'd been intended for the quality and had higher ceilings and longer windows than the rest of the buildings. There was a black-leaded range for cooking and heating and all her things from the cottage had fitted in somehow, the couch and the rocking chair, the sewing machine and her mother's little piano. Madge's mother had been a village schoolmistress before her marriage and had given Madge her love of music and reading which she had tried to pass on to her daughters. All the girls played the piano, but the tenants of Catherine's Land were more impressed by the sewing machine. Though Madge took

16

no money, she often ran up things for her neighbours, much to Gramma's disgust in the early days. 'No' sewing for they Finnegans again, or they Rossies?' she would scold. 'They'll take the skin off your back, if you let 'em, Madge!'

'They certainly haven't got much on their own backs,' Madge serenely replied. 'I don't mind sewing for them.' Indeed, she sewed for anyone, the Rossies, the Kemps, the Muirs, the Erskines, Lily MacLaren, and Sheena. It was a pleasure to sew for Lily, so slim and beautiful, with her cloud of dark hair and her grey eyes clear as water, young Sheena the same. Everyone knew that though Lily called herself Mrs MacLaren, she had never had a husband and Sheena, now thirteen, was a love-bairn, but there was nothing unusual in that. Even Gramma Ritchie, pillar of the Kirk, made allowances. 'I'm no' one for judging,' she told Madge, who smiled secretly at Gramma's idea of herself, 'but it was a soldier, they say, and her only fifteen, you canna judge poor Lily.'

'No,' Madge agreed fervently, 'I'd never judge her.'

All the same, she was not too pleased to see Lily swinging in the rocking chair that evening, with Sheena lolling against her shoulder.

'Why, Lily,' Madge murmured, kissing Jennie and Rachel and taking off her coat, 'what brings you here?'

'Can you spare a drop o' milk?' asked Lily. 'Save me going to Kay's?'

Which is just down the stair, thought Madge, vexed, but she unpacked her shopping bag and said, yes, she'd milk to spare and seeing as they were already there, Lily and Sheena might as well stay for their tea. She had been hoping to keep back a few of the sausages for the next day, but at the look in Sheena's eye, put them all into the pan Jennie had brought her.

'Madge, we couldna do that,' said Lily, making no move. But Sheena cried, 'Mammie, we could, we could!'

'I've got the range hot,' Jennie said softly, 'and I've peeled the tatties.'

'Potatoes,' Rachel corrected. 'Ma says potatoes, Jennie. You sound just like a Scot.'

'Never mind what we call them, let's get them on to boil,' said Madge, tying on her apron. 'Oh, you know, I think first I'd love a cup of tea.'

'Aye, that'd be nice,' said Lily.

Though Madge's oval face was white and her blue eyes shadowed with weariness, Lily stayed on and on. When the girls had washed up and retired to the bedroom to talk and giggle, she made yet another cup of tea and settled herself back into the rocking chair, Madge's chair, for another nice long 'crack'.

'I was thinking about your Will,' she remarked. 'He must've been a very special feller. I mean, for you to stay a widow so long. Is it no' eight years since he went?'

'Yes, it's eight years,' Madge agreed stiffly.

'Have you niver thought of getting wed again? There'd be plenty want you, Madge.'

'Oh, Lily . . .' Madge stirred her tea and looked away. First Annie, now Lily. She didn't want to talk about herself or Will, especially not to Lily.

'Have you no seen that new feller who's moved in on your stair?' Lily persisted. 'He's a house painter, they say. And a widower.'

'Mr Gilbride? Yes, I've met him. He's got two sons.'

'Malcolm and Rory. Rory's the handsome one, like his da. Do you no' think Jim Gilbride's good-looking?'

'Lily, I'm not interested in Mr Gilbride.'

'He'd be just right for you, Madge, I can tell. And what's the poor man to do, then, wi' no wife to look after him? They say she died of the Spanish influenza, like your ma-in-law.'

Madge kept her eyes down, feeling again the stab of grief. Two years on, she still couldn't believe she would never see again the tall figure of her mother-in-law, see the dark eyes so like Will's, so like Abby's, the head of coarse black hair scarcely touched with grey and swept up high with pins and combs that never dared to loosen. For months after Gramma had gone, Madge kept thinking she could hear her light step on the stair, her voice at the door, 'Madge, here's a bit pie, mind the gravy!' 'Madge, I've made you girdle scones, put the kettle on!' 'Lily, d'you mind?' Madge suddenly rose to her feet. 'It's my turn for the copper, I have to get my sheets in.'

'Oh, you shoulda said!' Lily unwound herself from her chair. 'Sorry, hen.' She gave Madge one of her lovely smiles. 'Sheena, let's away! Say thanks for your tea, now.'

Poor Lily, thought Madge, watching her make her way slowly up the stair with her jug of milk, Sheena following. How does she manage, then? There was a cleaning job which Lily herself, knowing her style of cleaning, said was a bit of a joke and it certainly didn't bring in much, but she did other things. A bit of pressing for Archie Shields, a bit of ironing, this and that. If Madge had her own ideas what the this and that might be, she never expressed them. Lily never brought a man back to Catherine's Land.

As Madge was about to close her door, she saw Mr Gilbride coming up the stair and felt embarrassed as he said good evening. After what Lily had said she scarcely dared to look him in the eye, but his own brown eyes which had a fiery glaze to them did not mind resting on her. He knew she was a widow, of course; no doubt he felt the same sort of sympathy for her as she felt for him.

'No' so bad, eh?' he remarked, taking off his cap to reveal a head of thick brown hair. 'No' so foggy.'

'Oh? That's good, then.'

The gas jet on the stair shone down, lighting their pale features, two people, bereaved. Then Mr Gilbride replaced his cap and opened his door and Madge, drawing back, closed hers.

Chapter Three

It was strange, but after that meeeting with Mr Gilbride on the stair Madge found she couldn't seem to get him out of her mind. She might be putting teacakes into paper bags or giving change or doing her work at home, and suddenly she would see again the tall, erect figure coming up the stair, the good-looking face with its straight nose and high cheekbones, the brown eyes that seemed to burn as they rested on her, and she would feel curiously excited and at the same time dismayed. She had scarcely looked at the man, yet here was his image constantly appearing and reappearing, why should that be? It was all Lily's fault, embarrassing her with her matchmaking. It was only because of what Lily had said that her new neighbour had entered so much into her thoughts. Even so, she never opened the street door without wondering if she would see his straight back in front of her; she never came out of her door without thinking he might be coming out of his. Sometimes she did see his sons, the plain and clever Malcolm, the handsome Rory, but it wasn't until a fine golden Sunday towards the end of October that she saw Jim Gilbride again.

It was such a beautiful afternoon they had decided to meet Abby coming from the West End and walk with her through Princes Street Gardens. As soon as the Sunday dinner was washed up and cleared away, they joined the crowds promenading down Princes Street.

'Supposing we miss her?' asked Rachel. 'She'll come home and find we're not there.'

'She never gets away before two o'clock and it's only that now,' Madge replied. 'I'm sure we'll see her at Maule's Corner.'

Maule's department store at the West End of Princes Street was a great meeting place and also a good vantage point; Madge knew that if they reached there before Abby, they would see her coming along Queensferry Street on her way from Glenluce Place.

'I see her!' cried Jennie, before they needed to cross to Maule's. 'She's talking to someone.'

'It's that old parlourmaid,' said Rachel, narrowing her fine dark eyes, 'Miss Whatsername.'

'That's no way to speak of Miss Givan,' Madge rebuked. 'Mind your manners, Rachel. Poor soul, I feel so sorry for her. Abby says she has no family, never has anywhere to go on her afternoon off.'

But the girls were not interested in Miss Givan, who had turned away, they only wanted to see Abby, who was speeding towards them.

How tall she was, thought Madge, how like her grandmother! In her Sunday skirt and jacket, with a brimmed hat pulled over her dark hair, Abby seemed to have grown prettier, even since last week. Seventeen. It was a lovely age. If only she had not had to spend it as a housemaid.

'You've come to meet me!' Abby exclaimed, 'I was just thinking how nice it would be if we could all walk back through the gardens!'

'Far too warm to stay indoors,' said Jennie, winding her arm round Abby's, as Madge asked quietly, 'How've things been, dear?'

Abby's face darkened and she shrugged. 'Madam's thrown one or two of her little rages, Mrs Moffat's thrown three or four. Apart from that, everything's been fine.'

'Oh, Abby—'

'Don't worry, Ma. I told you, didn't I, I've got my plans? As soon as I can, I'm going to get out of Glenluce Place.'

'How?' asked Rachel. 'How will you get out?'

'By qualifying myself for something better, that's how.'

'You mean studying?' Rachel made a face. 'How awful, Abby!'

At which, Abby's face cleared and she laughed.

They moved down a flight of steps to the formal gardens that had been laid out on the site of the old Nor' Loch, drained so long ago. Above them, the Castle on its volcanic rock, basked in the autumn sunshine. All around them people of the city, so starved for the sight of green, walked the paths between the flowerbeds or sat on benches, revelling in the rare warmth. Madge suggested they too should sit down for a while, but Abby had her eye on the ice-cream seller who was doing a good trade. 'Let's get cornets!' she cried. 'Come on, I'll treat you!'

As the girls ran to join the queue, Madge found a bench and sat down to rest her aching feet, sighing with relief. For a moment she closed her eyes. . . then sat up with a start. A man was leaning over her, taking off his hat, and the sunlight was catching a head of thick brown hair and turning it to copper.

'Afternoon, Mrs Ritchie,' said Jim Gilbride.

He was dressed in a dark Sunday suit with a stiff-collared shirt and a blue tie. As Madge looked up, he seemed immensely tall, a great dark silhouette, topped by that head of shining hair. She immediately sat up straight, worrying that she might have been asleep. Hadn't been asleep, had she? Whatever had she looked like, then?

'Afternoon, Mr Gilbride,' she murmured.

'Grand day. Mind if I sit here a minute?'

'No, not at all. Well, my girls are just over there.' She waved her hand towards her daughters still at the ice-cream barrow, and Mr Gilbride, who had been about to sit down, straightened up. He looked at the fair-haired Jennie, so like Madge, at the pretty dark-ringleted Rachel, at their tall sister, quite grown up, and shook his head.

'Sorry, Mrs Ritchie, I'll no' take their seats – didna know they were with you—'

'No, please don't go,' Madge said quickly, as he replaced his hat. 'My eldest daughter, Abby, is home this afternoon, I'd like you to meet her.'

'She's in service?'

'In Glenluce Place.' Madge rose as the girls, carrying cornets, came back, laughing. When they saw Jim Gilbride, they fell silent.

'Here's yours, Ma,' Abby murmured, glancing quickly at the man she didn't know. 'Mind, it's melting.'

Rachel, licking her ice-cream, stood without speaking, while Jennie's clear blue eyes were looking past Jim, as though searching for someone.

'Hello, Mr Gilbride,' she said, breathlessly, 'is Rory with you?'

'Not today, Jennie. He's away to a meeting, as usual.'

Madge, trying to keep her dignity as she coped with her melting ice, introduced Abby to Jim. He again raised his hat and shook her hand.

'Hear you work in Glenluce? Grand houses, eh? Did a job there once – och, ma ladder wasna tall enough. The height of those ceilings, you'd never believe!'

'You don't need to tell me,' Abby answered, fixing him with a dark gaze, 'we clean them.'

He laughed, then turned to Madge. 'If you're walking back home, can I no' walk with you, Mrs Ritchie?'

'Well, I suppose we are going back. We'll have to get Abby's tea—'

'Don't worry about tea for me,' Abby put in promptly. 'I'd just as soon be out in this sunshine.'

'The sun'll be going down soon, Abby, we'd better be getting home. Thanks, Mr Gilbride, we'd like to walk with you.'

The three girls in front, Madge and Jim behind, the little procession wound through the gardens, past the floral clock, empty of its plants at the end of the season, and up the Mound. Though her daughters were talking animatedly together, Madge, very conscious of the man at her side, could think of nothing to say. Rory was at a meeting. What meeting? She didn't like to ask. And the other son, Malcolm, did he not care to walk out on a Sunday with his father? No doubt he was out somewhere with his own friends. Clearing her throat, she asked about him.

'Malcolm?' repeated Jim. 'He's studying.'

Madge looked interested.

'Aye, he's ambitious, wants to get on. Doesna want to be a brickie like his brother. Or a house painter, like me.' Jim shot Madge a sharp glance. 'Though I'd ma own business once, Mrs Ritchie. Before the war.'

'What happened?'

'All went wrong.' He shook his head grimly. 'When I joined up, I'd a business, a house, a wife. When I came back, I'd nothing. The customers had gone elsewhere, I couldna keep on the house, and ma wife – mebbe you heard – took the Spanish 'flu. Ill three days, then in her coffin. Can you believe that, Mrs Ritchie? Ill three days and then gone. And me left with two great lads to look out for!'

'I'm so sorry,' Madge said gently. 'I'm really sorry, Mr Gilbride.'

'Shouldna be complaining to you, though.'

'Yes, because I know what it's like, I've been through it myself.'

'Aye, that's true.' He hesitated. 'Was he killed in the war, your man?'

'No, in an accident. It was a crane – fell – in the dockyard. A long time ago now, Mr Gilbride.'

'And get's no easier, eh?' As they approached the door of Catherine's Land he said again, his fiery gaze softening, 'No, I shouldna be complaining to you, Mrs Ritchie.'

'Are you coming, Ma?' asked Rachel, turning back. 'We need the key.'

'Yes, I'm coming.' But Madge turned impulsively to Jim. 'Would you like to come in and have a cup of tea with us, Mr Gilbride?'

'It's very kind of you, but I'll no intrude.' He tipped his hat and grinned. 'Have ma chores to do on a Sunday!'

'Your chores? Look if there's anything I can do to help, I hope you'll ask me.' Madge flushed. 'I mean it.'

'Thanks all the same, but I think you've enough to do, Mrs Ritchie.'

'That's right,' Abby put in coolly. 'Ma does sewing and mending for pretty well the whole of Catherine's Land as it is.'

'Well, I'm no' asking her to do mine,' he answered evenly, 'so there's no need to worry, is there?'

Madge, biting her lip, gave her key to Abby and told the girls to go ahead and let themselves in. 'Abby shouldn't have spoken to you like that,' she said in a low voice, 'I'm sorry, Mr Gilbride.'

'She was only thinking of you.' He hesitated. 'Look, I was wondering – I dinna want to speak out of turn – but would you like to come out with me – one evening?'

'Out?'

His eyes were holding hers in the way she had already come to know.

'To the pictures, or something? D'you like the films?'

'Yes. Yes, I do.'

'They say there's a good one on at the Alhambra.'

'It's on now?'

'This coming week.'

She stared up into his handsome face, as he looked down at her, waiting. 'All right,' she said in a rush. 'I'll come, I'd like to.'

He gave a soft, whistling sigh. 'When? Tomorrow?'

'Not tomorrow. I do my washing on Mondays, it's my turn for the copper.'

'Tuesday, then?'

'Tuesday.'

'I'll call for you. Ha'past seven. Can you be ready?'

'Yes, that's plenty of time. Half past seven, then.'

Madge began to walk slowly up the stair and he followed. 'Goodbye, Mrs Ritchie,' he called from his door.

'Goodbye, Mr Gilbride.'

Three pairs of eyes watched as she took off her coat and hat and carefully hung them up.

'Why did you have to make us walk home with that man?' asked Rachel. 'We could have stayed longer in the gardens.'

'I told you, the sun wasn't going to last, we had to get home.'

'But you wanted to walk with him, didn't you? Why did you? I don't like him.'

'And I don't,' said Abby, 'I don't like his eyes.'

'I like him,' Jennie put in, 'I think he's nice.'

'Will you please stop talking about Mr Gilbride and help me get the tea!' cried Madge. 'You shouldn't be discussing him at all.'

'Aren't we even allowed to say what we think now?' asked Abby truculently.

'Not when you're rude about it, and you were very rude to Mr Gilbride just now, Abby. I felt ashamed for you.'

'Ma . . .' Abby looked earnestly into her face. 'I don't like him, I really don't. I don't think you should get mixed up with him.'

'Mixed up? What do you mean mixed up? How dare you speak to me like that, Abby?' Madge, scarlet-faced, shook a cloth with an angry flap and spread it across the table. 'What I do is my business, it has nothing to do with you.'

'Oh, Ma, it has, you know it has!' Abby's eyes filled with sudden tears. 'It's my day at home, I look forward to it all week – don't let's quarrel.'

Madge at once put her arms around her. 'Abby, I don't want to quarrel, when have I ever wanted to quarrel with you? This is all so silly, it's all about nothing.'

'Is it?' Abby released herself and began to help Jennie to set the table. 'Mr Gilbride likes you, Ma. He'll be asking you to go out with him next.'

'He has already asked me to go out with him,' Madge said quietly.

As Rachel caught her breath and Jennie's eyes widened, Abby turned slowly to look at her mother.

'He's asked you out? When? Just now? On the stair?'

'Yes, he asked me to go to the pictures on Tuesday, I said I would.' Into the heavy silence, Madge cried, desperately, 'Look, what's the matter with you? Do you begrudge me a night out? How often do I go anywhere? You seem to be treating me like a criminal for saying I'd go to the pictures. I don't understand you.'

'You do understand,' Abby said flatly.

'No, I don't! Where's the harm in going to the pictures?'

'Yes, where's the harm?' asked Jennie. 'I don't see why Ma shouldn't go out if she wants to.'

Abby turned her head away. 'Is that kettle boiling?' she asked over her shoulder. 'I could do with a cup of tea.'

It was time for Abby to go. Madge said she would walk with her to the tram.

'There's no need, Ma.'

'I want to.'

'Can't we come?' asked Jennie.

'No, I won't be a minute.' Madge was putting on her hat, her face heavy with concern. 'You could make a start on the washing-up.'

'That means you as well, Rachel,' warned Abby, giving her sisters one last hug.

'Oh I do hate it when you have to go,' sighed Jennie and Abby managed a wry smile.

'Not as much as I do. Come on then, Ma.'

'I wanted to talk to you without the girls listening,' Madge said hurriedly, as they came out into the Lawnmarket. 'I didn't want us to part with bad feeling.'

'There's no bad feeling, Ma. I'm sorry I spoke to you the way I did.'

'I just think you're reading too much into this, you see. Mr Gilbride has only asked me to go to the pictures.' Madge tried to laugh. 'Not Gretna Green.'

'I know.' Abby was relieved to reach her stop and see the tram approaching. 'Here's my tram, Ma. I'll see you next week.'

'Take care, dear,'

'And you.'

When Abby was once again borne away by her tram, Madge walked slowly home and mounted the stairs. I needn't go on Tuesday, she told herself. I could say I'd changed my mind. But she knew she would not say she had changed her mind, she would not say she couldn't go. Whatever her girls thought, she wanted to see Jim Gilbride again. And why should she not?

Chapter Four

Next morning, Abby woke at five as usual and lay staring into the darkness of the basement room she shared with Tilda Beal, the under-housemaid. She knew she should get up, get on with her studies, but she was thinking about her mother. Until yesterday, whatever else was unsure in her life, her mother had been her rock. Always there, always the same, steady and true, the one person who would never change. Then, as though someone had waved a terrible wand, a change had come over her. And Abby and her sisters had seen it happen. One minute they were all together in the gardens, Ma just the same as usual; the next a man with red-brown eyes had appeared and blotted out the sun. Nothing was ever going to be quite the same again.

'Mr Gilbride has only asked me to go to the pictures,' Ma had said, 'not Gretna Green.' Maybe not, but he would have liked to take Ma to Gretna Green, or anywhere they could be married. Oh, yes, he would, Abby could read it in those hard brown eyes of his that seemed to flame, as his hair flamed in the sunlight. Jim Gilbride wanted her mother, and the awful truth was that her mother seemed to want him.

With a troubled sigh Abby quietly put back her bedclothes and lit a candle. It wouldn't do to light the gas and wake Tilda, lying now with her mouth slightly open and her blonde-lashed eyes tightly closed. She would sleep like that until the alarm went at six, which would give Abby just under an hour. With a shawl around her shoulders as protection against the basement's chill, Abby sat at the dressing table she used as a desk and began to set down columns of figures to tot up, a task she always enjoyed and always got right. Numbers were magical to her, she could never understand why Jennie and Rachel should frown and sigh over their sums and fail to see what was so clear to her. On the other hand, Jennie would be happily stitching away while Abby was still trying to thread her needle, and no one could draw like Rachel. Each to her own, thought Abby, but she was grateful for what she could do. She felt in her bones it would take her far. But not yet, of course. Her exercises over, she opened her textbook on book-keeping and settled down to solid work.

'Abby, is that you?' came Tilda' s wail, as the alarm clock shrilled into the silence. 'What you doing?'

'You know what I'm doing,' Abby answered over her shoulder.

'They sums again?' Tilda, fair and plump, sat up, yawning. 'I canna think why you waste your time on that stuff, Abby, it'll no' do you any good.'

'That's for me to decide.' Abby lit the gas and blew out her candle. 'Tilda, you'd better see if Edna's got the range going yet, you know what she's like for oversleeping.'

Edna Wright was the young kitchenmaid who slept off the pantry and had a habit of not hearing her alarm, which meant she would be late making the morning tea for upstairs and Mrs Moffat, the cook.

'If Mrs Moffat doesna get her tea, she'll be in a state,' Tilda groaned, as she and Abby washed shudderingly in cold water. 'Then we'll all catch it.'

They dressed quickly in heavy underwear, lavender print dresses and white aprons, black stockings and black strap shoes, then Tilda hurried along to the kitchen while Abby nipped into the maids' lavatory before Sarah Givan beat her to it. She was twisting her long dark hair into a knot and fastening on her cap, when Tilda came in to say that Edna had not woken up, had not got the range going, and had not made the tea.

'So now there'll be fireworks, Abby, you just wait and see. Och, ma hands are freezing!'

'Never mind your hands, did you get the range started?'

'Aye, and I pulled Edna out of bed and all. She's got the kettle going and the porridge on.' Tilda was studying herself in

29

a hand mirror. 'Will you look at ma face, Abby? Black as soot from that range! And ma hair? Listen, I'm thinking of having a bob.'

'Me, too,' said Abby, making her bed, 'it'd save time.'

'Madam might complain.'

'Can't make us put it back, once it's been cut.'

'That's true.' Tilda giggled. 'Shall we, though?'

'Sometime. Now we'd better get upstairs and make a start. And keep out of Mrs Moffat's way!'

Every day, their routine before breakfast was the same. Clean out the downstairs grates and light the fires, dust the dining room, brush down the stairs and rub up the brass rods, sweep the hall and front steps, polish the bell and letterbox and lay out the post on the silver salver on the hall table. These chores done, they were free to fly down the basement stairs to their own breakfast in the kitchen, where on that Monday morning, they found Edna crying because Mrs Moffat had boxed her ears.

'As though it was my fault I slept in,' Edna sobbed, when there's no diff'rence 'tween night and day wi' the shutters closed and all!'

'Och, you sleep like the dead,' Mrs Moffat exclaimed. 'Do you no' hear your alarm?'

'I'm too tired to wake up, I work too hard,' the elfin-faced Edna returned, at which Mrs Moffat grew purple and had to be soothed by Sarah Givan and told to think of her heart. Sarah was thin and elegant and liked, as she put it, everything 'nice'. She had worked with Mrs Moffat for many years and could usually calm the peppery little woman who had been Gramma Ritchie's friend, but this was becoming increasingly difficult as age made Mrs Moffat's job harder and her temper shorter. Her complaint today, as she slapped down their plates of porridge, was one they had all heard before: she should have been given one of they new gas cookers years ago, only Mrs Ramsay was too mean to buy one, so if her morning tea was late it was all her own fault. And Edna's, of course. Here a fierce look caused Edna's tears to start afresh, but Tilda said kindly, 'Never mind, Edna, Abby can wake you, she's aye up at five these days.'

30

Sarah turned a bright gaze on Abby. 'Oh? Why's that?'

'I just like to read,' Abby murmured, looking away.

'Likes to study!' cried Tilda. 'Studies every morning, reg'lar as clockwork.'

'Abby,' asked Mrs Moffat sternly, 'is this true?'

Abby flushed angrily. 'If I like to study in my own time, why shouldn't I?'

Mrs Moffat shook her grey head. 'If your grandma could hear you now, Abby Ritchie! She'd no time for booklearning when she was in service and you shouldna have neither. If you're no' getting your sleep, you'll no' be able to do your work.'

'No one's ever complained I can't do my work,' Abby retorted, 'and until someone does, I'm not giving up my studies.'

'But, Abby, what are you studying for?' Sarah asked quietly.

Abby stared at her plate and said nothing.

'Got her reasons,' said Tilda, 'always has.'

'Will you really wake me, Abby?' Edna whispered, and Abby looked up with a smile.

'I will, Edna, I promise.'

Mrs Moffat pursed her lips and took down the frying pan for the family's breakfast bacon. 'Off wi' you!' she cried. 'It's time for prayers.'

Family prayers were always said by Mr Ramsay in the morning room, a handsome oak-panelled room next to the library. Across the hall was the dining room, heavily furnished in mahogany which had belonged to Mr Ramsay's parents, the original owners of the house, for Glenluce Place was later than the New Town, Victorian, not Georgian. The L-shaped drawing room, large enough to host a dance, was on the first floor next to the principal bedrooms, while on the top floor were the old nurseries, now converted into bedrooms for the Ramsay boys, Mr Lennox and Mr John. All the work of the house was carried on in the double basement, the upper floor containing the kitchen, pantries and maids' rooms; the lower floor the wine, coal and storage cellars. At the back of the house was a strip of grass for hanging out the maids' washing, but most of the household laundry was sent out, for which blessing Abby gave private thanks.

Mr Ramsay, now reading from the Bible, was a lawyer, a tall, balding man in his forties, whose grey eyes beneath overhanging brows were small and cold. Sitting in front of him with her sons at her side was his wife Amelia, pretty-faced and plump, with fair hair elaborately pinned and coiled. She gave the impression of being good-natured but, as her family and staff knew, this was not the case. Her temper far outshone Mrs Moffat's and carried more weight; when she chose to display it, even Mr Ramsay bowed before the storm and her sons had early learned to scatter.

Abby, standing with the other maids at the back of the room, studied the turkey carpet at her feet and as usual let her thoughts wander until the delicious smell of frying bacon wafting up from the kitchen gave notice that the service was nearly over. Mrs Moffat, who never attended prayers, knew to the minute when to have family breakfast ready.

'Praise ye the Lord,' droned Mr Ramsay, in his strangulated Edinburgh tones. 'Praise Him with the sound of the trumpet.'

'Praise Him,' echoed Mrs Ramsay.

'Praise Him,' echoed the Ramsay sons.

'Let everything that hath breath praise the Lord,' finished Mr Ramsay and closed his Bible. 'Let us go in peace to serve the Lord.'

'Amen,' said everyone, and Mrs Ramsay led the way to the dining room where she rang the bell to give Mrs Moffat the warning she didn't need and the family took their places at the table. As Abby and Tilda helped Sarah to bring up the porridge, another day appeared to be following its usual boring course. So Abby thought.

It was her duty, one she had given herself, to 'do' the library, and when Mr Ramsay had departed for his office, Mrs Ramsay had left for coffee in town and the boys had gone to school, in went Abby with her feather duster, her polish and her cleaning rags. She always cleaned the room conscientiously, but when work was done she did not hurry away. No, for this was her one chance to choose another book to read at night by candle-light, when her studies were finished and Tilda slept. Mr Ramsay's library was quite extensive, but though he sometimes worked in the room after dinner, Abby knew his books were scarcely ever read. In spite of feeling a little guilty over borrowing without permission, so few books came her way she had long ago decided that the opportunity was too good to miss. After all, she worked hard for the Ramsays, she didn't see why she should deny herself this one small perk.

That morning, though looking for a novel, her eye was caught by one of Mr Ramsay's old school prizes, a book on arithmetic which looked interesting. Putting her feather duster under her arm, she sat down to read. Only for a moment, she told herself. But the library clock ticked away and she turned page after page, quite lost to her surroundings, until a hand descended on her shoulder. 'And just what do you think you're doing?' a voice whispered in her ear.

She leaped to her feet, the colour flooding her face as she looked into the narrow grey eyes of Lennox Ramsay. He was the older of the Ramsay brothers, a solemn-faced boy of seventeen, with his mother's blond hair and his father's long upper lip, a senior pupil at the Academy, destined for university and then a place in the family firm. When she took any notice of him at all, Abby thought he looked like a young lawyer already; she couldn't imagine him as a schoolboy, playing a schoolboy's games.

'Mr Lennox,' she murmured, 'I – I thought you were at school.'

'I have a dentist's appointment, but never mind about me. What are you up to with my father's books?' He took the textbook from her hand and read aloud its title. '*Principles of Arithmetic*? Why the blazes did you take this? I bet you were reading it upside down, weren't you?'

Abby's flush deepened and her dark eyes flashed. 'As a matter of fact, I found it quite interesting,' she answered, her voice trembling. 'I've always liked working with numbers.'

'Working with numbers?' Lennox Ramsay burst into laughter. 'Oh, that's rich! Wait till I tell the fellows at school that our housemaid is a mathematician! They'll say you ought to be written up in *The Scotsman*!'

'If you'll excuse me, sir, I think I should be getting on.' Abby, so angry she could scarcely speak, knew she must get out of Lennox Ramsay's presence before she did something foolish, such as wiping the smile from his face with the back of her hand. Satisfaction of that sort would end in her being given notice and she wasn't ready for that yet. 'If you please, sir,' she said woodenly, trying to move round him, but he caught her by the wrist and held her fast.

'Hang on a minute, Abby, what do you think my dear mother is going to say when I tell her about this?'

Abby grew cold. 'I don't know, Mr Lennox.'

'I don't suppose she'll be too pleased, do you? One of her maids lounging in the library, reading the master's books instead of doing her work?'

Abby ran her tongue over dry lips, but said nothing. Lennox smiled down at her.

'Well, maybe I won't tell her, if you don't tell her about this.'

He suddenly bent his head and pressed his mouth to hers with such force, she could do nothing but let it happen. When it was over, she took a step away from him, staring at him with enormous dark eyes, her fingers to her bruised lip, while he stood smiling again, pleased it seemed, with her reaction.

'Come on, what's a kiss?' he asked, lightly. 'You should be flattered I'm attracted. You've suddenly become quite pretty, did you know that? Just the sort of girl a fellow might notice. Now don't tell me that isn't more interesting than arithmetic?'

While she stood, mute, he put his hand round her right breast and squeezed it hard, then he strolled to the door.

'Please replace my father's book carefully,' he called back to her, 'he's awfully proud of all his prizes.'

Abby felt as though she were on fire. Humiliation burned through her like a destroying flame and she could not move, only let it consume her. To think that because his father paid her wages, a boy could treat her as Lennox Ramsay had treated her, not only kissing her so contemptuously, but laughing at her, making fun of what she held dear, letting her see that as a person she did not exist. She was a housemaid, therefore she could not object if he wanted to ridicule her, wanted to amuse himself by kissing and fondling her, she must just put up with it, if she wanted to save her job. I won't, though, she thought fiercely. I don't care about my job, I'll give in my notice, I'll leave! But then she would get no reference, she would have worked for nearly four years for nothing. The door of the trap that held her seemed to clang in her ears. It was real enough to do that, wasn't it? Oh, yes, it was real.

'Abby,' came Tilda's voice from the hall, 'are you no' coming down for your tea?'

When Abby stormed into the kitchen, Mrs Moffat looked up from the kitchen table where she was drinking tea with Sarah.

'What's up with you then?' she asked calmly. 'You look fair skewed.'

'That sickening Lennox Ramsay has just had the nerve to kiss me,' Abby burst out. She gingerly put her finger to her lip which felt swollen and raw. 'I won't stand for it, I won't!'

As Tilda and Edna squealed aloud together, Mrs Moffat and Sarah exchanged glances.

'Well, aren't you going to say something?' cried Abby. 'Mrs Moffat, what have you got to say?'

'Say?' Mrs Moffat slowly lifted the heavy brown teapot and filled two more cups. 'I say, watch yourself, that's what I say.'

'Watch myself? What do you mean?'

'These things happen,' Sarah put in nervously.

'You mean he's kissed you?' asked Abby.

Spots of colour rose to Sarah's thin cheekbones. 'No, of course not!'

'And he's certainly no' kissed ME!' Mrs Moffat said with a throaty laugh. 'Nor Edna.'

'Nor me!' cried Tilda. 'Och, I'd just die if that skemp laid a finger on me!'

'So, what do you mean, Mrs Moffat?' Abby pressed. 'What do you mean, saying watch myself? You must have meant something.'

'Do you no' remember Millie?' Mrs Moffat asked, after a pause.

Abby stared. Millie Robinson, who had been upper housemaid when Abby first went to Glenluce Place? Of course she remembered Millie, a pretty girl with curly toffee-coloured hair and a wide smile. Some months before she had suddenly said she wanted to return to Dunfermline where her parents lived, and then Abby had been promoted.

'Of course I remember Millie,' she told Mrs Moffat. 'What about her?'

'If you'd no' had your head stuck in so many books, you'd have known what about her,' the cook retorted contemptuously. 'Was she no' big enough when she left for anybody to know?'

Abby's eyes grew wide. 'You mean she was going to have a baby? Millie left to have a baby?'

'Seems you've no eyes in your head.' Mrs Moffat glanced at Sarah and shrugged. 'Aye, you're no' so clever as you think you are, Abby. Why d'you think she was given that ten pounds on top of her wages, then?'

'Ten pounds?' Edna cried. 'Millie got ten more pounds? I never knew!'

'Because Lennox Ramsay was the father?' Abby asked slowly. 'I can't believe it!'

'Happens a' the time, son of the house, pretty housemaid.' Mrs Moffat laughed grimly. 'Even if Master Lennox doesna look capable! Aye, he cost his da ten pounds and poor Millie a gey lot more. Poor soul, she was lucky to get anything out o' they Ramsays. I know girls was put out into the street without a penny to their names.'

'I canna bear to think about it,' Tilda murmured, but Abby's eyes were stormy, her face still darkly flushed.

'Why does no one care?' she cried. 'Why does no one do something to help? Have people like us no rights at all?'

'People do care, Abby,' Sarah said earnestly, 'but what can anyone do? It's the way of the world.'

'It needn't be! If enough of us tried to do something!'

'Do what?' asked Mrs Moffat. 'It's like Sarah says, there's no way things can be changed. The folk upstairs pay the piper and they ca' the tune. That's a' there is to it. Now, let's get on, there's work to be done.'

But Abby still sat staring into the cup of tea that had grown cold. Sarah put her arm around her.

'Try not to worry, Abby. You know what to watch out for now and so does Tilda. You can be on your guard and that's half the battle, isn't it?'

'Oh, yes, but if we don't do what Lennox Ramsay wants, what then?' Abby asked bleakly.

Sarah gave a long, troubled sigh. 'Will you tell your ma about this?' she asked, quietly.

Abby shook her head. 'No, I shan't tell Ma.' She pushed away her cup and stood up. 'Ma's got plenty on her mind as it is.'

Chapter Five

Seeing Jim was what was on Madge's mind. As their meeting drew nearer, she grew more and more nervous and when it was time to get ready she felt even worse. It was never easy getting ready in Catherine's Land. There was water laid on but no bathroom. Baths were taken in a tub laboriously filled with kettles, washing was managed from a jug and basin. For Madge who had to wash and change in her daughters' room, dressing was effort enough without having to worry how she looked for Jim Gilbride.

On that Tuesday evening she had decided to wear her best pleated skirt and a blue lace-collared blouse she had made herself. Her mother's amber necklace didn't look right with the blue of the blouse and she took it off, then she put it back again.

'What do you think?' she asked the girls. 'Does this go?'

'Looks lovely,' said Jennie.

'Doesn't go,' said Rachel.

'Maybe I don't need it, just for the pictures?'

'No, you don't.'

Madge took off the necklace. 'Well, I think I'm ready, then. You'll be all right on your own?'

'Oh, Ma, why shouldn't we be?' they groaned.

'Just don't open the door to anyone, that's all.'

'Not even Mrs MacLaren?'

Madge hesitated. The last person she wanted to know she was going out with Jim Gilbride was Lily MacLaren.

'If she comes down, just say I've popped out for a minute,' she said, at last, and did not miss the knowing look in Rachel's eye.

At half-past seven precisely, Jim Gilbride's strong knock sounded on the door and Madge, her nerves jumping, buttoned on her winter coat and put on her hat. 'You'll be all right?' she asked again, but Jennie gave her a little push.

'Better go, Ma, Mr Gilbride's waiting.'

Walking beside him, keeping up with his long stride, Madge felt quite unreal, as though this woman walking with this man through the streets of Edinburgh could not be herself, were some stranger Madge was only watching. It came to her now with a pang of conscience that she had not been honest with Abby. She had pretended not to understand Abby's anxieties, had tried to make out that a visit to the cinema with a man like Jim Gilbride was of no significance, while knowing very well that it could be very significant indeed. She and Jim were not seventeen-year-olds, they were people who had already experienced love and marriage and could be ready for love and marriage again. Especially Jim. There was no doubt that widowers usually remarried, they needed wives as maybe widows didn't need husbands. She had coped alone for many years, he for only two, yet Abby had seen, as Madge was afraid to admit, that he was already willing to 'like' another woman and that woman was herself. He might have only asked her to go to the pictures, not Gretna Green, as she had tried to joke to Abby, but going to the pictures together was for many people the first step in the ritual of courtship. Abby knew that, Madge knew it too. As she glanced sideways at Jim Gilbride's firm profile, she felt panic engulf her. Did she want to take that first step? She might as well be seventeen, she thought, she felt as untried, as vulnerable. Then she remembered Will and guilt succeeded panic. I shouldn't have come, she told herself, as they reached the Alhambra Cinema in Leith Walk. I wish I hadn't, I wish I hadn't come.

'It's a Lillian Gish picture, Mrs Ritchie,' Jim was murmuring. 'D'you like Lillian Gish?'

'Oh, yes, she's very good, isn't she?'

'Two ninepennies, please,' Jim said to the girl in the box office.

They moved into the darkness of a different world.

At first, Jim sat stiff as a post beside Madge, watching Lillian Gish suffer her way through *Broken Blossoms*, as the unseen pianist strummed away in accompaniment. Halfway through the film, however, without taking his eyes from the screen, he felt for Madge's hand and took it in a strong, dry grasp. An electric shock of feeling immediately raced through Madge's body. Here it was, the second step. She had been expecting it but when it came she still didn't know how she should respond. In fact, she was astonished by the feelings roused by that physical contact and not knowing how to regain control simply left her hand in Jim's. They continued to sit, hand in hand, until the film ended and the lights went up when, according to convention, Jim removed his hand and smiled politely at Madge as though there had been no contact between them.

'Enjoy it, Mrs Ritchie?'

'Very much, thank you.'

Aware that she had played her own part in the ritual by not removing her hand from his, Madge could not look at Jim. When he asked if she would like some refreshment, she refused, and when he took out his cigarettes and offered her one, she shook her head and said she didn't smoke.

'Dinna mind if I do?'

'Oh, no, Mr Gilbride, not at all.'

'Could you no' manage to call me, Jim?' he asked, narrowing his eyes in the smoke of his cigarette. 'Seeing as we're here together?'

'Jim,' she said obediently.

'And you'll let me call you Madge?'

'If you want to.'

'I do, then.' He took a few puffs of the cigarette, then stubbed it out. 'Shall we no' stay for the second picture?' he asked, abruptly.

Madge stood up at once, filled with a great rush of relief. 'If you're sure you don't mind? I don't want to be too late.'

The lights were beginning to dim for the second feature as they made their way out into the fresh air. Jim, as though it was the natural thing to do, took Madge's hand again and tucked it into his arm.

'I want to thank you, Madge, for coming out with me

40

tonight,' he said seriously. 'It's meant a lot to me. First time I've been out with anyone since ma Rona died.'

'First time for me, too,' she answered, very conscious of his arm beneath her hand.

'First time in all these years?' His eyes, very dark in the light of the streetlamps, searched her face. 'Why me, then?'

'I don't know.'

He gave a short laugh. 'That's no' what you'd call a compliment.'

'All I can say is that when you asked me to go out with you, I wanted to.'

'And when other fellas asked you, you didna?' He grinned. 'That's better, Madge, that's more like it.'

The night was cold, but fine and clear, the sort of night when Edinburgh's skyline, all towers and points and jagged silhouettes, seemed like a theatrical set, something quite unreal. Yet nothing could be more solid than Edinburgh stone, nothing more down to earth than its people. Was that part of the city's spell, Madge wondered, that contrast between its look of fantasy and its reality? She still felt a little unreal herself, holding Jim's arm. She still hadn't quite come to terms with the fact that she was out with a man and the man was not Will, even though she had held that man's hand all evening, even though she knew every time she met his eyes how he was beginning to feel towards her. But how did she feel towards him?

For some time they walked in companionable silence, from the east end of Princes Street to the station, up the Waverley Bridge and through the old closes into the High Street.

'It's a strange, grand place,' Jim observed, pausing to let Madge take breath.

'The High Street?'

'The Royal Mile.' He turned his deep gaze on her. 'Have you no' heard it said there's the whole of Scotland's history here?'

'Yes, Will's mother told me that.'

'Mind, when it's chucking out time at the pubs, you dinna think of history!' He laughed, but the laughter soon died. 'Madge, I used to think of this place when I was in France. All the riots and fights and famous folk, all the kinda thing you can still feel here – if you're a Scot – and I used to think,

41

where's Scotland's history now? Away in France with the English, for God's sake! I tell you, I used to wonder what in hell I was doing out in they trenches, excuse ma language. And when I came back, I still didna know.'

'It was a just war, Jim, everyone says so.'

'Is that right? Is that what they say?' His expression softened, as he held her hand. 'You dinna mind me talking against the English, Madge? I keep forgetting you're no' a Scot.'

'I'll forgive you.' She smiled up at him, relieved his mood seemed lighter. But then she added perhaps they should be getting on home, and immediately his face darkened again.

'Home,' he repeated, 'Aye, well I never thought I'd have to call a place like Catherine's Land home. When I'd ma own house, Madge, ma own garden!'

'I'm sorry, Jim.'

He shook his head. 'There I go, telling you ma troubles again, when you've enough of your own. Why do I no' count ma blessings, eh?' He waved a hand to the high windows above them. 'There's one blessing, anyway. At least we dinna have to dodge the slops coming out of the windows every night. Did your mother-in-law tell you about the folk crying, "Gardy-loo!"? And the poor devils below shouting, "Haud your hand!" If they were no' too late?'

'She did,' Madge answered, laughing, yet wondering at the changing moods of the man who walked at her side. One minute up, the next, down. She had had no experience of such a nature, for Will, though forthright, had been of even temperament. For a moment, she was apprehensive. 'I don't think you should get mixed up with Mr Gilbride,' Abby had said. Was she right? Maybe, but outside Madge's door, under the flickering gas jet, Jim's mouth found hers and as they gladly took the next step in the ritual, Madge knew she didn't care.

The girls were still awake and came out in their nightgowns to interrogate her the minute they heard her key in the lock. Was it a nice picture? Had she had ice cream? Had she had a good time?

Madge, taking pins from her hair, smiled. It was a lovely picture, she had not had ice cream, she had had a very good time.

'And will you be going out with Mr Gilbride again?' asked Rachel.

'Perhaps.'

'That's no answer, Ma.'

'All right, then, I will.' Madge began to brush her hair with long strong sweeps of her brush. She could not stop the smile still curving her lips. 'I will be going out again with Mr Gilbride.'

When Abby came home the following Sunday and repeated Rachel's question, Madge gave her the same answer. Yes, she would be going out again with Mr Gilbride.

'I see,' Abby commented tonelessly.

'Abby, you needn't worry.'

'If you say so.'

Madge said sharply, 'Look, is there anything wrong? You don't seem yourself.'

'I'm all right. By the way, don't bother about seeing me to the tram tonight. Frankie Baxter said he'd like to walk down with me.'

'Frankie? When did you see him?'

'Oh, on the stair.'

'Abby, I'm sure he's a nice lad—'

'He is, he's very nice.'

'But I know Mrs Baxter worries about the drinking. I mean, it goes with that sort of job, doesn't it? Piano playing in pubs?'

'He's only taking me to the tram, Ma,' Abby answered pointedly. 'Not Gretna Green.'

Madge coloured and said no more.

Chapter Six

After that first tentative evening, Madge and Jim began to see each other regularly. Sometimes they would go to the Empire, to see a few 'turns', sometimes to the cinema, sometimes, more rarely, to a dance hall, for Jim did not care for dancing. What they liked best was just to walk the dark streets, holding hands, kissing if there was no one to see, then kissing again at Madge's door when the time came to part. They never went further than those sweet snatched kisses and sometimes, lying alone in her bed-recess, Madge would wonder what it would be like if they did. Or she would begin to wonder and then stop, for there was always her Will at the back of her mind, there was always Jim's Rona. She still wasn't sure she wanted to replace Will with Jim, or whether Jim wanted to replace Rona with herself. She thought he did, but he never said. Even though his eyes seemed eloquent, he never spoke of love in words. Perhaps a man like Jim would never put feelings into words and she must just wait for time to tell her what he wanted. If only she knew what she wanted herself.

Once at the cinema during the interval between pictures, Jim spoke of Rona. Madge had been telling him about meeting Will at a friend's house in Southampton. 'It was love at first sight,' Madge said softly. 'There was never any question about it. We knew from the start.'

'Aye, that's the way it was for Rona and me,' Jim murmured. 'Only—' He broke off, staring at the back of the dusty plush seat in front of him. 'Only, I didna always appreciate her. You ken how it is, Madge? When they're gone, you think on what you mighta done or said? D'you ken what I mean?'

'Everybody does that when they've lost someone, Jim. You mustn't blame yourself.'

'But in the night – sometimes, I feel so bad—'

Madge pressed his hand. 'Me too, Jim.'

His eyes leaped to hers. 'Madge, how d'you always manage to make me feel better?' He suddenly put her hand to his lips and kissed it. It was an action so strange for him, so romantic, that a thrill went through her which he must have sensed, for his gaze grew more ardent and he leaned towards her – then the man next to him said, 'Excuse me, please,' and pushed past them to the aisle.

'Och, you great GOWK!' cried Jim, his face black with rage. 'Come on, Madge, for God's sake, let's away out of this!'

Outside in the street, he walked fast, pulling Madge along as she clung to his arm, but the night air seemed to cool his temper and gradually he slowed his step. By the time they were climbing the Mound, he was easy again, looking down at Madge tenderly as she lifted her face to his.

'Trouble is, we're never alone,' he whispered, ''cept in the street like this. We've always got other folk to worry about, at the pictures, at home—'

'I know, I know,' said Madge, 'I've got the girls—'

'And I've got Malcolm. Studying, studying – och, he's always there! Never goes out for a drink, never sees a pal . . .'

'He's like Abby for studying.'

'Aye.' Jim set his mouth grimly. 'Doesna like me, your Abby, does she?'

'She doesn't know you, Jim.'

'Doesna need to. She'll never like me. Because I like you.'

'Jim, let's be getting back, the girls will be waiting.'

'It's like I said, they're always waiting!'

'Well, they are. There's nothing I can do about it.'

'So, let's just talk for a minute, eh? Once we get back to Catherine's Land, we canna talk, Madge.'

There was a bench at the entrance to one of the closes and they sat huddled together, enduring the cold, both shivering, not just with the cold.

'I never thought I'd be talking like this to another woman after ma Rona went,' Jim said quietly. 'Folk used to say, you'll get over it, Jim, you'll find somebody else, but I never believed them. Was it the same for you, Madge?'

'Yes, the same.'

'It's only been two years for me.' He fixed her with his dark, holding stare. 'Mebbe you think that's no' so long?'

'I don't know, Jim. Everybody's different.'

'It's been a lifetime,' he groaned, 'I'm telling you, a lifetime. But, now – well, I've met you.'

She was silent, staring at an old man wavering past, crooning to himself.

'I'll no' go too fast for you,' Jim was saying gently, 'it'll all be the way you want it. Just say you'll give us a chance, Madge. Mebbe Abby's no' happy, but she'll come round, she'll see you've a right to your own life, eh? All I'm saying is, let's see each other, let's go out, have a bit of happiness – Madge, what do you say?'

She leaned against him as though she were weary and instantly his arms went round her, holding her close. For some time they sat, locked in that quiet embrace, then, still without a word, they rose and walked slowly home to Catherine's Land.

Madge's living room was warm and filled with shadows cast by the one gas light she had left burning low. Everything was quiet and orderly and it seemed to her that she was the only thing in it that was not, for Jim's kisses burned on her lips and Jim's words burned in her mind. She felt strange and not herself and sat down in her rocking chair, thinking of how her life might change, of how it had already changed. Jim had told her what he wanted. Her heart beat fast as she rocked in her chair. Dear God, she thought, I want it too.

'Ma,' came a voice at her side, 'why are you still wearing your hat?

'Rachel!' Madge jumped from her chair. 'What are you doing out of bed?'

'You're so late, Ma. I've been waiting and waiting, listening for you. You said you were only going to the pictures.'

'Well, I didn't go anywhere else.'

'So why were you so late?'

'You're mistaken, Rachel, I wasn't late. Now you run back to bed.'

'It's warm in here, it's nice.' Rachel lingered, staring at her mother. 'Was it a Mary Pickford picture, Ma?'

'Yes, she looked very pretty.'

'I sometimes think she's a bit like you.'

'Come on,' Madge said firmly, 'back to bed!'

When she had kissed Rachel goodnight and glanced at the sleeping Jennie, Madge undressed as quickly as possible. In spite of what she'd told Rachel, she had been late getting home and would have an early start in the morning, she must try to get some sleep. But when she was in her bed-recess, listening to the sounds of Catherine's Land at night, Jim Gilbride's face came into her mind, superimposed over Will's, and she knew sleep would not come soon, would perhaps not come at all.

Some days later, as another long day at Mackenzie's was coming to an end and Miss Dow was shutting the door, Jim in his paint-spattered clothes appeared and asked if he might come in.

'We're closed,' Miss Dow snapped, 'it's after six.'

'I just want to speak to Mrs Ritchie,' Jim said, taking off his cap and after giving him a hard stare, Miss Dow grudgingly allowed him in. 'Madge, there's someone to see you,' she called frostily, and shut the door with a bang.

Both Madge and Annie swung round from the bread shelves, Annie all interest, Madge immediately embarrassed.

'Why, Jim, what brings you here?' she stammered. 'There's nothing wrong, is there?'

'Finished a job up the street, thought I'd walk you home.' Jim fixed her with the dark, intense gaze Madge knew would not be missed by Annie. 'Are you no' ready, then?'

'Well – not quite.' Madge glanced quickly at Miss Dow. Annie cried, 'Madge, there's no more to do! You go get your hat and coat!'

'Annie!' warned Miss Dow. 'I think I am in charge here, am I not?'

'Sorry, Miss Dow,' said Annie.

'Sorry, Miss Dow,' Madge echoed, and Jim said curtly that he would wait outside.

'Well, who was that, then?' Annie asked eagerly.

'A neighbour.'

'What's he doing here, though? Are you walking out? Madge, you dark horse – niver saying a word!'

'Annie, will you hold your tongue?' exclaimed Miss Dow.

'Mr Gilbride's a friend,' Madge said, in a low voice. 'He must've just thought we could walk home together. If there's nothing else, Miss Dow . . . ?'

'Yes, yes, you get off,'' Miss Dow answered irritably. 'I've still the cash to do, but that's no' your worry.'

'Better not keep him waiting in the cold,' Annie whispered, giggling, as Madge with great relief let herself out of the shop.

Jim was waiting for her under a streetlamp. When she joined him, he took her bag and linked her arm to his, but did not smile.

'No' exactly the big welcome,' he commented quietly. 'Did you no' want me coming into your shop, Madge?'

'It's not that, Jim—'

'What, then?'

'Well, it's just that Annie Lossie is such a gossip, she'll go on and on about you tomorrow.'

'And you're no' keen to talk about me?'

'Not to Annie.'

He looked down at her, his expression set and hard.

'Because I'm no' important to you, is that it?'

'Jim, what's the matter? Why are you talking like this?' Madge searched his face with troubled eyes. 'You know you're important to me.'

'Funny way of showing it, haven't you? I come to walk you home, I think you'll be pleased, but you canna even introduce me to the folk you work with, canna get me out of the shop fast enough. I tell you, I didna know where to look.'

'Oh, I'm sorry, I'm really sorry! Look, I should have introduced you. I don't know what I was thinking of, it's just that you took me by surprise. Jim, please don't be like this!'

He made no answer, but dropped her arm and walked on with his usual long stride, leaving her struggling to keep up, bewildered by the new storm that had blown up between them. It died down as suddenly as it had come and as they reached the entrance to Princes Street Gardens, Jim turned and snatched Madge's hand. 'Sorry,' he whispered, 'I ken you didna mean to upset me. It's just me, I'm no' easy, never have been. Say you forgive me.'

'Jim, there's nothing to forgive!' she cried, her heart rising again. 'I was in the wrong, I embarrassed you.'

'Never mind, never mind,' he murmured fondly. 'Ah, Madge, I want to kiss you – you've no idea what it's like for me – looking at you, wanting you . . .' He pulled her close. 'Shall we go in the gardens?'

'Jim, it's late, I should be back—'

'Just for a minute, so I can kiss you. Only a minute or two, please!'

People were hurrying past them on the pavement, jostling them as they stood together, their hands clasped, their eyes locked.

'Only for a minute,' Madge whispered.

It was crazy, going into the gardens with him when she should have been at home, getting the tea, but Madge could offer no resistance. Still holding hands, they went together down the steps into the deserted place of wet leaves, wet grass, and sighing trees. Only a few weeks before, they had stood here in sunshine while the girls bought ice cream, and they had known perhaps even then that what might come was this shivering delight that gripped them now, making them sway as the trees swayed, kiss and part and meet again, murmur words that meant nothing and everything. Then as Jim's hands began to undo Madge's coat, search for her breasts, Madge forced herself away.

'Jim, we can't, I must go, I must!'

'For God's sake, Madge, d'you think I'm made of wood? You canna be with me like this, then say you have to go!'

'I know, I know.' She was almost crying. 'Do you think I want to go? But we can't make love here, can we? We can never be together, can we?'

He held her by the shoulders, his eyes glittering down at her through the shadows.

'Madge,' he said, hoarsely, 'will you marry me?'

Outside her door, there was the familiar pain of parting, but this time there was a difference. They had taken another step, the step that followed the holding hands and kissing; they were truly courting now, and the only step that remained was marriage. Both were very pale as they looked at each other, as though overcome by the decision they had taken, as though their new joy was too much to accept.

'Will you tell the girls tonight?' Jim asked, in a low voice.

'No, not tonight.' Madge leaned against him. 'I don't think tonight.'

'Well, we'll have to tell 'em some time. My lads and all.'

'Yes, but I was thinking, Jim, the girls don't really know you and I don't know your sons. How would you like to come in on Sunday afternoon? Have your tea and let's all meet?' Madge was becoming enthusiastic as the idea began to take shape in her mind. 'Abby will be home then, we could all talk and get to know one another.'

'Aye, it's no' a bad plan. But I dinna mind what we do, just so's we can be wed soon.' Jim grasped Madge's hand. 'You promise that, Madge? We'll be wed soon?'

'We'll be married soon,' she answered gravely. 'I promise.'

Chapter Seven

Jennie and Rachel, on their way to school, had stopped at the window of Mrs Baxter's sweetie shop. Although they both considered themselves almost grown up, they still liked to look in at the jars of 'boilings', the striped rock, humbugs and delicious sherbert lemons. At the back of the window were towering piles of Fry's chocolate and Palm toffee, and in cardboard boxes at the front, coconut kisses, liquorice allsorts and little bags filled with who knew what, known as ha'penny dips.

'Wish I could buy some sherbert lemons,' sighed Jennie, 'or else coconut kisses. I love coconut kisses!'

'We haven't any money and the shop's not open,' Rachel said dryly.

'Mrs Baxter's probably trying to wake up Frankie. Abby says he plays the piano half the night and never wants to get up till dinner time.'

'Lucky Frankie. Come on, Jennie, we'd better go. You know what we'll get if we're late.'

The two girls, shivering in the December chill, joined the streams of workers flowing down the Lawnmarket towards the High Street, men and women, red-eyed and pinched-looking, some coughing and spitting, others lighting cigarettes and blowing smoke that mixed with their breath on the frosty air. They saw the Kemp boys from the top floor of Catherine's Land, and Mrs Lindsay who stayed opposite Mrs MacLaren and worked in a draper's in the Canongate, Tam Finnegan, who was a road worker, and Jessie Rossie, who was a waitress somewhere near Holyrood. But no one waved, no one spoke, it

51

was too miserable, too cold, all anyone wanted to do was to get wherever they were going and hope it was warm.

'Listen, what do you think about Rory coming to tea on Sunday?' Jennie asked suddenly, and Rachel saw that her blue eyes were radiant.

'They're all coming, aren't they? All the Gilbrides?'

'Yes, well I think it's nice, I think it's nice to have people in.'

'By people, you mean Rory.' Rachel hunched her shoulders against the wind, as the traffic rattled by on the setts of the High Street. 'What I want to know is why Ma's bothering to invite them in at all. It's not Christmas.'

'She wants us to get to know them.'

'And you know why that is, don't you? She's going to marry Mr Gilbride.'

Jennie stood still, while the wind tugged at her knitted beret and reddened the end of her nose. The radiance had quite faded from her eyes.

'Come on,' Rachel called, walking on, 'we don't want to be late.'

Jennie slowly followed her. 'That's a piece of nonsense, Rachel. What you said, it's nonsense.'

'I wish it was, then.'

'Ma's been married. Why should she want to marry again?'

'Plenty of people get married again. If they're widows, I mean.'

'But Ma's got us, Rachel. Why should she want Mr Gilbride?'

'I thought you liked Mr Gilbride?'

'Yes, but not for Ma to marry.'

'Ssh!' Rachel knocked Jennie's arm. 'Sheena's coming – don't say a word.''

Sheena came up behind them and twined her arm in Jennie's. She was wearing a long hand-me-down coat which had two buttons missing, thin black shoes and black stockings, and a large blue crocheted hat. She looked rather dirty, rather comic, and quite lovely. Rachel and Jennie looked at her in silence.

'Och, it's freezing, I canna get ma hands warm!' she cried, blowing on her fingers, for she had no gloves. 'Why'd you no' wait for me this mornin'?'

'Thought you might be late,' Rachel answered.

'I'm no' late! I was right behind you all the way down the street!' Sheena's eyes shone. 'Saw your ma last night. Saw her coming back with Mr Gilbride.'

The sisters stared straight ahead and said nothing.

'I was by maself so I was sitting at the window, and I saw your ma and Mr Gilbride, holding on to each other, like they were drunk.'

'They weren't drunk!' Rachel cried angrily. 'They'd only been to the pictures!'

'Aye, well mebbe they were only cuddling.' Sheena laughed. 'Mam says they'll be getting wed soon, then you'll be having a new dad. He's awful good-looking, Mr Gilbride. I should think you'd be pleased.'

'We have to go now,' Jennie said, pulling her arm from Sheena's, 'we're going to be late.'

'It's no' time, the bell hasna' gone!' Sheena cried. 'Wait for me, wait for me!'

But the sisters were hurrying away towards the school gate, and they were taller than Sheena, their legs were longer, she could not catch them. After a moment or two, she gave up and turned to look at Alex Kemp, who had appeared at her side. He opened his hand to show he had two toffees. 'Want a sweetie?' he asked hoarsely.

Graciously accepting his homage, she gave him one of her lovely smiles and popped the sweet between her full red lips. Why worry about the Ritchie girls? She could see them any time.

In the schoolyard, the children were playing their games, the boys at one side rolling marbles, or wrestling and scuffling, while the girls opposite skipped and giggled together and kept out of the boys' way until the bell rang for assembly. Jennie, who was due to leave school soon, normally looked on at the games with an indulgently adult air, but now she stood near the girls' entrance with her head bent and looked at nobody.

'Don't take on, Jennie.' Rachel whispered, 'I might be wrong about Ma and Mr Gilbride. I bet I am wrong. There's no need to worry.'

'I'm going to tell Abby, soon as she comes home. She'll know what to do.'

'But there might be nothing to tell.'

'I'll ask her to talk to Ma. If she's not happy, Ma won't upset her. She never wants to upset Abby.' Jennie blew her nose as a teacher came out and began to ring the school bell with a terrible clangour. Rachel took Jennie's arm.

'I did say I might be wrong. Let's wait and see what happens, shall we?'

As she and Rachel were borne into school on the tide of their fellow pupils, Jennie prayed, 'Please God let Rachel be wrong, and if she isn't, please God let Abby know what to do.'

Chapter Eight

Abby was feeling easier in her mind. Since that one skirmish in
the library, Lennox Ramsay had not come near her. Nor was
he likely to, for she and Tilda had taken to doing their work as
a pair, rather like policemen patrolling tough areas. Tilda
giggled about it but, as Abby reminded her, she too was at
risk.

'Mrs Moffat told me to watch myself, so now I'm telling you
to do the same, Tilda. Don't let Lennox Ramsay try anything
on with you.'

'Abby, I'd rather die!'

'Yes, but he might give you presents. Now I think back, I'm
sure Millie had a lot of little brooches and scarves and things
she didn't have before.'

'As though I'd let anybody kiss me for a brooch or a scarf!'
Tilda cried. 'Abby, I'm ashamed you'd say that to me.'

'All right, I'm sorry, but you know what happened to Millie.
You can't be too careful.'

'Aye, and I bet your young man'd have something to say, if
Mr Lennox tried anything with you again.'

'What young man?'

'D'you think I've no' seen him? The one that walks you back
from the tram on Sundays.'

Abby flushed and laughed. 'Tilda, how d'you manage it? It's
dark when I come back.'

Tilda's blue eyes sparkled. 'Go on, Abby, tell me who he is,
then!'

'He's just a boy I knew at school. His name is Frank Baxter.
His mother keeps the sweetie shop at Catherine s Land.'

55

'And he's sweet on you, Abby. Even in the dark, I could see that.'

It was comforting to Abby to think of Frankie Baxter. They only met on Sundays, yet already he was becoming important to her. She knew if he were not to be waiting for her on the stair she would feel quite lost, which was strange, for she hadn't thought of him in years. He had only come back into her life a few weeks ago. There was nothing remarkable about him, they had nothing in common, but there it was, Sundays had become days for seeing Frankie as much as for seeing her mother. In fact, seeing Ma was really rather bitter-sweet now. While one part of Abby rejoiced in knowing her mother was happy again, another despaired because the happiness stemmed from Jim Gilbride. On the first Sunday of December, as she helped to clear away family breakfast, Abby asked herself, Will it be today Ma tells me she's engaged?

Later that morning when the family had returned from church and was getting ready for luncheon, Sarah setting the dining-room table gave Abby a call.

'Abby, would you run down to the cellar and fetch me a bottle of the claret? I'll need to be opening it soon.'

'Right you are, Miss Givan.'

'Thanks, dear. One from the rack near the door'll do.'

Abby, glancing at the grandfather clock in the hall, thought, Not too long to my time off, and her heart was as light as her step as she raced down the curving stone staircase to the lower basement. She was surprised to see that someone had already lit the gas, but maybe Tilda or Edna had been down earlier to fetch something for Mrs Moffat. All the preserves were kept here. Rows of home-made jams, marmalades and chutneys, bottled plums and apricots, together with eggs in pails of isinglass, strings of onions, bunches of dried herbs, jars of spices. There was always someone running up and down, yet it could still be frightening, hurrying through the shadows cast by the gaslight, watching out for mice or black beetles. The wine cellar was nearest to the foot of the stairs and Abby quickly dived in and picked out a bottle of the claret Mr Ramsay liked to have with the Sunday joint. She was turning to run back up, when she heard voices. Low, murmuring voices, then a giggle. Oh, God, thought Abby, I know that giggle!

She set the bottle on the lowest step and tiptoed along the flagged passage towards one of the great deep larders, from where the voices were coming. As she reached out and pulled the door open, Lennox Ramsay and Tilda stared into her stricken eyes.

For a long moment, the little tableau remained frozen, then Tilda, scarlet in the face, sprang away from Lennox and began frantically to pull her dress together, while her long hair, freed of its cap and pins, streamed down and tangled in the buttons she was trying to fasten. 'Oh, Abby,' she wailed, while Lennox, fully dressed in his Sunday suit without a blond hair out of place or even his tie undone, gave a sardonic smile.

'He niver give me anything, Abby,' Tilda gasped, 'dinna think that, he niver give me a thing!'

'Come on, let me pin up your hair,' Abby said quietly. 'Where's your cap, then? Where's your apron?'

As Lennox watched, leaning against the wall, Tilda's appearance was restored to respectability, though her face was still moist and flushed and her eyes full of tears.

'I canna go up the stair,' she whispered, 'dinna make me, Abby.'

'Yes, you can. You must. There's a bottle of claret you have to take to Miss Givan, she's waiting for it.'

'I canna, Abby, I canna!'

'Look, just say your eyes are red because you've got a cold, say anything – come on!'

'But what are you going to do, Abby?'

'Yes, what are you going to do?' Lennox echoed. 'Not going to tell my parents, I hope? That would be very unwise.'

'Abby, you wouldn't!' Tilda shrieked. 'Oh, Abby, you'll no tell them, will you?'

'Tilda, I have to tell them. This can't go on.'

'If you tell them, you know what'll happen,' Lennox said lightly. 'I've got things to tell, too.'

'I'll have to take my chance on that,' Abby replied.

The smile faded from his eyes. 'Look, you're a bright girl. Why risk losing your job? You know my people will take my part, whatever I've done. Is it worth being thrown out, just to get back at me?'

Abby raised her eyes to his. 'Yes,' she said simply.

When Abby entered the morning room, she found Mr and Mrs Ramsay sitting either side of the handsome chimneypiece, taking sherry.

'Yes, Abby?' said Mrs Ramsay, as Abby hesitated before them.

'I'm sorry to disturb you, ma'am – sir.' Abby cleared her throat. 'I wondered if I might speak to you for a moment?'

Mrs Ramsay's eyes went to the clock in the corner of the room, as though to remind Abby that it was almost time for luncheon and she had better not delay it.

'Very well, Abby, what is it you wish to say?'

Abby's mouth went dry, her throat seemed to be closing. Now that the moment had come to expose Lennox Ramsay, she was beginning to wonder if it was worth it, after all, to risk getting the sack. It was true she wanted to leave Glenluce Place anyway, but only when she was ready, when her studies were completed and she had a good testimonial in her pocket. Was it worth throwing all that away to get back at Lennox, as he had put it? Yes, because it wasn't a question of getting back at him, it was a question of rights, it was a question of protection. She thought of Millie Robinson and raised her eyes bravely to Mrs Ramsay's face.

'Abby, we are waiting,' Mrs Ramsay said coldly.

'I have a complaint to make,' Abby brought out, 'a complaint against Mr Lennox. He has been trying to – he has been – I don't know how to put it . . .'

At the look of outrage in Mrs Ramsay's eyes Abby's nerve failed and she floundered to a halt, until Lennox himself came striding in, at which her courage came flooding back. He was so obviously intent on getting his story in first, she thought, Be damned to him! I won't be beaten! Swinging round on the Ramsays, she cried, 'Do you want us all to end up like Millie Robinson?'

Mrs Ramsay rose from her chair and pushed back her carefully dressed hair with a trembling hand. 'How dare you come in here like this and accuse my son of having anything to do with a girl like you?' she cried, and caught her husband by the shoulder. 'John, you're a lawyer, tell her what the penalties are for slander, tell her she will be in the most severe trouble if she—'

'Oh, my dear, please say no more,' Mr Ramsay groaned. He turned his small eyes on his son. 'Lennox, what have you to say to this charge?'

'Only this,' Lennox answered solemnly. 'I caught Abby wasting her time in the library the other morning, reading your books, Father, instead of doing her work. She was extremely insolent when I spoke to her about it and I suppose this is her way of getting back at me.'

'There you are!' Mrs Ramsay's face was triumphant. 'The girl has concocted this story out of spite. Lennox has just proved it. Imagine it – reading your books, John, instead of doing her work! I've always suspected that Miss Abby Ritchie thought herself a little too good to work for us, with her put on English accent and all her airs and graces!' She turned a glittering blue eye on Abby. 'Well, my dear, you don't need to worry about working for us any more. You can leave this house today. Your box and wages will be sent on, but do not ask for a character, as I shall not provide one.'

'My dear—' Mr Ramsay began, but his wife quelled him with her hand.

'That will be all,' she finished, as Lennox stood with his eyes cast down, but Abby, trembling, held her ground.

'No reference?' she cried. 'But that's not fair, it's not right! I'm entitled to a reference, I've always worked hard and you've never found any fault!'

'Did you or did you not read my husband's books instead of doing your work?' Mrs Ramsay asked.

'I – I – did look at one or two books, but I always did my work first, I never failed in my duty—'

'Oh, yes, you failed in your duty, Abby, and I have a perfect right to dismiss you. So please don't waste any more time arguing, just go. I want you out of this house *now*.'

It was quite apparent that Mrs Ramsay was working herself up into one of her rages, and as her voice rose and her face crimsoned, Lennox took a step backwards, pulling Abby with him.

'I told you how it would be,' he said in a low voice, 'you'd better go.'

'Yes, Abby, please go,' Mr Ramsay murmured hurriedly, 'as your mistress said, your box and money owing will be sent to your home—'

'To Catherine's Land!' cried Mrs Ramsay. 'Is it any wonder she behaves as she does, coming from a place like that! I should never have taken her on in the first place, but I listened to that stupid cook – oh, wait till I see Mrs Moffat!'

'I demand my reference,' Abby called, shaking aside Lennox's hand. 'You can't deny it to me, it's my right—'

'You are not to be trusted, you have no rights!' Mrs Ramsay shouted, 'will you go? Will you go now?'

From the hall came the sound of a gong and Sarah appeared at the door of the morning room.

'Luncheon is served,' she announced, then as she took in Abby's ashen face and Mrs Ramsay's look of thunder, her jaw dropped.

'Abby?' she whispered.

'Abby Ritchie is leaving us, Sarah.' Mrs Ramsay was leaning on her husband's arm, her hand theatrically to her heart. 'Do not mention her name to us again.'

Abby, pushing past Sarah, made for the basement stairs and found Lennox following.

'You fool, why didn't you listen to me?' he asked harshly. 'There was no need for you to lose your job.'

'Just like there was no need for Millie Robinson to lose hers?' Abby cried furiously.

'Come on, these things happen, it's the way of the world—'

'So everyone says. Maybe it's the way of your world now but it won't always be.' She looked him straight in the eyes. 'But I'm warning you, Lennox Ramsay, I'm going to keep in touch with Tilda, and if I find you've harmed her in any way, I'll do something about it, I promise you!'

'Such as?' he asked, a little nervously.

'Don't you worry, I can cause trouble for you, and I will. Now get away from me – I have to pack my box.'

Mrs Moffat was at the kitchen range, scarlet-faced and breathing hard as she transferred the Sunday joint to a serving dish.

'Abby, what's going on?' she shouted, as she saw Abby running past the door. 'Come here, now—'

But Abby was already in her room, where Tilda was sitting with puffed eyes and her hand to her head. 'Oh, Abby, I feel so awful – Abby, what're you doing?'

Abby was hauling her trunk from behind the wardrobe. 'What do you think I'm doing? I'm packing.'

'You've no' got the sack?'

'I have. I'm leaving today. They're going to send my box on.'

'Oh, you shouldna have said anything, you shouldna!' Tilda rocked to and fro. 'I knew you'd be in trouble, I knew they'd niver take your part!' Suddenly, her rocking halted. 'Abby did you – did you say anything about me?'

'No, you needn't worry, I kept you out of it.' Abby was rapidly folding clothes for the open trunk. 'But why were you such a fool, Tilda? You knew what happened to Millie. Why didn't you come to me and tell me what was going on?'

'I was too scared, Abby, scared of losing ma job. I'm no' strong like you, I canna fight back and he kept coming and finding me, and then he said he was goin' to get a motor for his birthday in January and he'd take me for a drive on ma day off, and I've niver been in a motor . . .'

Abby gave a groan and banged the lid of her trunk shut. 'Listen, I'm not going to be here to help any more, but if he tries anything else, go to Mr Ramsay. Not Mrs, whatever you do. Go to him, because he knows what Lennox is like and I think he'd help. But keep in touch with me, Tilda, write to me, don't forget.'

'I'm no' much good at writing, Abby.'

'You can manage a postcard. Anyway, I'll write to you.' Abby untied her apron, tore off her cap and threw them on her bed. 'There, that's me, finished with this place. Finished for ever. As soon as the others have got the lunch over, I'll say goodbye.'

'Oh, Abby,' wailed Tilda, and dissolved once more into tears.

'It's a mercy your gran didna live to see this day,' Mrs Moffat groaned, when Abby, in her coat and hat, was ready to leave. 'I canna believe what's happening!'

'Her gran would've been proud of her,' Sarah said, quietly. '"Abby's done nothing wrong, she's only told the truth.'

'Aye, well mebbe that's a lesson for her. The truth's not always something that should come out.'

'The worst thing is no character,' Tilda whispered. 'Abby, what'll you do? How will you find another job?'

Abby shrugged. 'I'll find something.' She took a last look round the vast dark kitchen, now scrubbed and tidied after Sunday luncheon, at the table where she had sat so often with the others for hurried meals and cups of tea, at the row of bells that had ruled her life. Please, God, she said to herself, may I never have to work in a place like this again.

'Goodbye, everybody,' she said, aloud, 'I'm away for the tram.'

They kissed and hugged her, Tilda, Sarah, Edna, even Mrs Moffat, and Sarah also slipped an envelope into Abby's hand.

'What's this?' Abby asked, embarrassed. 'Oh, Sarah, you're not trying to give me money, are you?'

'No, but it's something you might find useful.' Sarah gave a wobbly smile. 'Oh, Abby, we're going to miss you! But you're going to do well, you know, don't let what's happened here upset you.'

'I won't.' Abby gave a sob and flung her arms around Sarah's thin frame. 'Thank you, Miss Givan, thank you. Take care, take care, all of you!'

As Tilda sobbed and Edna sniffed, Abby picked up her canvas holdall and walked up the area steps to the street without looking back. It seemed like any other Sunday afternoon, going home to Catherine's Land, yet there was all the difference in the world.

On the top deck of the tram, she opened the envelope Sarah had given her. Inside was a cutting from *The Scotsman*. It was an advertisement for the post of Junior Accounts Clerk with Logie's, a well known Princes Street store. Across the top, Sarah had written, 'Am I right, this is more in your line than service, Abby? Good luck, and don't forget us. Sarah Givan.'

'Fares, please,' said the conductor, climbing the swaying stairs, 'Och, that's an awfu' cold you've got there, lassie!'

'Isn't it,' Abby agreed, blowing her nose.

Chapter Nine

So, here she was back at Catherine's Land, this time to stay. Abby's heart sank as she went up the worn steps and pushed open the front door. She was on the point of remembering Mrs Ramsay's painful words and letting herself get worked up into another rage, when she smelled carbolic. Ma had been cleaning the stair again. No one else ever cleaned it, though folk stepping round Madge with her brush and pail would always promise they'd be taking their turn. 'Aye, dinna worry, hen, next week!' And Madge would wring out her cloth and smile and next week would do it herself.

I will get Ma out of here, Abby promised herself, but she knew she had said that many times before and was no nearer managing it. What hope had she? At the moment, she didn't even have a job. And then there was another thought nagging at the back of her mind. Would Ma want to go? Now that she had Jim Gilbride?

The door of the flat was ajar and Abby went through, steeling herself to break the news that she would not be going back to Glenluce Place. Instead she stopped short, staring around .

'What's going on?' she cried. 'It's no one's birthday, is it?'

It was not only that the whole room appeared to have been spring-cleaned, washed and polished until it shone, with the range newly black-leaded and even the great kettle scraped of its soot, but the table, covered with Gramma Ritchie's white lace cloth and Madge's wedding-present china, was groaning with food. There were plates of boiled ham, pork pies and tomatoes, egg sandwiches, potted meat sandwiches, sliced bread and butter. There were teacakes, a plum cake, glass dishes of tinned pears, and a huge, quivering jelly, expertly unmoulded to make a splendid centrepiece.

'Oh, Abby!' Madge, in her best dress, ran to greet her. 'I didn't see you come in, dear. Girls, Abby's home!'

Jennie, also in her best dress, made by Madge, of dark red wool, flew to Abby and clung to her as though she were some sort of lifeline. 'Oh, Abby, I'm so glad you're back,' she whispered.

'I'm usually back on Sundays,' Abby replied. 'What's up?'

'Nothing. It's just that we're having Mr Gilbride to tea. And Rory. Look at all the things we're going to have.'

'I'm looking.' Abby turned to her mother. 'Gone to a lot of trouble, haven't you, Ma?'

'Well, most of it was cut price from Mackenzie's,' Madge said defensively, 'though I made the plum cake.'

'I made the sandwiches,' said Jennie. 'Rachel, where are you? Abby's here!'

Rachel emerged from the bedroom. Instead of her Sunday dress, she was wearing the jumper and skirt she wore for school, and her lovely face was dark. 'Isn't it awful, Abby, we're having those Gilbrides to tea? Malcolm and Rory. I hate them both.'

'Rachel, please spare us that kind of talk!' cried Madge. 'You know you don't hate the Gilbride boys.'

'They're not *boys*,' Rachel retorted scornfully, 'Malcolm's nineteen and Rory left school ages ago. They are both boring.'

'Rory's not,' Jennie said, flushing, 'he's very handsome, he's the best-looking person I know.'

'That doesn't stop him being boring.' Rachel's eye was caught by Abby's holdall. 'Why've you brought that, Abby? Are you staying the night?'

Abby opened her mouth to speak, then closed it again, as a knock sounded at the door. Madge caught her hand in a nervous grasp.

'Abby, you will be pleasant?'

'Of course, Ma.'

'I want us all to get to know one another.'

'I've said I'll be pleasant. What more can I do?'

Jennie ushered in the three Gilbrides, stiff in their Sunday suits. Madge took Abby across.

'Jim, you remember Abby?'

'Aye, I do.' Jim and Abby shook hands without enthusiasm.

'And this is Malcolm, and this is Rory.'

The two brothers nodded, but did not offer their hands. Both were as tall as their father, but where Malcolm was plain and sandy, with small eyes and a thin narrow nose, dark-haired Rory was extravagantly handsome, with the sort of profile normally seen on coins. Jennie couldn't take her eyes off him as he accepted one of the chairs brought in from the bedroom, but he seemed to Abby to be quite uninterested in his surroundings and sat with his fine head bent, as though he had better things to think about. Malcolm, however, was polite and attentive, especially towards Rachel, but her expression as he tried to talk to her about school was stony. It was a relief when Madge suggested they should all sit down at the table.

Abby, next to Malcolm, asked him what he did for a living.

'Study,' said Jim, with a laugh, 'seems to me.'

'You're at the university?' Abby asked in surprise. 'I hadn't heard that.'

Malcolm turned his small eyes on her. 'I'm a clerk with a firm of accountants, working for my articles. I plan to be an accountant myself.'

'Quite the toff, our Malcolm,' said Rory. 'Talks like one already, eh?'

'Rory, watch yourself!' snapped Jim.

'I'm no' interested in the class war,' Malcolm said smoothly, though his eyes glinted at his brother. 'All I want is a good career and a decent way of life. Is that too much to ask?'

'Yes, if it's at the expense of the workers!' Rory retorted, but Jim was colouring up and drawing his brows together and at these signs of rising temper, Rory subsided.

Madge said hastily, 'Abby's studying, too. She's learning book-keeping.'

'Book-keeping?' Malcolm paused in cutting his cold ham. 'Why, I thought you were in service?'

Abby looked down at the sandwich on her plate. 'I have plans, too,' she said obliquely.

'Abby was always top of the class at school,' Madge went

65

on proudly. 'All her teachers thought she should have gone to university.

Malcolm said nothing, but his lips trembled into a smile.

'You think that's funny?' Abby asked, dangerously calm.

'No, no.' He drew back from the brink. 'I ken fine there's plenty girls get to college these days.'

'But not housemaids like me, you're thinking?'

He shrugged. 'It's all a question of money, would you no' say?'

'Well, let's say I'm like you. All I want is a good career and a decent way of life. Is that too much to ask?'

Malcolm laughed, but Jim said comfortably, 'Och, you'll soon be wed, a pretty lassie like you. A career'd just be a waste of time.'

'Excuse me,' said Abby, leaping to her feet. 'I'll fill up the teapot.' She splashed hot water on to the tea and set down the kettle with a thump. 'More tea, Mr Gilbride?' she asked icily, standing over him with the large brown teapot.

'Aye,' he replied blandly. 'Thanks.'

As Abby poured the tea, making no further comment, Madge breathed again.

The meal was almost over when there came a light tap at the door.

'I'll go!' cried Jennie, while Madge bit her lip. 'I know that knock,' she murmured to Jim, 'it's Lily MacLaren.'

She was right. Lily, pale and lovely in a grubby blue shawl, came gracefully in, holding Sheena by the hand. At the sight of the visitors, her clear eyes opened wide.

'Och, you've company, Madge, we'll no' stay. Sheena, come away.'

'Why?' asked Sheena. 'Why'd we have to go?' She was wearing a print dress that was too big for her, but her slender neck and delicate face rose from the wide collar like a flower and as she lolled against her mother in the way she had, Abby saw Rory's dark blue eyes move to her and stay.

'You'd better come in.' Madge said resignedly. 'I'll make some more tea.'

'Madge, I only looked in for a bit chat.' Lily took the chair Jim set for her. 'Hello, Mr Gilbride.'

'Mrs MacLaren.'

She gave him a languid smile. 'Everybody calls me Lily.'

'You'd better call me Jim, then. D'you know my two sons?'

Lily's eyes travelled from Malcolm to the handsome Rory. 'Met on the stair, haven' we?'

They agreed. Everybody met on the stair in Catherine's Land.

As she rose to fill the kettle, Madge's heart sank. With Lily's arrival, the whole point of her efforts to bring together Jim's family and her own was lost, for when Lily was present in some mysterious way she always dominated the scene. She scarcely seemed to open her eyes, yet fascinated everybody in sight, and Sheena it was plain, could already do the same.

'Still, I'd better make them a sandwich,' Madge sighed, 'they've probably not had much to eat today.'

'Will you no' give yourself a rest?' came Jim's voice at her shoulder as she stood, carving ham, and his hand came down on hers. 'Let the girls do that, you've been on your feet all day, am I no' right?'

Her heart rose like a bird in the sky and she laughed up into his face.

'Jennie,' she called, 'will you take this ham to Mrs MacLaren?'

Malcolm was the first to break up the party, saying he had to get back to his books, couldn't spare any more time.

'Aye, and I've a union meeting tonight,' said Rory, rising but still keeping his eye on Sheena, who was now contentedly eating plum cake.

'Rory works for a builder,' Jim explained. 'Seems he's got collared for union work by they brickies already.'

'Why, he's still only a boy!' Madge exclaimed.

'I'm sixteen, I'm no' too young,' Rory said impatiently. He moved to the door. 'But thanks very much for the tea, Mrs Ritchie, it was grand.'

'And thanks to the girls, too,' said Malcolm, smiling at Rachel.

'I didn't do anything,' she responded coldly.

'Can I see you to your tram, Abby?' Jim asked politely, but she thanked him quickly and said that that wouldn't be necessary. He turned to Madge.

'I'll no' forget your tea,' he whispered, 'you went to a lot of trouble. Shall I see you soon?'

'Yes, soon. Good night, then.'

Jim held the door. 'You coming, Lily?' he called back. 'Madge's got plenty to do.' And as the surprised Lily and Sheena tore themselves away and drifted up the stair, Madge gave a sidelong glance at Abby to see if she had noticed Mr Gilbride's thoughtfulness.

'Is Frankie waiting to take you to the tram?' she asked.

'Not tonight, Ma.' Abby's voice shook a little. 'I'm not going back to Glenluce Place tonight. I'm not going back at all.'

Chapter Ten

'Girls,' said Madge to Jennie and Rachel, 'will you start the washing-up?'

'Oh, Ma!'

'Abby wants to talk to me. I'll help you later.'

'But why do we have to go?' asked Rachel.

'Just do as Ma says,' Abby said shortly, and with rebellious backward looks the younger sisters removed themselves. Madge looked at Abby.

"You'd better tell me what's been happening," she said quietly, and Abby told her.

'But why didn't you tell me before?' Madge cried, when she had finished. 'I'd never have let you stay another day! Oh, I know that sort of thing goes on, but I thought you'd be safe with people like the Ramsays. Gramma Ritchie knew Mrs Moffat, there was never a hint, a whisper—'

'Lennox Ramsay was probably a sweet little boy when Gramma knew Mrs Moffat.'

'Oh, Abby.' Madge shook her head. 'When I think of that poor Millie! What's happened to her? Who's taking care of her?'

'She's all right, she's with her folks. And the Ramsays gave her ten pounds on top of her wages.'

'And they think that's all they need do? It's disgraceful.' Madge caught at Abby's hand. 'Abby, it might have been you!'

'Don't worry, Lennox never got very far with me. I just hope I've frightened him away from Tilda.'

'But now you've been dismissed without a reference? Abby, it isn't fair! What are you going to do?'

Abby showed Madge Sarah's cutting. 'First, I'm going to apply for this. I'll use Miss Taylor's reference from school. It should count for something, even if it is three years old.'

'I wish I could do something to help, Abby.'

'I was wondering – could you make me something new to wear? In case I get an interview?'

Madge leaped to her feet. 'I'll get some material tomorrow. There's still some of Gramma's money left, I can pay out of that. Shall we look at my patterns?'

Abby hesitated. 'If you don't mind, Ma, I'd just like to go down the stair – see if Frankie's waiting.'

He was leaning against the locked door of his mother's shop, his hat on the back of his head, his hands in his pockets, whistling one of the tunes he played at the cinema. When he saw Abby, his blue eyes danced and he swept her into his arms.

'I thought you were niver coming, are you no' going to miss your tram?'

His lips were sweet on hers and for a moment she clung to him, letting herself enjoy the moment of being with him again, before she drew away.

'I'm not going back to Glenluce Place, Frankie. I've been given my notice.'

'Notice? You?' He shook his head in astonishment, 'I dinna believe it, Abby. Why'd they want to give you notice?'

'I was caught reading Mr Ramsay's books instead of doing my work.'

'And they sacked you for that?'

She nodded. It was partly true and she had decided not to tell Frankie the whole truth about her dismissal, in case he felt like punching Lennox Ramsay. The sight of Lennox with a bloody nose would have been satisfying, but she didn't want Frankie up on an assault charge.

'I don't care, anyway,' she went on, swinging Frankie's hands in hers. 'I've wanted to do something better for a long time and now's my chance.'

'You'll no' move away?' he asked quickly.

'No, there's an accounts job at Logie's and I'm going to apply for it.'

'Accounts.' In the dim light of the streetlamp, Frankie's

expression seemed subdued. 'Aye, well you're clever enough to do anything you've a mind for, Abby. You'll no' have to earn your living playing a piano.'

'Frankie, don't talk like that, you're very talented.'

He gave a crooked smile. 'Will you still marry me if I'm selling sweeties in Ma's shop and you're running Logie's?'

She laughed and kissed him. 'Who's talking about marriage?'

'I might be.'

'Oh, Frankie, we're both too young, we'd be crazy.'

'Well, you know me, I am crazy.' He held her close. 'I'm no' talking about next week. Just one day, eh?'

'One day.' They kissed again, long and passionately, then Abby said she must go. 'My first evening back, I have to talk to Ma and write my application.'

'Aye.' He walked with her up the stairs to her mother's door. 'Shall I see you tomorrow, Abby?'

'You can go with me to Logie's. I'm going to deliver my application by hand.' She ran her hand down his face. 'But you'll have to get up early, Frankie, no staying in bed till dinner time!'

He grinned. 'Anything for you, Abby.'

When Abby let herself back into the flat, she found Madge and her sisters sitting round the table, now covered with its usual chenille cloth. At the looks on their faces, Abby, who had been on wings, fell instantly to earth. Something was up and she could guess what it was. When Madge asked her to sit down, she had something to tell her, Abby slowly pulled up a chair.

'You know I've been seeing Mr Gilbride,' Madge began, staring at her folded hands. She stopped and cleared her throat. 'Well, we've got to know each other very well, we've become friends – more than friends – and the thing is – what I want to tell you is – that he has asked me to marry him.'

There was a silence. The girls studied the chenille tablecloth.

'And I've said yes,' Madge finished.

Abby raised desolate eyes. 'It's funny, I've been expecting this,' she murmured, 'but I'm still surprised.'

'I'm not!' cried Rachel. 'I just don't believe it, that's all. I don't believe it!'

Jennie said nothing. She had gone rather pale.

'I know it must seem strange to you,' Madge said desperately, 'having a new father—'

'We don't want a new father!' Rachel cried. 'We don't want Mr Gilbride!'

'It's Ma's life,' said Abby, 'she has a right to marry again if she wants to.'

'But not him, Abby, not Mr Gilbride. He's horrible, he's got horrible eyes that stare, and a terrible temper, everybody says so. Ma wouldn't be happy with him, I know she wouldn't. Oh, Ma, please don't take him!'

Madge put her hand to her brow. 'I'd no idea you felt like this, Rachel, no idea at all.'

'You knew we didn't like him, Ma.'

'Jennie' – Madge turned to her quickly – 'you like Mr Gilbride, don't you? I remember you said so. And you like Rory and Malcolm, too. You'd be happy to have them as brothers, wouldn't you?'

'Brothers?' Jennie's pallor turned to a deep scarlet. 'Rory as a brother?' She gave a sob and jumping to her feet, ran into the bedroom, slamming the door behind her with a crash that shook the people at the table like a physical blow.

'Jennie!' Madge sprang up, would have run after her, but Abby held her arm. 'Leave her alone, Ma. Can't you see what's the matter? Don't you know how she feels about Rory?'

'Feels about Rory? Jennie's only a child, she can't have feelings about Rory!'

'She's got feelings, Ma, and they're not for Rory as a brother. Didn't you see the way she looked at him today?'

Madge slowly shook her head. It seemed to her, as she stared from Abby to Rachel, that her children had suddenly grown up behind her back, that she didn't know them at all.

'I must talk to Jennie,' she murmured, 'I can't leave her in there on her own.'

'Well, I don't know what you can say.'

'She really does care for Rory?'

'Everybody knows that,' said Rachel.

Everybody except me, thought Madge. She'd been so

72

wrapped up in her own affairs, she had not seen what was happening to her daughter.

'I am going to talk to her,' she announced. 'I'll make her see that it can still be all right. Rory isn't her real brother, it won't make any difference if I marry Mr Gilbride.'

'Jennie won't see it that way,' Abby told her. 'You said Mr Gilbride was going to be her new father, so Rory must be her brother.'

Madge looked about her, distractedly, then moved towards the bedroom.

'I'll talk to her, Abby, it's all I can do.'

Jennie was lying on her bed in the darkness, her quilt pulled up to her chin.

'Jennie, it's Ma,' Madge whispered, sitting on the bed.

'It's no good coming to talk to me, Ma. Talking's not going to make things different.'

'I'll just light the gas, shall I?'

'No! I don't want the light. Just leave me alone.'

'Listen to me, Jennie. I've come to tell you there's no need for you to get upset like this, I promise you, there isn't.'

'Yes, there is. You're going to marry Mr Gilbride and he'll be our new father. That's what you said, isn't it? So if he's our new father, Rory will be my brother.' Jennie burst into tears. 'And brothers can't marry sisters.'

'Marry? Jennie, what are you talking about? You're only a child still and Rory's a boy. By the time you're old enough to marry, you'll have forgotten all about Rory.'

'No, I won't, I shall never forget about Rory. He's the only person I'll ever want to marry.' Jennie sat up in bed, her eyes glittering in the half-darkness. 'I mean that, Ma, I'll never marry anyone but Rory. But if you make him my brother, I won't be able to, and I'll never forgive you!'

'He won't be your real brother, Jennie! Only your step-brother, that's not the same. I don't know the law, but I can't see why stepchildren shouldn't marry if they want to.'

'I don't care about the law.' Jennie flung herself back against her pillow. 'I only know, if you marry Mr Gilbride, Rory will think I'm his sister and he'll never want me, that's all I know.'

'Oh, Jennie—'

'Ma, I don't want to talk any more. I just want you to leave me alone.'

'You'd better have some tea, Ma,' Abby said, when Madge came drooping from the bedroom. 'You look terrible.'

'I feel terrible. I don't know what's to be done.'

'You could give up Mr Gilbride,' said Rachel.

Abby moved the kettle across to the heat. 'I've told you, Rachel, Ma must do what she wants to do.'

'You have to remember that you girls will have your lives,' Madge said quietly, 'I should have mine.'

'Yes, but not with him!' cried Rachel. 'Abby, you agree, don't you? Ma would never be happy with Mr Gilbride?'

'I don't like him, I'm not going to say I do.'

'You don't have to like him!' Madge cried with sudden spirit. 'Though why you shouldn't, I don't know. He's never been anything but nice to you.'

'I don't trust him.' Abby made the tea and set out cups and saucers. 'I'm sorry, I wish I did.'

'Let's just have that tea and go to bed,' Madge said after a pause, 'it's been a long day.'

When she was alone, Madge went about her usual night-time duties, damping down the range, lowering the gas, setting the table for breakfast, with no consciousness of what she was doing. She had not felt so low since Will died, and now she was bitter, too. A door had been opened, a door to love and fulfilment, but her daughters it seemed wanted it closed. They did not like Mr Gilbride, so she was not to like him, either. Jennie had a childish attachment to Rory, so her mother must give up her real attachment to his father. Almost certainly, what Madge had told Jennie was true; by the time she was ready for marriage, she would have quite forgotten Rory and Madge's sacrifice would have been for nothing. As for Abby and Rachel being so against Jim, why should they be? He had a temper, it couldn't be denied, but it never lasted. It flared and it died and then he was himself again, the man she loved and wanted, the man who could give her happiness again. Everyone was entitled to happiness if it was offered, and how often would love like Jim's come her way?

I have the right, Madge thought, trembling, I have the right to take it.

But then she remembered Jennie and her face in the shadows, so young, so grieving – this must seem like the end of the world to her. Poor Jennie, poor child. And Abby, so despondent, Rachel, so incensed. Madge had brought an end to all their worlds that night. Yet, she loved Jim and had said she would marry him. He had rights, too.

As she undressed for bed, Madge decided she would not try to come to any decision just then, she would think about things, weigh them up, be sensible and practical.

She felt as though she was being torn to pieces.

Next morning, Jim caught her as she was running down the stairs, already late for work.

'Madge, I wanted to thank you for that grand tea you gave us,' he told her, smiling. 'The lads really appreciated it.'

'I'm glad.' Madge tried to smile back, conscious of her pallor and the shadows beneath her eyes; she had scarcely slept. 'Jim, I've got to go, I'm late.'

'Yes, but listen, did you tell the girls? Did you tell 'em about us?'

'No,' she said at once, 'I didn't.'

Jim's brow darkened. 'Why not? I thought sure you'd tell 'em last night. I told the boys.'

'What did they say?'

He laughed. 'What you might guess. They were thrilled. Canna wait to get you into the family. We've been on our own too long.'

'And they like the girls?'

'Aye, they've always wanted sisters. Madge, when will you tell 'em?'

'Soon, but the thing is . . .' Madge, trying to placate him, remembered Abby. 'The thing is, Jim, something's happened. Abby's been dismissed and it's – you know – upset us.'

'Dismissed? A fine girl like her? What for?'

Madge lowered her voice. 'There was a young man – the son of the house – made advances. When she complained, they told her to go. Without even a character!'

Jim's face went red with anger. 'Tell me his name,' he said

tightly. 'Tell me the feller's name, I'll go down and teach him a thing or two!'

'No, no, that wouldn't do any good. Please calm down, Jim, it's all over. Abby's left and says good riddance, she's trying for another job and I'm going to make her something to wear for the interview.' Madge was hurrying down the Lawnmarket. 'Look, I must go, but I promise I'll tell the girls soon, I will!'

Jim caught up with her and grasped her arm. 'I'll be waiting,' he whispered, close to her face, 'because I want you. But I'll no' wait too long. You ken that, eh?'

Oh, God, thought Madge, leaving him, what am I going to do?

Chapter Eleven

On Tuesday, Abby's box arrived, together with an envelope containing six pounds.

'See, they've docked me three pounds!' she exclaimed to Madge. 'I get thirty-six pounds a year now, that's nine pounds the quarter. They haven't paid me for December.'

'Well, I suppose it's fair in a way, if you're not working in December.'

'Ma, they threw me out! I didn't ask not to work in December!' Abby sighed in exasperation. 'Oh, well, I suppose there's nothing I can do about it. And at least I can pay you for my keep now.'

'Let's get on with your two-piece,' said Madge, spreading a clean sheet over the table. 'I'm really looking forward to this, Abby.'

Together they rolled out the fine blue woollen tweed Madge had managed to buy from Archie Shields for only six shillings a yard with lining thrown in, for Archie had always had a soft spot for her, even if she had never agreed to work for him. Madge always liked a bargain and even in her worried state gave a little smile remembering it, as she took her tape measure from her work basket.

'Stand still, Abby, I'd better just check your measurements.'

'I feel so bad, Ma, getting you to do this for me,' Abby murmured, obediently lifting her arms and turning as her mother ordered. 'If I hadn't been such a terrible needle-woman, I could have done it myself.'

'Can't be good at everything.' Madge laughed a little. 'Look at me, I can scarcely give the right change!'

'But couldn't we get Jennie to help you, Ma? She's very good, she could do a lot, and you'll be tired when you come home from work.'

'Oh, I don't think we should ask Jennie to do anything,' Madge said quickly. 'She's not speaking to me at the moment.'

'That is so ridiculous!' Abby strode to the bedroom door and shouted, 'Jennie, here a minute!'

'She won't come,' Rachel called from her chair by the range where she was reading *Little Women*. 'She doesn't want to talk.'

'Jennie!' cried Abby again, ignoring Rachel. 'Come here, I want you to help Ma with my two-piece.'

Jennie, very pale, with reddened eyelids, appeared at the door of the bedroom.

'Why should I?' she asked.

'Because I want you to, because Ma wants you to.'

'Well, I don't want to!' Jennie cried, and went back into the bedroom, slamming the door behind her.

'I told you,' Rachel said with satisfaction.

'Honestly!' Abby's face was red with anger. 'She'd get the strap from some parents, Ma, talking like that!'

'As though I'd use a strap on any of you!' Madge cried. 'You know why she's upset, Abby.'

Abby sat down. 'Yes, I know. I didn't mean I wanted you to punish her. I suppose we're all a bit on edge.'

'You are,' said Rachel.

'I think we should just leave Jennie alone for the present,' Madge murmured, 'she'll come round.'

'When you're married to Mr Gilbride?' asked Rachel.

'Will you be quiet?' Abby hissed, as Madge, her face coldly set, assembled her paper patterns over the material and took up her tailor's scissors. For a moment she hesitated, the blades of the scissors poised in her capable hands over the new blue cloth, then, as Abby and Rachel watched in fascination, she began to cut.

'Ma, I'll pay you back for the material,' Abby said quietly. 'I've got my money now and I don't want you to use up Gramma's savings on me.'

'Your money has to last some time, I don't want you to pay me back. Gramma meant that money to be used as needed and you need it now. You have to look smart for your interview, Abby.'

'If I get one.'

'Of course you'll get one.'

'I've no proper qualifications, Ma.'

'It's only a junior post, they won't expect any.' Madge looked up from her work. 'And look how much you've done on your own, anyway. I think they'll be impressed.'

'I've no reference from my last job,' Abby said glumly. 'What do I say about that?'

Every morning, Abby waited for a letter from Logie's, and every evening, as she sewed and pinned and treadled away, Madge waited for a knock on her door from Jim Gilbride. He would be wanting to know if she had spoken to the girls yet and she would say – what would she say? She longed to see him, longed to be with him, yet the thought of his knock filled her with dread. 'All a bit on edge,' Abby had said. Madge felt they were walking on glass.

On Friday morning, Abby ran down the stairs as usual to sort through the letters the postie had left. A few minutes later, she tore back to the flat, half laughing, half crying, her dark eyes ablaze.

'Ma, I've got one!' she shrieked. 'I've got an interview! Oh, can you believe it?'

Madge, who had been putting on her hat before leaving for work, gave a cry of joy. 'Abby, that's wonderful, oh, that's really wonderful! I knew all along you'd get one, but it's wonderful all the same.' She flung her arms round Abby and kissed her. 'When do they want you?'

'Monday morning at ten.' Abby sat down at the table where the porridge plates lay waiting to be cleared. She shook her head dazedly. 'I can't believe it. Monday morning at ten. At Logie's. Me.'

'Oh, Abby, that's not much notice,' Madge said, worriedly. 'Your costume – it's not ready.'

'There's all the weekend, there's plenty of time.' Abby jumped up. 'I'll wear my white blouse and my black gloves and my strap shoes – and I can borrow your blue hat, can't I, Ma? Oh, Rachel – Jennie . . .' Abby danced around the room. 'I've got an interview at Logie's!'

'I always knew you'd get one,' said Rachel.

'So did I.' Jennie turned to her mother. 'Ma, I'll do the buttonholes, shall I?'

'Oh, Jennie!' Madge held her close. 'Jennie, you've come back!'

Into the scene of kissing and hugging, a shadow fell. Jim Gilbride had come in through the open door.

'What's going on?' he asked, smiling. 'Somebody got some good news?'

Jennie and Rachel sidled away to school, while Abby disappeared with the porridge plates. Madge, picking up her shopping bag, said hastily, 'Oh, Jim, I'm late again. Will you walk with me?'

'Seems that's as far as we get these days.' Jim took Madge's arm as they went out together into the street. 'Have you no' been wondering where I've been?'

'Yes, I have. What's been happening?'

'Big office job in Lothian Road, had to get done by yesterday.' Jim whistled and shook his head. 'Meant working all hours, by electric light and all, had me spinning, I can tell you. Listen, have you missed me?'

'I have,' she answered truthfully.

'Well, I'll be free tomorrow, we can go out tomorrow. ' He pressed her hand. 'Seems a lifetime since we were out, eh? Where'll we go?'

'Jim, I'm ever so sorry, I can't go out. Not this weekend. I've got sewing to do for Abby.' Madge looked nervously away. 'She's got an interview at Logie's on Monday and I'm making her a new costume, a two-piece, you know, a really difficult pattern, and it's taken longer than I thought. But I could see you on Monday, Jim, it'll all be over by then.'

'Oh, yes?' With a sinking heart, she saw that his face had taken on a hard, brickish flush and his eyes had the intense brightness that always accompanied his anger. 'You can see me on Monday because your sewing'll be finished by then, will it? That tells me where I stand, eh?'

'You said you couldn't see me lately because of your job, Jim. This is just the same. It doesn't mean I don't want to see you. I'm longing to see you!'

'Aye, when you've finished working yourself to death for

that girl of yours. You'd lie down in the street and let her walk all over you, if that's what she wanted. Och, it makes me sick to think of it! You and me engaged, practically wed, and you canna fit me in before Monday because you have to do some bloody sewing for a girl that should be doing it for hersel' anyway! You call that a job? You say that's the same as my job, when I have to earn the money to live by what I do? Where's the truth in that, Madge?'

'I'm sorry, it was a silly thing to say, of course it's not the same.' She tried to take back the hand he had snatched away, but he wouldn't allow it, was striding ahead in the way he had, his head in its spattered cap held high, his boots ringing on the pavement.

'Jim, wait!' she cried, hurrying after him, aware of the stares from people passing by. 'Please try to understand!'

He stopped and turned to face her. 'Seems to me I understand anyway, Madge. In your life, your girls come first, and me second. Is that the way it's always going to be?'

'No, no!' She twisted her hands together, not able to look at the pain in his eyes. 'If you'll just let me get this done, I'll be able to go out with an easy mind, Jim. You know how it is, when there's something you have to do?'

As usual, as suddenly as it had risen, his anger left him. He looked away, down the Mound, at the crowds hurrying under the dark winter sky.

'I only want to be with you, Madge, that's all I can think about.'

'Well, shall we meet on Monday, then?'

'Aye, on Monday.' He began to walk away from her. 'Same time, eh?'

'Same time.' Madge took a deep breath and walked on fast to Thistle Street. She felt she had been reprieved.

'You're late, Madge,' Miss Dow said sharply as Madge unbuttoned her coat. 'There's all the trays to do, you know.'

'I'm sorry, Miss Dow, it won't happen again.'

Annie, already setting out tea loaves and currant buns, winked as Miss Dow turned her back. 'Naughty girl, Madge! Ha' you been chatting to your man, then?'

'I overslept,' Madge answered, 'that's all.'

Annie happily pursed her lips. 'I'll believe you!' she cried.

As she helped to fill the bakery shelves, Madge's mood did not lighten. She felt weighed down by the strain of the meeting with Jim, by the burden of her love for him, by her anxiety for the girls. Jennie had come back to her and that was wonderful, but how long would she stay? Then there was Abby. She must be given her chance, no matter what it cost. Afterwards, Madge could decided what to do.

It was a shock to arrive home that evening and find that Abby had had her hair cut.

'Oh, Abby, what have you done?' cried Madge, collapsing into a chair.

'I think it looks lovely,' said Jennie. 'It suits her, and it's all the thing.'

'Yes, it's good.' Rachel swung Abby round and studied the bob with critical eyes. 'Makes you look – like a girl who goes out to business!'

'That's exactly what I want to look like,' Abby replied. 'Come on, Ma, it's not a crime to cut your hair.'

'But you had such lovely thick hair.' Madge sighed. 'Oh, I can't get used to these modern ideas. It's a good job your Gramma can't see you.'

'I bet Gramma'd have been the first to try out something new when she was young. Anyway, I want to please the people at Logie's, that's why I've had it done.'

'Has Frankie seen it yet?' asked Rachel, and Madge's eyes flickered.

'I don't think we need worry what Frankie thinks,' she said, a little coldly.

'He hasn't seen it,' Abby answered, 'but, as I said, I did it for Logie's. Oh – every time I think of Monday morning, I get butterflies in my stomach. I wish it was all over!'

Madge, rising to look at the stovies Abby had put in the oven for tea, thought, And what about Monday evening for me?

Chapter Twelve

Logie's of Princes Street was one of Edinburgh's finest stores, on a par with Jenner's and Forsyth's. Rumour had it that Queen Mary had been known to shop there, and it was certainly grand enough for royal custom, with its smart commissionaire, its high-ceilinged, oak-fitted departments, its hydraulic lifts, and respectful staff. Joseph Logie had founded it back in 1869 and there had been grand half-century celebrations after the war – though Joseph had died by then and had handed over the store to a Board of Trustees and his sister's son, Stephen Farrell. Mr Farrell, a handsome man with thick silver hair cut to show his well-shaped head, was as distinguished-looking as any of his customers – or clients, as he liked to think of them – and he ran Logie's with an efficiency even more impressive than his uncle's. One of the practices dear to his heart was to sit in on interviews for all staff, however humble their position in the hierarchy. That way, he said, he could be sure that only people of the right calibre were appointed. 'Only the best for Logie's, only the best at Logie's', was the framed motto hanging over Mr Farrell's desk, and on the wall of the waiting room into which Abby was shown on Monday morning. When she read it, her heart sank to her black strapped shoes. How could they possibly consider her the best? The two young men already waiting were much more likely candidates, both looking composed, with well-brushed hair and wearing good dark suits. She picked up a magazine and stared at it with unseeing eyes.

Before she had entered the portals of the great store, she had been feeling quietly confident. It was true what Rachel had said of her, she looked like a girl who went out to business, and the blue two-piece, with its shorter skirt and stylish jacket (buttonholes beautifully worked by Jennie) made her look, as Abby put it to Madge, her 'absolute best'.

'Ma, I can never thank you enough,' she had murmured, as she gave her mother one last hug before Madge left for work. 'I only hope I can get the job and pay you back one day.'

'I told you, Abby, I don't want any money.'

'I wasn't thinking just of money, Ma,' Abby told her.

Frankie Baxter had walked with her as far as Logie's doors but, nervous at seeing the commissionaire again, had said maybe he wouldn't wait.

'No, don't wait,' said Abby, 'there's no point.'

'I'd like to walk you home, though.'

'You won't know when it's over, will you?' Abby swallowed and touched Frankie's hand. 'I'll let you know the minute I get back.'

He had murmured good luck as she waved and passed through the revolving doors and the commissionaire had touched his hat. As though I could afford to shop here, she had thought with awe, but when she asked directions for the interview, his expression changed and her spirits fell.

What am I doing here? she asked herself, as she was taken up in the lift by a lady assistant who didn't speak to her. It's all a mistake, I'm a fraud and they'll know. What am I going to do?

A clock in the little room ticked loudly, its hands showing three minutes to ten. The two young men studied their finger nails and over her magazine she gave them covert glances. One, she saw now with guilty satisfaction, had spots. The other was blond, with a small moustache and a smoothness about him that made her choose him as the one who would be appointed. There was something in his manner that showed he had already decided that for himself.

As the clock began to strike ten, the door opened and an elegant, thin faced young man appeared.

'We're taking you in alphabetical order,' he announced with an easy smile. 'Mr Cameron, would you like to come this way, please?'

The blond young man rose without change of expression and was ushered into a larger office opening from the waiting room. When the door had closed on him, the young man with the spots looked across at Abby.

'Mind if I ask your name?'

'Abigail Ritchie.'

'You'll go in before me, then. My name's Alan Talbot.'

'Might be an advantage to go in last.'

'Won't matter when I go in. I'm hopeless at figures.'

Abby stared. 'Why are you applying for this job, then?'

'My dad's idea. He's a trustee here. Thinks I should start this way and work my way up.'

'I see.' Abby was beginning to revise her ideas on who would be the successful candidate. 'So what would you rather do?'

'Be an actor. No, don't laugh.'

'I'm not laughing. I think it would be wonderful to be able to do something like that.'

'Who says I can?' Young Mr Talbot was suddenly very serious. 'All I can say is, it's all I want to do.'

'You should do it, then. Why don't you?'

'Maybe I will. What about you? You really want this job?'

'More than anything.'

'Well, I hope you get it. There's not many girls want to work in accounts.'

'I do,' she said quietly.

The clock ticked. They stared at their magazines. Suddenly, the door opened again and the blond young man reappeared. A voice said, 'Miss Ritchie, please.'

Two people were facing her from behind a long oak table. One was a handsome silver-haired man in his fifties; the other a woman of about forty, heavily built, with dark grey hair and spectacles. On the wall over their heads was a portrait showing a strong-faced, elderly man wearing Victorian dress, standing against a background of Logie's famous Princes Street façade.

'Our founder, Miss Ritchie,' said the man who had shown her into the office and she saw that he too was handsome, in the way of the man with silver hair. 'Joseph Logie.'

'Oh, yes,' Abby said huskily. She tried to sit gracefully on the chair placed for her, as the two people at the oak table smiled at her.

'Good morning, Miss Ritchie,' said the woman with the spectacles. 'May I present Mr Farrell, the Senior Partner of Logie's, and Mr Gerald Farrell, a partner in the firm?'

The man with the silver hair inclined his head and the younger man nodded and took his seat behind the table.

'I am Miss Inver, Chief Accounts Clerk,' the woman went on, 'and I shall be conducting your interview.' She shuffled some papers before her. 'Now, Miss Ritchie, I see that you are soon to be eighteen years old and that you live in Catherine's Land?'

'Yes, that's correct,' Abby replied. 'We moved there from Southampton when my father died.'

'Ah, you're English?' asked Mr Farrell. 'We are quite happy with that, quite happy. I went to school in England myself.'

Miss Inver waited politely, then went on; 'I must tell you, Miss Ritchie, that we were most impressed by the presentation of your application, and by your headmistress's testimonial. It's what you could call glowing, in fact.'

'Thank you, ma'am.'

'We also liked your initiative in studying book-keeping on your own, particularly as the duties of this post will be mainly general book-keeping. Can you tell us how you came to take up these studies?'

'I thought I should try to qualify myself. I've always wanted to work with figures in some way.'

'That's interesting. Of course, people with Logie's receive training, anyway, and are encouraged to take the public examinations. You'd want to do that?'

'Yes, ma'am, I would.' Abby's heart was beating fast, sweat was breaking out on the palms of her hands. It was all going so well, so unbelievably well. Too well? She was beginning to feel rather afraid.

Miss Inver looked down at her papers again. 'There is one point, however, we're not clear about, Miss Ritchie . . .'

Abby froze.

'If you left school at fourteen and are now nearly eighteen, what have you been doing in the past four years?'

Abby looked into Miss Inver's intelligent eyes.

'I was in service.'

There was a short silence. 'Service?' repeated Miss Inver. 'Here, in Edinburgh?'

'Yes, I was upper housemaid to a family in the West End.'

'We appear to have no reference from your employer, Miss Ritchie.'

'No, ma'am, I wasn't given one.' Abby took a deep breath. 'I was dismissed without one.'

All three persons facing her sat back in their chairs, their eyebrows raised, and Mr Gerald Farrell shook his head, as though in disbelief.

'Dismissed without a reference? For what reason?' Miss Inver was leaning forward again, her blue eyes behind her glasses very serious.

'They said it was for reading my employer's books instead of just dusting them,' Abby said valiantly.

'And did you?' Mr Farrell asked, his mouth twitching a little.

'I always did my work first, sir, but the books were there and yes, I suppose I did read them – from time to time.'

'They can't have sacked you just for that,' Mr Gerald observed. 'Come, Miss Ritchie, what was the real reason?'

Abby looked down at her hands holding her gloves. 'I'd rather not say,' she said at last, gripped by a quiet despair. Instead of managing to gloss over the episode, she had presented herself in the worst possible light, had made it seem she was one who wasted her employer's time, who would give no satisfactory account of why she had been sent packing. But if she had given the real reason for her dismissal, would they have thought any better of her? A housemaid accusing the son of her employers? They might have thought she had encouraged him, or made the whole thing up, as Mrs Ramsay would certainly have told them if they had asked her. I might as well leave now, thought Abby wretchedly, put myself out of my misery.

'Miss Ritchie,' said Miss Iver, softly, 'may I ask you – was there a young man in the household where you worked?'

Abby's head jerked up, her cheeks flushing scarlet. She could not speak.

Miss Iver nodded. 'I see there was. Well, perhaps we should

leave this, turn to other matters. You've told us you've studied book-keeping. Can you tell me what you would expect to find in your department, if you were asked to keep the books for a firm like this?'

From the depths, Abby's spirits rocketed. She had been let off! They weren't going to press on her dismissal, they had understood, or at least Miss Inver had understood, and now they were only interested in what she knew. And she could tell them. She began to pour out all that she had learned in those long cold hours when the rest of the house slept, when her candle guttered and her hands sometimes grew too cold to hold the pen. What would she expect to find? The journal, the ledger, the daybook, the invoice book, the cash account, the bank account – the terms came tripping off her tongue so fast she could hardly hold them back, and a world of double entry and balance sheets seemed to be opening up before her, when Mr Farrell held up his hand.

'Thank you, Miss Ritchie, I see you know your subject. In theory. But I'm a practical man, as my uncle was before me. I go by what people can do.' There suddenly appeared in his hand a long sheet of paper. 'Here are some figures from a balance sheet. As you'll see, there are the usual columns, liabilities, assets, but no totals. Would you be so good as to total them up for me and tell me if they balance?'

Abby took the paper. 'Now, sir?'

'If you please, Miss Ritchie.'

Only the muted sound of traffic outside the office windows broke the silence, as Abby stared down at the figures she had been given. They were for large sums of money in pounds, shillings and pence, all neatly written in ink. Three pairs of eyes, as she was well aware, were watching, waiting to see if she was as good as she had made herself out to be.

No, I'm not, she thought, as panic descended, I can't do it. I can't total these up with those three watching me, it's impossible. Even as she studied them, the figures appeared to be merging, running into a darkness she could not fathom, and she was about to cry out, 'I'm sorry!' – when the darkness faded, the figures separated again, became only the kind of figures she had worked with many, many times. It's my practice time, she told herself, this is just another exercise, I can do it and I will. She saw that Mr Farrell had placed a pencil before her on the table and with a hand she made steady, she picked it up and began to tap down the columns, adding as she went, finally pencilling in her totals, which tallied.

'They balance,' she announced. 'I make the totals, eight hundred and seventy-five pounds, seven shillings, and no pence. Is that right?'

Instead of answering, Mr Farrell glanced at Miss Inver, who said, pleasantly, 'Would you mind waiting outside, Miss Ritchie? We have to see Mr Talbot now.'

Chapter Thirteen

She was back in the waiting room, her cheeks burning. her thoughts whirling. Had she made a fool of herself in there, babbling out all that textbook stuff she'd put into her head?

'I see you know your subject. . . in theory,' Mr Farrell had said, and had made it plain enough that everything was going to depend on that practice balance sheet. If only he'd said whether she'd got it right! Abby was in torment because she couldn't be sure that she had.

Her gaze went to Mr Cameron, staring into space. Why was she wasting her time worrying about the balance sheet? If the job didn't go to the trustee's son, the nice would-be actor, it would go to this blond fellow. He was so perfect, with his good suit and confident air; he looked as though he had never so much as set foot in a place like Catherine's Land, never mind lived in one. Yet, to be fair, the interviewing board had seemed to take no interest in where she lived. Abby heaved a long sigh. No, they were much more interested in that balance sheet.

'What did you get?' she was astonished to hear herself asking. 'What total for the balance sheet?'

He lifted his fair brows. 'Balance sheet?'

'Yes, didn't they give you one to total?'

'Oh, that.' He shrugged and in his Morningside accent said lightly, 'I'm afraid I don't remember precisely.'

'Well, did you get the totals to balance?'

'I believe I did. Yes, I got them to balance.'

'I did, too.' Abby tried to smile. 'Not that that proves anything.'

'No.' Mr Cameron returned his gaze to space and they did not speak again.

Alan Talbot was soon back, wearing a rueful grin.

'Don't ask how I got on,' he said to Abby, 'I think they're going to offer me Carpets.'

'Carpets?' jerked out Mr Cameron. 'You mean that's an alternative?'

'It's just another department. I expect I could start there, if I wanted to.'

'But you don't want to, do you?' asked Abby as Alan Talbot sat down. His grin faded.

'No, I don't. Maybe I'll do what I want to do instead.'

'Miss Ritchie?' came Mr Gerald's voice from the door. 'Would you mind stepping this way?'

She was flying to Thistle Street, or so it seemed. Miss Ritchie, they had said, we'd like you to start on Monday, December 13th, your salary will be £54.12s per annum, you will be entitled to one week's paid holiday a year and discounts on purchases at a fixed percentage, you will be instructed in your duties by Miss Inver and encouraged to take the professional examinations, provided you study in your own time. Miss Ritchie, welcome to Logie's! (And, yes, Mr Farrell had told her, you got it right.)

Welcome to Logie's. She couldn't believe it. No more sweeping and dusting, or making beds and cleaning the brass, no more answering bells, or worrying about working for people like the Ramsays, no more keeping out of the way of a fellow like Lennox. But Tilda – Abby slowed down a little – she would still be looking out for Tilda. Not everyone could escape, as Abby had escaped. It would be up to her to do something for those who were left. She quickened her step, hurrying towards Mackenzie's and Madge.

'Ma, I've got the job!' she cried, bursting into the shop and, in front of Miss Dow's scandalised eyes and Annie's astonished grin, she kissed her mother, who dropped a customer's bag of teacakes and shed a few tears. Then it was up the Mound to Catherine's Land, to find Frankie coming running, while his stout, forbidding mother clicked her tongue and asked what all the fuss was about.

'I've got it, Frankie,' Abby told him. 'I still can't believe it. They didn't mind about my reference, they didn't seem to mind about anything.'

'Did I no' tell you?' he asked, taking her hands, trying to match her joy and failing. 'I said you could do anything you wanted to!'

'I was lucky, Frankie, they could easily have turned me down.'

'Not you.' They began to walk down the street, away from his mother's shop and his mother's eyes. 'They'd have been crazy to turn you down. Listen, shall we go celebrate? Have a bite to eat somewhere?' He put his hand in his pocket and rattled some coins. 'Come on, I'll treat you, eh?'

'Oh, Frankie, that would be lovely!'

'And tonight you can come to the Palace – all of you – I can get you free seats.' His eyes were dancing again. 'Want to?'

'You mean Ma and the girls as well?' Abby's hand was shaking as she put it into his. 'Frankie, I can't believe all this is happening. It seems too good to be true.'

'Luck has to turn some time, Abby.'

'It doesn't for everybody, though.'

'Let's no' think about everybody, Abby. Just you and me.'

But that evening Madge said she couldn't go to the Palace Cinema. She'd promised to meet Mr Gilbride.

'Oh well, that's that, then,' said Abby flatly.

'Ma, it'll spoil everything if you don't come,' cried Rachel.

'Maybe Mr Gilbride could come, too,' Jennie suggested, but Abby frowned and Rachel shook her head.

Madge said quickly, 'No, no, that wouldn't do. You go, girls, and I'll be here when you get back. Go on, it'll be lovely, the three of you.'

When the girls had left, starry-eyed with excitement, Madge paced her floor with nervous steps. Then she left her flat and crossed to Jim's.

'There's no one in, they've gone to the pictures,' she told him, and saw his eyes light up.

'You mean we needn't go out? I can come over?'

'Yes,' she said quietly, 'come over.'

Chapter Fourteen

He came in, warily at first, as though he couldn't believe they were alone, as though he expected one of the girls to leap out from behind Madge's rocking chair. When it became clear that there was only Madge waiting, he grinned.

'You clever woman,' he whispered, drawing her into his arms, 'how'd you think of it? Why'd we no' think of sending them out before?'

'I've never liked Jennie and Rachel to be out on their own, Jim. Abby's with them tonight, that's the difference.'

'For us, too, eh?' His arms held her, his mouth was on hers. It was what she had longed for and yet feared, for the more they clung together, feeling the pleasure of their contact, the harder it was to pull apart.

'Jim, wait, I want to talk . . .'

His face was softening before her gaze, changing from the hard front he put on to the world, melting with the love he felt and the desire. 'No talking,' he murmured fondly, 'you're no saying you're going to waste time talking when we're alone like this?'

'I don't want to, Jim, but I have to.' With a supreme effort, she pulled herself from him. 'I have something to tell you.'

Something in her tone made him instantly alert. 'Tell me? Tell me what?'

'Let's sit down.' She moved towards her chair, but did not sit down and neither did he.

'What d'you want to tell me?' he asked quietly.

'I – don't know how to begin.'

'No' good news, then?'

She shook her head, keeping her eyes down, yet aware that the soft light of love had already died from his face and that if she looked up the strong hard mask would be back in place.

'D'you want me to guess what it is?' he asked, in a curious, light tone.

'No!' She put her hands to her face, all her rehearsed speeches going from her mind. 'Oh, I'm sorry, Jim, I'm sorry! I can't marry you, I shouldn't have said I would. It'd never work, it'd never do. Jim, I'm so sorry!'

'Sorry!' At the explosive sound of the word whistling between his teeth, her head jerked up and she snatched a quick, terrified glance at his face. It was white. Set. A stranger's face. And she was seized by terror.

'Don't look at me like that!' she cried, and he gave a short bark of laughter.

'How d'you expect me to look at you, Madge?' He caught her by the shoulders. 'You lead me on, you give me your word, you say we'll be wed, then you change your mind – and you're SORRY?' He shook her, hard. 'What d'you think I am? Some great gowk you could play the fool with?'

'No, no! You know that's not true, Jim, that was never true! I love you, I do—'

'Shut up, will you?' He thrust her away from him. 'One minute we're kissing, we're promising to wed, the next, och, no, we canna wed, it wouldna work, it wouldna do! What's happened, then? What's changed? Is it the girls? Is it your Abby?' He took her by the wrist, holding it in such a vice, she cried out with pain. 'Is it Abby, Madge? Has she been blethering behind ma back? Is she the one's put you off? Come on, tell me! I've a right, I've a right to be told!'

'It isn't Abby,' she gasped, 'it isn't the girls.'

'What, then? What made you change your mind?'

'Jim, you're hurting me. Please, let go of me!'

'I'll no' let you go till you tell me the truth.'

'I love you, Jim, everything I said I meant, but I just got to thinking, I didn't want to marry again. It's been too long, I – I could never get used to it. I'm sorry, I'm sorry!'

For a long terrible moment, he was silent as he still held her by the wrist.

'You bitch,' he said, at last, 'I thought you were a lady, I

94

thought you were something sweet, something special' – she burst into tears, swaying in his grasp – 'but you're no better than that Jezebel up the stair, you're worse, because Lily MacLaren never offers a man love.'

'How can you talk to me this way?' Madge cried. 'How can you, Jim? You know what you mean to me – why won't you try to understand?'

'Understand?' His eyes were full of fire, burning into her. 'Do you no' understand what you've done to me, Madge? Do you no' understand what some men'd do to you? To pay you back?

'Jim, no,' she whispered, shaking with terror. 'No,please—'

'You needn't worry,' he answered disgustedly, 'I've never wanted a woman that didna want me.' He dropped her wrist and looked into her face, then he put up his hand and ran it swiftly down her cheek. 'Who'd ha' thought you'd be like you are, Madge, when you look like you do?' As she closed her eyes, wilting before him, he struck her twice with his fist. 'I niver want to see you again as long as I live,' he whispered, and jerking her from him, ran from her flat and down the stairs, through the playing children and out into the street.

Chapter Fifteen

When the last film ended, Frankie played the National Anthem and went to the back of the cinema to find Abby and her sisters.

'I'll no' go for a drink,' he told them, 'I'll walk you girls home.'

Jennie and Rachel were thrilled. Thrilled by the films, thrilled by Frankie, thrilled just by being out late at night. As for Abby, she was on the moon. Or, might have been. She wasn't sure where she was, except that it was somewhere way off the ground.

'Like the show, girls?' asked Frankie, as he shepherded them out into Princes Street. 'Like my playing?'

'We liked everything!' Rachel told him promptly. 'Specially your playing.'

'It must be so hard,' said Abby, 'I mean, to get the music to match what you see.'

'Aye, it's no' as easy as folk think.'

Jennie was drifting along the pavement in a dream. 'Didn't you think Edna Purviance was pretty in the Charlie Chaplin?' she murmured. 'Didn't you think she looked like Ma?'

'I think Mary Pickford looks like Ma,' Rachel replied, 'it's her lovely hair.'

'Abby used to have lovely hair,' Frankie said with a laugh. 'Once.'

Abby half withdrew her arm from his. 'You don't like my hair, Frankie?'

'I like what there is of it. But why'd you want to look like a boy?'

'It suits me, everyone thinks so. I thought you did, too.'

'All right, I do, then. Och, you're no' going to get mad at me tonight, Abby? Not tonight?'

Her expression relaxed. 'Not tonight. No, I can't be mad at anyone tonight. Oh, do you know, it still hasn't sunk in? I'm going to work at Logie's!'

They slowly made their way home through the chill December air, Jennie and Rachel going on ahead, Abby and Frank following, arms linked. At the entrance to Catherine's Land, Jennie turned and called for the key to the flat.

'It won't be locked,' Abby replied. 'Ma said she'd be home early.'

'She might not be, though. Come on, Abby, give us the key.'

'All right, you go up. I'll just have a word with Frankie.'

'Thank the Lord,' Frankie whispered, drawing Abby to him, as her sisters, exchanging knowing looks, ran up the stairs. 'I thought they'd niver go!'

But though his kisses seemed as passionate as usual, Abby soon released herself from his arms.

'What is it?' she asked quietly. 'What's different, Frankie? Is it my job?'

'Aye.' His smile was rueful. 'It's no' going to be the same, once you start at Logie's.'

'I don't know what you mean. Why shouldn't it be the same?'

'Well, it's no' like being in service, or working in a shop, is it? It's a man's job, it's a career.'

'And only men should have careers? Is that what you're saying, Frankie?'

'No, I'm no' saying that,' he answered patiently. 'It's fine for women to have careers. But they canna marry, can they? You canna be a teacher and be married. I bet you'll no' be allowed to stay on at Logie's, either. If you marry.'

'I'm not sure,' she said slowly. 'I know it's true there are rules in a lot of professions—'

'And you'd no' want to give up a job like that to marry me, would you?'

'Frankie, I told you we were too young to think about marrying.'

'I know I've no money,' he muttered.

'It's nothing to do with money. You don't want to tie your-self down yet, do you?'

'I want you, Abby, that's what I want.'

'Well, we can still see each other, Frankie!'

'I couldna stand one o' they long engagements, Abby, niver ask me.' He shook his head. 'If we canna be wed, I think maybe I'll go back to Glasgow.'

'Frankie, you wouldn't!' She was staring at him, quite taken aback, when there were flying feet on the stairs and Jennie was beside them, her face paper white, her eyes staring.

'Abby, it's Ma!' she screamed. 'She's hurt!'

Frankie was first at the door of the flat, but Abby cried, 'No, let me see what's happened!' and he stepped back.

'It's all right,' she told him, reappearing quickly, 'nothing to worry about. Ma's just had a fall. Hurt her eye.'

'Hurt her eye?' Frankie looked at Abby dubiously. Everyone who lived in Catherine's Land knew what it meant when a woman 'hurt her eye', but Mrs Ritchie – surely what happened to other women had not happened to her?

'Can I help?' he asked hesitantly. 'Fetch the doctor, or something?'

'No, no, she doesn't need the doctor.' Abby took a deep breath. 'She just tripped, you see, tripped over the end of the mat.'

He nodded, still gazing at Abby, who said she'd better go.

'Thanks for a lovely evening, Frankie.' She brushed his lips with hers. ''Bye, then.'

'Can I see you tomorrow, Abby?'

'I expect so. I'll have to see how Ma is.'

She waited, clearly longing for him to go, and after a moment he turned slowly away.

Madge was lying on the sofa, holding a cold compress to one side of her face, while Jennie and Rachel hovered near, staring at her with enormous eyes.

'It's not as bad as it looks,' she murmured thickly, as blood began to seep again from her cut lip. 'Jennie's making me some tea.'

'Got the kettle on,' Jennie whispered. 'Oh, Abby, what can we do?'

Abby gently took the cloth from Madge's hand and looked in silence at the livid bruises down the side of her mother's face, and the dark, fast-swelling eye.

'Shouldn't we get the doctor?' asked Rachel.

'No,' Madge said at once. 'I only tripped, haven't broken anything.'

'I'll change this cloth and get a plaster for your lip.' Abby glanced at the kettle. 'Jennie, make the tea as soon as you can.'

'I feel better already,' Madge said, wincing as she sipped the tea.' Don't worry, girls, this swelling'll soon go down and then I won't look such a fright.'

'You won't be able to go to work tomorrow, that's for sure,' said Abby. 'I'll go down and tell them, shall I? Tell them you tripped over the mat? If that's what you did.'

'I said so, Abby.'

'What did Mr Gilbride do?' asked Rachel. 'When you tripped over the mat?'

'He – wasn't here,' Madge said, after a pause.

'What a pity.' Abby's mouth twisted. 'He could have helped you, couldn't he?'

Madge looked at the clock above the range. 'Girls, you'd better go to bed, it's getting late. I'm sorry, I never asked you about your evening. Did you enjoy the pictures?'

'Oh, Ma, for heaven's sake!' cried Abby. She pushed her sisters towards the bedroom. 'You two go and get ready for bed. I'll help Ma.'

But when Jennie and Rachel were out of the room, Abby made no move, only stood staring down at Madge with a hard, suffering gaze.

'He did this, didn't he? Jim Gilbride did this to you, Ma?'

Madge made no reply. She put her hand to her brow and closed her eyes.

'Why did he do it?' Abby persisted. 'Was it because you said you wouldn't marry him?' When Madge still said nothing, Abby flung herself down at the side of the couch and took her hand. 'Oh, it makes me sick, Ma! It makes me so sick! To think of someone like you, who never hurt anyone, being treated like this!'

Madge's eyes opened. 'I hurt him. That's why he hurt me.'

'So, it's all right that he beat you, is it? You deserved it? You're going to say you quite understand and forgive and forget?'

'No.' Madge's voice rang with sudden strength. 'I'm not going to do that.'

Abby was sighing and rising to her feet when the knock came. A light, fearful knock at the flat door. Abby and Madge exchanged glances, as Jennie and Rachel appeared from the bedroom in their nightgowns.

'That'll be him,' said Abby.

'Mr Gilbride?' cried Jennie. 'Do you mean Mr Gilbride?'

'Don't let him in!' said Rachel, 'Abby, don't!'

'Madge,' came Jim's hoarse voice, 'are you there?'

Madge, putting aside her cold compress, rose to her feet.

'No, Ma, you are not to go to that door!' cried Abby. 'I'll go, I'll tell him—'

'I will go,' said Madge, in the tone of voice she seldom used, but which was always obeyed. 'Abby, will you excuse me, please?'

He had been drinking, she could smell the beer on his breath, but he was not drunk. When she closed the door behind her and he saw the face she turned to him, he gave a groan and lowered his eyes.

'Oh, Madge, what've I done? Oh, God . . .' He tried to take her hand and she let him, but it was lifeless in his clasp and he let it go. 'Madge, will you believe me – what I did, it wasna me – it was ma temper, only ma temper. It comes over me, like a fire, burning, and I canna see straight, canna think straight.' He leaned against the wall and the gaslight shone down, exposing the lines of strain marking his handsome face. 'You know I'd never want to hurt you, Madge, if I was in ma right mind. It was just the thought of never having you, you see, after you'd said we could be wed, I couldna accept it, couldna stand it.'

'I know I hurt you,' she said, quietly. 'I hurt you badly.'

'Aye, and I wanted to hurt you back.' He shook his head. 'But to hit you – ruin your face—'

'It's not ruined, it'll get better.'

'Do you hate me? Do you hate me, Madge?'

'No, I don't hate you.'

'You understand it was ma temper made me do it? Only ma temper? All the stuff I said, all the names I called you, I didna mean them, Madge, I didna mean any of it. Do you believe that?'

'I believe you, but I can't forget it, Jim.'

'But if I didna mean it, Madge?'

'You think that makes it all right?' Madge was swaying on her feet, so exhausted she could hardly stand, yet she stayed where she was, fixing Jim with such a dark terrible gaze from her unharmed eye, his own gaze dropped before it.

'Is that how you used to treat Rona?' she asked softly. 'When she did anything that didn't suit?'

'No! No, that isna true. She felt ma temper, she niver felt ma hand. Madge, I swear it!'

She looked at him doubtfully, and he cried, passionately, 'I loved her! I loved Rona! Just like I love you!'

'In all the years I was married to Will,' Madge said steadily, 'he never once struck me.'

Jim swung back to look at her. 'Did I no' say why I did it, Madge? It was ma temper, it wasna me, can you no' understand that?' He moved to try to take her into his arms. 'I'll niver do it again, I promise, I'll niver hit you like that again. Just say it's no' over, Madge, for God's sake! Say it's no' all over for us?'

'Oh, Jim.' She pulled herself away from him. 'It has to be.'

Physically she was throbbing with pain, but inside she felt numb. Tomorrow her love for him would probably come flooding back – you couldn't turn love off like a tap, there would be bad days ahead, they couldn't be avoided. But in her heart she had already decided, she would never let herself be vulnerable to him again.

'Can't you see?' she whispered, feeling for the handle of her door. 'I could never be sure?'

He looked down at her marked face. 'Aye, well, I canna blame you.'

Oh, don't, she thought, don't be reasonable, don't be sweet and tender, don't try to make me change my mind.

'I'll always care for you, Madge,' he said in a low voice, watching her, 'you'll always be special.'

'Good night!' she cried, and, squeezing herself round her door, closed it in his face.

'Are you all right?' asked Abby, as she sank once more on to her sofa.

Madge nodded. She felt too exhausted to talk any more, yet knew there was still something she had to say.

'I want to tell you – I want to tell you now that I've decided not to marry Mr Gilbride.'

Her three girls stood very still and said nothing.

'It'll be for the best,' Madge went on, 'so now let's say no more about it.' She put the cold compress back to her face. 'Girls, will you go to bed?'

'Shall I help you, Ma?' asked Abby.

'I think I can manage, thanks, dear.'

'So, shall I tell the bakery tomorrow you won't be coming in?'

'I might be a lot better by tomorrow.'

'I'm afraid you won't look better, Ma.'

Madge thought of Annie's grin, Miss Dow's frown.

'Well, say I'll be in the next day, I've just had a bit of a fall.'

'They'll be sure to believe you,' said Abby.

Chapter Sixteen

In fact, Madge being Madge, so quiet, so much a 'lady', her story was accepted. Annie might giggle and Miss Dow sniff and ask why a grown person couldn't keep herself upright, but they didn't believe Madge had been the victim of some man's fist, any more than the tenants of Catherine's Land believed it. Mrs Ritchie one of the poor women seen every weekend nursing their injuries? The idea was unthinkable, so they didn't think it. Only Lily MacLaren shook her head over Madge's yellowing bruises and whispered, 'Hen, I made a mistake, he wasna right for you, was he?' But Madge made no answer to that and Lily expected none.

The December days went by and one Monday morning Abby began her new job at Logie's. Madge could not help worrying over how she would get on working in a place like that when she'd only been used to service. And would the other assistants patronise her because she came from Catherine's Land? Abby was so full of joy over her appointment Madge couldn't bear to think she might be let down, but she need have had no fears. From the first day, Abby slipped into her new surroundings like a hand into a glove. As she told Madge, she felt she might have been born to the place, and though Miss Inver could be sharp, she was always fair, while her colleagues in Accounts made her feel very welcome. Best of all was her new found status. She was no longer 'Abby', she was 'Miss Ritchie'; she was entitled to staff lunches; she was greeted politely by the grand comissionaire, and if she met any of the trustees or partners, they always inclined their heads and smiled. Mr Gerald, Mr Farrell's nephew as she had discovered, was particularly pleasant to her; always stopped if they met on the stairs to ask how she was enjoying her work and whether she had any problems. People said he was engaged to a lawyer's daughter and there would be a big wedding soon, which would mean a celebration for Logie's staff, and Abby was looking forward to it. There was only one worry on her horizon and that was Frankie.

He pretended to be just the same and had said no more about going to Glasgow, but Abby had the feeling he was trying to distance himself from her. Sometimes when she suggested meeting he would say he had to see his friends for a drink, or he had promised his mother to do a few jobs, the sort of excuses he would never have made at one time if there had been a chance of seeing Abby.

'I think he's trying to get used to doing without me,' Abby told Madge one evening when she was helping her with her modest household budget. 'I'm sure one day I'll come back and that awful mother of his will tell me he's gone to Glasgow.'

'I never did care very much for Mrs Baxter,' Madge admitted, 'but she's a widow, too, she's had a hard life. The thing is, Abby, it will be just as well if Frankie does put you out of his mind. You're too young to get serious over anyone and you have your job now.'

'He knows that, Ma. But I'd miss him if he wasn't around, I really would. I know you don't think he's anything, just a piano player—'

'I never said that!' Madge exclaimed. 'It's the drinking I worry about. You know what damage that can do.'

'But you're secretly hoping I'll meet a nice clerk with paper cuffs and boiled collars, aren't you?' Abby asked, only half laughing.

'Abby, I just want you to be happy,' Madge said tiredly, and Abby quickly pressed her hand.

'I am happy, Ma. Come on, let's have a look at these figures.' Abby cast her eye down the columns of her mother's worn cash book. 'Rent, five shillings; groceries and meat, nine and six; coal, one and six; gas, two shillings; doctor's club, one shilling; soap, sevenpence; matches, tuppence; clothes, two and six. That comes to twenty-two shillings and threepence for weekly payments. And coming in you have, eighteen shillings, wages, three shillings, Dad's work fund, and seven shillings and sixpence from me. You're in credit, Ma. What are you worrying about?'

'I was all right until the rent went up,' Madge answered, 'but now, you see, I'm short. Without your seven and six.'

'But you've got my seven and six.'

'Yes, but I don't like to count on it.'

'Why ever not? I've always given you something, Ma, even when I was in service, that was only fair. Why shouldn't I pay you for my keep, now I'm at home?'

'I'm just thinking you won't always be here, Abby. You go out to business now, you'll need a room of your own.'

Abby shook her head. 'Ma, I'm earning good money, I'll always help you. And if you're talking about moving, I'd like us all to move. Right away from Catherine's Land.'

Madge's eyes widened. 'Move away from Catherine's Land? We could never afford to do that, Abby! Anyway, I've got used to it, I don't mind living here.'

Even with Jim Gilbride across the stair Abby wanted to ask, but held her tongue. Jim Gilbride's name was never mentioned.

'Don't worry about me going anywhere,' she said, after a pause. 'There's plenty of time to think about that.'

'Oh, I know, I'm just preparing myself.' Madge smiled faintly. 'Like Frankie.'

Since that terrible night when she and Jim had parted, Madge had never seen him and was grateful. The truth was, a part of her loved him still and as she had foreseen, all the loving and wanting had come back, hurting so much that most nights she lay awake, either staring dry eyed into the darkness, or weeping salt tears that stung her face and made her feel worse in the mornings. But she remained steadfast, she would never take him back. And that was not just for Jennie's sake, although it was for Jennie she had originally given him up. Whenever she thought of the future she might have had with him, she felt as though she had been standing on the edge of a volcano, had only by the sheerest good fortune not fallen into the flames. But there was still that love for him trapped in her heart, she did not want to risk seeing him again and, every time she went out or came back, would quicken her step, shivering in case she should see his tall figure ahead, see his eyes fire up at the sight of her, hear his voice: 'Madge, say it's no over, please, say it's no' over, please, say it's no' over!'

'It is over!' she cried, stopping her ears in her imagination. 'It's over, Jim!'

Christmas was approaching and though some of the Scots thought more of Hogmanay, there was still the feeling of something exciting in the air. Madge had made a cake and puddings long ago and stored them away. Now she and Abby bought a little tree and dressed it with the glass toys Madge's mother had saved to buy long ago, and the girls made paper chains and small presents. On Christmas Eve, Jennie and Rachel hung up stockings for Madge to fill later with oranges, nuts and sweets.

'Don't you want a stocking?' she asked Abby, who laughed.

'I'm a bit old for a stocking, Ma! Anyway, I've got my best present already, and you know what it is.'

'Doing sums at Logie's?' Rachel asked with a groan. 'Ugh, rather you than me, Abby!'

'Oh, yes,' agreed Jennie, who was not going to say that she'd had her best Christmas present, too, which was that Ma was not going to marry Mr Gilbride. Of course, there was another present she'd like, but she did not expect it yet. One day, though, Rory might notice her and ask her out, might feel about her as she felt about him. Soon there would be a new year and who knew what that would bring?

'My best Christmas present is for us all to be together,' said Madge, as they set off for the midnight service at St John's. 'That's really all I want.'

The tall, elegant church in the West End was always cold, and on this third Christmas Eve after the end of the Great War was not festive. Too many of the faces in the congregation were marked with grief, too many ghosts joined those at prayer.

Madge bent her head and thought of Will. Since her break with Jim, at least she had not had to feel guilty about her dead husband. Not that she would have forgotten Will, anyway, and sometimes it seemed to her that he would have understood if she had wanted to marry again. He might have said it was time for her to be happy again. But not with Jim Gilbride. Perhaps not with anyone now. She had made one venture into the real world. Now she felt like withdrawing into the safety of her memories. For the time being, at least, she would leave the pain and joy of love to other people.

When they came out of church, rain was falling that might turn to sleet, maybe even a little snow, but no one was hopeful for a white Christmas. On the walk home, the girls talked of the old days when they had believed in Father Christmas, although Rachel wasn't sure she had ever really believed in him.

'Though I never told you, Ma,' she said to Madge, hugging her arm.

'I did wonder how he could get down every chimney,' Jennie added, 'and what happened when the fire was on.'

Abby laughed, then stiffened. Two people ahead were crossing the road to the Lawmarket, the man tall with a straight back and a soldier's step, the woman slim and graceful, leaning on his arm as though she belonged there. But then her daughter had that trick, too, hadn't she?

'What is it, Abby?' asked Madge, although she had already seen Jim Gilbride and Lily MacLaren.

Abby, glancing at her mother, saw there was no need to pretend, but still said, 'Let's slow down.'

'Why should we? We want to get home, don't we?' Madge, her eyes very bright, her face yellowish in the streetlights, abruptly stepped up her pace. When Jim opened the door to Catherine's Land and helped Lily through, the Ritchies were just behind, yet neither Jim nor Lily seemed to notice. Lily, gliding up the stairs, relinked her arm to Jim's, and it was not until his door was reached that she looked back and saw Madge. Her clear eyes lit up.

'Merry Christmas, Madge!' she called down. 'Merry Christmas, girls!'

Then, at last, Jim Gilbride turned his head and rested his dark burning gaze on Madge's face.

'Merry Christmas,' said Madge, trembling, while her girls moved closer to her.

He took off his hat, he seemed about to speak, then he

107

grasped Lily's arm and together they continued up the stairs and out of sight.

So Lily had brought a man home at last, thought Madge, as she unlocked her door. What did it matter? As her daughters watched uneasily, she took off her outdoor things and turned up the gaslight.

'Come on,' she called cheerfully, 'let's get the range up and heat the mince pies. Move the kettle over, Jennie, then we can make the tea.'

'Are you all right, Ma?' Abby asked quietly.

'I'm all right. We're together, aren't we? Didn't I say it was all I wanted?'

They sat listening to the noises from the street, the cries and creaks and steps on the stair that were a part of Catherine's Land, the sound of a church bell pealing in the distance for Christmas, and when the kettle came up to the boil, Jennie made the tea.

Part Two
1925–1927

Chapter Seventeen

Jennie was sitting in the June sunshine, dangling her legs from a flat-topped gravestone in the kirkyard of Greyfriars Church. It was a historic place. In 1638 the National Covenant for religious and civil liberties had been signed there. Forty years later, after a battle they had lost, a thousand Covenanters waited among the tombs to be transported or hanged. There should have been ghosts, but Jennie did not feel them. Nor did Rachel, lying in the grass with her hat off, nor the crowds of city people eating their lunches out of paper bags. Greyfriars was somewhere to come for a breath of fresh air in summer; to forget your troubles at work if you had a job, or if you didn't have a job to forget that too, for a little while. Times were hard in 1925.

The Ritchie girls had jobs, they were lucky. Jennie, now eighteen, had been apprenticed ever since she left school to Miss Watson, a dressmaker with premises in Victoria Street. Rachel, seventeen, worked in an art materials shop in Candlemaker Row. On a fine day like this they would meet to have their sandwiches together, sometimes being joined by Sheena from the tobacconist's off Chambers Street. They were waiting for Sheena now.

Jennie, so like her mother, still looked much the same as she had looked at thirteen, except that her hair was short. But Rachel without her ringlets was quite changed. Madge said her shingled hair was enough to make anyone weep, but Jennie thought her sister dazzlingly attractive. As attractive as Sheena, though Sheena's style was all her own. She had not cut her hair or shortened her skirts, but that didn't stop the

111

men from hanging around her. Jennie wasn't envious. She had admirers herself, she was taken to dances and the cinema. She scarcely ever thought of Rory Gilbride.

It was in January, 1921, that Jim Gilbride had quietly removed himself and his sons from Catherine's Land. Malcolm had found a flat somewhere over on the south side, but Jim had gone to Glasgow and so had Rory. Jennie had been distraught, had wept for days, could never look at the elderly couple who had taken Jim's flat without bursting into fresh sobs. If Jennie ever thought about that now it was with an indulgent smile for her younger self. How could she have been so foolish? But people said first love was the sweetest and hurt the most. Jennie was glad hers was over.

'No sign of Sheena,' she told Rachel from her vantage point. 'I wish she'd hurry up. Miss Watson gets so shirty if I'm not back on time.'

'You know Sheena, always late.' Rachel stood up and picked grass from the blue cotton dress Jennie had made for her. 'Why don't we start without her? I'm hungry.'

Jennie looked in their paper bags. 'There's cheese, or boiled ham. Which do you want?'

'Both. I mean some of each.' Rachel, fanning herself with her hat suddenly became alert. 'I think I see her, Jennie. She's got someone with her.'

'Oh?' Jennie, shading her eyes with her hand, slid down to stand next to Rachel. She was interested, wondering who Sheena had got in tow this time, for she often arrived with adoring young men who were rarely seen more than once. 'Who is it, then?'

'Don't know, can't be sure.'

As Rachel gave her a sidelong glance, Jennie stiffened. She did know, she was sure.

'Jennie—' Rachel began.

'I know.' Jennie was very unconcerned. 'I've seen him too. It's Rory Gilbride.'

Sheena came drifting up the path between the graves, attracting and ignoring glances from everyone she passed. She wore a long floating dress of green silk which someone had given her mother years ago, and a large floppy hat, chosen, Rachel guessed, to look as different as possible from the cloche

112

hats all the other girls were wearing. There were those who thought Sheena didn't try to be different, but Rachel knew better. Her difference added to her attraction and Sheena strove hard to achieve it.

Rory was attracting glances, too. My goodness, thought Rachel, observing his dark suit and formal collar and tie, he doesn't look like a brickie today, what's he done to himself? One thing was sure, he was more handsome than ever. She glanced again at Jennie, whose eyes were riveted on the face she always said she had forgotten. Clearly she was remembering it well enough now.

'Look who's here!' cried Sheena as she reached them. 'Came into the shop and wouldna go, so I said he could come up here and share ma piece.' She pulled out a large packet of sandwiches from a carrier and looked up at Rory, standing speechless beside her. 'Come on, then, Rory! Do you no' remember the Ritchie girls?'

'Hello, Jennie,' he muttered, not meeting her eye, 'hello, Rachel.'

'Why don't we all sit down?' asked Rachel coolly. 'Jennie's bagged that gravestone, but there's plenty of grass.'

'Oh, Rachel, I don't mind where I sit!' Jennie, flushing, sat down on the grass. When after a moment's hesitation Rory sat down next to her, she said quietly,

'Rory, it's nice to see you again. What are you doing away from Glasgow?'

'He's no' in Glasgow now,' Sheena told them, lounging full length on the gravestone. 'He's got a new job in Edinburgh, he wants a place to live. I say he should come back to Catherine's Land.'

Catherine's Land? Rachel and Jennie exchanged glances.

'Is your dad coming with you?' Rachel asked bluntly.

'No.' Rory took a sandwich from the packet Sheena offered him. 'Sheena, I dinna want to take your piece.'

'Och, I've plenty, dinna be so soft!'

'We have some to spare too,' said Jennie. 'Cheese or ham?'

'So, what's the new job, then?' Rachel pressed Rory. 'Have you given up the building trade?'

'I have.' Rory's classically handsome face was suddenly

alight, his deep blue eyes shone. 'I'm going to work for the Labour Party!'

'Labour Party?' echoed the girls in surprise. Even Sheena seemed at a loss.

'It'll no' pay much, a job like that,' she commented. 'I mean, what'll you do?'

'It's a new job, it's a grand job,' Rory answered sharply, stung by the dubious expressions on the faces around him. 'I'll have plenty things to do, I can tell you! Getting folk to join, organising elections, helping the agents – it's just the sort of job I want!'

'Looks like you've done well,' Rachel said. 'No more carrying bricks for you.'

'That's not the way I see it!' he cried. 'I niver minded working as a brickie. I wanted to be one. I wanted to be with the workers, doing what I could in the union. But I couldna turn down a job like this, it's too important. It's getting to be where the power is. Can you no' see that?'

'Power?' Rachel took another ham sandwich, as Sheena lay with her eyes closed and Jennie sat, silent. 'Where's the power in the Labour Party, Rory? They lost the last election, didn't they?'

'Aye, after we'd had a Labour government for the first time in history!' Rory cried, so agitated now, his sandwich stayed uneaten in his hand. 'Dinna forget that!'

'Rory, people are looking,' Jennie murmured.

'Let 'em look! I'm just trying to remind you that we did have a Labour Prime Minister. Ramsay MacDonald got us in and he'll get us back, you'll see, he'll take us back and we'll be stronger than before!''

'All right, all right,' Rachel said hastily, 'no need to shout. The thing is, you're wasting your time with us. We don't get the vote till we're thirty.'

'Och, thirty,' moaned Sheena. 'Canna bear to think of it.'

'Abby says they're sure to change that law,' Jennie put in. 'Why should women have to wait for thirty to vote?'

'When we get in we'll make things better for women,' Rory said firmly. 'We believe in equality, we'll see women get it.'

'And I'll vote for you,' said Rachel, 'as long as I don't have to wait until nineteen thirty-eight!'

114

Rory relaxed a little, letting the angry light die from his eyes. As the girls continued to ply him with things to eat, he told them he was staying for the time being with Malcolm, who was doing well in his firm and had a fine flat in Newington. So was Abby doing well at Logie's, the Ritchie sisters were quick to reply. She had been promoted to Senior Accounts Clerk and had her own flat in Marchmont.

'Aye, they're both the type to get on,' Rory murmured. He lowered his eyes. 'And how's your ma?' he asked, after a pause.

'Very well,' Rachel answered shortly.

'Manageress at Mackenzie's,' said Jennie. 'Miss Dow was moved to another shop and Ma was offered her job.'

'Has to have Abby to check her accounts, but she's quite pleased with herself.' Rachel fixed Rory with a hard stare. 'So what about your dad, then?'

'He's fine.' Rory cleared his throat. 'As a matter of fact, he got married again a couple o' years back.' Into the silence he added desperately, 'She's a bit of a tartar.'

'D'you no' get on?' Sheena asked softly.

He shook his head. 'I've no' lived at home since they were wed.'

Suddenly Jennie leaped to her feet. 'People are leaving, it must be getting late. Rory, have you got a watch?'

'Aye, got this for ma twenty-first.' Rory consulted a large wrist watch. 'It's half past one.'

'Oh, no, Miss Watson'll kill me!' Jennie began to gather up their paper bags. 'Rachel, are you coming?'

'Suppose so, though old Jackson could manage a bit longer without me.'

Sheena yawned and stretched. 'So can Mr Duffy do without me. We'll no' go back yet, eh, Rory? Why don't we go and look at that room in Catherine's Land? It's your grandma's old room, Jennie, the one Mrs Lindsay left. It'd do fine for Rory.'

Jennie and Rachel walked together as far as the statue of Greyfriars Bobby at the top of Candlemaker Row. At one time Jennie used to shed tears over the story of the terrier who would not leave his master's grave, but of course she was quite over that sort of thing now. Today she did not spare the memorial a glance.

'I'd better run, Rachel, see you tonight.'

'No, wait – I wanted to ask you – what do you think of Rory, then?'

'You mean coming back? Doesn't bother me.'

'Sure?'

'Rachel, I know I used to be silly about him, but that was years ago. I was still at school!'

'Seemed to be taken with Sheena. Did you see the way he was looking at her?'

'I thought he was talking more to you.'

'Talking to me, looking at her.'

Jennie, hurrying away, only called again, 'See you tonight!'

'Oh, what a long way off,' sighed Rachel.

Sunshine she decided, arriving home that evening, did not suit the Lawnmarket. Mist and rain, yes, the perfect weather for the ancient stone, but sunlight, even soft evening light like this, exposed every fault so cruelly it was like looking at some old wrinkled body without clothes. Rachel, who had a painter's eye, did not shrink from what was harsh or ugly, but when it came to her home missed desperately the beauty she did not need in art.

She pushed open the unlocked door of Catherine's Land, wrinkling her nose at the familiar smell of stale air, stale beer and other people's cooking, and began to climb the stair. The O'Hanlons had gone now but the Finnegans were still in their first floor flat, the younger children replacing older ones in spilling out of the door, playing mysterious games, asking for pennies or sweeties from anyone who passed. That evening their mother, Marty, was leaning against the wall, watching and smoking a Craven A. She adored Madge, who had helped deliver her last two babies, and she didn't mind Jennie, but stuck-up Rachel she despised and she gave her no smile or word of greeting as she came up the stair. Aware of Marty's opinion, Rachel said hello anyway and when she received only a brief nod in reply, gave the children a coin and moved on. She didn't expect to be liked by the Marty Finnegans of Catherine's Land and didn't care when she wasn't.

The long windows were open in her mother's flat but the room still seemed airless. At the sight of Madge taking a large meat pie from the oven, Rachel groaned.

'Oh, Ma, couldn't we have had a salad?' she cried. 'It's so hot!'

Madge, now forty-one, still pretty if a little heavier, with her fair hair still unbobbed, looked crestfallen.

'I'm sorry, Rachel, I never thought. But there's not much in salad and this is a very good pie.'

'I'll eat it,' said Jennie, setting out knives and forks. 'I'm hungry.'

'All right, I'll wash my hands,' sighed Rachel.

When the three of them were at the table, Rachel looked across at Jennie. 'Did you tell Ma the news?'

'What news?' asked Madge with interest.

'You mean about Rory?' Jennie shook her head. 'No, I didn't.'

'Ma might as well know. Rory Gilbride's back in Edinburgh, he's thinking of taking Gramma's old flat here.'

Madge looked down at her plate. 'He's on his own?'

'Yes, his dad's not coming.'

'When did you see him?'

'Today. Sheena brought him up to Greyfriars. He went into her shop for cigarettes, ended up sharing our sandwiches.'

'He's a nice lad,' Madge said quietly. She looked at Jennie who was eating stolidly, not raising her eyes. 'Is he looking for a building job?'

'Oh, no, he's white collar now,' Rachel told her. 'Working for the Labour Party. Some sort of organiser.'

'The Labour Party?' Madge frowned. From the time she had been eligible to vote, she had always voted Liberal. 'I'm not sure I like the sound of that. Some people think the Socialists are no better than the Communists. They supported the Russian revolution, anyway.'

'I'm sure Rory's not a Communist,' Jennie said, at last raising her head. 'I'm sure he'd never want a revolution!'

'Wouldn't he?' thought Rachel.

After they had done the washing-up, Madge and Jennie settled down to sewing while Rachel sat flicking through sketchbooks, her face taking on the expression of discontent Madge so feared to see.

'What's the matter, Rachel?' she ventured to ask.

'Oh, I'm so bored!' Rachel tossed her books aside. 'And tired of working in that awful shop.'

'Why, I thought you didn't mind the shop!'

'Well, I do. Everybody thinks it's just the place for me because I meet artists, but I hate meeting artists when all I do is sell them paint and canvases. I mean, I should be an artist too. I've got the talent, I know I have.'

'You draw and paint anyway,' Jennie remarked. 'Doesn't that make you an artist?'

'Not a professional,' Rachel said scornfully. 'I don't just want to paint for a hobby. I want to go to art school and be properly taught.'

'Well that takes money and Ma hasn't got it. Stop going on.'

'I wish I did have the money,' Madge said unhappily. 'You know I'd send you to college if I could, Rachel, but even Gramma Ritchie's savings have gone now.'

'Oh, I know, I'm not saying it's your fault.' Rachel's dark eyes gleamed. 'Listen, do you think Abby would lend me something? I could pay her back later. Ma, do you think I could ask?'

'No, I don't.' Madge's tone was firm. 'Abby's wages aren't as good as all that yet and she has a lot to pay out for her flat. I'm sure she won't be able to help.'

Rachel sank back, the lines of her mouth hardening. 'That's it, then, isn't it? There's no hope anywhere.' She gave a theatrical sigh and stood up. 'Maybe I'll just go and see Sheena. Find out what Rory has decided about the flat.'

'I'll come too,' said Jennie. 'You won't mind, Ma? We won't be long.'

'Why should I mind?' Madge smiled. 'I'll make some tea when you get back.'

There had been a little coldness between Madge and Lily after that Christmas when Lily had been seen around with Jim, but it had quickly passed. Lily, lovely as ever, still came down to have a 'bit crack', as she put it, and Madge still patiently endured it, but tonight she very much hoped that Lily would be otherwise occupied. The talk of Rory's return to Catherine's Land had stirred unpleasant memories for Madge. She did not want to have them further stirred by Lily.

118

Jennie, at the door, halted and suddenly ran back.

'Rory told us something else, Ma,' she brought out quickly. 'His dad has got married again.'

'I thought he would,' Madge said calmly. 'He'd made up his mind to find somebody.'

'Rory says she's an awful tartar. He left home as soon as they were wed.'

'Fancy.' Madge folded up her sewing. 'Well, you go on up to see Sheena. Find out what's happening.'

'I think Ma's all right,' Jennie murmured to Rachel as they mounted the stair. 'She doesn't care for Mr Gilbride any more.'

'Like you and Rory, then.'

'Yes,' agreed Jennie, with a limpid look at her sister, 'the same.'

Chapter Eighteen

Earlier that evening Abby had left Logie's, stepping out from the staff exit at the back of the building into still-warm sunshine. At the end of a long day it was good to be in the fresh air and she stood for a while enjoying it, watching some of the Logie girls running out to meet their young men, walking off arm in arm, talking and laughing. There was no one waiting for her.

Usually she didn't mind. She had her job, she had her flat, and until recently she had had her studies. But now she had finished her exams and she was free. Hours of free time stretched away, the beautiful evening beckoned. To what? She had nowhere to go but home.

It was a long walk to Marchmont, but the queue for the tram looked endless. Could she face strap-hanging anyway? She decided to walk and set off at a good pace, thinking for no particular reason of Frankie Baxter. Or perhaps there was a reason. If things had worked out differently he might have been outside Logie's waiting with those other young men. She too might have gone off with someone, arm in arm, talking and laughing. But Frankie had gone south more than three years before and their old feelings had faded. Abby had only seen him once since then when he had returned for his mother's funeral. Mrs Baxter had died of pneumonia, very quickly, and the sweetie shop was now leased to Jessie Rossie, who allowed all the children in whether they had pennies or not and, like Madge, had to call in Abby to help her straighten out the books. Frankie and Abby had had a little time together before he left Edinburgh, but the meeting had been bitter-sweet and they both knew it meant nothing. Frankie said he was doing well, playing the piano in London pubs, and had plans to move on to something new but wouldn't say what.

'And you're still happy at Logie's?' he had asked, his gaze on her very bright. When she said she was he had kissed her briefly and said he'd keep in touch, but he never had. There was really no point in thinking any more about Frankie.

Abby's feet in their city shoes were beginning to hurt. By the time she reached George IV Bridge she was beginning to think she might after all have to wait for a tram, but someone suddenly called her name and she saw a car drawing up beside her at the kerb.

'Miss Ritchie?' Gerald Farrell was looking at her from the driving seat. 'Can I give you a lift?'

Her heart bounded. What a bit of luck! Mr Gerald's sports car, open-topped, glittering with expensive metal, seemed as inviting as the glass coach to Cinderella and as he leaped out and opened the door for her, she delightedly took her seat.

'This is lovely,' she told him. 'I'm most grateful.'

'My pleasure. Where can I drop you?'

'Marchmont, please. Spinney Road.'

'Not Catherine's Land?'

'I've moved. I have my own flat.'

'Really? That must have happened while I was in America, then.'

He had not long been back from a tour of American department stores and looking now at his handsome, rather long, quizzical face, she realised she had missed him. Not that she saw him often, but when she did he was always so charming, always treated her with such old-fashioned courtesy, Logie's had been just a little duller without him. That evening he was elegant in a well cut suit, with a tweed cap over his light brown hair, and Abby was glad she was looking presentable in a navy two-piece and dark silk blouse (Logie's sale bargains). It was well known that Mr Gerald's usual effect on people was to make them check their appearance.

'I hope I'm not taking you out of your way?' she murmured, as they roared through the traffic. She knew he had a house in the West End, which was in the opposite direction.

'Not at all,' he replied, but did not say where he was going. 'Spinney Road, was it? What number?'

Abby's flat was the ground floor of a converted Edwardian villa in a quiet street. She had a bay-windowed sitting room, a double bedroom, a second bedroom that served as a study, a tiny kitchen and a bathroom. There was a small garden at the front, which belonged to the elderly widow who lived upstairs, and a strip of lawn at the back, which was Abby's. Here she put out her chair on summer evenings and read, or lay back looking up at the sky, thinking how lucky she was.

'Very nice,' Gerald Farrell commented. 'Do you live here alone?'

'Oh, yes, I'd never want to share. Takes all my money to pay the rent, but I want my independence.'

'I thought your mother might have joined you.'

'My mother is still in Catherine's Land. With my sisters.' Abby picked up her bag and her summer cotton gloves. 'Thank you ever so much for the lift, Mr Gerald. I did appreciate it.'

'What do you intend to do now? Cook yourself a meal?'

'I'll probably just have a salad.'

'I know a restaurant down the road from here.' He turned a reflective gaze on her flushed face. 'Miss Ritchie, would you care to have dinner with me?'

She couldn't believe it. Her flush deepened, her dark eyes grew wide. Gerald Farrell, of all people! He had been married for four years. She remembered his wedding, to the statuesque, golden-haired Miss Monica McIver. There had been a grand reception for the staff of Logie's, with champagne and smoked salmon, no expense spared, and everyone had been sure that the handsome couple, like a fairytale prince and princess, would live happily ever after. Surely, they had, but even if they hadn't, it seemed inconceivable that Mr Gerald, the perfect gentleman, should have asked Abby to spend time with him behind his wife's back. She stared at him, letting him read the message in her eyes. She made no reply.

'Ah, you're upset,' he said, gravely. 'You think badly of me. But is there anything wrong in offering you dinner? Why shouldn't we have a meal together?'

'You make it sound right, but I think it isn't.'

'Please' – he put his hand lightly on her arm – 'try to see it my way.'

She saw that there were lines of strain round his mouth, an emptiness in his eyes she hadn't appreciated before. It came to her with a little shock that Gerald Farrell was suffering. Why, she couldn't even begin to guess, but it seemed clear that behind his suave elegant exterior was no Lennox Ramsay, but a man who simply didn't want to be alone.

'I'm sorry,' he was saying, withdrawing his hand from her arm, 'I shouldn't have asked you. It was selfish. Why should you risk your reputation for me?'

'My reputation? Mr Gerald, this is nineteen twenty-five, not nineteen hundred and five. I'm not worried about my reputation!'

'You say it wouldn't be right for us to have dinner together.'

'I'm thinking about your wife,' she said, in a low voice, and he drew back.

'Miss Ritchie, so am I.'

Nothing more was said until he had parked the car in the next street and helped her out. What am I doing? thought Abby, but her steps moved with his to the little restaurant he said he knew. She had passed it often but had never been in.

'Would anyone know you here?' he asked.

'What a question! I can't afford to go to restaurants.'

'I was naturally assuming you'd be taken.'

'No,' she answered, biting her lip, 'I haven't been to this restaurant.''

It was fashionable, it was expensive, no one she knew would ever have taken her there. When she looked round the shadowy interior it seemed so crowded she thought with relief they wouldn't be able to stay, but a waiter took one look at Gerald Farrell and found them a table. When the menu was brought, Gerald asked if he should order for them both. Abby, having glimpsed the prices, said faintly, 'Yes, please.' It made her smile wryly to watch him make his choice, wasting no time. He was the only man she'd ever met who could order a meal without first having to work out the bill. There were really only two sorts of people, she decided: those who needed to worry about

123

money and those who didn't. Yet not having to worry about money was clearly not enough to keep Gerald Farrell happy.

Now that he had won his battle and had her with him, he seemed to be trying to behave in conventional fashion, making small talk, telling her how good she was at her job.

'I knew you would be, as soon as I called you for interview. You were very nervous – do you remember being nervous?'

'I remember,' Abby murmured.

'But you still came in with all guns firing, didn't you? The opposition never had a chance!'

'I think that's enough about me,' she said uneasily.

'Abby – I may call you Abby? – you must know you are rather a remarkable person.'

'Because I was brought up in Catherine's Land?'

'I didn't say that.'

'No, but that's what you meant. There are plenty like me in the tenements, Mr Gerald. They only need education and a little money.'

'I wish you'd call me Gerald,' he muttered.

She looked him in the eye. 'I've agreed to have dinner with you, but I can't call you Gerald. Please don't ask me.'

'I don't understand you. Here with me, you're the same as anyone else—'

'Using the right knife and fork? I learned that in service. I learned a bit about food and wine, too, and this is a very good dinner. I'm enjoying it.'

'Thank you,' he said blankly, and for a while they ate in silence.

The June night was growing dark at last and when the waiter brought the coffee he lit a candle at their table. The soft light was flattering, making Abby feel more at ease, but Gerald Farrell's unhappiness still stretched between them like a barrier, preventing her from reaching out to him as she was beginning to want to do. If only he would tell her what was wrong, let her help him. But he said nothing.

When they left the restaurant the night air was still warm with no hint of an Edinburgh breeze, no whisper of mist.

'Might be somewhere abroad,' Gerald murmured. 'The south of France, perhaps, or Italy.'

'I've never been abroad.'

'You'll go one day.'

'There are a lot of things I'm going to do one day.'

They walked slowly back to Spinney Road and stopped at her gate. There were lights in the upstairs windows and Abby wondered if Mrs McKay was peering through her curtains, trying to see who was down at the gate with Miss Ritchie. Thank heavens it was too dark for her to see Gerald Farrell's face clearly. Abby gave him a quick glance. Should she ask him in? He surely wouldn't expect it, yet she found she wanted to. He solved the problem.

'Abby, I'll say good night.' He shook her hand and let it go. 'Thank you for this evening.'

'I'm the one who should thank you.'

'No, I gave you dinner but you gave me much more. I don't mind telling you, I was pretty low when I met you, didn't really know what to do with myself. I was just driving – anywhere.' He gave a long bitter sigh. 'You got me through.'

'I'm glad, then.'

'And Abby – there's something I'd like to tell you. About my wife—'

Abby moved a little away. 'Mr Gerald, you don't have to—'

'No, it's all right. I just want to say I do love her. She means all the world to me.'

'Yes, of course. Look, I'd better go. Thank you again for a lovely evening. Good night, Mr Gerald.'

'Still Mr Gerald?'

'I think it's best.'

'But we are friends? We've known each other a long time, you know.'

Friends, thought Abby, are equal. 'Yes,' she said aloud, 'we're friends. Good night again.'

'Good night, Abby.'

In her flat she put on the lights and drew the curtains but did not sit down. She felt restless, moving from room to room, still scarcely able to believe she had spent the evening with Gerald Farrell. Had she really said she was his friend? It was ridiculous. Yet she couldn't stop trembling with excitement.

To calm her nerves she lit the gas flame on her little cooker and boiled the kettle to make tea. So much wine, so much coffee, yet her throat was parched. The tea was comforting.

She drank it standing up, as her mind went over every look Mr Gerald had given her, every word that had been said, until his last words at the gate about his wife. 'I do love her, she means all the world to me.'

I do love her, she means all the world to me. Obviously, Monica Farrell was the cause of his unhappiness. She had not gone to America with him, she had not been in Edinburgh to greet him on his return, she was 'away' in Berwick. Doing what? Seeing someone else. That was the only explanation.

I do love my wife, she means all the world to me.

Lucky, lucky Monica, thought Abby, setting down her cup with a sudden angry movement. How dare she throw such luck away?

Chapter Nineteen

Gerald Farrell did not come into Logie's next day. Abby looked for him, but his secretary said he had gone to Glasgow on business. Gone to Berwick, thought Abby, and was annoyed that she minded. To convince herself that nothing had changed for her, she threw herself into work like some sort of tornado, feeling all the more nettled when young Donald Rennie asked, 'Are you feeling all right, Miss Ritchie?' Donald had been appointed to her old post of Junior Accounts Clerk. He was nineteen, red-haired, freckled and walking out with a young lady from Haberdashery. He and Abby had always got on well, but this morning she gave him a look set to freeze.

'All right? Of course I'm all right! Why shouldn't I be?'

'I just thought you were looking a wee bit peaky. No' your usual self.'

'I am exactly my usual self!' Abby slapped a pile of invoices on his desk. 'There's no need for you to worry about MY health, Mr Rennie, thank you all the same.'

When he flushed and lowered his eyes, she bit her lip.

'Sorry,' she said, quickly, 'didn't mean to snap.'

'Nae bother, Miss Ritchie.'

He picked up the invoices and Abby, moving back to her desk, caught Miss Inver's eyes resting on her in mild surprise. Her colour rose. What a morning this was turning out to be! She had never felt so much at odds with her world.

It was a relief to leave the office at lunchtime and walk the sunny streets, stopping at a greengrocer's to buy lettuce and tomatoes and some early strawberries. She had decided to go and see her mother for tea. It always made her feel better, to see Madge.

The evening was warm again. Trudging up the Mound to the Lawnmarket, Abby thought of the night before. 'Miss Ritchie, can I give you a lift?' There was no sports car stopping at the kerb for her now. She took off her hat and paused for a moment. Two young men were coming towards her.

The Gilbride brothers! She hadn't seen them for years but recognised them instantly. What were they doing here? Didn't Rory live in Glasgow? She felt an apprehension it wasn't hard to understand. To her the name of Gilbride spelled trouble. If Rory and Malcolm had been back to her mother's, no good could come of it. Keeping her face averted, she turned aside and the brothers, deep in conversation, passed her without recognition. In spite of the heat, she quickened her step to Catherine's Land.

Jennie and Sheena were on the stair, laughing together. Both looked excited and Abby's heart sank.

'Jennie!' she called sharply, and her sister's face lit up.

'Abby! I didn't know you were coming today! Sheena, it's Abby!'

'I can see that,' Sheena answered languidly. 'Hello, Abby. Och, you're as red as a beetroot, ha' you been running?'

'Jennie, I've just seen the Gilbrides.' Abby nodded briefly to Sheena. 'They haven't been here, have they?'

'You've seen Rory?' cried Jennie. 'Oh, but didn't he tell you? He's coming back!'

'I didn't speak to him. Coming back where?'

'To Catherine's Land!' Sheena said triumphantly. 'To your gran's old room, Abby, up the stair.'

'It's all right, Abby,' Madge said placidly. 'It's only Rory who's coming back, not his father. As a matter of fact' – she hesitated – 'Rory told Jennie that Mr Gilbride has married again.'

'What poor soul has taken him on, then?' Abby unpacked her carrier bag, laying out her lettuce, tomatoes and strawberries. 'I hope you haven't made anything for tea yet, Ma? I thought we'd have salad, maybe get some ham at Kay's. All I can say is I'm not happy about any of the Gilbrides coming back here, even Rory.'

'Why do you say that?' cried Jennie. 'Why shouldn't Rory come back if he wants to? He has to find somewhere to live, he's going to be working for the Labour Party. Why shouldn't he live here?'

'It's you I'm thinking of, Jennie.' Abby gave her a long, steady look. 'I don't want to see you get hurt.'

'I shan't get hurt! Rory doesn't mean anything to me now. What I used to feel' – Jennie blushed and stumbled – 'that's all over. Rory's just a friend.'

A friend. Abby winced. 'All right, let's wash this lettuce. Ma, have you got any boiled ham, or shall I run down to Mr Kay's? When's Rachel coming back? Shouldn't she be here now?'

What's the matter with Abby, thought Madge, looking in her old leather purse for a shilling, she seems all on edge. 'Ask for a quarter of ham, no, say six ounces, and see if he has any cream,' she said aloud. 'I'll give you the money.'

'Oh, Ma, put your purse away,' Abby said impatiently, 'you know I'll pay.'

By the time Rachel arrived home, the table was set, the cold ham and tomatoes sliced, the lettuce crisped, and Madge was adding diced potatoes left over from yesterday's dinner.

'It's just like the old days,' she said happily, 'the four of us together. We do miss you, Abby.'

'Why d'you come?' asked Rachel, spinning her hat into the corner. 'We weren't expecting you today.'

'I often come, don't I? Needn't have a reason.'

'You're looking pale, though. Sort of peaky.'

'I am not looking peaky!'

'Rachel, hurry up, we're all waiting,' Madge ordered. 'And we've got strawberries to follow.' She hesitated. 'Do you think we should keep a few for Sheena and Lily?'

'Ma, they can buy their own.' Rachel took her place at the table. 'You don't have to worry about them now.'

'Ma likes to worry.' Jennie turned towards Abby. 'But she's not worrying about Rory and me, so why should you? I mean, he's not coming here because of me.'

'No, because of Sheena,' Rachel declared 'Any fool can see that.'

Abby raised her eyebrows. 'Oh, you didn't tell me that bit, Jennie.'

'Well, I don't know if it's true.'

'It's true, believe me.' Rachel nodded. 'You only have to see the way he looks at her.'

'All right, it's true then,' snapped Jennie. 'But I don't care, that's the point.'

There was a short silence, then Madge said, 'Let's get the strawberries. Rachel, will you pour the cream into a jug?'

'I bet it's off.'

'No, it's all right,' Jennie replied. 'Everything's all right, thanks to Abby.'

Rachel's velvet-dark eyes rested on Abby's face. 'Yes, Abby's very generous,' she murmured.

'For buying a few strawberries?' Abby stared in surprise, but Rachel said no more.

'When's Rory moving in, then?' asked Abby, as the sisters did the washing-up.

'Tomorrow!' Jennie's eyes were shining. 'He brought his things round today. Malcolm came over to give him a hand.'

'I wonder how Malcolm feels about Rory's Labour Party job? Probably won't want his colleagues to know his brother's a Socialist.'

'You think Malcolm's a Tory?' asked Rachel.

'I'd take a bet.'

'What about you?'

'Me?' Abby hung up the tea towel. 'I don't go in for politics.'

'Thought you used to say you wanted to help working people to have better lives?'

A shadow crossed Abby's face. 'I did say that. I was think-ing of helping them myself. Haven't done much, have I?'

'You got Tilda a job with Ma,' Jennie said loyally. 'And she's really happy, isn't she, Ma?'

'What's that?' called Madge, from her rocking chair.

'Isn't Tilda happy, working at Mackenzie's?'

'Oh, yes, Tilda . . .' Madge smiled. 'She's very happy. No better than me at giving change, but very popular with the customers. One of these days she'll be off with one of the clerks, like Annie.'

'Married, you mean?' Rachel wrinkled her fine nose. 'That's not for me, thanks. I can think of better ways of earning a living.'

'Wives don't earn a living, Rachel,' Jennie said, laughing, but Rachel laughed too.

'Don't they?'

When Abby went into the bedroom to put on her hat, Rachel followed.

'Abby, could I ask you a favour?'

'Of course.' Abby studied her reflection. 'I do not look peaky,' she said again. 'What do you want, Rachel?'

'Could you lend me some money?'

'Money?'

'Ssh!' Rachel put her finger across Abby's lips. 'Don't let Ma hear you. She told me not to ask you, but you're my only hope, there's no one else.'

'What do you need the money for?' asked Abby, in a whisper.

'For art college. I really need to go. To become a professional. There's no other way. If I just carry on by myself, I'll get nowhere and it's not fair, because I'm good, I'm sure I am. Oh, Abby please say you'll help me?'

Rachel's voice, so low, yet so filled with passion, was a revelation to Abby, who had no idea her young sister was capable of such feeling, could appear so mature.

'Oh, Rachel, I wish I could help you, I really do, but I've no capital, only a few pounds in savings. Apart from that, just my salary.'

'But it's a good salary, isn't it? You could spare something, couldn't you?'

'Only a very little, not enough for college fees. My rent takes pretty well all I have. Oh, love, I'm so sorry.' Abby tried to put her arms around Rachel, but she pulled herself away.

'If you won't, you won't,' she said harshly, her pretty face crumpling, 'there's no more to say.'

'It's not that I won't, I can't. Please try to understand. Look, there are trusts that exist to help poor students. I thought of applying to one myself, for university, but I knew

131

Ma needed me to get a job. Maybe we could try for you, though?'

'No, it's hopeless. You need a good leaving certificate from school and I haven't got one. You know I could never do anything but draw.'

'Well, what about an art scholarship, or something of that sort?'

'I'd never get one. I probably don't do the sort of thing they want, and I couldn't bear to be turned down, I couldn't!'

'If you're good, there'll be people who'll know. You can't be sure what they'll say if you don't ask. Let's find out how you apply—'

'No, I don't want to, I tell you! I don't want my work taken apart and sneered at! I want to pay my own way, so I can do what I like.' Rachel seized Abby's arm in a hard clawing grasp. 'Abby, I'd pay you back, I promise I would. You wouldn't lose out, as soon as I began to make money, you'd have every penny back.'

'Rachel,' Abby said quietly, 'I can't do it.'

'All right, then, don't!' cried Rachel, and ran out of the flat, banging the door after her, while Madge and Jennie stared after her.

'Poor girl,' Madge murmured. 'I suppose she's been asking you for money, has she, Abby?'

'But why should she expect Abby to pay for her art lessons anyway?' asked Jennie.

'The fact is, I can't. I wish I could.' Abby heaved a great sigh. 'Didn't Malcolm Gilbride once say everything comes back to money in this world? Maybe I'll vote Labour after all. Only I haven't a vote.' She kissed her mother. 'Ma, I've got to go. Don't worry about Rachel, she'll come back as soon as she's cooled off.'

'Running out like that,' Jennie muttered, '*and* without a hat!'

'I feel so bad,' Madge murmured, 'I feel I've failed. All your lives I've had to say no, haven't I? No, you can't have this, no, you can't have that. All I've ever wanted was to give you the best."

'Look around you, Ma,' Abby said quietly. 'Compare us with other folks here. We've never really had to go without.'

'You bought the strawberries,' Madge said, with a watery smile.'

'You know what I mean. Come on, cheer up. What Rachel's after is the icing on the cake, that's all.'

But as she walked with Jennie to the tram, Abby knew she wasn't being honest. What Rachel wanted was something more than luxury, something more even than a way of earning a living. It was fulfilment as an artist, and why should she be denied it because she was poor? If only she would consider trying for a scholarship! There weren't many but there were some, and if she was really good, she'd succeed. But Rachel could never face the possibility of failure.

'Has to be the best,' Jennie said shortly, echoing Abby's thoughts. 'That's Rachel.'

'Try to talk to her,' Abby murmured. 'I know she's difficult.'

'Difficult!'

'Well, do what you can.' Abby put her hand on Jennie's shoulder. 'And look out for yourself, too.'

'You mean with Rory? I keep telling you, you've no need to worry. Oh, but listen, Abby, Sheena says if the weather stays good, why shouldn't we all go to Portobello on Sunday? We could take a picnic, it wouldn't cost much.'

'Who do you mean by all?'

'Well, Sheena and me, Rory and Malcolm, Rachel and that artist fellow she sees. And you, of course.'

'What about Ma?'

'She's going to a band concert in the Meadows with Mrs MacLaren.'

Abby thought for a moment. Portobello, a small seaside town now part of Edinburgh, had fine sands and a golf course and was a good place to go for a blow in winter. In warm summer weather, however, it was sure to be crowded and Abby didn't think she fancied the idea of joining up with half Edinburgh and the Gilbride boys, even if she might have liked a day with her sisters. She shook her head.

'I don't think I'll come, Jennie, thanks all the same. Sunday's my day for getting on with things in the flat.'

'But it won't be the same without you!'

'Maybe another time.' Abby gave her sister a hug. 'Here's

my tram, I'll see you soon. You know, I sometimes think Edinburgh folk spend their lives climbing in and out of trams!'

Except for those with large shining open-topped motor cars. A sudden sharp pain pierced Abby's heart as she remembered Gerald Farrell and though she smiled and waved to Jennie from the tram, she looked so woebegone that Jennie asked herself, as Madge had done, what's wrong with Abby? But walking back to Catherine's Land, she decided there couldn't be anything wrong with Abby. Her sister could always deal with anything that came her way. No doubt she only had a bit of a headache. Jennie herself was filled with a very pleasant feeling she couldn't at first account for, but then she remembered. Rory was coming back to Catherine's Land tomorrow, coming back to live! Just the thought of seeing him every day put to the back of her mind what Rachel had said about Sheena and when she ran up the stair she was singing. And there was Rachel herself. Thunder-faced, not speaking, but not wandering the streets either.

'Cheer up,' Jennie whispered, putting her arm round her. 'You'll work something out, you'll get to college, you'll see.'

'No I won't. I've no money, I'll never have any money.'

'Maybe that fellow you know – Tim – could lend you something? His folks have money, haven't they?'

'His father's thrown him out, because he wants to be an artist instead of a lawyer.' Rachel spoke with what seemed a kind of gloomy satisfaction in her hopelessness. 'He hasn't a penny.'

'Maybe there'll be someone else, then, someone you meet in the shop.'

'There won't, there won't!' Rachel flung herself into the flat. 'Oh, Jennie, why is everything so *unfair*?'

Back in Marchmont, Abby took off her hat and sank into a chair. What's the matter with me, she asked herself drearily, I've worked so hard, I've got what I wanted, but it all seems so pointless.

She closed her eyes, was trying to empty her mind, think of nothing, when her doorbell rang and she leaped to her feet.

For a crazy moment she wondered – no, it wasn't Gerald Farrell, it was Mrs McKay from upstairs.

She was a lady of the old school. Elaborately pinned grey hair, hawk-like features, a tight little voice breathing from a tight little mouth. 'Oh, Miss Ritchie, I'm glad I've caught you at last!' She made it sound as though Abby was constantly out on the tiles. 'I have a parcel for you.'

'A parcel?'

'Well, it's a box.' Mrs McKay suddenly produced a long white box from behind her back. 'From the florist.'

'Oh.' Abby took the box in trembling hands. Flowers? For her? There must be some mistake.

'Your birthday?' asked Mrs McKay, watching her closely.

'No – I . . .' Abby stepped back. 'Thank you, Mrs McKay,' she said firmly. 'It's very good of you, to take this in for me, I appreciate it.'

'No trouble,' Mrs McKay replied frostily. 'Any time.'

When she had closed the door, Abby stood for some moments staring down at her name on the long white box. There it was, plain as plain. Miss Abigail Ritchie. There could be no mistake. She cut the string and lifted the lid of the box. Inside were a dozen red carnations that began to fill the house at once with a beautiful, clove-like scent. And there was a card.

'Thank you for yesterday,' it read. 'May we meet again soon? Could it be Sunday?' There was no signature.

Chapter Twenty

Sunday was cool and breezy, but fine enough for the trip to Portobello. Everyone met at the General Post Office to catch the tram.

Jennie and Rachel were in summer dresses and cloche hats and carried the picnic in large shopping bags. Sheena was wearing her floating green dress, but instead of a hat had crushed a velvet Juliet cap over her dark hair, making herself look even more interesting than usual and causing Jennie and Rachel to exchange sidelong glances. Rory was in a Sunday suit that was too warm and too smart, but still looked like a god who had suddenly fallen to earth, while Malcolm in sports jacket and flannels was making a big effort to look casual. Tim Harley, a slender young man with silky blond hair, looked satisfactorily like an artist in a cream linen suit and floppy bow tie.

'I hope it's going to be warm enough for you girls to wear your bathing dresses,' said Malcolm, as their tram eventually rattled into view.

'We are not wearing bathing dresses,' Rachel replied coldly.

'I niver wear one,' said Sheena, and smiled into the silence as the men pondered this remark.

'I'll get the fares,' Malcolm offered, as they found seats in the tram. Rachel said they should all get their own, but when Malcolm insisted she did not argue. Rory raised his eyebrows, as though surprised by his brother's generosity.

'I'll bet there won't be room to move on the sands,' sighed Jennie. 'That's probably why Abby wouldn't come, she hates crowds.'

'Not much fun staying at home, though, and cleaning the flat,' Rachel commented.

'If that's what's she's doing,' murmured Sheena, sitting close to Rory and half leaning her head on his shoulder.

'I never thought you'd come,' Gerald Farrell murmured.

'Nor did I,' said Abby.

She met his gaze as he stood by his car at the end of her road, then looked away. He was perfectly dressed in a light jacket and cavalry twill trousers, while Abby was in a new, rose-coloured frock that made her look vividly attractive. She knew they appeared a well-matched couple all set for a day out without worries and only wished it were true.

When she first read the card with the flowers she'd been so flattered she'd thought she couldn't say no to a meeting on Sunday. But the next day at Logie's, when a second note appeared on her desk suggesting a time and place, reaction had set in. Dinner after a casual meeting was one thing. A planned meeting, a whole day out spent together, was quite another. Gerald Farrell had not asked her to reply to his note, only to come at eleven o'clock to the end of her road where he would be waiting. If she didn't want to come, he would understand.

All along, she had been quite clear in her mind what she would do. She would sit in her flat and watch the clock and when the hands moved past eleven, she would be able to relax and feel proud of herself. She was strong, she could do it. She was also intelligent enough to see that there was no point in doing anything else. Gerald Farrell was a married man who loved his wife. He had no right to ask her out. She had no right to go. At five minutes past eleven she went.

'You changed your mind,' he guessed softly, as he opened the car door for her. 'I'm glad.'

Abby stared straight ahead, furious with him, furious with herself.

'Where are we going?' she asked abruptly.

'That depends on you. Where would you like to go?'

'I don't mind. Well, not Portobello.'

'I'd like to take you up the coast Aberlady way, there are some wonderful little beaches in that direction.' He laughed and the laughter made him seem like a boy. 'In heaven's name, what made you think we might go to Portobello?'

The sands at Portobello were not as crowded as Jennie and the others had feared, but people were arriving all the time and they decided to walk as far as they could while there was still space left. To begin with they walked together, the girls' unsuitable shoes sinking into the sand, the men crushing their hats under their arms and letting the wind take their hair.

'Does this no' make you feel good?' cried Malcolm. 'I could eat that picnic already. What's in it, girls?'

'Wait and see,' answered Jennie. 'But I'll tell you now it's mostly from Mackenzie's.'

'Any beer?' asked Tim Harley.

'No, you'll have to make do with lemonade.'

'Doesna bother me,' said Rory. 'I'm no' a drinking man.'

'I am,' said Tim. 'Wish we could've gone to the pub.'

'What an idea, this is Sunday, remember,' Malcolm reproved and Tim, shrugging, caught Sheena's eye and grinned.

'I'm in disgrace,' he whispered.

'So am I.'

'Why, what have you done?'

'Nothing. I'm just in disgrace anyway.' She laughed, twirling round him in her green silk dress. 'For being me.'

Jennie didn't see how it happened, but suddenly they weren't in a crowd any more, they had separated into pairs. And not the pairs she would have expected. Sheena and Tim were drifting together in the distance, Rachel had taken off her shoes and stockings and was walking at the water's edge with Malcolm. Jennie unbelievably was with Rory.

'Who is that fellow?' he asked, narrowing his eyes at Tim Harley's distant figure.

'One of Rachel's admirers. He's at the art college.'

'I suppose he considers himself a gentleman.' Rory's tone was contemptuous. 'You can tell he's got money.'

'Rachel says he hasn't. His father's an advocate, but he's thrown Tim out because he wants to be a painter.'

'But somehow he's at the art college and somebody's paying his fees? Surprise, surprise! Jennie, that kind is never cut off, they've always got family in the background, propping them up while the rest of us have to work.'

'Well, I think he seems nice.'

'Does Sheena?'

'How should I know what Sheena thinks?'

'She canna help attracting men,' Rory muttered. 'She's like her mother, it's born in her.'

There was an ashen taste in Jennie's mouth, there were clouds over the pale sun. 'We shouldn't talk like this about Sheena,' she said in a low voice and struggled ahead through the dry sand.

'You're right, I'm sorry.' Rory caught up with her and lightly touched her arm. 'You're a good friend, Jennie, you're loyal. I wish you were with us.'

'You mean in the Labour Party? I haven't a vote.'

'You could still help, we need all the help we can get. Och, Jennie, can you no' see what needs to be done? Do you niver look round at the poor bairns? At the folk struggling? There's niver any change, things niver get better. Does that no' bother you?'

'Yes,' she whispered, 'oh, yes, it does, Rory. I do care, don't think I don't.'

'Well, will you join us, then?'

'But what can I do?'

'I could give you some things to read, pamphlets and books – if you're interested.'

'I am interested. Yes, I'd like to read the books.'

'They'll make it all clear, show you what we want to do. The Party's the only hope for change, the only chance we've got, can you understand that, Jennie?'

'Yes, I think I can.'

He smiled and for Jennie it was like sunshine after storm. She was basking in his approval when she saw that he was already turning away, shading his eyes with his hand, and she knew he was looking for Sheena.

'Can you see her?' he asked, and didn't even have to say her name.

'No, I can only see Rachel,' she answered. 'Rachel and Malcolm.'

At another time she might have been intrigued to see them

still together, her sister and dull Malcolm, but now she could only think of herself and of how the trap was closing on her again and she mustn't let anybody see. Abby had known how it would be, she should have listened to Abby. But it wouldn't have done any good. Rory would still have come back, whatever her own feelings were. He would have come back for Sheena.

'Hello!' voices called through the crowds and Jennie raised her eyes to see Sheena and Tim coming towards them.

'Where've you been?' cried Rory. 'You've been gone for hours!'

'About fifteen minutes,' Tim answered, raising his eyebrows. 'Anything wrong with that?'

'We've come back for the picnic,' Sheena announced. 'We're starving! Come on, let's find a place to sit. Rachel! Malcolm! Come away now, we're going to have our picnic!'

'After we've had lunch, we can walk by the sea,' Gerald Farrell was telling Abby. They were sitting in the lounge of a small hotel, studying menus over sherry. 'The coast's so beautiful here, so wild, so unspoiled. And the good thing is there's usually no one about.'

'Isn't that lucky?' Abby commented coldly. She looked around at the few elderly couples sharing the lounge with them. 'But there are people here – are you sure you don't mind?'

A flush rose to Gerald's high cheekbones. He set down his glass and sat in silence. Abby felt a sudden compunction. Throughout the drive here she had punished him by her silent resentment; now she seemed to be taking pleasure in making him feel guilty. Yet she was here with him, she had agreed to come. She felt herself a hypocrite.

'I'm sorry,' she said jerkily, 'I shouldn't have come.'

'I shouldn't have asked you.' He raised his eyes. 'But I said I was selfish, didn't I?'

'I wish you'd just tell me what's wrong.'

'I can't. At least, not here.' He called the waiter. 'Let's order, shall we?'

The lunch was perfect, but Abby had no idea what they ate or what they talked about. All they both wanted, it was plain, was to get through the meal and be alone.

'I'll show you the path to the sea,' Gerald said, when they

left the hotel. 'Are you sure you'll be warm enough? There's usually a cold wind on this part of the coast.'

'I've got a jacket, I'll be all right,' Abby answered, shivering all the same.

The way to the beach led through rough grass and stunted trees bending in the wind. Sand was already blowing in around their feet, fine white sand that seemed never to have been wet, and when they came out on to the beach itself there was the same white sand, miles of it, stretching away into the distance, running down to an inky blue line that was the sea.

'Well,' Abby said softly, 'this is different.'

No deck-chairs, no ice cream, no people. Only the gulls, screaming. And themselves.

'I've never seen a beach without people before.'

'You don't like crowds?'

'No. That's why I like the seaside in winter.'

'You can come here anytime, it's never full. My father used to take a house on this coast for the summer, I know it pretty well.'

'You were lucky.'

Gerald picked up a pebble and turned it in his fingers. 'I suppose I was. Sometimes my parents would drive over in a pony and trap, but my father really came for the golf and Mother used to like to meet her friends. So my brother and I would usually ride our bikes to the beach. We'd trawl the rocks, play in the dunes for hours.'

'I didn't know you had a brother.' Abby stooped to slip off her shoes. 'Does he live in Edinburgh?'

Gerald looked down at the pebble in his hand, then he flung it hard away from him. 'Hugh never came back from Mons,' he said shortly.

'Oh!' Abby caught at his cold hand. 'Oh, I'm so sorry!'

His fingers closed round hers. 'I used to feel guilty, that I came back and he didn't. Damned silly, but a lot of us felt that way.'

'But think of your parents – if they'd lost you too!'

'As it happened, I lost them. They both died in 1919.' He let her hand go. 'Apart from my uncle, I have no family now.' When she stared at him, words trembling on her lips, he smiled coldly. 'What's the matter? Are you thinking of Monica?'

Immediately, Abby looked away, down to the sea. She

wished he had not spoken his wife's name. Never name names, people said, but Monica was between them now, she couldn't be unsaid, her cool beauty was driving them apart.

'You don't understand!' Gerald cried. 'Monica's left me. She wants a divorce.'

They began to walk along the drifting sand, Abby carrying her shoes, Gerald his cap. For some time, neither spoke, then Gerald at last began to talk.

Children were what it was about. Not having children. Monica's not having children. Gerald's fault in not giving Monica children. It was true they had not been married so very long. Four years was no time at all, the doctors said. Just relax, don't worry. But what Monica wanted, she wanted now, she was not prepared to wait any longer. Gerald had failed, Gerald would have to go and, though there was no other man in her life at present, she wanted to be free. The social stigma of divorce seemed not to worry her; for the hope of a second chance for children she was prepared to endure it, and Gerald must endure it too. At present she was with friends in Berwick, 'thinking things over', but there was really no question what she was going to do.

'Every day I expect her telephone call,' Gerald said to the wind. He turned to look at Abby. 'I think I'd be almost glad to get it now.''

'Poor Gerald,' Abby said gently, and his face lightened.

'That's the first time you've said my name.'

'I wanted to.'

'You feel differently towards me now?'

'I'm not sure how I felt before, it's hard to say.'

'There's my careful Abby. You know you disapproved of me, a married man, asking you out. On the way here you made me feel – I don't know – like some sort of villain out of a melodrama—'

'Oh, don't!' Her fine dark eyes searched his face. 'I shouldn't have treated you like that. I knew you were just very unhappy. All I really want to do is help you.'

'You've already helped me.' He ran his hand down her face. 'I want to tell you something. When I went home after we'd had dinner, for the first time I found myself not thinking of Monica.'

142

'Oh?' She was trembling, not trusting herself to say more.

'You were in my mind, Abby. You still are.' He was drawing her gently into his arms. 'That's why we're here now, because I had to see you again. I'm still selfish, you see.'

'But I wanted to see you, too, Gerald. That's the truth of it.'

'Not just to help me?'

'Not just to help you.'

They hesitated, both knowing that if they kissed they would cross some sort of barrier, then with one mind kissed anyway. For a long time they stood together on the lonely shore, while the gulls called overhead and the inky sea moved slowly closer. Then Gerald said reluctantly, 'Maybe we should go back.'

From the stop opposite the General Post Office, the little group watched their tram swaying away. The trip to Portobello was over.

'Has it no' been a grand day?' asked Sheena, putting a sticky hand into Rory's. 'Have we no' been lucky?'

'Very lucky,' Rachel agreed, with a mysterious smile at Malcolm.

'So, what do we do now?' asked Tim, but no one answered. 'Rachel,' he pressed, 'don't you want to come back with me?'

'Think I'd better get home, Tim. Ma will be wondering where we are.'

'I'll come and see you at the shop, then?'

'If you like.'

'I might look in, too,' said Malcolm. His face was shiny with sweat, he had slightly caught the sun, but his eyes on Rachel were alight. 'Might take up painting, eh? Sunday hobby?'

'And sell your paintings at a profit, I suppose?' Rory muttered. 'Let's away, girls.'

'What's going on?' Jennie asked Rachel, as they followed Sheena and Rory home. 'You took Tim to Portobello and spent the whole time talking to Malcolm.'

'Why not? I suppose I can talk to Malcolm if I like?'

'You've never wanted to talk to him before.'

'I wouldn't say that.' Rachel was very cool. 'Anyway, I've discovered he's more interesting than I thought. He knows how to make money.'

'Rachel!'

'Oh, stop looking at me like that! There's nothing shocking about making money.'

'Yes, but Malcolm's only got his wages. If he says he's got money, he must be having you on.'

'He wouldn't dare. No, the thing is, he's got in with a crowd who know about stocks and shares and all that sort of stuff. He's picked up tips, he's got what they call a flair. And you know what he told me? He'll soon be able to buy a house of his own! He's thinking about Morningside!'

'You're not interested in a house in Morningside,' Jennie said quietly.

'I'm interested in anywhere that's not Catherine's Land,' Rachel retorted.

'Yes, but you're going to try to borrow money from Malcolm, aren't you? For your art college fees?'

Rachel's lovely mouth curved into a smile. 'I might.'

'I don't think you should, Ma wouldn't like it.'

'Jennie, don't you dare say a word about this to Ma! What I do is my business, leave Ma out of it.'

'You're not twenty-one, you can't do as you please.'

'Wait and see what I can do.' Rachel ran ahead to join Sheena and Rory at the door to Catherine's Land. When she looked back at Jennie slowly following, her dark eyes were full of warning.

'Gerald, I wish you could come in for a minute,' Abby said, as they drew up at the end of her road.

'So do I, but it wouldn't do.'

She understood, of course, but where was the harm in a cup of coffee when she knew now that Gerald's wife didn't want him, that they were not hurting her by being together? Only two nights ago, it was true, Gerald had said he still loved his wife, but he had been still pretending then that he and Abby were only friends. A man couldn't kiss a woman as Gerald had kissed her and love someone else. Those words had meant nothing.

'I'd better say good night, then.' She touched his hand and he instantly turned and took both her hands in his.

'Oh, God, Abby, I don't want to say good night to you!'

'We could just have a cup of coffee. I mean, that wouldn't compromise me.'

'Abby, don't make it hard.'

'All right, I won't say another word.' She felt for the door handle and immediately he was at the door, opening it for her.

'We can meet again?' he asked urgently.

She nodded, keeping her face averted, and ran to her flat without looking back.

An hour later her doorbell rang. She had been sitting where she had dropped, staring at the carnations Gerald had sent her, drinking in their heady scent.

'Mrs McKay,' she groaned, rising to answer the door.

But it was Gerald.

'I've been driving round and round Marchmont like a fool,' he gasped. 'I couldn't go home. Oh, Abby, darling, may I come in?'

Chapter Twenty-One

On a sultry evening in August, Lily MacLaren came gliding down the stair with a flush of excitement touching her usual pallor. It was a Monday, Madge's wash night, but now it was Jennie who was working in the basement, while Madge sat gratefully in her rocking chair, darning stockings.

'Come in,' she called to Lily, who had tapped at her open door, 'the door's on the latch for Jennie.'

'Hen, I've some news!' cried Lily. 'If you canna guess it, I'll tell you anyway. Sheena's got herself engaged!'

Madge sat up and put aside her mending. 'To Rory?'

'Aye.' Lily sat down on the couch, fanning herself with Madge's evening paper. 'Och, it's so hot, eh? There'll be thunder before the night's out. What d'you think, then, Madge?'

'It's very good news,' Madge answered promptly. 'Rory's a fine young man, he should make Sheena very happy.'

A frown puckered Lily's brow. 'I dinna ken, Madge, she's difficult. Wants a lot. And he's no' got much.'

'He's ambitious. I think he'll go far.'

'Wi' Labour?' Lily sniffed. 'No money there, Madge. And he didna even want to buy Sheena a ring.'

'Sheena wanted an engagement ring?' Madge asked in surprise. Very few in Catherine's Land could aspire to such a thing.

'Did I no' say she wants a lot? Well, he wasna keen, but I says to him, you want Sheena, you buy her a ring, a ring with a stone she can show to all her friends, or she'll no' take you.' Lily gave a satisfied smile. 'He got the ring.'

'Fancy.' Madge shook her head. 'He must be doing well, then.'

'Och, he borrowed the money from his brother. Malcolm's the one wi' the moneybags. Is there a cup of tea in the pot, Madge?'

As Madge was boiling the kettle on her new gas ring, Jennie appeared. She smiled when she saw Lily, but there was a defeated look about her, as though she already knew she had lost her particular race.

'Keep an eye on the weather,' she told Madge. 'I've hung the things on the green.'

'Shouldna done that, pet,' Lily said cheerfully. 'Might be a storm.'

Jennie only shrugged and flung herself into a chair.

'I hope Rachel's all right,' Madge said worriedly, pouring the tea. 'She's out somewhere but I don't know where. Never tells me anything.'

'Aye, there's girls for you,' sighed Lily. She glanced at Jennie and then significantly at Madge.

'Have you heard the news, Jennie?' Madge asked, taking her cue. 'Sheena and Rory are engaged.'

'I know. Sheena told me yesterday.' Jennie drank her tea and stood up. 'Ma, I'll just be in the bedroom. 'Bye, Mrs MacLaren.'

'But Jennie, ha' you seen the ring?' cried Lily, half rising from her chair. 'A bonnie diamond—'

Jennie had already gone.

'Poor girl.' Lily sat down again. 'She's aye been sweet on Rory, eh?'

'Oh, but not now,' Madge said quickly. 'She knows Sheena's the one for him.'

'It's different when there's wedding bells. No hope then they'll change their minds.'

Madge gave a long sigh and gazed out of the window. 'Looks as though the storm's passed over, anyhow. Maybe the washing'll dry, after all.'

'Madge, you're a wonderful woman!' Lily cried. 'I think you'd find something good to say about Judgment Day!'

'Why, yes. All our troubles would be over by then,' agreed Madge, laughing in spite of herself.

'Or just beginning,' said Lily.

*

'Jennie, what are you doing?' asked Rachel, coming into the bedroom some time later. 'Ma says you've been in here for ages.'

Jennie looked up from her bed where she had spread a number of pamphlets. 'I'm reading. Any law against that?'

'Reading what? All that stuff Rory gives you?' Rachel picked through the titles: *Forward With Labour*, *What Labour Can Do For You*, *Why You Should Vote Labour*. 'Oh, Jennie, this is such a waste of time!'

'I don't know what you mean?'

'Well, Rory's not going to forget Sheena because you're calling yourself Labour, is he?'

'As though I'd think that!' Jennie cried passionately. 'Haven't you heard they're engaged?'

'Engaged?' Rachel sat down on her own bed and kicked off her shoes.

'You mean it's official? Ma never said.'

'Yes, it's official.' Jennie stacked her magazines together and put them beside her bed. 'Sheena told me yesterday.'

'And you never told me?'

'Didn't feel like it.'

'Has he bought her a ring?'

'Oh, yes, a diamond. Borrowed the money from Malcolm.' Jennie shot a quick glance at her sister. 'You mean Malcolm didn't tell you?''

'No, he never said a word,' Rachel answered frowning.

'You're not the only one with secrets, then. Have you fixed up your loan yet?'

'It's none of your business, but no, I haven't.'

'Better hurry up, in case Rory needs to borrow some more. Were you out with Malcolm tonight?'

'No, with Tim.' Rachel jumped up. 'Look, I've had enough of these questions. You're getting down in the dumps, sitting here by yourself. Come out and have some tea.'

'I don't want any more tea. Anyway, I've got to get the washing in. You could help me.'

Rachel made a face. 'Do I have to? You know I hate going out the back. Tell you what, if you bring it in, I'll share the ironing.'

'You should do that anyway.' Jennie moved to the door. 'All

right, I'll get the washing in this time. But we'll have to leave the ironing till tomorrow. The stove's not on so we can't heat the irons.'

'What a shame,' sang Rachel.

It was growing dusk when Jennie went out to the drying green at the back of the tenement carrying her large wicker clothes basket. Here the Ritchie laundry was hanging in sullen stillness, for though there had been no rain, there was no breeze and nothing had dried. Jennie didn't care, didn't care about anything. Her face set and stony, she began pulling off pegs and tossing sheets into the basket. She didn't hear Rory's step as he came ducking through the lines until he reached her. When he said her name, she swung round with a start.

'Rory, what are you doing down here?'

'Came to see you. I wanted to tell you about Sheena and me.'

Jennie tore down a pair of towels. 'Sheena's already told me. I hope you'll be very happy.'

'Thanks. The thing is, it's no' going to make any difference to us. I mean, our talks and that.' He put his hand on her arm, seeming not to notice her flinch at his touch. 'It's very important no' to give up, Jennie, no' to lose interest in what we have to do.'

'I shan't lose interest,' she said hoarsely. 'You can still lend me the books.'

'Aye, Sheena'll no' mind.' His gaze never left Jennie's face. 'You're needed, you see. Everybody's needed. There's bad times ahead.'

'You mean strikes?'

'Aye, a miners' strike. Mebbe a general strike. The pit owners are planning to cut the men's wages to lower the price of coal. Can you believe that? When they get so little anyway? But we'll fight it, we'll no' let those fellers get away with it. So, dinna give up on us, eh, Jennie?'

She gave a shrill little laugh. 'Rory, there's not much I can do.'

'There'll be marches – meetings – women'll be needed as much as men.'

'Oh, yes, I'll be needed for marches and meetings.' Jennie bundled the rest of the laundry into the basket and snatched it up. 'Rory, will you just leave me alone!' she cried. 'Just leave me alone!'

Staggering with the weight of the basket, she left him to stare after her while she ran across the green, down a flight of mossy steps and through the basement door, which she slammed behind her with a resounding clang. Faces appeared at windows, laughter drifted down, then Sheena's voice from Lily's high window cried, 'Rory, Rory, are you no' coming up?'

Rory, running his hands through his black hair, strode swiftly into the house.

During the next few weeks wedding talk occupied Lily and Madge, though Jennie and Rachel kept aloof and Rory said he just wanted the whole thing over so that he and Sheena could be together.

'The funny thing is,' Madge told Abby, one Sunday morning, 'Sheena doesn't seem a bit interested in the wedding herself.'

They were walking back from St John's together, for Abby to please her mother occasionally joined her at church; Jennie rarely attended now and Rachel never. The September morning was pleasantly warm and they were taking their time walking back towards the Lawnmarket.

'I should've thought she'd be thinking of nothing else,' Abby remarked.

'Yes, but when I offered to make her a wedding dress, she just said, "Oh, Ma'll find me something second-hand, thanks all the same".' Madge's blue eyes were wide on Abby's face. 'Wouldn't you have thought she'd like a new dress?'

'She may have been thinking of the money, Ma, but she's always liked old clothes anyway. I expect she'll turn up in some Edwardian lace thing and still look wonderful.'

'I daresay. You've heard it's to be a register office wedding?' Madge shook her head in disapproval. 'Rory doesn't hold with church weddings and Lily's never been a churchgoer. I don't suppose Sheena's ever set foot in a church in her life. They've fixed the date for November.'

Abby bent a stern gaze on her mother. 'Promise me you

won't go getting involved, Ma. I don't want to hear that you're doing the reception or baking the cake or anything of that sort.'

'But Abby, I can't leave it all to Lily!' Madge paused for breath as they neared Catherine's Land. 'You know she has no money. I said she could bring a few folk back to my flat and I'll get the cake through Mackenzie's and do some sandwiches and pies. Rory says he'll get the drink, so we needn't worry about that.'

'I knew it, I knew you'd get involved.' Abby sighed in exasperation. 'And Jim Gilbride,' she added in a lower tone, 'are we going to have to see him?'

Madge walked faster. 'I suppose so. It's his son who's getting married.' She looked back. 'There's no need to worry, Abby. Seeing him won't bother me at all.'

Abby had said she could stay for Sunday dinner but must leave soon afterwards, she had to meet a friend.

'Oh, that's good.' Madge stopped to look at the potatoes Jennie had earlier put in the oven. 'I'm glad you're getting out again, Abby. You seemed so lonely at one time. Is it that young man with the nice car today?'

Still bent over the range, Madge did not see Abby's face turn pale, but Jennie did and wondered.

'I'm not sure what you mean,' Abby said, after a moment.

'Well, someone said they'd seen you in a lovely car with a very smart young man.' Madge straightened up. 'Was it Sheena, Jenny?'

'It was Sheena.' Jennie stared across at Abby. 'Said she'd seen you with a fellow who looked like a toff. Certainly had a toff's car.'

'A toff?' Abby laughed. 'It was only Mr Gerald. That's Mr Farrell's nephew. He's a partner in the firm. He sometimes gives me a lift.'

'Is he married?' asked Jennie.

'If it's of any interest, yes, he's married.' Abby began to set the table with quick deft movements.

'What a shame. So it won't be him you're seeing today?'

'Jennie, what's the matter with you?' asked Madge. 'Speaking to Abby like that! Go and tell Rachel we're nearly ready.'

Madge turned to Abby. 'You know what it is,' she said in a

low voice, as Jennie marched into the bedroom to find Rachel. 'She'll be better when the wedding's over.'

'Will she? I thought Sheena and Rory were going to stay on in Catherine's Land in Gramma's old flat?'

'Oh, they'll have to move soon. That little room'll never do for a couple. And then there'll be children.'

'Sheena doesn't want children, Ma,' Jennie called from the bedroom door. 'She told me that herself.'

'Everybody wants children,' Madge said firmly. 'And Sheena's very young.'

'No younger than you, Ma, when you got married.'

A slow smile crossed Madge's face, as she stood, flushed from the heat of the range with the gravy spoon in her hand. 'I suppose that's true.'

Rachel came up and put her arm around her mother's waist. 'We know you wish it was one of us getting married, Ma,' she murmured, 'but maybe we'll surprise you one of these days.'

'Pretty girls like you? Why should I be surprised if you get married?' Madge asked, laughing.

But when Abby was getting ready to leave, she said quietly, 'Would it upset you, Abby, if you had to leave work? I mean if you did get married?'

'Of course it would, Ma. I don't see why women should have to give up good jobs just because they've found husbands.'

'Well, it would put the men out of work, you see, if women took the jobs, and the men are the breadwinners, aren't they?

'They needn't be.'

'Oh, Abby, you're just like Rory, aren't you? You want to change the world!'

'Yes, I do, but just at the moment I don't want to get married, so that's all right, isn't it?' Abby kissed her mother. 'Bye, Ma. Take care. Bye, Jennie, bye Rachel.'

'Have a nice time with your friend,' Jennie murmured, and spread out a paper pattern on the table.

'Aren't you going out yourself?' Abby asked, smoothly.

'No.' Jennie bent her head. 'I've got to cut out my bridesmaid's dress.'

Chapter Twenty-Two

With the coming of October, it had become too cold to go to Greyfriars kirkyard and Jennie no longer met Rachel and Sheena in her dinner hour. Sometimes she went out window-shopping; more often she stayed in Miss Watson's back room with Sally Bone, the new apprentice, while Miss Watson herself, a plump, fussy little woman rested upstairs in her flat. It was to the back room that Sally admitted Sheena, on a day so windy she was almost blown in and could scarcely get her breath.

'Sheena, I don't want to go out today,' Jennie said at once. 'It'll be miserable up the kirkyard.'

'I'm no going to the kirkyard. Thought we could go somewhere for a cup o' tea.' Sheena was wearing a long grey coat and a black beret pulled rakishly over her flowing hair. While Sally, young and tongue-tied, stared at her in astonished admiration, Jennie's gaze was cold.

'I can make you a cup of tea here if you like,' she said with reluctance. 'Though I'll catch it if Miss Watson comes down, we're not allowed visitors.'

'So, let's go out, then.' Sheena pulled Jennie to her feet. 'Come away, get your hat, I want to talk to you.'

They battled against the wind to a nearby tearoom, where Sheena chose a table behind the door, away from other customers. 'I'll have to keep ma voice down,' she whispered, 'but what'll you have? Girdle scones or teacakes? Ma treat, Jennie.'

'What's all this about?' asked Jennie. 'Why all the mystery?'

'Ssh!' Sheena put her finger to her lips as the waitress

153

brought a plate of buttered scones and a pot of tea. 'You'll just have to wait till I've had something to eat. I'm falling through maself and that's no lie.'

Jennie watched amazed as Sheena ravenously ate her own scones, then finished Jennie's, too. 'D'you no' want that one, Jennie? I'll have it, eh? Shall we have some more tea?'

As Jennie poured more tea, Sheena finally pushed her plate away and licked her buttery fingers. 'I bet you can guess what's wrong with me, then? I either eat like this, or I'm sick as a dog. That's the way it takes some folk, they say.'

'What does?' asked Jennie.

Sheena glanced round the tearoom but seemed satisfied no one was listening.

'Being in the family way,' she answered calmly.

'Sheena, you're not! You can't be!'

'Keep your voice down, will you? It's true.' Sheena's lip trembled. 'I wish it wasna.'

Jennie was fighting a nausea of her own. Sheena and Rory. Making love. Starting a baby. They were engaged, she'd always known she'd have to face dark images after the wedding, but now it seemed they hadn't waited for the wedding and she'd had no idea, no idea at all. What a fool she'd been, how stupid, how green.

'Are you sure?' she asked dully.

'Aye, I'm sure.'

'So what does Rory say?'

'Rory?' Sheena s water-clear eyes grew wide. 'It's no Rory's, Jennie! He's no' the type to jump the gun. I'd no' be worrying if it was Rory's.'

'Sheena, what are you saying?' Jennie's eyes were blazing. 'You got engaged to Rory and all the time you were seeing another man?'

Sheena stood up, gathering her big coat about her. 'We'll have to go. I'll get the bill.'

Outside in the windswept street, she turned to face Jennie. 'It happened before I got engaged, Jennie. Musta been some time in July. I didna have any idea when Rory give me ma ring.'

'Oh, Sheena—'

'Och, I niver thought for a minute – I mean, he was so much the gentleman, asking me to sit, saying it would all be in

154

costume, I wouldna have to take ma clothes off – I niver dreamed I'd end up like this, Jennie, niver in the world!'

'Who asked you to sit?' cried Jennie, 'Sheena, who are you talking about?'

'Tim Harley, of course.'

'Tim Harley! You mean Rachel's young man?'

'He's no' her young man, she's given him the push.' Sheena was shivering in the wind and stepped for shelter into a shop doorway, dragging Jennie with her. 'The cold-faced devil! He'll no' marry me, Jennie, and he'll no' pay.'

'Marry you? Of course he can't marry you! You're going to marry Rory!'

'Aye, but it's Tim Harley's bairn, he's the one I should wed. But he'll no' help me, he'll no' pay. Says he's no money till he gets his ma's allowance and that's no' till November, but I've got to have the money now, I canna wait.' Sheena gripped Jennie's arm hard. 'Jennie, will you lend me something? Only a few pounds? I'll pay you back, I swear, but I've got to have the money now!'

'A few pounds? Sheena, I couldn't lend you a few shillings. I would if I could.'

'Can you no' see I'm desperate?' Sheena asked quietly. 'There's this woman I know, she's a nurse, she's good. She'd do it for five pounds, if it was cash. It's no' so much, is it? Five pounds?'

'It's a fortune, I don't know anyone who could spare it.' Jennie could scarcely meet the intensity of the beautiful gaze fixed upon her face. 'But Sheena, what's it for?'

'Och, I feel so sick.' Sheena had turned a cheesy white and let go of Jennie's arm to put her hand to her brow. 'It's they scones, I should niver have ate them. Jennie, dinna play the fool, you ken what the money's for. Let's walk on, mebbe it'll go off. Och, I feel so bad!'

'You're going to get rid of the baby?' Jennie asked in hushed tones, as they turned to walk down the street with their backs to the wind.

'I'm no' having it, that's for sure. I'm no' gonna be like Ma, saddled with a bairn and iverybody pointing the finger. And no' just at her.'

'Sheena, your ma thinks the world of you. She'd never've wanted to be without you!'

'Aye, but you dinna ken what it's like to be a love-bairn, Jennie. You've no dad, but your ma has a wedding ring and there's all the difference in the world.'

'You'll soon have a wedding ring,' Jennie murmured.

'No' if I dinna get some money. Can you see Rory marrying me with another man's bairn on the way? He'd kill me first.'

'Sheena, that's a wicked thing to say! Rory would never harm you.'

'You canna tell what men'll do, Jennie, and I dinna trust they Gilbrides.' Sheena's colour was returning, but she still looked unwell and afraid. 'Listen, do you think you could ask your Abby to help me? She's getting good wages, she might have a bit put by?'

'Everybody thinks of Abby, but she's not rich, she couldn't help Rachel.'

'Aye, but Rachel would want more than me, eh? I only want five pounds. Please, will you ask her, Jennie? Ma has no money and I havna dared to tell her anyway. Please, I'm at my wits' end!'

Sheena's hand on Jennie's arm was icy cold and she shrank away. 'I'd have to tell her what it was for.'

'Tell her, then, I dinna care. Abby can keep a secret. Just say you'll ask her!'

'All right.' Jennie gave a long troubled sigh. 'I will, I'll ask her.'

Showboat, the Jerome Kern musical was coming to the Empire Theatre and Abby had offered Jennie and Rachel a pair of reduced price tickets she'd bought through Logie's. It would be a good opportunity Jennie decided, to pick up the tickets and speak to Abby at the same time, though how she was going to say what she had to say she had no idea.

Abby made her very welcome, drawing her into her pleasant sitting room where a fire was crackling in the elegant grate, table lamps were softly glowing and bronze chrysanthemums stood straight in a tall vase. How well Abby had done to live like this, thought Jennie, how far she had come from Catherine's Land. Why, there was even a smell of coffee drifting in from the kitchen! People in Catherine's Land couldn't afford coffee. Tea was what they had, always tea, from a heavy old teapot on the side of the range, where there was usually a great

156

crusted kettle and a blackened cloth to lift it with, as at the Ritchies' flat, even though Ma had a gas ring now.

'You're very quiet, Jennie,' Abby commented. 'Anything wrong?'

'No, no. I just came for the tickets.'

'I could have dropped them in for you, but it's lovely to see you, anyway. Would you like some coffee? And some Logie's shortbread?'

The coffee was delicious, so was the shortbread. If only all she need do was sit here peacefully with Abby, thought Jennie, and became aware of her sister's eyes on her.

'Come on, tell me why you've really come,' Abby said quietly. 'Not just for the tickets, right?'

'Abby, it's awful to ask you, but have you got five pounds to spare?'

'Five pounds? Whatever for?'

'For Sheena. She – needs it.'

'Something to do with the wedding?'

Jennie groaned. 'I wish it was. She's going to have a baby and it isn't Rory's'

Abby gave a long sigh and set down her coffee cup. 'The silly little fool,' she whispered.

'I know, and the wedding's next month. She's desperate. Rory'll never marry her, if he finds out.'

'You're worried about that?' Abby asked wryly.

'Yes, because I don't want him hurt. I think it would kill him.'

'More likely, he'd feel like killing Sheena.'

Jennie's eyes flashed. 'Sheena said that, but I told her it was wicked to talk like that about Rory. He's not violent, he's never been violent!'

'His father is.'

'Well, he's not. He's like his mother, he's kind and caring, that's why he wants to help the workers. Abby, I know him!'

'All right, you know him. But whatever happens, there'll be trouble over a thing like this.' Abby rose and made up the fire, watching the flames die for a moment and the smoke rise. 'Who's the father?'

'Maybe I shouldn't say. He won't help, anyway.'

Abby sat back in her chair again and fixed Jennie with a

sombre gaze. 'So Sheena needs five pounds for an abortion and I'm the only one who can help?'

'There's no one else. Sheena won't tell her mother, I daren't ask Ma, Malcolm might let it get back to Rory. There's only you.'

'I'll tell you frankly I don't approve. I don't want to get involved. Apart from being against the law, it's dangerous. Supposing Sheena died?'

'Died?' gasped Jennie.

'Women do. Back-street abortions can go wrong. How would we feel then?'

Jennie closed her eyes. If Sheena were to die . . . Rory might . . . She put the shameful thought from her.

'I think Sheena'll risk it,' she said breathlessly. I know it seems a terrible thing to do, but she's just so desperate—'

'I'm not saying I don't feel sorry for her,' Abby said, slowly. 'The whole thing's a nightmare.'

As Abby stared into the fire, Jennie said nothing but anxiously watched her.

'Have you got five pounds?' she asked at last.

Abby nodded. 'In the Post Office.'

'Couldn't you let her have it, then? And leave it to her to decide what to do?'

'I suppose I'll have to. Oh, Jennie, what a mess! Poor Sheena. You can tell her I'll get her the money as soon as I can.'

'Oh, Abby, thank you!'

The sisters clung to each other in a sudden rush of emotion, each feeling they were entering the dark waters of an unknown experience which was not even to be their experience, yet somehow must be shared.

Jennie said she'd better go, she would just visit the bathroom first. Abby's bathroom was so wonderful she usually liked to linger, smelling the scented soap, looking at herself in the mirrors, but that evening with so much on her mind she could take no interest. She was turning to go after drying her hands on one of the splendid Logie towels, when she noticed Abby's blue dressing gown on the back of the door. Hanging next to it was another robe, a brown one, of excellent quality, with silk piping and cord and a monogram on the pocket. Jennie left the bathroom, carefully closing the door behind her. She knew the brown dressing gown belonged to a man.

She said nothing, of course, when she rejoined Abby, but Abby was quick to read what she could not hide.

'Oh, dear,' she murmured, 'I should have put it away, shouldn't I? Are you thinking I'm a silly fool, too?'

'I'm not thinking anything,' Jennie answered in a low voice. 'It's nothing to do with me.'

'I know you know what that dressing gown means, but it's not as bad as it looks. The . . . person who owns it . . . he's not free at the moment, but his wife wants a divorce and as soon as it's through, we'll be married.'

'I see.'

'Jennie, you won't tell Ma, will you?'

'As if I would!'

Abby hugged her. 'Thanks, Jennie. I know I can trust you.'

Oh, yes, everybody can trust me, Jennie thought drearily, as she waited for her tram. I keep everybody's secrets. Maybe I'd like a few of my own.

Later that evening, Abby put her lips to Gerald Farrell's long, elegant back, and whispered, 'Gerald, I think I should tell you, my sister, Jennie, knows about us.'

She had waited until they made love before telling him because when they were spent and ecstatic and floating on joy, there would be the chance that he would say, 'What does it matter? Soon everyone will know.' And then they could drift into contented sleep before Gerald had to steal away in the early morning, escaping Mrs McKay's keen ears and gimlet eye.

But her little plan failed. As soon as she had spoken, Gerald came instantly awake and asked quickly, 'How did she find out?'

Abby sat up against her pillow, pulling the sheet over her breasts in an oddly defensive movement. 'I'm afraid she saw your dressing gown.'

'Oh.' He relaxed. 'But she wouldn't know it was mine, would she?'

'No, but we have been seen together. In the car. I just said you'd been giving me a lift.'

'You told them my name?'

'I didn't think it mattered at the time.'

'And now your sister has put two and two together?'

'I think she has.'

Gerald switched on the bedside light and reached for his cigarettes. 'A little indiscreet, weren't you, Abby? There's never any need to name names.'

'Jennie won't say anything, this won't get out, I promise you.'

'That remains to be seen. I have to say, I'm not happy about it.'

'I'm sorry, then.' Abby's tone was sharp. 'But if it's going to come out one day, why worry now?'

'Abby, you know the situation. If my uncle were to find out about us before I'm ready to tell him, there'd be all hell to pay. Logie's is an old-fashioned firm, it has an old-fashioned clientele. For me to be having an affair with—'

'An accounts clerk?'

'I was going to say before I'm a free man. I'm afraid my uncle wouldn't understand at all.'

'So, when are you going to be a free man?' Abby got out of bed and pulled on her blue dressing gown. She tied the cord round her waist and looked back at Gerald, whose eyes in the smoke of his cigarette were narrowed and considering. 'I thought divorce proceedings would have been started by now.'

'These things take time.'

'Has Monica – has your wife seen the lawyers?'

'Oh, yes, she's had preliminary talks.' Gerald's gaze moved to Abby and softened. He stubbed out his cigarette and left the bed to take her in his arms. 'Come on, darling, don't look at me like that, huge great eyes, accusing . . . you know my marriage is dead. You know I love you.'

'I know you like making love to me,' Abby said quietly. 'Maybe that's all I know.'

'That's not fair.'

'Well, I sometimes think you ask a lot of me, Gerald.'

'I do.' He stroked her dark hair. 'But things will work out for us, I promise. We'll just have to be patient. I know it's hard, but it won't be for ever, you must believe that.' He kissed her long and deliberately. 'Shall we go back to bed now?'

160

'I don't think so. It hasn't been a good evening, I've a lot on my mind. Maybe you should go now."

"All right, if that's what you want." He studied her gravely. 'But I'm sorry you're worried. Is there anything I can do?'

'No, it's just a family thing. I can sort it out. Would you like a drink before you go? Some of your whisky?'

'My guess is you'd rather have some tea, wouldn't you?'

'I would, I've a headache coming on.'

'Poor darling.' Gerald reached for the brown dressing gown that had caused their first real coolness. 'I'll make the tea, then, and you can lie back and be waited on. Don't ever say I'm not domesticated, Abby. I make the best tea in Edinburgh.'

She laughed, very willing to have the mood lightened. Gerald could always charm her. Not because he set out to, but because he was so different in his ease and elegance from any other man she had known. It thrilled her that she alone had the power to make him happy, to change him from despairing rejected husband to fulfilled ecstatic lover. When he spoke of a future together she knew it could happen because it was what he wanted, and as she sipped the tea he brought her she gave herself back to happiness and peace of mind. Maybe he needn't go early, after all, she told him, her headache was much better.

The next day in her lunch hour she withdrew five pounds from her Post Office account.

Chapter Twenty-Three

Sheena was dancing like a child with a Christmas toy. Everything was going to be all right, her problems were over, the world was a beautiful place again. She threw her arms around Jennie's neck, pouring out her thanks.

'Tell Abby I'll niver forget her for this. And I'll niver forget you either, Jennie. Now I canna wait to get it over.'

'What will you do?' asked Jennie uneasily.

'See Mrs Smith, of course. Fix a time.'

'Mrs Smith? This woman calls herself Mrs Smith?'

'It's her name. Why should she no' call herself by her name?'

'You know it's a crime, what she does for a living? She could get sent to prison.'

'Aye, well she's no criminal, she's a very respectable woman.' Some of Sheena's elation was fading. She looked down at the money in her hand. 'Jennie, you'll come with me, eh?'

Jennie stared, aghast. 'Come with you? Sheena, I couldn't! You'll have to ask your mother. She's the one should go with you.'

'I canna ask her, have I no' said? She doesna approve, she'd niver let me do it.' Sheena's eyes were large with fear. 'Jennie, you'd no let me go on ma own?'

'What else can I do? I'm terrified to think of it.'

'Jennie . . .' Sheena gave a long shuddering sigh. 'So am I.'

But as she had known she would, Jennie gave in. On Saturday afternoon, her half-day, she agreed to go with Sheena to Mrs Smith's house in the Canongate.

'But, Sheena, I'm just going to wait for you,' she warned. 'I'm not – you know – going to be there.'

'Och, no!' cried Sheena, wonderfully returned to high spirits. 'I'm no' asking that. Somebody to go home with, that's all I want.' Again she threw her arms around Jennie. 'I'll niver forget this, Jennie, niver!'

'Neither will I,' said Jennie.

The worst thing was not being able to talk to anyone. Everyone round Jennie was blissfully unaware and must be kept so. Sheena's mother, her own mother, Rachel, and of course Rory. Jennie couldn't bear to look at Rory and wondered how Sheena could. But Sheena seemed to be good at concealing her feelings. Only to Jennie had she let the mask slip and even for Jennie the mask was now back in place.

On Saturday morning as Jennie left for work, Sheena was waiting for her on the stair.

'I'll meet you at Mrs Smith's,' she said in a hoarse whisper. 'Now you ken where it is? Over the haberdashery?'

'I know where it is.' Jennie moved uneasily in the shadows. 'Sheena, what about your ma? What about Rory?'

'What about them?'

'They'll wonder where you are when you don't come home this afternoon.'

'I'll be coming home, Jennie! It'll no' take long, Mrs Smith said so. Anyway, Ma'll be out cleaning.'

'But supposing Rory wants you to go out somewhere?'

'He's away to a meeting in Glasgow, he'll no' be back before six. Then I'll tell him I'm no' well.' Sheena fixed Jennie with a hard gaze from her beautiful eyes. 'Jennie, you'll no' let me down? You'll be there at two?'

'I've said so, haven't I?' Jennie lowered her voice as Donnie Muir ran past them, grinning. 'But listen, it's not too late to change your mind, you know. I mean this could be dangerous. You might die.'

'Die!' Sheena's voice was contemptuous. 'Jennie, there's nothing to it, I'll no' die.'

'But you might get caught, then you could go to prison, too.'

Sheena tossed back her long dark hair. 'Just be there at two, eh, Jennie? Like you said.'

Jennie felt strange all morning, brooding on what she saw as her guilt. If anything happened to Sheena, it would be her fault. It was true she had warned Sheena, but that didn't count, she had known full well that Sheena would not back out. And it was through her that Sheena had got the money, even though all the time there had been at the back of Jennie's mind the terrible thought that if Sheena were to die Rory might turn to her. But she wouldn't think of that, she really didn't want that. She didn't want anything to happen to Sheena and that was the truth. But if she hadn't helped Sheena to get the money, her conscience would have been clear. What was to happen in Mrs Smith's rooms in the Canongate would have had nothing to do with her. Now it had everything to do with her. So reasoned Jennie, trying to sew, her face paper white, her hands grown large and clumsy.

'Will you look at they stitches!' cried Miss Watson, leaning over Jennie's shoulder. 'I wouldna accept them from Sally, niver mind you, Jennie. What's got into you? Take them out, take them out!'

'Sorry, Miss Watson,' Jennie murmured, while Sally concealed a smile and the hands of the clock moved inexorably on.

One o'clock struck and Jennie put aside her work, watching Sally go off on her carefree way and Miss Watson climb the stairs to her flat. Then she made a cup of tea in the back room and tried to eat a sandwich, but the bread stuck in her throat. The quarter struck, and then the half-hour, and she washed her face in cold water and put on her jacket and hat. She might as well go. It wouldn't take her long to get to Mrs Smith's but she didn't want to be late, didn't want to keep Sheena waiting if just for once she was early for an appointment.

They arrived together, Sheena very pale and waif-like in her long grey coat and black beret. The autumn sunshine glinted on the little diamond in her ring as she put her hand on Jennie's arm.

'You came,' she whispered.

'I told you I would.' Jennie looked up at the windows over the haberdashery shop. 'That's it, is it? Where's the stair?'

'At the side, I'll show you.'

The stairs like those of Catherine's Land, were of worn dirty stone. There was the familiar smell of old cooking and outside the door at the top was a can of milk already covered with small specks of dust.

'Better knock, then,' Jennie said shakily, as they stood staring at the door.

'Aye.' But before Sheena could raise her hand, the door opened and a woman came out. She wore a black dress and a print apron. Her hair was greyish blond, cut raggedly short, and her eyes were very pale. Though she gave them both a welcoming smile, Jennie disliked her on sight and would have given the world to run away. But Sheena was already moving eagerly forward.

'I've brought the money, Mrs Smith,' she said breathlessly. 'Five pounds, eh?'

'That's right, dear, but who's this, then?' The pale eyes rested on Jennie. 'I'm no' doing two for the price o' one, you ken!'

While Jennie's face flamed, Sheena tried to laugh. 'Och, no! This is ma friend, she's going to wait for me.'

'Canna wait here,' Mrs Smith said firmly. 'I havena the room. Come back later, eh?'

'When?' asked Jennie, but Mrs Smith only shrugged.

'When you like. It'll no' take long.'

Jennie hesitated, unwilling now to leave Sheena, but Mrs Smith was already drawing her inside. There seemed nothing for Jennie to do but go. She looked down at the can of milk, however, and asked just as the door was closing,

'Isn't this your milk here, Mrs Smith?'

'Och, that milkman, the great loon, leaves me ma milk and niver knocks on ma door – thanks, hen.'

As Mrs Smith stooped to pick up the can, Jennie touched her arm. 'My friend – she will be all right? You'll see she's all right?'

Mrs Smith's pale gaze was chill. 'She's gettin' what she wants, is she no'? What've you got to worry about?'

Jennie, biting her lip, turned away.

It was cold in the street and she didn't know where to go or what to do. Shoppers jostled her as she wandered down the Canongate, wondering if she should try to get a cup of tea somewhere, but she still didn't feel like anything to eat.

'Jennie, what are you doing here?' she heard a voice cry, and it was Rachel's. She swung round to find her sister standing arm in arm with Malcolm Gilbride, staring at her with bright curiosity.

'It's my afternoon off,' she retorted. 'I suppose I can look round the shops if I want to? Anyway, shouldn't you be at the art shop, Rachel?' Unlike Jennie, Rachel had to work on Saturday afternoons and was permanently cross about it.

'My lunch hour,' Rachel answered airily.

'Pretty late back, aren't you?'

'Old Jackson won't mind.'

'Twists him round her little finger,' Malcolm said fondly, 'like she twists us all.'

Rachel laughed and Jennie thought how pretty she looked and how much at ease. Malcolm looked well, too; well and happy and prosperous. Jennie turned away, her face bleak.

'I'd better get on. I'll see you later, Rachel.'

'Will you tell Ma I shan't want any tea? Malcolm's taking me to the King's tonight, we're going to have something to eat after the show.'

Jennie nodded and walked on. Lucky Rachel. Going to a show, not in love with Rory, not involved with Sheena. It must be nice to be Rachel. But Jennie could not spend time thinking of her sister, she had to run up the Canongate with her heart in her mouth, she had to go back to Mrs Smith's, to whatever awaited her there.

At first she was filled with great bounding relief. Sheena was at the foot of the stair, leaning against the wall. She was all right, she'd come through, she hadn't died! Jennie was not going to be made to suffer for her shameful thoughts. But then she saw the look on Sheena's face and felt again that cold touch of her hand.

'Oh, Jennie,' Sheena whispered, 'it's no' over. I thought it would be, but it isna, it isna!'

'What do you mean?' cried Jennie, filled with sick apprehension. 'What happened, then? Didn't she do it?'

Sheena closed her eyes for a moment. When she opened them they were wide and staring. 'Aye, she did it.'

'So, what's wrong?'

'Jennie, she makes it come but it doesna come straight away. She niver told me, she niver explained. I thought I could stay with her, but she doesna let you wait. She said I'd to go home, just go away home.' Sheena burst into tears. 'What am I going to do?'

'Maybe it'll come in the night?' Jennie suggested, desperately.

'But supposing it comes before, when Rory's there! Jennie, can you no' think of something?' In the fading afternoon light, Sheena looked pale and ill. 'Could I maybe go to Abby's, do you think?'

'She won't be back from Logie's for another two hours.' Jennie shook her head. 'Sheena, you'll just have to go home and tell your ma, there's nothing else you can do.'

'Jennie, I'm too scared, I'm too scared of Rory!'

'If he comes back, I'll keep him out, I'll say you're ill.' Jennie was counting the coins in her purse. 'Look, I've enough for a taxi, let's get you home before anything happens here in the street.'

Lily's flat was in its usual disarray but Lily herself had not yet arrived home and they thanked God for that.

'What should I do?' Sheena asked, standing woefully in the middle of the room. 'Should I go to bed?'

'I don't know. I don't really know anything about it.' Jennie gave Sheena a fearful look. 'What did Mrs Smith say?'

'She said it'd be like a miscarriage, just sort of come away.'

'You won't need a doctor?'

'Och, no! D'you want me arrested?'

'He wouldn't know what you'd done, would he?'

'He might guess. I'm no' going to risk it.' Sheena collapsed into a chair. 'Jennie, will you no' make us a cup of tea?'

But it was while Jennie was boiling the kettle on Lily's stove that Sheena gave a little scream and doubled up with a spasm of pain.

'Jennie, I think it's starting! Och, Mrs Smith niver said it might be so soon! What'll I do? Ma might be home any minute!'

'But Rory won't be home till six.' Jennie put her arm round Sheena and helped her to her bed in the tiny room off the living room. 'It might all be over before he comes.'

'Way I feel, it'll niver be over.' Sheena sat despairingly on the bed while Jennie helped her to undress and put on a nightgown and at Sheena's direction found old towels and strips of sheeting in the chest of drawers.

'If the kettle's boiling,' Sheena added, 'I'd still like some tea.'

'Sheena, I wish you'd let me get somebody to help,' Jennie said worriedly. 'I can't do anything, I don't know what to do.'

'Jennie, I can manage. Other folk do. Just make us some tea, eh?' Sheena lay back and closed her eyes.

For some agonised moments Jennie looked down at the colourless face with its fine mist of sweat, then she said, with decision, 'I'm going for Ma.'

On Saturdays, her mother finished early. Please God, let her be back, prayed Jennie, running down the stair, let her be back, please! And she was, just taking off her hat, her shopping bag still unpacked on the table. Never in her life had Jennie been so glad to see anyone and she caught at her mother's hands.

'Come on, Ma, quick, up the stair!'

'Jennie, what is it? What's happened?' cried Madge, her eyes filled with fear.

'It's Sheena. Oh, Ma, don't waste time, just come!'

'Oh, poor girl, poor girl,' Madge murmured, taking in the situation as soon as she saw Sheena. 'Oh, my goodness, I'd no idea there was a baby on the way. Jennie, if there's some boiled water in Lily's kettle, I'll just wash my hands. And will you run down and get me a clean pinny from the cupboard?'

'Ma, shouldn't I fetch a doctor?'

'No doctor!' cried Sheena, wildly. 'I tell you, I can manage!'

'It's all right, dear, no one's fetching a doctor,' Madge said soothingly. 'You're going to be all right, but you're going to lose the baby, you know that, don't you?'

'Aye, I know,' Sheena answered, her eyes glistening with tears. At something in her tone Madge glanced sharply at Jennie and drew her into the living room out of Sheena's hearing.

'Has Sheena done something, Jennie? Has she brought this on?'

Jennie nodded, not daring to meet her mother's eye.

'But why? When she's going to marry Rory anyway?'

'Ma, it isn't Rory's.'

'Not Rory's? Oh, the poor silly girl!' Madge shook her head in disbelief. 'Jennie, where's Lily? Does she know about this?'

'She's at work, she doesn't know anything. Promise you won't tell her?'

'Jennie, she isn't going to need any telling,' Madge said dryly. 'Will you go and fetch that pinny?'

It was a wonderful feeling to know that she was no longer alone and as Jennie ran down the stair, she felt as light as thistledown because her mother was sharing her burden. There was still plenty of time before Rory was due home; if their luck was in, he need never know what had been happening.

But their luck wasn't in. When Jennie came flying out of the flat with her mother's clean apron over her arm, Rory and Lily were already ahead of her, climbing the stair.

'Rory!' screamed Jennie, and stood like a stone.

'Hello, Jennie.' Lily looked back, smiling. 'Just met Rory at the door and look what he's give me!' She held out a bunch of yellow chrysanthemums in tissue paper, while Rory grinned.

'Half price at the station, I couldna resist them. Is Sheena up the stair, Jennie?'

'You're early!' Jennie burst out. 'You weren't due home till six!'

'I caught an earlier train.' Rory's dark blue eyes were puzzled. 'Is everything all right, Jennie?'

'Yes, yes, of course it is. Only Sheena's not so well, she has a headache—'

'No' so well?' cried Lily. She turned and began to hurry up the stair. 'Come on, Rory, we'll go see her.'

'Aye, poor lassie,' said Rory, following, without a backward glance at Jennie, who stood stricken at the foot of the flight of stairs, the gaslight flickering down on her bent blonde head. The street door banged and Rachel came running up, her face flushed with the cold, her eyes sparkling.

'Hello, Jennie, whatever are you doing there?'

Without waiting for an answer, she hurried into the flat, calling over her shoulder that she was just going to change.

Jennie stayed where she was, listening to the sounds of Catherine's Land. People talking, laughing, a baby wailing. She strained her ears to hear what might be happening in Lily's flat above, but could hear nothing. Then a door somewhere opened and closed. There were steps on the stair. Rory's? Jennie's heart was thudding. But it was only one of the Kemps.

'Jennie, what you doin' on the stair?' Jamie Kemp asked good-naturedly.

She shook her head mutely, not caring what he thought. Was someone crying? In Lily's flat? She couldn't be sure, there were so many noises. But that was surely another footstep on the stair.

'Rory!' Pushing past Jamie Kemp she ran to him. 'Oh, Rory!'

She tried to take his arm, but he only looked at her with burning eyes and put her from him. As Jamie stared after them, they both ran down the stair and out into the street, Jennie stumbling after Rory, calling his name. 'Rory, wait! Rory, wait!'

But the night was full of people and none of them Rory. Though she waited and waited back in Catherine's Land, he never came home.

The next morning it was discovered that Lily MacLaren had done a 'flit'. Aye, said the tenants standing about in groups, enjoying the gossip because they'd no work to go to, she'd flown. Got Archie Shields to find her a taxi, taken all she could carry and Sheena in blankets and flitted away before the dawn was breaking. Scared of the polis, it was said, and it was right enough that Peggie Kemp had seen Sheena coming out of Mrs Smith's and everybody knew what that meant. And then Lily'd been keening and Rory'd gone running. It didna take too much of a mind to work out what young Sheena'd been up to, eh? No wonder Lily'd done a flit. No wonder she'd put the miles between her Sheena and a son of Jim Gilbride's! Like father, like son, and Jim was a man who'd go dancing mad if you so much as looked at him the wrong way. Aye, you had to feel sorry for poor sweet Lily, then, and poor wee Sheena. You had to pray to God Rory never found 'em, and Amen to that!

But Rory had not gone looking. On Monday evening when Jennie was coming home, she saw him ahead of her under the streetlights. Her heart leaped, she wanted to call out, but this time did not dare. He looked back and saw her.

'Hello, Jennie,' he said quietly.

'Hello, Rory.' She could see his eyes and they were not burning now, were dead, as though there would never be fire in them again.

'Like some pamphlets?' he asked. 'I've got some new ones.'

His voice was shaking, he was like a stranger, but a great rush of joy flooded Jennie's being.

'Yes, I'd like some,' she said faintly. They walked slowly towards the door of Catherine's Land. Jennie cleared her throat. 'Would you like to come in to Ma's, Rory? Have something to eat?'

'No, I can't. Not tonight.' There were beads of sweat on his brow as he looked up the stair. 'Mebbe some other time, eh?'

'Any time,' said Jennie.

Chapter Twenty-Four

After the storm came peace. The lives of the Ritchies marked
time and Madge felt a great relief, though she missed Lily
more than she had thought possible. Even Rory appeared to
have settled into a life without Sheena, though her name was
never mentioned in his presence and where she and her mother
had flown was not known. Rory came often to have meals with
Madge and the girls and seemed to like to spend time with
Jennie, but it was clear to everyone that he was filling his empty
heart with work, of which there was plenty. 1926 was without
doubt going to be the year of a general strike, the first great
test of trade union power. 'Not a penny off the pay, not
a minute on the day', was the slogan of the miners when
told they must work longer hours for less money, and every
workers' union would support them in their struggle.

'Thank God,' said Rory, 'it's coming at last.'

'What will it mean?' asked Jennie.

'A complete shutdown. The country'll see for the first time
they canna manage without the people who do the work!'
Rory's eyes were shining in a way Jennie had never thought to
see again. 'Are you no' excited?' he asked.

'I am,' she answered sincerely. For some months she had
been working for the women's section of the Labour Party,
even though she had no hope of a vote for years to come. 'I
know things can't go on as they are. I see the misery.' She
gave a wry smile. 'I live in Catherine's Land.'

'There's worse places than Catherine's Land. And you girls
and your Ma, you've niver had to live on the edge.'

'Neither have you, Rory. Doesn't mean we don't care.'

He fixed her with a sombre look. 'You care, Jennie, but your Rachel – doesna give a damn, eh? And Abby, working at Logie's, she's no' one for the poor.'

'Abby's always been on the side of the poor!' cried Jennie. 'She remembers what it was like to be in service!'

'Aye, well she got her three meals a day there all right, if I'm no' mistaken. And I've seen her with that feller in his grand car. I bet they go out for slap-up dinners that'd feed a miner's family for a month.'

'Rory, he's just a friend to her.' Jennie lowered her eyes. 'As I am to you,' she added.

'Yes, you're a friend,' Rory agreed softly. He covered her hand with his. 'You've made ma life bearable these past months, d'you ken that? I sometimes think I wouldna have got through without you.'

She brightened, pressing her fingers in his. 'Oh, I'd like to think I'd helped you, Rory!'

'Nobody could help to begin with,' he muttered. 'I just wanted to kill maself. Or sometimes I wanted to kill her.'

'Rory!'

'Aye. I wanted to do to her what she'd done to me. I wanted to make her suffer.'

'I don't like to hear you talking like this, Rory. It's not you.'

'No, because I didna do it, did I?' He laughed harshly. 'Och, I ken full well Lily MacLaren left because she was afraid of me, but she'd no need to be. I soon got over all that. I thought, why should I swing for a little bitch like Sheena? She's no' worth it.'

'You're not being fair, Rory. It – it happened before she got engaged to you, she told me so herself.'

'Mebbe so, but she kenned all along I loved her. I worshipped her. Even before she got ma ring, she was ma own girl and I thought I was her man, but I wasna. There were others, there were always others.' A hard flush had risen to Rory's cheek, his eyes were burning darkly. 'And there always would have been. So when I felt like jumping off George the Fourth Bridge, I'd tell maself that. And I'd go on living.'

'Oh, Rory.' Tears rose to Jennie's eyes, partly for him, partly for herself. He didn't realise it, but no one knew better than

173

she what he had suffered over Sheena. But he was getting over Sheena. And Jennie was suffering still.

'Jennie and Rory are so sweet together,' Madge told Abby one spring evening. 'So friendly and easy. I don't know if it's really what Jennie wants, but it's nice to see.'

'I'm sure it's not all she wants,' Abby replied, 'but she'll settle for it.'

'Have you had to settle, Abby?' Madge asked quietly, and Abby, taken by surprise, could not meet her mother's gaze.

'I don't know what you mean, Ma.'

'Well, aren't you seeing somebody you don't want me to meet? I don't want to pry. I just want to be sure you're happy.'

'I'm happy. I'd tell you if I wasn't.'

They both knew that that probably wasn't true, but it made them feel better that it was said.

Am I happy? Abby asked herself, walking to the tram. No, nor friendly and easy with Gerald. Their relationship was foundering on rocks that had been submerged and now were beginning to be revealed. There had been no more talk of divorce and Abby had decided she would not ask about it again, she would not put herself in the position of the nagging mistress. She hoped Gerald still loved her. If he did not, she would have to find the courage to make the break. Yes, she promised herself, she would have the satisfaction at least of being the first to say goodbye.

Gerald came round later that evening, bearing a bottle of wine and a spring bouquet. Paper-white narcissi, yellow tulips, perfect, early-flowering lilies.

'Always lovely flowers,' she said with a smile. 'You spoil me.'

'Impossible,' he answered, kissing her.

They had a light supper during which it seemed to her that he was on edge, but she might have imagined it; she was perhaps too much on the lookout for change. But after supper when he had lit a cigarette, he began, 'About Monica . . .'

As though they had just been talking of Monica, when they had not mentioned her name for weeks! Abby, pouring coffee, felt washed by a cold wave of apprehension.

'Here's your coffee, Gerald,' she said evenly. 'What about Monica?'

He stirred his coffee, round and round, round and round,

until Abby could have screamed. 'She wants to come back to Selkirk Terrace,' he said, without looking up.

'What do you mean? I thought she was looking for a place in Berwickshire.' Abby had gone white. 'She can't come back to your house if there's going to be a divorce.'

Gerald drank his coffee and lit a cigarette. 'Seems she's changed her mind.'

'About the divorce?'

'Seems so.'

'And that's all right, is it?' Abby's voice was trembling. 'All right by you, Gerald?'

'No, of course not – I mean . . .' He put his hand to his brow and the cigarette between his fingers wreathed his face in smoke. 'The thing is, her parents have stepped in. They've always given her a good allowance, that's why she thought she could go her own way. But now she's told them about the divorce they've threatened to cut her off, won't have a divorce in the family whatever the reason.' Gerald glanced quickly at Abby and away. 'So, you see the position.'

'Very clearly. Monica wants children, but not as much as all that.' Abby laughed. 'So where do you fit in, Gerald? Do you come with the allowance and the Selkirk house? Things she might as well keep?'

'Monica has never said she didn't love me,' he replied, with dignity. 'That was never the reason for our parting. I thought you knew that.'

'I don't know what I know any more!' she flashed. 'I thought I knew you loved me, but obviously I got that wrong, didn't I? You were just filling in time with me, using me—'

'No!' He took her in his arms. 'No, Abby, darling, that's not true! I never used you. I do love you, you're very special to me, always will be—'

'Only you just have to go back to your wife.' Abby pulled herself free from his embrace. 'I suppose it's a very old story. I wonder why I thought it was something more? Goodbye, Gerald.'

'Abby!'

She picked up the coffee tray and took it out to the kitchen, calling over her shoulder, 'Don't forget to take your dressing gown this time, will you? And you might as well take those flowers. Put them in Monica's room, make her feel welcome.'

'I can understand your feeling bitter,' he began, then shouted, 'Oh, for God's sake leave the flowers! They're yours, I brought them for you. Abby, will you listen to me? Maybe you're right, we should end things, but I want you to know that it won't make any difference at Logie's. You've no need to worry about that.'

'No need to worry?' Abby's face was turning scarlet, her dark eyes were smouldering. 'Why should I even think of worrying, Gerald?'

'You needn't, that's what I'm saying. What's happened between us is not going to affect your career in any way.'

'I should hope not! My career is nothing do to with you!'

'That's not quite true, Abby, I am on the board. But it's quite likely that Miss Inver will be returning to Dundee in a year or so – she has elderly parents she wants to be near – and I shan't hesitate, I promise you, to recommend you for her post.'

A mist was forming before Abby's eyes, she could scarcely see the look of appeal in Gerald's eyes, the nervous smile that was hovering round his lips as he tried to placate her.

'Recommend me!' she cried. 'Don't you dare! I don't want your recommendation, I don't need it. I'll get my promotion on my own merits or not at all. Is that clear?'

'Perfectly,' he replied quietly. 'But can't you see we're talking about your merits anyway?' He took a step towards her. 'If there had never been anything between us, don't you think I'd have recommended you anyway?'

Her gaze fell and to her horror, tears began to roll down her still scarlet cheeks. 'Oh, just go,' she said thickly. 'Please, Gerald, just go.'

'Abby—'

She turned away and stood with her back to him, trying to gain composure, and after a while she heard the door open and close and knew she was alone.

Later she found his dressing gown still on the back of the bathroom door; he had forgotten it, after all. She tore it down and bundled it into a carrier bag. Now she would have to get that back to him at the office without his secretary seeing. What would dear Monica have said if she had returned it to the house? At least Gerald needn't worry she would do anything of that sort. Probably that was why he had risked an affair with her in the first place. Abby, exhausted, sat down by the fire and found his cigarettes lying on the table in front of her. It gave her a small feeling of satisfaction to throw them into the flames and watch them burn.

Chapter Twenty-Five

All the troubled year of 1926, Jennie was at Rory's side. When the General Strike collapsed in May after only ten days, Jennie was there to support him in his bitter disappointment. When the miners decided to stay out after everyone else went back, Jennie suffered with him over their hardship. Six months later when they were forced back to work by hunger, it was Jennie who followed as Rory ran into the night, shouting he couldn't breathe, couldn't live, in a world that was so unjust.

'They've had to crawl back,' he muttered, standing at the top of the Mound looking over Princes Street. 'Had to crawl back to the owners. For less money, for longer hours. You ken that's what it was all about in the first place? No' a penny off the pay, no' a minute on the day.' He shook his head. 'I canna take it, Jennie, I canna take it any more.'

'I know, I know.' She slipped her hand into his, as the night wind buffeted their still figures. 'The thing is, you can't give up, Rory. You just have to keep on, that's all there is left.'

'Aye, it's easy to say. But the government plays with a loaded dice. The workers niver have a chance, they'll niver have a chance.'

'They will, they will. Things'll change, they always do.'

Rory stood with his shoulders hunched and his eyes fixed on the lights below. 'Look at it, Jennie, look at the city. Auld Reekie. See the smoke? Even at night you can see it. That's from fires. Hundreds and hundreds of fires, all burning coal. And it has to be cheap coal, you ken. If a man has to kill himself to dig it out, it's still got to be cheap, so that all the New Town folk can have a fire in every bloody room. Cheap,

cheap coal, and niver mind what others have to pay, eh?' He swung round and looked down at Jennie with fiery eyes. 'And you tell me to keep on. Keep on doing what?'

'Working for the Party, I suppose,' Jennie answered uneasily. She had not seen Rory so low since he parted with Sheena and wasn't sure now what she could do to help. She felt as desolate as he did, but it was understood that he wouldn't try to comfort her, it was up to her to comfort him. For the first time, she felt weary of so much comforting.

'Let's go back,' she said quietly, 'it's cold.'

'No, I want to walk. I just want to walk. Are you no' coming with me?'

She shook her head, moving aside to let people go by, people hurrying home to be warm and comfortable, to sit beside those fires that cost so much. 'You go on, Rory. I'm going back.'

'You don't want to walk with me?' he asked sternly.

'Not just now.'

'Goodnight, then.' He strode away, his head down against the wind, and though a part of her wanted desperately to call after him as she had always called before, 'Rory, wait for me!', this time she let him go.

'You're back early, dear,' Madge observed as Jennie let herself into the flat. 'I thought you were out with Rory.'

'No.' Jennie lit the gas under the kettle. As she felt Madge's speculative gaze on her, she began to hum a tune from *Showboat*.

Maybe Abby's wrong, Madge thought, maybe Jennie's decided not to 'settle', after all. Better not say anything, though. Not just yet.

Two days passed like years. Sometimes Jennie was on the point of giving in, she couldn't stand it any longer, she would have to go and see him. But then why shouldn't Rory come to see her? He didn't.

Another day went by and she was coming slowly out of Miss Watson's into the evening chill, when she found him waiting for her. She hesitated, poised to run to him, to bury her face in his rough damp coat, but she made no move. She said, evenly, 'Rory? What are you doing here?'

'Hoping to see you.'

'Well, I think you know where I live.'

'Jennie, dinna be like this. I've missed you.'

'So've I missed you, then.'

'Would you like' – he hesitated, as though not used to finding the right words – 'to go for a bite to eat?'

She stared up into his face, quite taken aback. They never ate out, they couldn't afford it.

'I've a few shillings,' he told her, reading her mind. 'There's plenty cafes open.'

'Ma'll be expecting me home.'

'I had a word with your Ma in the shop this dinner time.'

'You told her I wouldn't be back? How did you know what I'd say?'

'I said I would ask, that's all.' Rory put Jennie's arm in his. 'Och, Jennie, come away, eh?'

Everything was rose-coloured, there were wings on her feet, as she ran with him up Victoria Street, across George the Fourth Bridge, down the High Street and into a little cafe that served fish suppers and pots of tea for one and sixpence. Food for the gods, when she was sitting looking at Rory and he was looking at her, and just for once they were not talking politics. She knew it couldn't last, they couldn't put their troubles aside for ever and tomorrow must think of the miners again, but this evening belonged to her and she was going to enjoy its every moment.

'Jennie, I've been thinking,' Rory murmured, as she poured the tea, 'I've no' been fair to you.' He put up his hand as she opened her mouth to speak. 'No, this is hard to say, let me say it. I've been thinking, this past couple of days, I've been thinking I've no' deserved what you've done for me.'

'You told me I'd helped you,' she said quickly.

'Aye, once. But you've always been there for me, haven' you? To listen, get me through? Why've I niver said how much that meant?' His fine eyes rested tenderly on Jennie's face and though to see such a look was all she'd prayed for, now that it was there she couldn't meet it. Dreams didn't come true. Not for her.

'I'm no good at putting things into words,' Rory was continuing. 'No' this kind of thing, I mean. Och, I can spout on ma soap box . . .' He laughed and Jennie laughed, too. She'd never seen this side of Rory before and couldn't believe she was seeing it now. Rory laughing at himself? Rory lost for words? He was looking round the crowded cafe, at the people eating, the flushed waitresses taking orders, no one casting even a glance their way, and suddenly he stretched across the table and took Jennie's hand.

'Shall we get wed?' he asked abruptly.

She had not been able to say a word, had sat there so shocked, he had hastily stood up and said he would pay the bill. Now they were in the Lawnmarket, walking together, her arm in his, her eyes on his face, but she still had not said a word.

'I ken it's no way to propose,' he murmured uncertainly, 'but can you no' give me an answer, Jennie? We'd be so right for each other, we've got the same ideas, we'd work for the same things—'

'Rory,' she interrupted hoarsely, 'do you love me?'

He stopped at the entrance to one of the closes and drew her into its shadows. 'Goes without saying, Jennie.'

'But you have to say it. You always have to say it.'

'I'll say it, then. I love you, Jennie. Do you love me?'

She brought his face down to hers and kissed him on the mouth, uncaring that someone was wandering past them, that others might be following. Her prayers had been answered, her dream had come true, nothing in the world mattered to her then but Rory.

'Can't you tell from that?' she asked breathlessly, as she let him go.

'Aye, but you have to say it,' he teased her. 'Do you love me, Jennie?'

'I love you, Rory.'

As they climbed the stair in Catherine's Land, their arms twined together, he said, with sudden darkening mood, 'Jennie, I'm sorry, I canna give you a ring.'

For the first time that evening something other than joy entered Jennie's mind. Sheena's lovely face danced before her eyes, Sheena's diamond ring cut through her happiness like a knife.

'I don't want a ring!' she cried passionately. 'You need never worry about a ring for me, Rory!'

'She took it off,' he whispered, 'did you ever hear that? I said, tell me his name, I just want his name. But she niver said a word. Just took off the ring and threw it on the bed.'

'Oh, Rory,' Jennie sobbed, 'what did you do?'

'I left it.' His eyes flamed. 'Did you think I'd take it?'

'No, no. Oh, let's not talk about it, let's not think about it!' Jennie pulled him into her arms, holding him close, willing him to see nothing, remember nothing.

'Let's go in,' he said gently. 'And tell your ma.'

It was a familiar scene that greeted them when they opened Madge's door. Madge, in her rocking chair, turning the heel of a sock for one of the Finnegans, Rachel on the couch, reading, on this occasion an art monograph, for she was now a full-time student at the College of Art, courtesy of Malcolm Gilbride. Madge had not been pleased at first that Rachel was borrowing money from Malcolm, but Rachel said she would pay him back as soon as she was earning. As she had already sold a painting to a gallery in Dundas Street, she was sure it would not be long.

'Someone's paid good money for those squares you paint?' Madge asked wonderingly. 'Oh, well then – but I wish you'd draw things I could recognise, Rachel.'

'I can recognise everything I draw,' Rachel replied.

They looked up as Jennie and Rory came in and Madge only had to take one look at Jennie's face to drop her knitting and run to her.

'Oh, Ma,' Jennie whispered, 'we're engaged. I can't believe it, but it's true.'

'Jennie!' Rachel flew across the room to kiss her. 'Oh, I'm so happy for you! And you, Rory! Listen, if you're going to be my brother-in-law, I'm going to kiss you too.'

When Rory had bent his handsome face to be kissed by Rachel and by Madge, Rachel went rooting in the cupboard and found some sherry given to Madge by Malcolm the previous Christmas which she'd never opened.

'Now's the time!' she cried. 'Will you do the honours, Rory? Ma, where's the corkscrew?'

When four dusty glasses had been washed and the sherry poured, Rachel stood with a strange expression on her heart-shaped face. 'To Jennie and Rory!' she called. Madge echoed, 'To Jennie and Rory!' Then added, 'A wedding in the family – oh, how lovely!'

'A double wedding,' Rachel said quietly.

There was a silence. Rory sharply raised his head. Jennie and Madge were staring at Rachel with the same kind of astonishment in their blue eyes.

'Rachel, what do you mean?' asked Madge.

'I think I know,' said Rory.

'Right.' Rachel smiled. 'You're going to be my brother-in-law in more ways than one, Rory. I'm going to marry Malcolm.'

'Rachel, what are you thinking of?' cried Madge. 'You've only just started at the art college.'

'I don't have to give up the art college, Ma. I can be a married student if I like, I'm paying my own way.'

'You mean Malcolm is paying,' Jennie said flatly. 'Rachel, why are you doing this?'

Rachel shrugged. 'Why are you marrying Rory? Don't ask silly questions.'

Jennie, flushing, looked up at Rory. 'Maybe we should drink another toast,' he said slowly. 'To Rachel and Malcolm.'

'To Rachel and Malcolm,' Madge murmured. 'Maybe I'll make some tea. Rory, would you like a sandwich?'

They all had sandwiches and Mackenzie's fruit cake. No one spoke again of Rachel's engagement.

Later, when Jennie and Rory had self-consciously excused themselves to say good night on the stair, Madge said softly, 'She's so happy, isn't she, Rachel? I never thought I'd see it.'

'You don't mind, Ma, that we 're marrying Gilbrides?'

'No, I don't mind.' Madge busied herself putting things away. 'I've no interest in Jim Gilbride.'

'You'll have to see him again at the wedding. And his wife.'

'I'm sure we'll all be very polite to one another,' Madge said serenely. As she picked up her knitting and began to count stitches, Rachel lay back on the couch.

'Do you think Rory will make Jennie happy?' she asked lightly.

'He's the one she wants.'

'Malcolm says he's a fanatic, he could be very difficult to live with. Now Malcolm's quite different.'

'And you think he'll make you happy?'

'Oh, yes. I know what I'm doing.'

Madge looked up. 'Will you tell me the truth?' she asked, quietly. 'Are you marrying him because you owe him money?'

'No, because he's going to buy a nice house in Morningside.' Rachel laughed. 'Oh, I'm teasing, Ma! Of course I'm marrying him because I'm fond of him. We'll get on fine, you'll see.'

'I hope so.' Madge's face was still troubled but when Jennie came back, walking lightly as though dancing, she brightened. 'Girls, we must talk about your plans.'

'Oh, not tonight,' Rachel sighed, 'there's plenty of time.'

'That's true. You're both very young, you can afford to wait, save up—'

'I didn't say we wanted to wait. There's no point in waiting.'

'We don't want to wait, either, Ma,' Jennie put in, quickly. 'And we don't want a big wedding, there's no need to save up.'

'But I want you both to have a nice 'do',' Madge protested. 'I want to give you the best I can.'

'You're a widow, Ma, no one expects you to have money to spend on weddings.' Rachel spoke with decision. 'Anyway, Malcolm's already offered to help.'

'Seems we can't do anything in this family now without Malcolm Gilbride,' Madge commented coldly.

'He's only thinking of you, Ma.'

'Yes, all right, I'm sorry.' Madge tried to smile. 'The main thing is that you girls are happy. If only Abby—' She stopped.

'Abby?' Rachel repeated. 'Don't worry about Abby, Ma. She's married already, to Logie's.'

'I don't know about that,' said Jennie, lowering her eyes.

Rachel stood up, yawning. 'Let's talk about things tomorrow. That sherry has made me sleepy. I'm going to bed.'

'It hasn't made me sleepy,' Jennie murmured. 'I feel I'll never sleep again.'

But some time in the small hours, she did sleep, drifting away into a vivid dream in which Sheena had died and came

184

back to Catherine's Land as a ghost, wringing her hands and weeping.

'Sheena, what are you looking for?' Jennie asked in her dream, and Sheena's dead eyes were large and tragic.

'I want ma ring,' she answered. 'I've come back for ma ring.'

Chapter Twenty-Six

Madge was bitterly disappointed when Jennie and Rachel both chose to be married in the register office, rather than St John's. She had always pictured her daughters exchanging their vows in church, wearing traditional white wedding dresses made by herself, looking their best on their special day. Now wasn't that what every woman wanted? Not Jennie, it seemed. Not Rachel.

'I would have liked a church wedding,' Jennie explained, 'but Rory's dead against it. He's against all religion, he says it gets the people nowhere.'

'And all my friends would think I'd gone crazy if I turned up in a veil and all that orange blossom nonsense,' said Rachel. 'Malcom fancied a church wedding because it's supposed to be the done thing, but I told him he'd have to do what I wanted, as it's me he's marrying.'

'But we do want you to help us with our outfits, Ma,' Jennie said eagerly. 'We've chosen the patterns already. I thought I'd make mine in blue, Rachel wants cream.'

'And I suppose you've also planned the wedding breakfast?' Madge asked sarcastically, and they cheerfully agreed that they had.

'We thought we'd book that hall off the Canongate and get a firm in to cater,' Rachel announced. 'Now don't look like that, Ma! You know you can't manage such a big do yourself, you'll just have to leave it to us.'

'And who is going to pay? Malcolm?' Madge's eyes filled with tears. 'It should have been your dad and me.'

'Oh, Ma!' Jennie threw her arms around her mother. 'Don't

be upset. Rory and Abby are going to chip in, too, it's not only Malcolm. We just don't want you spending all your savings on us, do we, Rachel?'

'No, we don't. Try to understand, Ma.'

'I usually do, don't I?' asked Madge, in defeat.

Afterwards she told herself she shouldn't complain. Compare her lot with poor Lily MacLaren's! Her daughters had brought no tragedy into her life, they were marrying the men they wanted, they had every chance of being happy. But she still grieved that she was not to see her two lovely girls floating down the aisle in white dresses paid for from her own savings, made by her own needle. Maybe Abby – oh, it was no use thinking of Abby. Rachel was right, Abby was married to her career.

The tenants of Catherine's Land were naturally taking an interest in the Ritchie girls' double wedding. Jennie was popular and it was generally agreed that Rory Gilbride would be a lot happier with her than with that little baggage, Sheena, but uppity Rachel and snobby Malcolm deserved no better than each other. As for the wedding breakfast, what was Madge Ritchie thinking of, paying out for catering and a hall, not to mention a four-piece band for dancing! With so many hungry folk walking the streets, was it no' a shocking waste of money? All the same, everyone waited to see who would be invited.

'Do we really have to have all these Catherine's Land folk?' Malcolm asked Rachel in confidence. 'I mean, can you see Mr Abbott, our senior partner, making conversation with Mrs Finnegan and Jamie Kemp?'

'Ma's known them all for years, she couldn't leave them out,' Rachel answered.

'But they won't know what to do and they won't have anything to wear. Don't tell me your mother's planning to make 'em all wedding outfits?'

Rachel gave a burst of laughter. 'She'd like to! No, of course they'll just have to wear what they've got. They like weddings, they'll do their best, Malcolm.'

'Well, we surely don't have to send them all formal invites. Those cards cost money, you know.'

'Oh, what's a few shillings?'

Malcolm looked hard at Rachel from beneath his sandy brows. 'I hope you're not going to think like that when you're housekeeping, Rachel. The only reason I have money is that I know it doesn't grow on trees.'

Rachel stiffened and drew back. 'If you're marrying me to get a penny-pinching housekeeper, you'd better think again,' she said icily, and Malcolm instantly capitulated.

'Och, I'm marrying you because I love you! I've loved you since your hair was in ringlets, you ken that full well.'

'Just as long as you understand what I'm like, Malcolm.'

His answer was to pull her into his arms and spend the next few minutes happily kissing her, while she looked over his shoulder with a cold expression in her lovely eyes. Nothing more was said about sending invites to the tenants, but later that week Madge herself went round and asked everyone to the reception. For the ceremony at the register office, only close family would be present. Including Jim Gilbride, Madge thought with a sinking heart.

The March wedding day was cold and blustery, but everyone said for a register-office wedding the weather didn't matter. They all had other worries, anyway.

Jennie was terrified in case Sheena should walk in; Malcolm that Rachel might say she had changed her mind; Rachel that her artist friends would find everything too conventional, especially her outfit, which she should never have let her mother make when she could have designed something spectacular for herself. Madge kept rehearsing in her mind the cool and collected greeting she would make to Jim Gilbride, while Rory got through the hours by keeping himself busy – packing his case, cleaning his shoes, brushing his new suit made by Archie Shields at reduced price – and never letting the thought of that other planned wedding, that other bride, enter his mind. Nobody wanted anything to eat.

At two o'clock Abby arrived at Madge's flat, wearing a smart jumper suit in burgundy red wool with matching hat. Jennie and Rachel were still in the bedroom getting ready but Madge cried 'Abby, you look lovely! But haven't you lost some weight?'

'No, I'm fine.' Abby smiled as she glanced down at her suit.

'Logie's best, of course. I'm trying not to look too much like the older sister on the shelf.'

'Abby, you'll soon find someone!'

'Don't want anyone. Ma, you look wonderful.' Abby turned her mother round, admiring her dove-grey frock with short box-pleated skirt.

Madge blushed. 'You don't think the skirt's too short?'

'It's just right. You've got nice legs, why not show 'em?'

'I suppose I'm not used to showing my legs. And then there's my hat. It seemed all right in the shop, but now I can't get it to fit over my hair.'

'I told you you should have had your hair cut!' came Jennie's voice from the bedroom. 'Modern hats aren't meant to go over great knots of hair!'

'And you must be the only person in Edinburgh still using hat pins!' added Rachel, at which Abby grinned. 'I'll help you with it, Ma. Come on, you two, time's getting on!'

The bedroom door opened and Rachel appeared, wearing her cream dress and deep-brimmed hat, followed by Jennie in blue. They both stood self-consciously waiting to be admired, but Madge immediately dissolved into tears and Abby seemed quite taken aback.

'I – I don't know what to say,' she stammered.

'Bad as that?' asked Rachel.

'I mean, you both look so beautiful.'

'Well, that'll do, I'll settle for beautiful, won't you, Jennie? Now, where are the flowers, Ma?'

As she pinned a spray of red roses onto Rachel's collar, Madge thought it was true, both her daughters did look beautiful. Maybe Rachel with her rich colouring and great dark eyes might be said to eclipse the paler looks of her sister, but to Madge's eyes it was Jennie who had the bride's true radiance that was so special, that came only from love.

'Now your turn,' she murmured, taking up the white rose buttonhole, marvelling that things had worked out for Jennie just as she had always wanted. 'I'll never forget Rory, he's the only person I'll ever want to marry,' she had said long ago and it had seemed only childish nonsense at the time. Yet here she was, marrying him! She had endured Rory's love for Sheena, she had stood by him in the terrible time after

189

Sheena's betrayal, and now they had both come through to the joy of their marriage. Leaning forward to smell the scent of the white flowers, Madge whispered, 'I'm so happy for you, Jennie.' And Jennie, who had now quite stopped worrying about Sheena's possible arrival, serenely kissed her mother's cheek.

'Are you two ready?' Rachel asked from the window. 'I can see the taxi!'

'Oh, Abby!' cried Madge. 'Help me with my hat!'

Rachel and Jennie were well on their way downstairs by the time Madge and Abby got to the door of the flat, yet Madge still lingered.

'Come on, Ma!' cried Jennie, turning back. 'We mustn't be late!'

'I was just thinking' – Madge's face was suddenly blank – 'you girls'll never come back here to this flat.'

'Oh, Ma, of course we will!'

'No, not to live. We'll never be here together, the way we used to be.'

'You left your mother,' Abby said gently. 'That's the way things go.'

'Oh, I know. It's the way things go.'

'For goodness' sake, Jennie's not even leaving Catherine's Land!' cried Rachel. 'Please hurry, Ma, the taxi's waiting.'

Madge sighed and closed the door, then slowly followed her daughters down the stair.

It seemed that the whole of Catherine's Land was at the street door to see them off. There were cheers and squeals from the children, cries of, 'Do they no' look bonnie, eh?' and 'Och, you're as pretty as your daughters, Madge!' and 'Your turn next, Abby, hen!' as they ran the gauntlet to the taxi, blushing scarlet.

'Good luck!' cried Mr Kay, from the grocery shop.

'Good luck!' cried Archie Shields. 'We'll see you for the dancin'!'

'Aye, we'll see you for the dancin'!' the others echoed, and as Marty Finnegan flung a handful of rice, Madge threw out ha'pennies for the children. Down the cracked pavement the coppers rolled, and away went the children of Catherine's

Land, whooping and shrieking after them, as the taxi bore the wedding party away to the register office.

The three Gilbride men were already there, pale and unsmiling in dark suits with carnation buttonholes.

'Well, at least they've turned up,' Rachel observed with a nervous laugh, and Jennie's eyes grew enormous.

'Why, I never thought they wouldn't,' she said faintly, glad this worry had not presented itself to her mind before.

As the taxi drew up, Malcolm hurried forward, his face happy and incredulous as though he still couldn't believe his luck, and Rory followed, handsome and solemn, but Jim kept back and did not raise his eyes. A tall bony woman had joined him from the door of the register office, and Madge, descending from the taxi, looked straight at her. She had round eyes and a tiny scarlet mouth and looked for all the world like a wooden Dutch doll. The second Mrs Gilbride, thought Madge, and her heart beat fast.

'Hello, Madge,' said Jim. He looked the same, yet indefinably older. Perhaps he had put on a little weight? Or maybe the brown hair that could flame in the sun was not quite so thick? His fierce gaze now turned on Madge had certainly not changed. All her little speeches went quite out of her head.

'Hello, Jim,'' was all she said.

'How are you keeping, then? You're looking well.'

'I'm very well, thanks. How about you?'

'Fine.' Jim touched the arm of the woman at his side. 'Madge, I'd like you to meet ma wife. Bella, this is Mrs Ritchie.'

The Dutch doll's round eyes snapped with interest, but it was impossible to tell how much she knew about Madge. 'Nice to meet you,' she said, in a deep Glasgow voice.

'I'm sorry we haven't met before,' Madge said awkwardly. 'I meant to ask you over—'

'I was meanin' to ask you.'

'Things happen so fast.'

'Aye, that's true.'

Nobody could think of anything else to say and all looked relieved when the photographer Malcolm had engaged called them over for the group photograph.

191

'Oh, you are lucky, going first,' Rachel whispered to Jennie when the time came to go inside for the ceremonies. 'I feel so nervous!'

'It's funny,' – Jennie gave a radiant smile and took Rory's arm – 'I don't feel nervous at all.'

Chapter Twenty-Seven

The excellent wedding breakfast had been enjoyed, Malcolm and Rory had each said 'a few words', the cake had been cut and the toasts made. Now the four-piece band was thumping its way through a waltz and the wedding guests – art students, clerks, accountants, Catherine's Land tenants – were moving together in a wonderfully good-natured mix, helped on by alcohol and the spirit of the occasion.

Mr Abbott, senior partner in Malcolm's firm, was watching Rachel as she danced by in her husband's arms and shook his grey head, smiling.

'She may be from Catherine's Land,' he murmured to Humphrey Blake, a junior partner of the firm, 'but she's a very attractive girl.'

'An artist, they say,' said Humphrey. 'Might lead young Gilbride quite a caper.'

'Think so?' Mr Abbott's gaze still followed Rachel until a young clerk cut in on Malcolm and she danced away with a toss of her dark head. 'Might be worth it.'

As the music changed to a reel, Tim Harley came to Jennie and asked her to dance. He seemed surprised when she refused.

'Oh, I say, what have I done, then?' he asked lightly, but, seeing the expression on her face, he flushed deeply.

'I see. Sheena told you, did she?'

'She did,' Jennie answered coldly.

'Look, I wanted to help her, but you must understand I really couldn't. I mean, I never could have married her, I wasn't in a position to, and anyway it wasn't that kind of relationship.'

'I don't want to talk about it. Will you excuse me?'

'No, Jennie, please wait.' He put his hand on her arm. 'Did she – did Sheena tell anyone else?'

'You mean Rachel?' Jennie shook off his hand. 'You're here, aren't you?'

'So Rachel doesn't know. . . you won't tell her, will you? I'd rather she didn't think too badly of me.'

'Tim, Rachel's just got married, I don't suppose she thinks of you at all.' Jennie, breathing hard, walked swiftly away

Abby was thinking that if anyone else said to her 'your turn next' she would scream, when a voice she knew spoke her name and she looked up. Frankie Baxter was standing before her.

'Frankie!' She leaped to her feet. 'Oh, how nice to see you! I didn't know you were in Edinburgh, I didn't know you'd be here.'

'I'm gatecrashing.' He had been a little wary, unsure perhaps of his reception, but now was relaxing, his eyes beginning to dance in their old way. 'Abby, you're as bonnie as ever.'

'You're looking very well yourself.'

'Now you're being polite.' He drew up a chair and they both sat down. 'I'm no' fit, I'm over weight, I canna deny it. No exercise, you ken. Canna get much exercise on board ship.'

'Frankie, you're never in the navy?'

'The navy? Me?' He laughed aloud. 'No, I'm playing the piano on a cruise liner. I'm what they call the entertainment. Beats playing for the pictures, I can tell you. Anyway, they say there'll be talkies soon. Then what's a poor pianist to do, eh?'

'Frankie, why didn't you write?' Abby asked softly. 'Didn't you think I'd want to hear what you were doing?'

He shrugged and said nothing.

She was studying him with delighted interest. It was true he had put on weight; he also seemed a little older and rather more weary, but none of that mattered. 'I can't tell you how glad I am to see you,' she said deliberately.

'And me you, Abby. Specially after the shock I got.'

'What shock?'

'Well, I'd got ma bit of leave, I'd come back to Auld Reekie, thought I'd look in on the old sweetie shop. Nobody there, everything shut up. 'No' dead?' I'm asking, when I find old

Kay and he says, 'No, all gone to the Ritchie girls' wedding.'
Can you imagine how I felt? There's only ever been one
Ritchie girl for me and that was you. I was just getting ready
to go out and hang maself, when the old feller tells me it's
your sisters' weddings he's talking about.' Frankie took
Abby's hand, laughing. 'So, here I am, gatecrashing.'

'Oh, Frankie!' She didn't know why but she felt she was
holding on to his hand as some sort of lifeline, as though she
never wanted to let it go. She felt so strange, happy, yet as
though she could burst into tears. Was it just the weddings that
had put her into this crazy mood? For she did feel a little crazy.
Or was it seeing Frankie again?

'Abby,' he was saying, urgently, 'can we meet? After this is
over?'

'Yes, I mean, I want to, but I think maybe I ought to go back
with Ma. She's going to be feeling pretty lonely.'

'Aye, that's true.' Frankie hesitated. 'Could we no' take her
with us? For supper, or something? Then afterwards, you and
me could walk, mebbe? Just the two of us?'

'Let's see what Ma says,' Abby answered tremulously, and
drew Frankie to his feet.

Madge had been wondering how long it would be before Jim
Gilbride came over to talk to her. Not long, she guessed, and
she was right. As soon as Bella was taken off to dance with
Malcolm, Jim appeared at Madge's side.

'I'll no' ask you to dance, Madge. You remember I was niver
a dancing man.'

'I remember.'

'But it's good to talk, eh?'

She watched Bella dancing, surprised somehow that she did
not move stiffly like the wooden doll she resembled. 'I don't
know that we've much to say,' she said, at last.

'Madge, turn round, look at me. D'you no' ken how much
you've been in my mind these past years?'

'I know you got married.'

'Aye.' He gave a grim smile. 'To somebody as different from
you as I could find. And shall I tell you something? I've niver
given her ma hand. Niver hurt a hair of her head. You were
wrong, you see.'

Madge moved uneasily on her chair. 'Jim, I don't want to hear this. It's private. It's between you and your wife.'

'Between you and me,' he said savagely. 'Because we could've been happy. If you'd trusted me. We could've been as happy as we'd ever been. But I slipped up once and that was it, wasn't it?' He moved his hand through the air. 'Over. finished. No more chances. I blame you for that, Madge, I do.'

'And that's what you want to talk to me about after all these years, is it?' Madge's eyes suddenly blazed. 'I told you we'd nothing to say to each other, Jim. Will you excuse me?'

'No, no, dinna go!' he cried, and as people turned their heads, she subsided into her chair. 'Listen, I'm sorry, I shouldna have said that, the last thing I want is to upset you, now that we've met again. And we'll be seeing each other often now, eh? Now that our kin's wed.'

'I don't think we need meet, Jim, even if our children have got married.'

'Why? Why should we no' meet?' His fiery eyes were holding her as they used to do in the old days. 'We're family now!'

'It wouldn't be fair on Bella,' she answered quietly. 'Be honest, Jim, you know it wouldn't.' She stood up. 'I see Abby coming over, Jim – I really will have to go.'

'Oh, yes, Abby.' He gave a short hard laugh as he turned away. 'Nothing's changed, has it, Madge? Nothing's changed.'

'Ma, look who's here,' said Abby, wondering if she sounded as strange as she felt, 'it's Frankie.'

'Frankie?' Madge turned her flustered gaze on him. 'Oh, how nice of you to come! We didn't know you were back in Edinburgh.'

'I owe you an apology, Mrs Ritchie,' he said humbly. 'I didna have an invitation, but I came anyway. I hope you'll no' mind.'

'Mind? Of course not. If we'd known you were here, we'd have asked you, wouldn't we?' Madge put her hand on his arm. 'Frankie, we still miss your mother in the sweetie shop.'

Trust Ma to come up with something nice to say, thought Abby. 'Frankie plays the piano on cruise ships now,' she told her mother. 'He's the entertainment.'

'I'm no' the sole attraction,' he put in, his eyes smiling, 'they do have other folk in the cabaret.'

'Oh, Frankie, what an interesting life!' Madge exclaimed. 'I've never been out of my own country, it must be lovely to travel. But how long are you here for?'

'Yes, how long?' asked Abby, her eyes meeting his.

'Only a few days,' he answered, and Abby's gaze fell.

'We were wondering, Ma, if you would like to come out with us for supper when this is over? You won't want to be on your own in the flat, will you?'

Madge looked from Abby to Frankie. Something had risen between these two, something she hadn't seen since the days when she used to tell Abby they were both far too young to be serious about each other. They weren't quite so young now. Were they serious still?

'That's kind of you, dear, but I'll be too tired to go out anywhere tonight. Why don't just the two of you go? You'll have a lot to talk about.'

She saw their eyes meet, felt Frankie breathe again, and was ready to give an indulgent smile when Tilda from the bakery came hurrying towards them, her face moist with the heat, her eyes shining.

'Mrs Ritchie, Mrs Ritchie, I think your girls are leaving!'

'Hello, Tilda!' cried Abby. 'I'm sorry I didn't see you before – how are you?'

'Och, I'm fine.' Tilda flung her arms around Abby in a quick hug. 'Working with your Ma, it's all I want.'

'Now that's not really true,' Madge said, laughing. 'Tilda's walking out with a nice young man, Abby. I don't think she'll be with us much longer. But did you say the girls were leaving, Tilda?'

'Come on,' cried Abby, 'we mustn't miss the going away!'

Rachel, as the focus of attention, had been having such a wonderful time she was loath to give it up but, as Malcolm told her, there was a cab waiting and a honeymoon. Jennie and Rory were already at the door, surrounded by well-wishers ready with the rice, and the driver was putting their luggage into the taxi.

'All right, all right, I'm coming,' said Rachel, flashing last smiles and waving to her friends. 'Don't fuss, Malcolm!'

'They're niver going on honeymoon together, are they?' someone asked, as the two grooms and the two brides ran through the hail of rice to the open taxi door. Another voice explained that they were all catching the London train but Rory and Jennie were only going as far as Berwick, from where they were to spend a few days in the Borders. Malcolm and Rachel were going south to catch the Channel ferry to Paris.

'Paris?' There was a whistle of surprise. 'Money's no object, eh?' asked one of Malcolm's colleagues.

'Rachel wants to see all the galleries,' another said, grinning.

'On her honeymoon?' Laughter rippled round, then people stared as Jennie came back to kiss her mother one more time.

'I won't be away long,' she said breathlessly. 'I'll be back before you know I'm gone.'

'Come on, Jennie,' Malcolm called severely. 'We have a train to catch.'

Goodbyes were called, more rice was thrown, and good luck paper horseshoes and confetti. Tin cans rattled on the back of the taxi as it began to move away and everyone waved, though Madge could hardly see through tears. She wiped her eyes and looked around for Abby, but over the heads of the waiting guests saw again Jim Gilbride's hot, dark gaze fixed on her face.

Chapter Twenty-Eight

Everybody was so kind, offering to keep her company, not wanting her to be lonely her first night without her girls. Jessie Rossie, Peggie Kemp, Archie Shields, Joanie Muir, all pressed Madge to join them. 'Now you come away with us, hen, we're going down the street for a drink' – 'Dinna stay by yoursel', Madge, come and have a cup o'tea' – 'D'you mebbe fancy seeing a picture, then, take your mind off things, eh?'

To them all, she gave the same answer. It was very nice of them to think of her, but she was so tired she was going straight to her bed. Maybe another night she'd join them? Aye, another night, they agreed, there'd be plenty lonely nights, eh, now that the girls had gone? Even though Jennie was only going up the stair, it wasna going to be the same for Madge.

Abby and Frank took her home in a taxi. 'I've never been in so many taxis,' Madge murmured, and Abby fussed around her, asking her over and over again if she'd be all right?

'Oh, go on with you, Abby! Anybody'd think I was ill! Like Jennie said, they'll be back before I know it.'

But when Abby and Frank had gone and Madge looked around her empty flat, desolation struck her like a blow. Only yesterday, they had been a family. Today, they were still a family, but a family that had divided, branched away, ready to make new growth; her daughters still her daughters, but also wives. Wives had to cleave to husbands, husbands to their wives. And parents? Parents had to let go.

Madge took off her hat which had been pressing on her knot of hair all day, and loosened some of the hat pins. The girls thought she should get her hair bobbed and maybe she

199

would. Maybe she would make herself look different for her different life ahead. She gave a long sigh and braced herself to go into the girls' room. All neat and tidy. Jennie would have seen to that. Beds stripped, sheets piled in the corner. Everything cleared from the dressing table except a handkerchief and a box of face powder, almost empty.

'You could sleep in here now, Ma,' Jennie had suggested. 'You could have your own room again, like you've always wanted.'

Her own room. Madge stared at the two empty beds and shook her head. Not tonight. Tonight, she'd sleep in her little alcove bed just as usual. Maybe when she began her new life, had her hair cut and everything, she'd move into the girls' room, but not tonight.

She changed out of her wedding outfit and hung it on the end of the wardrobe, then she poured some water into the washstand bowl and washed her face. Poor old tired face, she thought, looking into the girls' mirror. Had she really looked so woebegone at the wedding? Jim Gilbride's burning gaze came back to her and the colour rose to her cheeks. She had not looked woebegone. At least, not to him.

But she wouldn't think of Jim Gilbride. In fact, it was a relief that she needn't. He belonged to the Dutch doll now and it seemed that she could handle him a lot better than Madge ever could. She was just the sort of wife he ought to have, even if he didn't want her. It might be said that he had got his deserts, but Madge was not going to dwell on that. Dwelling a moment longer than was necessary on Jim Gilbride seemed to her a far too dangerous thing to do.

After all the rush and excitement of the day, the time seemed now to be passing very slowly. Madge, wearing her everyday blouse and skirt, went back into the living room and studied the clock. Could it only be half past eight? The clock must have stopped. It hadn't. She shrugged and turned up the range for it was beginning to feel quite cold, but she didn't need to put on the big old kettle for tea, she could make it on her gas ring. Yes, a cup of tea was what she needed. She'd feel much better after a cup of tea.

She didn't feel so very much better. She still felt empty inside, as though she had lost a very important part of herself.

Perhaps she should go to bed? Make up her own familiar bed and go to sleep, shut out this day that had brought to an end the best phase of her life. When she was needed.

It seemed easier just to sit back in her rocking chair, close her eyes and listen to the sounds of Catherine's Land. Some of the wedding guests were returning now, thundering up the stair, laughing, swearing, falling over. How Abby had hated that noise, and Rachel too! Well, they were away now. Only Jennie would be coming back and she had never minded the noise.

The clock ticked on. Rachel would still be travelling, but Jennie and Rory would have arrived at the boarding house where they were to spend their first night. People talked so much about honeymoons, Madge reflected, but they weren't always so blissful. She had adored Will, but really the bliss had come later, when she'd known what to expect. Maybe she should have talked more to the girls, but she could never seem to find the way to begin. Living in Catherine's Land they knew the facts of life, all right, but when it was you and your man, well, it was different, wasn't it? Madge wasn't really worrying about Rachel. Rachel was the sort to take care of herself. But Jennie was so much in love, so very vulnerable. Please God, prayed Madge, may Jennie be just as happy as she thinks she will be. But how would she get on in that one room of Rory's that had been Gramma Ritchie's? Surely when the children came, they would have to move. Rory might say he wanted to live like the people and it was true enough that some of the people lived crammed together like sardines in a tin, but Madge wasn't going to let that happen to Jennie. Something bigger would have to be found.

Something bigger. Madge stopped rocking. She looked slowly round the long living room, she thought of the spacious bedroom, and her heart began to bound. Something bigger. Why, it was right here! This very flat! She, Madge, could move into Rory's room, she needed no more space than Gramma Ritchie, while Jennie and Rory could take on this place. It would solve all their problems, and be just what Jennie wanted. When the children came she and Rory might even split the bedroom — Madge had often thought of doing that herself — and give themselves some privacy. They might not even have to use her own alcove bed.

Madge sprang up, suddenly very excited. She wished Jennie were back so that they could discuss her idea then and there. In the meantime, she would look round, see how they could make it work, decide what to take and what to leave. Then another thought came into her mind and made her laugh aloud.

'I could be Gramma Ritchie!' she cried. 'Gramma Ritchie up the stair! Heavens, how the wheel spins full circle!'

'So this is where you live?' asked Frankie, staring up at the Marchmont house by the light of the streetlamp. 'Grand, eh?'

'It's only a flat, it's only rented,' Abby said quickly.

'Aye.' He turned his head to look at her. 'But it's a long way from Catherine's Land. You've got what you always wanted, Abby.'

'You've come a long way, too, Frankie.'

'Maybe.' He shrugged. 'Well, I'd better say good night.'

'Say good night? What do you mean? Didn't we say we'd have coffee in my flat?'

'I'd rather have a drink.'

Abby hesitated. 'I might have some whisky.'

'You're sure you want me to come in?'

'Frankie, we arranged it.' Abby was trembling as she took out her key. 'But if you don't want to—'

He caught her arm. 'For God's sake, you know I want to!'

She showed him round and, when he had admired everything, asked him to put a match to the fire while she made the coffee.

'But there's whisky for you.' She set the bottle and a glass on the low table.

'You're no' having one?'

'Coffee will do me.'

By the time she returned with the coffee, the fire was beginning to flame and Frankie was sitting back in an armchair, looking quite at ease.

'Abby,' he murmured softly, holding out his arms.

'I'm just going to have my coffee, Frankie.'

The light died from his eyes and he folded his arms across his chest. 'D'you no' approve of me having a drink, then?'

'I'm only wondering if you have to have it.'

'I felt like one, that's all. It's no' a crime.'

'Frankie, you know what's in my mind.'

He left his chair and caught her to him. 'Abby, dinna spoil things by worrying about ma drinking. It goes with ma job, but I can take it. I'm no' an alcoholic, I promise you!'

'Oh, Frankie, I didn't think that! And I don't want to spoil anything!' As he looked long and ardently into her face, Abby faltered a little. 'I'm sorry – maybe I'm feeling nervy, or something . . .'

'Nervy?' He ran his hand down her cheek. 'Not like you, Abby.'

'No, but weddings are strange times, aren't they? People get weepy. I keep thinking of Jennie and Rachel . . . married . . .'

'It's no' our wedding night,' he whispered.

'Would you like it to be?'

'Abby, dinna tease.'

'I'm not teasing.'

It was true. She had never been more in earnest than in her lovemaking with Frankie. With Gerald there had always been the feeling that it was slightly unreal, that it couldn't be happening. Maybe because she knew so well that Gerald wasn't really hers, however much she might make herself believe he was. But Frankie was utterly and completely hers and she was his. There was no golden-haired wife in the background, no sense of not belonging. Frankie was a part of her, she felt he always would be.

'Why has it taken so long for me to know I want you?' she whispered, when she had taken him to her bed and their bodies had met in such smooth pleasure they might have made love together a hundred times. 'Why did I let you leave me?'

'Because you wanted Logie's,' he said into the darkness.

She lay very still. 'But Frankie, darling, I still want Logie's.'

'So I'll still have to leave you?'

'Maybe we could work something out?'

He was silent for some time, gently caressing her. 'Abby, sweetheart, if anybody could work something out, it'd be you,' he said, at last.

Madge in her bed was making plans. Tomorrow she would go up to Rory's room – he had left her the key, he wouldn't mind – and see where she would put her things. Then when he and

203

Jennie came back from honeymoon, she could put the idea to them fair and square. If they liked it but couldn't manage the rent, well she could help, just the way Gramma Ritchie had helped her in the old days. Everything was going to work out for the best. For Jennie. For Rachel. For Abby, too, if the way she and Frankie had been exchanging looks was anything to go by. In the darkness, Madge's lips curved into a smile.

On Monday, she'd quite decided, she would go to that little hairdresser's in Rose Street in her dinner hour and have her hair bobbed. It would be the start of her new life.

As the city clocks chimed the small hours, Madge, who had thought she would lie awake for ever, fell asleep.

Part Three
1933

Chapter Twenty-Nine

On May 26, 1933, Bobby Gilbride was five years old. His father, Malcolm, had promised to come home early for his birthday party. Auntie Jennie would be bringing his cousins, Will and Hamish, with dear Gramma Ritchie and maybe Auntie Abby, but Uncle Rory had to go to a meeting. Bobby's mother, Rachel, said no one would ever expect Uncle Rory to come to a children's party.

Rachel had taken time off from her painting to oversee the arrangements, though most of the tea had been prepared by her maid, Gillie, and the cake had been made by Mackenzie's. As it was fine, the games would be held in the garden, but the tea was laid in the dining room of Malcolm's solid, semi-detached villa in Morningside.

'All looks very nice,' Rachel commented, surveying the usual jellies, sandwiches and sausage rolls. 'You've done very well, Gillie.'

'Thank you, ma'am,' the maid replied coolly. She was an angular young woman with ginger hair and a strong jaw, and rather resented working for Mr and Mrs Gilbride, they not being what she described as the 'real thing'. Why, Mrs Gilbride came from Catherine's Land and her mother and sister lived there still! Of course Madam was very attractive, but she made a lot of extra work, trailing paint all over the place from that so-called studio of hers, that was only a top bedroom when all was said and done. And then her paintings! Great blocks and squares of colour she stuck on with a knife. Was it any wonder she never sold any!

Still, she had her admirers, as Gillie knew and, as she said to

Mrs Taylor who came in to do the 'rough', it just showed if you were pretty enough you could get away with anything.

'Doesna get away wi' much from the master,' Mrs Taylor replied. 'Och, no, he keeps her in order.'

'So he thinks,' said Gillie darkly.

It infuriated Rachel that her servants should have the nerve to look down on her. Abby might think that all maids were angels but everybody else knew that servants were the biggest snobs on earth.

'It's understandable,' Abby tried to explain. 'If you spend your life taking other people's orders it makes it easier if you think they've got a right to give them.'

'Oh, trust you to take their part!' Rachel retorted.

Today, on her son's birthday, Rachel was depressed. Although she loved Bobby dearly, his birthdays always brought back the misery of the first year of her marriage. The shock of finding out so early on that she – who never wanted children – was pregnant. The recriminations she had heaped on Malcolm's head for not 'taking care'. Hadn't he said over and over again that she would be 'all right'? And look what had happened! If there hadn't been so much fuss about Sheena, Rachel might have tried Mrs Smith's services herself. As it was she had to endure her mother's delight and Jennie's envy, (for Jennie hadn't started a baby until the following year), and then months of sickness and looking awful. It had been a complete nightmare. At the end had come the worst shock of all, when Malcolm dropped his bombshell. She had been sitting up in bed in the nursing home eating grapes, when he had told her quietly that she would not be returning to the art college.

'What do you mean?' she had cried. 'I've another two years to do at least. Of course I'm going back!'

'No, Rachel. You have a baby now, it's not possible.'

'But I can have a nanny, Malcolm! Women like me don't have to spend all their time looking after babies. I am going back to college and you are not going to stop me.'

'No.' The finality of his tone had made her turn cold. In the year she had lived with Malcolm she had already discovered that underneath his seeming indulgence lay solid rock. Now it seemed she could no longer rely on that indulgence. The wedding ring was round her finger but Malcolm was not.

'Will you please explain?' she asked icily.

'It's easy enough to understand. You're not going back to college because I'm not going to pay your fees. It is your place to stay at home with our son.'

'But you promised, Malcolm, you promised!'

'That was before Bobby was born. He comes first now.' Malcolm had tried to take her hand. 'I'm not saying you can't have help, Rachel. I'm a professional man, I don't expect my wife to wash nappies. But you must be at home to supervise. I'm not having our boy put at risk.'

She had flown into a passion, burst into tears, begged, threatened, but Malcolm had remained unmoved. With no money of her own, there was nothing she could do. She stayed at home.

At least Malcolm had not objected to her keeping on with her painting in what free time she could snatch for herself. In the good light of the top bedroom she doggedly worked away at her canvases, selling so few she didn't even cover the cost of her materials but she was determined never to give up. One day, she told herself, Malcolm would be sorry, he would realise she was a proper artist and should never have been subject to his petty rules and dictates. In the meantime, she had found other ways of getting even with him.

The telephone rang as she and Bobby were waiting for the party guests to arrive. Bobby, a good-looking boy with Rachel's dark eyes and Malcolm's light sandy hair, patted a balloon around the furniture and watched his mother as she went to answer it. He thought she looked very nice, with her dark hair all waves and her red dress covered in patterns. It was true, Rachel did look attractive in the Art-Deco clothes she designed herself, though Madge and Jennie privately thought them rather odd and in Gillie's view they were just another example of the way her mistress could get away with anything. 'If you design them yourself and get Jennie to run them up, why'd they cost more than if you bought them at Logie's?' Malcolm often asked, but Rachel never troubled to answer.

'Who is it, Mummy?' cried Bobby, when Rachel had been

talking for some time in a low tone he could scarcely hear. 'Is it about my party?'

'Ssh!' Rachel shook her head at him and for a moment put her finger to her lip.

'Got to go,' he heard her say, 'till tomorrow, then. Goodbye, Tim.' And she put the receiver down.

Half an hour later the party was in full swing. Jennie, in her element because she was with children, was helping Polly, the part-time nursemaid, to organise games on the lawn, while Rachel circulated among the mothers and Madge took Jennie's little Hamish on her knee and let him play with her amber beads.

'Oh, look at Will!' she cried to Rachel. 'Trying to join in, bless him, and him only four! He always wants to do everything Bobby does. Rachel, this is a lovely party.'

'Yes, we've been lucky with the weather.'

'Lucky in every way.' Madge's calm blue gaze surveyed the large secluded garden, the stone house beyond with its windows open to the May sunlight, its air of prosperity. 'You've done well, Rachel.'

'I suppose so.'

Rachel moved on and Madge, looking after her, thought, Ah, she's just the same, never content.

Madge was nearly fifty, but still a pretty woman, her oval face scarcely lined, her fair hair cut youthfully short. She always tried to look her best when she came to Rachel's, so as not 'to let her daughter down', but she never felt at ease in the Morningside surroundings. Always she dreaded the haughty looks from the maid, who liked to let Madge see that she knew she lived in a tenement and had once worked in a cake shop. It was much pleasanter visiting Abby in her cottage in South Queensferry, on the few occasions when Abby had time to entertain.

At Abby's insistence and with some financial help, Madge had given up her job at Mackenzie's and now did a little dressmaking from home, helping Jennie with commissions from Miss Watson and looking after the boys. The exchange of flats had been a great success, and Madge's idea of splitting the bedroom into two had been approved by the landlords and proved a great boon when the children came. Jennie was happy in her old home and it seemed to Madge that everything had worked out for the best, just as she had forecast. Even for Abby, even for herself. It was true that she had had to make sacrifices, Gramma Ritchie's room was not as comfortable as she pretended, but she had Jennie and the boys very close and she had her independence. Every time she met Jim Gilbride again – and she saw to it that they didn't meet often – she felt a little pang for the love she had lost but also a great relief that it had come to nothing. Malcolm said his father and stepmother were practically leading separate lives now but that was of no interest to Madge. All she knew was that she was better off on her own.

It was time for the birthday tea and the children ran, whooping and shrieking, into the dining room, followed dutifully by the grown-ups. Just before the candles on the cake were due to be lit, Malcolm arrived and swept Bobby up into his arms.

'Sorry I was late, Bobby,' he whispered, his dour features softening as he pressed his face against his son's. 'But I'm here now and that's all that matters, isn't it?'

'Let's light the candles, Daddy!' Bobby cried. 'We're all waiting to sing!'

'You mustn't sing,' Rachel told him, smiling. 'We sing to you.'

'No, no, I like to sing,' Bobby answered firmly, and loudly joined in with 'Happy Birthday to You, Happy Birthday to you, Happy Birthday, dear Bobby, Happy Birthday to You!'

'Silly to cry,' Madge murmured, dabbing her eyes, 'but they're so sweet at this age and the next thing you know is they're grown up and you're a grandmother.'

'Oh, thanks, Ma, I'll look forward to that!' Jennie, laughing, jumped up to hand round plates as Bobby and Malcolm cut the cake.

When the guests had gone home, the mothers sighing with relief, the children bearing their spoils of balloons and party sweets, Rachel offered to show Madge and Jennie her latest painting. Malcolm had gone up to change and in any case wasn't much interested in her work these days.

'We should really be going,' Madge answered, 'Jennie has to get Rory his tea.'

'He can wait for once, can't he? And you needn't worry about catching the tram, I'll run you back in the car.'

'I can never get over you driving a car,' Madge said admiringly.

'Or having one,' Jennie commented.

'All right, I'm lucky,' Rachel snapped. 'But Abby has a car too, I'm not the only lucky one.'

'Abby's worked hard for what she's got.'

'And I haven't, I suppose?'

As Rachel's eyes grew stormy, Jennie said hastily, 'I didn't mean that. Come on, let's see this painting, then.'

Rachel, still looking thunderous, told Polly to look after the boys, she daren't let them loose in her studio, and led the way to the top of the house. As usual, Madge took more interest in the fine house Malcolm had been able to afford than in the prospect of viewing Rachel's art work. She knew from experience that she wouldn't be able to recognise whatever it was that Rachel had produced this time, and she never felt comfortable in the clutter of the studio, with its stacked canvases, rags and jars, half-squeezed tubes of paint, brushes soaking in a terrible sink.

'Rachel, does that girl of yours ever come in here?' she asked now.

'You mean to clean? I let her in from time to time, but she never does anything but complain. Who cares?' Rachel took Madge by the elbow and guided her round a large easel to look at the picture in the best light. 'Jennie,' she called, 'come and see what you think of this!'

The picture on the easel struck both Madge and Jennie dumb. It showed nothing but a large black oblong towering into a grey sky. The paint laid on very thickly with a knife was still wet and glistening, but the only light in the picture came from small pale squares set at intervals into the darkness of the oblong. There were no figures – Rachel never painted people – yet in some mysterious way the towering oblong seemed to pulse with life, as though if it could have been removed from the canvas, crowds of chattering, laughing people would have been revealed.

'Oh, Lord,' Jennie whispered, 'I think I know what it's meant to be!'

212

'What?' cried Madge. 'What's it meant to be?'

Rachel laughed. 'Oh, Ma, can't you see? It's Catherine's Land!'

A long silence followed. Madge found a rickety wooden chair and sat down heavily. Jennie stood by her side, her fair face angrily set. Rachel, a little unnerved, stepped back as though to distance herself from them.

'I can't believe it,' Madge said at last. 'That's how you see your old home, Rachel? That great black block there?'

'Where we live?' asked Jennie coldly.

'Ma, it's stylised!' Rachel cried. 'It's not meant to be realistic, I know it doesn't really look like that!'

'It must look like that to you,' Madge answered steadily.

Rachel shrugged. 'I didn't mean to upset you, Ma. Or you, Jennie. Honestly.'

'I think it's time we went home,' Jennie said, taking Madge's arm as she rose from the chair. 'Thanks for everything, Rachel.'

Rachel bit her lip as they moved to the door. 'I'm really sorry you don't like it. I wish I hadn't shown it to you now.'

'It'd still exist, whether we'd seen it or not,' said Jennie. 'But I'm not going to say any more. If that's how you see a place with real people, people who matter to us, that's up to you. We see a different Catherine's Land, don't we, Ma?'

In a small silent procession they made their way downstairs.

'Actually, there was something else I wanted to tell you,' Rachel said, in a subdued tone when they reached the hall. 'I was in Glasgow the other day, in Buchanan Street—'

'Yes?' said Jennie impatiently.

'And I saw Sheena.'

All the colour drained from Jennie's face. She might have been turning to ice before their eyes. Madge put out her hands.

'Oh, no,' she whispered, 'not Sheena back again!'

'In Glasgow, not Edinburgh.' Rachel was feeling relieved she had found something to make her mother and Jennie forget the picture upstairs. 'I don't suppose she'll come here. She won't want to see anyone who knows what happened.'

'Was Lily with her?' Madge asked, as Jennie stayed silent, her eyes half closed.

'No, for once she was on her own.'

'Perhaps it wasn't her!' cried Jennie suddenly. 'Perhaps you made a mistake!'

'No.' Rachel was positive. 'I didn't speak to her, didn't let her see me, but it was Sheena, all right. She looked just the same, except that she'd had her hair cut.'

'I wonder where Lily and Sheena went?' Madge murmured. 'I wonder what they've been doing all these years?'

'As long as Sheena doesn't come back to Edinburgh, I don't care!' Jennie cried and, as Polly appeared with the boys, threw her arms passionately around her small surprised sons.

'I'll run you back,' Rachel muttered, 'just let me find my keys. Malcolm, are you there? I'm taking Ma and Jennie home.'

Malcolm came downstairs, having changed into a light jacket and flannels.

'Abby telephoned while you were in your studio, Rachel. Said she was very sorry, she can't get round to bringing Bobby's present this evening but she'll drop it in tomorrow. Malcolm gave Madge and Jennie swift goodbye kisses. 'Oh, and she said to tell you she'd some news. Didn't say whether it was good or bad.'

'I wish you hadn't told us that,' said Madge, 'now we'll have to worry.' She picked up Bobby and held him close. 'Goodbye, darling, happy birthday!'

'Oh, Gramma,' Bobby wailed, suddenly bursting into tears. 'My birthday's over!'

Chapter Thirty

Earlier that day Abby had been having elevenses in Logie's staff cafe, reading the paper and depressing herself with the news which seemed uniformly bad. Adolf Hitler seemed to be turning Germany into a one-man show. What was he after? There was talk that he wanted to get rid of all the Jews, which was absurd. Were his other plans as crazy? At home the unemployment figures were sky high and rising. The National Unemployed Workers' Movement was in fact planning a hunger march in June. People would be coming to Edinburgh from all over Scotland to demand that the Secretary of State did something to help. They didn't just want charity, they were asking that more should be done to create jobs. At the same time, they wanted the degrading Means Test abolished, rents reduced and an increase of benefits – three shillings a week for an adult, one and sixpence for a child. Abby folded the paper with a groan and lit a cigarette. Three shillings. One and sixpence. In God's name it wasn't much to ask. Couldn't something be done?

'Miss Ritchie?' A young secretary was at her table. 'Mr Gerald – I mean Mr Farrell – would like to see you in his office. When you have the time.'

When I have the time. Abby smiled to herself. When the Senior Partner of Logie's asked to see you in his office, you found the time.

'Thank you, Katie.' She put out her cigarette. 'I'll go up now.'

It was three months since Stephen Farrell had died of a heart attack on Murrayfield Golf Course and Gerald had assumed his mantle. There had been mourning, of course. Stephen Farrell had been well respected and well liked, but so was his nephew and the transition of power had been smooth and easy. Mr Gerald, now known as Mr Farrell, was poised to make changes, that was to be expected, but they would be sensible, for-the-best changes, and no one was afraid. Least of all Abby, who since the initial pain of her break with Gerald had had a strangely good professional relationship with him. Perhaps the word professional was the key to that. They were both professionals before all else and with love out of the way, work could come first and did. Sometimes when she saw the beautiful Mrs Farrell shopping in Logie's with her two adopted girls, a small dart of shame would pierce Abby's heart, but she always removed it. She and Gerald had not been blameless, but at the time of their affair had had a genuine need of each other. Monica had excluded herself from Gerald's life and it had not seemed wrong to him to give Abby the love his wife didn't seem to want. It had not seemed wrong to Abby to take it. All that was water under the bridge now, of course, and didn't even cross Abby's mind as she went to powder her nose and comb her hair before taking the lift to Mr Farrell's office.

'Come in, Miss Ritchie.' Gerald rose from his uncle's desk which still stood below the portrait of Logie's founder, remembered by Abby from her first interview. 'Thank you for coming. Won't you sit down?'

Gerald was over forty now, still elegant, a slight touch of silver at the temples adding a further touch of distinction to his good looks. As his secretary left them and Abby took a chair, he relaxed his formal manner and smiled at her.

'Nice to see you. Like some coffee?'

'No, thanks, I've just had some.' Abby lifted her dark brows enquiringly. 'What can I do for you, Gerald?'

'Cigarette?' He opened the box on his desk. 'No?' He closed it and sat down, while Abby watched him with sudden apprehension. It seemed to her that he was fussing around for no apparent reason. Why wasn't he coming straight to the point? These changes he would be making, perhaps she had been too complacent over them? He was a new broom. Was he going to start sweeping with her?

216

'Don't look so worried, Abby. What do you think I'm going to do? Hand you your cards?'

'It's not impossible.'

'Yes, quite impossible that we'd ever let you go. You know that.'

'Do I?' She smiled with relief and leaned forward to open his cigarette box. 'May I? I think I'll take one of these, after all.'

'And I'll join you.'

For some moments they smoked in silence, studying each other with friendly yet wary eyes.

'I do wish you'd tell me why you asked me up,' Abby said at last.

'You've no idea?'

'No idea at all. Could you please end the suspense?'

'I'm sorry, I'm not trying to tease. You know my moving on has created a vacancy for a junior partnership? I want to offer that partnership to you.'

Abby caught her breath. She put her hand to her lip and thought, It's true, people's jaws do drop. I can feel mine doing it. I must look a perfect fool—

'I hadn't realised you'd be so surprised,' she heard Gerald saying, as though from a great distance, and shook her head as though to shake herself back to reality.

'Are you serious?' she asked.

'Never more so.'

'Maybe I shouldn't ask' – she tried to laugh – 'but why? Why me?'

'There's no need for false modesty, Abby. You're the best one for the job. You're first rate in your own field – the Accounts Department has never been better run – and you've also got ideas – initiative – the sort of thing we have to have at Logie's.' Gerald leaned forward, his hazel eyes bright on her face. 'You thought of the Mercat Buttery, didn't you? And opening a department for Scottish gourmet foods? Both highly successful. You reorganised our ordering system, you found new suppliers – do you think the trustees don't notice that sort of thing?'

'Gerald, I'm flattered, but—'

'But what? Give me one good reason why I shouldn't promote you.'

217

'I can give you two. One, I'm a woman. That's not a reason in my book, but it might be for the trustees. Has any woman before me been offered a partnership here?'

'No, but there's always a first time. It's my job to do new things if they're worth doing. What's the second reason?'

'The second reason is that I shouldn't actually be working here at all.' Abby lowered her eyes and a deep flush rose to her brow. 'Gerald, I'm married.'

He sat back in his chair with such force she might have pushed him there. 'Married?' he stammered, his eyes riveted to her face. 'Abby, what are you saying?'

'It's true, Gerald.' She ran her tongue over dry lips. 'I've been married since nineteen twenty eight.'

'And you've never told me? Never said a word?'

'I know it was wrong, I've deceived you. I never wanted to do that, believe me.' She looked at him with desperate eyes. 'But when I got married you weren't the Senior Partner. If I'd told you, I'd have put you in an impossible position, you would have been duty bound to tell your uncle and you know what he'd have said. Women in my sort of post are expected to resign if they marry, they're supposed to be keeping the breadwinners out of jobs. That's general policy, isn't it? At Logie's, too?'

'Abby, if you'd come to me, discussed it with me, I could have put it to him—'

'I'd still have been expected to go and I couldn't face it. I thought it best not to tell Logie's anything about my marriage. In fact, no one knows the truth except my mother and my sisters.'

Gerald shook his head, dazedly. 'What about your husband? What does he feel about it?'

'He's gone along with it for my sake.'

'Who is he? Do I know him?'

Abby smiled faintly. 'You don't know him. He's what you might call a childhood sweetheart, we went to school together. Now he's a pianist on a cruise liner.'

'So away a lot?'

'Yes, that's how we've been able to work it. We took a cottage out at South Queensferry. We've kept ourselves to ourselves. No one really knows who we are or what we do.'

'And you've been willing to live like that all these years?'

'To keep my job, yes.' Abby despondently put out her cigarette. 'Now I suppose we've come to the end of it.' She raised her eyes to Gerald's. 'Look, I shan't blame you if you ask me to go. Maybe I should have admitted things from the beginning. I've explained why I felt I couldn't take the risk.'

'Abby, my uncle thought very highly of you, I still say he might have understood.'

'And he might not.'

'Well, the thing is, I agree with you, it's a pernicious system that pushes women out of the workforce.'

'So, I'll blame the system,' she said drearily. 'A system that punishes me for doing what men are allowed to do anyway.'

Gerald ran his hand through his hair. 'You know something? I wish you hadn't told me.'

'Well, I did tell you.'

'Because I offered you a partnership?'

She nodded. 'I don't think I could have kept it a secret much longer, anyway. It's been – hard.'

'But, Abby, what's to be done?'

She shrugged. 'I'm afraid that's up to you, Gerald.'

His gaze on her was steady. 'I'm not letting you go, Abby, I'll tell you that now. It would be crazy. We're going to get round this thing somehow.'

'I can't think how, unless you change the rules.'

'Well, why not? Why not change the rules? I make the decisions now, I keep forgetting that.'

'What about the trustees?' Abby asked, her voice trembling. 'Aren't you forgetting them? They don't have to accept a complete change of policy.'

'They will accept. I'll see that they do. Even if it's only for you.'

'I don't want it to be just for me. All married women should have the right to work.'

'I know, I know, but we must do what we can. If I could just push some clause into your contract – you know, on the lines of exceptional circumstances, something like that – damn it all, Abby, you're going to be a partner! That puts you into a special category, doesn't it?'

'I suppose it does.'

'Well, would you be willing to go along with that sort of compromise? Just for the time being?'

'Oh, Gerald . . .' Her smile was wide and radiant. 'I honestly don't think I could refuse.'

They celebrated with some of the late Stephen Farrell's best sherry, raising their glasses as they stood at the window looking down over Princes Street.

'To Abby Ritchie, partner,' Gerald murmured, and then laughed a little. 'Only you're not Abby Ritchie now, are you? Do you realise I don't even know your married name?'

'Baxter. My husband's name is Frank Baxter.'

'To Abby Baxter, then.' Gerald drank, keeping his eyes on her face. 'How are we going to tell people, Abby?'

'I don't know. I can't tell them I've been married since nineteen twenty eight, I just can't.'

'How about if you were to take some holiday? Go abroad, maybe, and when you come back say you got married while you were away?'

She hesitated. 'Would I have the nerve, do you think?'

'You have the nerve for anything.'

'It's not a bad idea.'

'Especially as your husband works on a cruise liner, anyway.'

'He does, but I could never afford to go on a cruise.'

'Maybe they'd give you special rates?'

'I doubt it. They might not even encourage the staff to bring their wives.'

'I think you could get round that.' Gerald hesitated. 'Look, I'd be willing to—'

'No,' Abby said, firmly. 'That's out of the question, thanks all the same.' She smiled, her dark eyes thoughtful. 'You know, I am drawn to the idea, though. Maybe I could scrape enough together to go second class? I could go away with Frankie, come back and say we'd suddenly decided to get married—'

'And then we could announce that the board had agreed to give you special permission to stay on.' Gerald heaved a deep sigh. 'Yes, I think that's a way it could be done. What a relief.'

'Have you forgiven me?' she asked quietly. 'For keeping you in the dark all these years?'

'If I'd been in your shoes, I expect I'd have done the same.' Gerald suddenly kissed her lightly on the cheek. 'Abby, I want to say I'm glad things have worked out for us. And I'm not talking about keeping you in your job.'

'I know what you're talking about. Are you happy, Gerald?'

'Very happy. And you?'

'I think I'm happier than I ever thought possible.'

They stood together, not touching, letting the warmth of their friendship wrap them close.

'I've always been so grateful to you,' Gerald murmured 'Never said so before, but a lot of women would have been so bitter . . .'

'I was, for a time.'

'But you never tried to harm me, you never hurt Monica.'

'You know I wouldn't have done that.'

'No, you wouldn't.' He pressed her hand and released it. 'The way I behaved I didn't deserve you, Abby.'

'Gerald, it's all in the past, let's not talk about it.'

'Just this once, because this is a special day.'

'A special day,' she repeated. 'Yes, it is special. And the really good thing is that Frank is home on leave at the moment. I'll be able to give him the news this evening.'

'And go out and celebrate?'

'And be able to tell the world we're married. That's what Frank will care about. He's wanted to do that for such a long time.'

'You may not care to tell him I said so,' Gerald told her, 'but I hope he realises he's a damned lucky man.'

Chapter Thirty-One

The cottage Abby and Frankie had rented was on the edge of South Queensferry, some eight miles from Edinburgh. It was pebble-dashed with a tiled roof, had tiny gardens front and back, and a spectacular view of the Firth of Forth and the magnificent Forth Bridge. Abby never tired of looking out at the vast expanse of sky and sea, at the great bridge dominating the little harbour town. After a busy day at Logie's and a tiring drive in her Morris saloon, to come home to the cottage refreshed her spirit she once told Frankie. 'Doesn't stop you wanting to go to Logie's tomorrow,' was his comment. 'Well of course not,' said Abby.

On that evening when she came back with her special news, she parked the car hastily and ran through the little house to find Frankie. He was sitting outside, smoking a cigarette and looking across the water. Beside him on the stone wall that bounded the property stood a glass tankard of beer, half full.

'Frankie!' she called, and he turned his head and smiled but did not leap up to sweep her off her feet and cover her face with kisses, as he might have done once. She felt a little dashed but not surprised. Ever since he'd come home on this latest leave, he had been subdued in spirits and she rather blamed herself. She should have taken some holiday to be with him, but there'd been so much to do after Stephen Farrell's death, it really hadn't been possible to get away. From now on, though, everything was going to be different.

'Frankie, I've some news!' she cried, kissing him.

'Good or bad?'

'Good. Can't you tell from the way I look?'

'You always look fine to me.'

She laughed, putting back her dark hair which was longer now and marcel waved. 'Maybe I'll make you guess. What would make me very happy?'

He shrugged. 'Being made Senior Partner?'

'Wrong. But partner would do.'

Frankie's eyes on her face sharpened.

'That's no' possible, is it?'

'You mean because I'm a woman?'

'And too young.'

'Plenty of people have been promoted who were only my age, all from Accounts, like me.'

'Aye, but all men, eh?'

'So, I'm the first woman.' Abby's joy was a little dampened. 'I won't be the last.'

'I daresay.' Frankie reached for his beer and drank deeply. 'Well, congratulations, Abby. You've done well, I'm proud of you.'

It seemed to her he didn't look very proud. She sighed and for some moments stood looking away towards the bridge. 'There's something else I want to tell you,' she said quietly.

'More good news? I canna wait.'

'I told Mr Gerald – I mean, Mr Farrell – that we were married.'

Frankie sat very still, his blue eyes fixed on Abby; they weren't dancing. 'Was that no' a bit risky? I thought you'd be given your cards the minute you let on.'

'With this offer of a partnership, I felt I had to tell him. It wouldn't have been right to keep it a secret any longer.'

'And what did the great man say? It's pretty obvious he didna give you the order of the boot.'

'He said he didn't want me to go, he said he'd make an exception.'

'And what about these trustees that go between you and your wits? Are they going to agree to that?'

'Mr Farrell says he thinks he can persuade them.' Abby reached forward and took Frankie's hands. 'Frankie, listen, he had another idea. He suggested I should go on holiday, maybe even on your liner if we could find the money—'

'On my liner? Are you crazy? We could niver afford that!'

'We've got savings, Frankie, I could go second class. And don't forget, I'll be earning more money now!'

'Oh, yes, more money,' he agreed coldly. 'And what happens when you've been on this cruise?'

'Well, I announce our marriage when we get back and Mr Farrell will say the board has given me permission to stay on. Oh, Frankie, it's wonderful, isn't it? That we can tell people at last? You're pleased, aren't you?'

Their eyes locked, then Frankie freed his hands from hers and stood up. 'Are we no' the lucky ones?' he murmured, looking down at her. 'We've only been wed since nineteen twenty eight, but now we can call ourselves man and wife because Mr Farrell says so. Is that no' grand?'

'Frankie, why are you talking like this?' Abby's eyes were bewildered. 'It's Bobby's birthday, I should have taken his present round but I came straight home to tell you the news. I thought you'd be over the moon!'

'Over the moon? You've no' the faintest idea what I'm feeling, have you? All these years married and we live out of sight like criminals because you want to keep your job, then Mr Gerald Farrell says abracadabra, we can say we're Mr and Mrs Baxter after all, and all the years of hiding and skulking have been just a bloody waste of time!'

'No, that's not true! It was Mr Stephen Farrell who was in charge before. He'd never have changed the rules for me, might never even have promoted me—'

'But Mr Gerald's different, eh?' Frankie's face was flushed, his blue eyes glittering. 'Because of old time's sake, eh?'

'I told you about Gerald and me because I thought I should be honest,' Abby cried. 'But it was all over years ago and there's nothing between us now. You know that perfectly well, just as I know there are things in your life that are over and done with. It's not fair to drag up the past!'

Frankie lowered his gaze. 'All right, I'm sorry. It's just that I'm sick of having ma life run by some feller in an office I niver even see. Why should what he says matter to me?'

'Frankie, will you try to understand? Things are going to be different now. We can announce our marriage, move back to the city if that's what you want, live like other people—'

'With me on liners and you out at work? You call that living like other people?'

'You could give up the liners, you could find a job in Edinburgh.'

'There's nothing I'd like better. If you'd let me earn the money and you'd stay at home!'

There was a quivering, stifling silence between them. Abby lit a cigarette with trembling fingers, keeping an intense dark gaze burning on Frankie's face.

'I want to work,' she said quietly. 'You know I always have. I explained it all before we were married and you accepted it.'

'I niver accepted it!' Frankie cried. 'You've no eyes in your head if you didna see that!'

She recoiled, as though he had struck her. 'What are you saying?' she whispered. 'I don't understand – all these years – why didn't you tell me?'

'Didna want to lose you.'

'But you wouldn't have lost me! We could have worked something out—'

'Like you worked things out for us before?' He shook his head. 'Abby, there's no point in talking any more. I want one thing, you want another.'

'We're not going to stop talking!' she cried. 'We have to tell each other the truth!'

'Let's go into the house,' he muttered. 'I could do with another drink.'

It was almost dark inside the cottage. Soon they would have to light the lamps – they had no gas or electricity – but now Abby led Frankie to his armchair and put herself on his knee.

'Never mind about your drink. Just tell me what you really want. Tell me the truth.'

He drew her close against him. 'I suppose I want what other men want. A wife who'd no' mind being at home, who'd want children – no, dinna leap up, Abby, hear me out. You said you wanted the truth, eh?'

'All right,' she said, with an effort. 'I'm listening.'

'I ken you're clever, Abby, and I'm truly proud of you. I'm glad you've been made partner, I dinna begrudge you that at

225

all. But I sometimes think you should've wed somebody different from me. Somebody who'd want your sort of marriage.'

For a long moment, Abby was still, scarcely seeming to breathe as she lay against Frankie's shoulder. Then she sat up.

'What you really mean is that I shouldn't have married anyone. I don't want to stay at home, I don't want to cook stews and bake bread, I don't want to make clothes, I don't want children. I'm not really a wife at all, am I?'

'Nobody can love like you, Abby!' he cried hoarsely. 'You've a right to be wed.'

'I wondered when you'd remember about love,' she said bitterly. 'I love you, Frankie, that's all that matters to me. If we haven't got the perfect marriage, I don't care, I just want you.'

'You say that, but it's not true. Abby. You wouldn't give up your job for me, would you?'

'I would if I really had to, but it's pointless to talk like that. I don't have to give it up, do I?'

He drew her back into his arms. 'No,' he agreed heavily. 'You don't have to.'

They lit the lamps and Abby cooked the steaks she had brought home for supper.

'I brought a bottle of wine, too,' she told Frankie. 'I was thinking we'd be celebrating.'

'We can still celebrate.' When he had filled their glasses, Frankie said he would make a toast. 'To you, Abby, and success in your new job.'

'No, don't drink to me,' she said quickly, and raised her own glass. 'To us, to our happiness.'

'To our happiness,' he repeated, solemnly and they both drank.

They made love that night, fiercely and violently, as though trying to convince themselves that passion would give them everything their marriage did not. Here we are, making love and it's wonderful, they seemed to be declaring. What could be wrong between people who can love like us? Nothing at all.

'Come in with me,' Abby said next morning when she started the car. 'We can have lunch together and after work we can take Bobby's present round. Want to do that?'

'Why not?'

'You've been too much alone this leave, that's been the trouble. Don't you agree?'

'I'll lock up, ' said Frankie.

'Going on a cruise?' Rachel repeated blankly. 'Well, you're the lucky one, aren't you?'

Frankie looked up from the toy soldiers he was helping Bobby to unpack from their handsome Logie's box. 'I think you're the lucky one, Rachel.' He put his hand on Bobby's sandy head. 'You've got this one.'

'My thoughts exactly,' put in Malcolm.

'Yes, but to be made a partner, so young and everything,' Rachel went on peevishly. 'I think Abby's lucky, whatever you say.'

'I agree with you,' said Abby. 'When I think what my life might have been like, I know I've been lucky.'

'Aye, there's plenty folk'd think we'd all been lucky, come to that,' Frankie murmured. 'Just to have enough to eat and boots to wear. Have you no' heard about the hunger march coming off next month?'

'Yes, Rory's involved and I wish he wasn't,' Malcolm replied. 'Seems to me to be Communist dominated.'

'I don't think so,' said Abby. 'It's being organised by the union for unemployed workers, they're not Communists.'

'And neither is Rory,' Frankie remarked, 'he's a right to be involved. You canna blame folk for marching, Malcolm, when they're starving and it's all they can do."

'Did I say I blamed them? I've no wish to see people starving because they can't get work, but there's a limit to what the government can do. We're in the grip of a world recession, jobs can't be pulled out of thin air.'

'It's the Means Test that upsets everyone,' said Abby. 'It's wicked and shameful that people are allowed hardly any assets at all before they can get help.'

'Aye, they're treated like criminals because they need a few shillings to feed their children.' Frankie scrambled to his feet. 'Come on, Bobby, let's go and play your ma's piano, shall we? You tell me what tune you want and I'll play it, eh?'

'Just needs the pint on the top, doesn't he?' Malcolm commented to Rachel, as Frankie settled himself at the upright

227

piano and Bobby looked on with adoring eyes. Rachel knocked Malcolm's arm in case Abby should hear, but she was already by the piano, watching Frankie's face as his hands moved over the keys. Every line seemed to have been smoothed away from his brow, his eyes were dancing, his mouth gentle and smiling. Would he ever again look like that for her? So happy, so serene? A stab of regret pierced her. If only she could have said, 'All right, I'll throw up my job tomorrow, I'll stay at home, we'll have a baby.' She knew she never could. Tears misted her eyes, as Bobby's voice rose high and clear over Frankie's accompaniment.

'If you go down in the woods today, you'd better go in disguise, if you go down in the woods today, you're in for a big surprise, for every bear that ever there was is gathered there together because, today's the day the teddy bears have their picnic!'

Chapter Thirty-Two

Rory was checking arrangements for the arrival of the Scottish hunger marchers in Edinburgh, still fuming over the decision of the Labour leadership and the TUC not to give official blessing to the march. There would be hundreds of Labour people and trades unionists involved, yet the officials held back, claiming the march was Communist organised. What a piece of nonsense! Everybody knew that the National Unemployed Workers Union, the true organisers, were independent of the Communist Party. Rory thanked God that very few were following the official line on this. He himself had gladly given his services to the reception committee and had been working flat out for weeks, Jennie had scarcely seen him.

Now at last he was home for a while, sitting at Madge's old table, checking lists, drinking tea he had let grow cold while Jennie sat near him, with a faraway look in her eyes. It was Thursday evening; Catherine's Land for once was quiet. At the long windows, Madge's curtains stirred in the breeze, while in their cots in the divided bedroom, the two little boys slept soundly.

'Tomorrow the marchers'll get on the road,' Rory murmured. 'They'll be coming from all over Scotland, a thousand at least. Is that no' something?'

'M'm', said Jennie.

'They've all got their instructions. By four o'clock on Sunday they should be at the meeting place, Corstorphine. They'll have their own field kitchens, so that's no worry.' Rory made a tick on one of his lists and went on, 'Next thing'll be the march to the Mound – we're expecting a good turn out there – for the speeches. Councillor Paton'll give the welcome, then the organisers will reply. Then comes our bit, the meal at the ILP Hall, Bonnington Road. Are all the women quite happy about the arrangements for that?' As Jennie did not answer, Rory looked up, 'Jennie are you no' listening to me?'

'Yes, yes I am!'

In fact she had been thinking about Sheena, brooding again on Rachel's report of seeing her in Glasgow, looking just the same except that she had had her hair cut. Sheena in Glasgow. Alive and well. Why shouldn't she come to Edinburgh, then? Edinburgh was the place she knew, she was almost certain to come back to her native city, especially if she thought enough time had gone by for Rory to have forgotten her. I must be prepared, thought Jennie, I must be ready at all times to meet Sheena again. She twisted her hands together. As long as Sheena didn't meet Rory.

'I was talking about this meal the reception committee's putting on,' Rory was saying. 'It's a big job – a thousand people arriving – we canna afford to let them down.'

'It's all taken care of, we won't let them down,' Jennie answered patiently. 'Why don't you stop worrying, Rory? You'll do all the better tomorrow if you take a rest tonight.'

'You know me, I canna rest if there's something like this ahead of me.' Rory sat back in his chair and put a hand through his black hair. 'Och, if only it'd do some good, Jennie! If only we could get it through to that bonehead Secretary of State he's got to do something! Take this embargo the government's put on Russian goods – we're losing orders all the time because the Russians canna put them in. Sixty thousand engineering workers canna do their jobs and the government doesna bloody care!'

'It's the children I care about,' Jennie murmured, drawing her mending basket towards her and sorting out socks. 'There has to be more help for them.'

'You try telling that to Sir Godfrey Collins,' Rory groaned. 'I bet he doesna even agree to see the marchers. When they get to the Scottish Office, he'll no' be there. Och, I think you're right.' He pushed aside his papers. 'I've done enough for tonight.'

'Want another cup of tea?'

'No, thanks.' For some moments Rory watched Jennie's skilful needle weaving in and out as she darned one of his socks. 'I meant to tell you,' he said quietly, 'I saw Sheena today.'

The needle stopped and Jennie slowly raised her eyes. At what he read there, Rory leaned forward and grasped her hand.

'Dinna look like that,' he said gently. 'She's no' that important.'

'She was once.'

'But not now. What there was between us – it's dead as a doornail.'

Jennie was silent, her eyes searching his handsome face which seemed to her strangely blank, as though he was keeping his emotions strictly in check. But she might be imagining that.

'Did you speak to her?' she asked at last.

'I wasna going to, but there she was, behind the counter—'

'What counter?'

'In Atkinson's Stationer's. She's working there. I'd gone in to reorder some of our headed paper, and there she was. I couldna believe ma eyes.'

'It's what happened before, though, isn't it? When you went into that tobacconist's all those years ago?'

'It's no' the same at all. I was a young lad then, ready to fall in love. I've had ma fingers burnt since then. I'm also married.' He gave one of his rare, sweet smiles. 'Very happily married.'

Jennie smiled back, she melted a little. 'Tell me what happened.'

'Well, to begin with, she was a wee bit nervous. Couldna be sure what I'd do, I suppose. As though I'd want to do anything after all this time! But I was quite polite. I told her what I wanted, she wrote it down, then asked me how I was.'

'And you told her you were married to me?'

'Aye, and that we'd two boys. She was amazed.'

'I don't see why!' cried Jennie. 'Why shouldn't we be married?'

'Och, she was just making conversation. Anyway, then she told me she'd been living in Galashiels, that's where her ma took her because she had a sister there. And Lily MacLaren's

231

married now, to a joiner, and Sheena was married too, but her husband died.'

'Died! He must have been very young.'

'They were married two years, then he got peritonitis and the doctors couldna save him. Sheena went back to live with her ma, then decided to come here.'

'Rachel saw her in Glasgow the other day.'

Rory raised his eyebrows. 'You never told me that.'

'No.'

'Were you afraid, or what?'

'I just didn't want to talk about her.'

Rory was silent for a while. 'Canna make her go away by not talking about her,' he said at last. 'She works at the Atkinson's shop in Glasgow one day a week, the rest of the time she's here.'

'And lives here, I suppose?'

'Aye, got a room in the Canongate.'

Near Mrs Smith's? thought Jennie and felt her cheeks burn. 'Did she say anything about me?'

'She did, she's keen to see you, and your ma. She says she'll call round soon.'

'I'll look forward to it.'

At the curtness of her tone, Rory again reached for Jennie's hand. 'I tell you she's no' important. She's just somebody we once knew, that's all.'

'How can you say that? After what happened? After what we all went through?'

'It was a long time ago,' he said quietly. 'Doesna do to brood on things for ever. Anyway, Sheena's different now.'

'How – different?'

'More serious. And she's had her hair cut.'

'Oh, well, that'll make a lot of difference, won't it?' Jennie pulled her hand from Rory's. 'I'm not sure we should see too much of her, Rory. She's from the past and she should stay there.'

'The thing is, she's got interested in politics. She's actually joined the Labour Party. Can you believe it?'

'No,' Jennie said shortly, 'I can't.'

'It's true, and she wants to help on Sunday, when the marchers come.'

232

'She's welcome to come to Bonnington Road then and help me peel the tatties.'

'No, she wants to march with us to the Mound,' Rory answered, seriously. 'Women are very welcome, you ken that, and we need everybody we can get.' He stood up, yawning and stretching. 'I can hardly believe it's coming at last, Jennie. We've waited so long, worked so hard . . .'

'It'll be worth it, Rory, you'll see, some good'll come of it.'

'I hope to God you're right.'

They were both bone-weary, but when they were lying together in the double bed they had bought on the never-never, neither could sleep. Rory lay thinking of the men and women who would be leaving their homes next morning, carrying their blankets and haversacks, striking out behind the marching bands, to make their great statement to the capital of Scotland. None of them knew what they would find, how their demands would be met, even where they would be able to sleep; all they knew was that they had to do something to keep body and soul together. What they really wanted was work, but if there was no work, then there must be relief. Only the government could provide it, and they'd better, they'd better, thought Rory, turning and groaning against Jennie's slim body. As she murmured in return, Jennie was seeing only Sheena. Seeing her as in those early dreams, searching for her ring, Rory's ring. Had she found it? Was she still in secret wearing it? There had been another man since Rory, a husband too, but he was dead. And Sheena was alive. And free.

The dawn was breaking before sleep came to them and when they woke neither felt refreshed.

Madge was sympathetic and encouraging when Jennie talked to her next morning. Jennie could be sure Rory meant what he said. What he had felt for Sheena was long dead, he was a happily married man now with two little boys. Jennie had nothing to fear.

'I wish I could be sure that was true,' said Jennie.

'Jennie, people change as they get older. They want different things. Rory'll look at Sheena now and wonder what he ever saw in her.' Madge floured her rolling pin and rolled out her pastry, while Jennie glumly watched.

'He was so crazy about her, though, Ma, and then she hurt him so badly, I can't understand why he'd ever want to look at her again.'

'Well, I think it's a good thing that he doesn't mind seeing her. It proves she doesn't matter to him any more. You'd have more to worry about, if he hadn't been able to face meeting her again.'

'Yes, that's right.' Jennie was looking brighter. 'I just don't want her stirring up memories again and upsetting him.'

'He's got you, dear, you'll look after him.' Madge sliced apples, sprinkled in sugar and carefully set a pastry lid over her pie. 'But fancy Lily being married, then! And never a word from her. Sometimes I think I wouldn't mind seeing Lily again.'

'First, I've got to meet Sheena,' said Jennie with a sigh.

She came on Saturday evening. Jennie had been on edge all day, half expecting her.

'Hello, Jennie.'

'Hello, Sheena.'

Their eyes met and slid away. Jennie thought, She hasn't changed. Her bobbed hair was different, her little scrap of blue frock was different, but the magic of her attraction that even Jennie could feel was still there and always would be, whatever clothes she wore, however she did her hair. But at least she wasn't wearing Rory's ring, only a plain gold wedding band. Jennie felt relieved enough to smile and hold wide the door.

'Come in, Sheena. I was just getting the boys to bed.'

It made it easier that the boys were there, all chubby and rosy in the pyjamas Jennie had made for them, staring round-eyed at the lady visitor. Sheena was ecstatic.

'Och, they're grand wee boys!' she cried. 'Both like you, Jennie, that lovely fair hair – or is this little one like his dad, then? Aye, he's got Rory's dark blue eyes, hasn't he? You canna mistake them.'

How can she talk so easily about Rory? thought Jennie, taking Will and Hamish to their cots. It was as though nothing had happened for her, as though she'd parted with Rory the best of friends.

'I've brought the weans some sweeties,' said Sheena, settling herself on the sofa. 'Better keep them for the morning, eh?'

'That's kind of you.' Jennie placed the packets of sweets on the shelf over the range where her mother's clock still ticked. 'I'll put the kettle on, shall I? I expect you'd like a cup of tea.'

'Such lovely boys,' Sheena murmured, her lip trembling. 'You're so lucky, Jennie. I can niver have any children now, I've been told. After you know what.' She lowered her eyes.

'Oh, Sheena, I'm so sorry!' Jennie, setting out cups and saucers, caught her breath in genuine sympathy. Never to have children? She couldn't imagine the misery. 'And I was so sorry to hear about your husband, too. That was terrible, to die so young.'

'Aye, went quick.' Sheena sighed. 'Just as well, eh? I canna stand illness.'

She looked around Madge's old flat, noting the new chairs and matting, the wireless in the corner, the wedding photograph on the piano. For some time her eyes rested on that photograph but she made no comment, only asked, 'Where's Rory?'

'Out with the committee. The marchers are due tomorrow, remember.'

'He'll be up to his eyes, eh?' Sheena took a cup of tea from Jennie and stirred in sugar. 'Is this no' nice, Jennie? Meeting up again after all these years?'

'We thought about you,' Jennie answered carefully. 'Wondered what you and your ma were doing.'

'Did Rory say we went to Galashiels? Auntie Betty put us up but her and Ma didna get on and Ma found us a room of our own. Then she met this feller who'd his own business, fell for Ma like a bag o' hammers. Next thing I knew they were wed! Och, I niver thought Ma would settle in a place the size o' Galashiels, but I might ha' settled there maself, if ma Douglas had no' died.'

'Tell me about him,' Jennie said softly.

'He was nice, Jennie, a real nice feller. Worked in a bank. Aye, a collar and tie man, quite the gentleman!' Sheena laughed. 'Couldna figure me out, though, kept trying to make me like everybody else. But we were happy, all the same. We were really happy.'

'What happened?'

'He took this pain – I still canna believe it – took this pain one day, was dead the next. And me a widow!'

'Oh, Sheena!'

'Aye. I went to live with Ma for a bit, but I couldna settle. I says, it's me for the city, Ma, and she says, Sheena you do right to go back to a bit o' life. So here I am, back in Auld Reekie. Seems like I've niver been away.'

Jennie hesitated. 'Did you ever think – I mean did it worry you at all – about meeting Rory?'

'At first,' Sheena replied, after a pause. 'But then I thought, Edinburgh's a big city, why should I see Rory? And what happened – that was all so long ago. You canna keep on remembering forever, can you?'

'So when you did see him, it was all right?'

'Why you ken fine it was! I could see straight away the past didna mean a thing!'

Jennie bent her head. She made no reply.

'You're no' holding it against me?' Sheena asked quickly. 'I mean, what happened? You were so good to me, I'll niver forget what you did for me, but you'd no' let it come between us now, eh? I want us to be friends, just like we used to be.'

'Things have changed, Sheena.'

'You mean you and Rory are wed? Aye, well you were always right for him and I wasna. But that need make no difference to us. I'd no' like to think you didna want me as a friend because you married Rory.'

'Of course I want you as a friend,' Jennie answered, her heart sinking, 'only—'

'Only, what?'

'Nothing. Look, let's not think too much about the old days. I want to tell you about Abby and Rachel.'

When Sheena had expressed herself suitably impressed by the achievements of Abby and Rachel, she stood up and said she must be going. But first she'd like to nip up the stair and see Jennie's mother.

'Is it no' grand your boys have got their own Gramma Ritchie up the stair, then? It'll be just what your ma wants, eh?'

'Yes, it's worked out well.' Jennie moved with Sheena to the door. 'But what about tomorrow? Are you going to join the marchers?'

'Aye. Rory gave me this form.' Sheena scrabbled in her bag and took out a piece of paper. 'You canna march unless you fill this in.'

'It's just to promise to keep the discipline and to say you understand what all the demands mean,' Jennie explained. 'We've all signed it. So you'll be going to Corstorphine tomorrow?'

'I wouldna miss it. See all them people marching in to Edinburgh from all over Scotland, what a grand thing, eh? Och, the government'll have to give in, they'll have to do something, they canna let the people starve!'

Maybe she has changed after all, Jennie thought, listening to Sheena sounding so like Rory; the plight of the unemployed had never bothered her in the old days. This must have been the side of herself she had shown Rory and so impressed him. If it was genuine, Jennie could only feel pleased. There was no reason why it shouldn't be genuine. It was true what Ma had said, people wanted different things as they grew older and Sheena had joined the Labour Party before she'd even met up with Rory again. A sudden warmth consumed Jennie for her old friend, for if Sheena had made Rory suffer, she had certainly suffered herself and, in spite of all her looks and powers of attraction, she still remained rather a pathetic figure. Jennie flung her arms around her and as Sheena's own arms wound round her tight, she knew she was committed again.

'I'm glad you're back,' she whispered, 'though I'll have to admit, I was a bit worried when I first heard.'

'You niver had any need to worry, Jennie.' The clear eyes met hers. 'I'll go to your ma, shall I? Up the stair, just like the old days!'

She laughed, and Jennie laughed too, as she watched Sheena mounting the stair. Just like the old days. The past seemed all around Jennie as she went into her flat and closed the door, but only the past she wanted to remember. The rest was fading mercifully from her mind.

Chapter Thirty-Three

All Edinburgh waited for the marchers on Sunday, June 11th. The well-to-do were apprehensive. These gaunt battalions descending on the city, what might they not get up to? The poor, however, were thrilled and made proud by the action the unemployed had taken. They saw the march with its brass bands and scarlet banners as a great gala of colour and excitement, they couldn't wait to line the streets to cheer the marchers on. By the time the leaders were making speeches on the Mound, two thousand Edinburgh people were up there too, trying to hear, not minding if they couldn't, anxious only to show support. When the marchers eventually moved on to the ILP hall where they were to be given a meal, euphoria was the order of the day.

Jennie had wanted to go to the Mound herself, not so much to see the marchers or hear the speakers, but to be with Rory. He would be sure to be in a state of great excitement now that things were happening and she should be by his side, but of course she had promised to help with the marchers' dinner and couldn't let the committee down. As she chopped meat and peeled potatoes, she too was excited, quite strung up in fact by the atmosphere of the day and the air of expectancy that filled the hall. It was as though she and all the helpers were athletes reaching the end of a race they had been running in their minds for weeks.

'Oh, I wish they'd come!' cried one young woman, laying out knives and forks with a trembling hand.

'Here they are!' someone shouted from the door, and as the first of the marchers arrived, foot-sore and pale from exhaustion, a great sigh of relief moved from one woman to another as they began to serve the meal.

Jennie had no time to think of Rory but suddenly he was before her, a plate someone had given him in his hand, his eyes shining with triumph.

'It's all going so well, Jennie!' he whispered. 'Couldna have gone better if we'd tried it a hundred times. You should've seen the crowds at the Mound! My God, if the leadership doesna want this march, there's plenty who do!'

'Oh, Rory, I'm so glad!' Jennie cried. 'You see, all your hard work's paying off, just like I said!' She took his plate. 'But now, what'll you have to eat? You must eat something, I'm sure you've had nothing all day.'

'Later, I'll have something later.' He was turning away, his eyes raking the hall with feverish excitement, when someone touched his arm and he looked down and smiled. 'Why, Jennie, look who's here!'

It was Sheena. In a trailing blue dress with a small hat set on the back of her head, she stood out from the weary marchers like a star in the night sky, but while they stared at her in obvious admiration, she smiled only at Jennie. And Rory.

'Sheena!' he cried, shaking her hand. 'Did you march from Corstorphine, then? Och, I niver thought you'd do it!'

'Sure I did! And I marched here from the Mound. Did you no' see me?'

'If I'd seen you, I'd have remembered. But now you're here you'd better have something to eat. Jennie, give Sheena some of that pie, eh? Looks good.'

Sheena who had never been known to refuse food, obediently held out her plate to Jennie, who, after a moment's hesitation, piled it high.

'You too, Rory,' Sheena ordered. 'Come on, now, dinna hold back.'

'He doesn't want anything to eat,' Jennie said tightly. 'Rory, you're going to have something later, aren't you.'

'Well, I'm no' sure now, that pie's tempting me – did you make it, Jennie?'

'Yes I made it. Do you want some then, or not?'

'He wants some.' Sheena took the spoon from Jennie's hand and served Rory herself. 'Have to be firm with this feller, Jennie. Shall we go and sit down, Rory?'

'I canna be long, I have to help find accommodation for these people tonight. We've been offered the Waverley Market, but we're no' taking it.'

'Eat your dinner first,' Sheena said, imperiously, and led him away to join other marchers at one of the trestle tables, while Jennie watched them, standing quite still.

'Are you dishing out that pie or not, then?' someone called, and with a start she came back to her surroundings and continued serving out the food.

She was determined not to let her imagination run away with her. Rory and Sheena were only sitting together, weren't even talking to each other, only to the other people at the table. There was no need to see things that weren't there. All the same, when Rose McLeod, one of the helpers, said she was looking tired, she should go and have a cup of tea in the back room, she agreed. It would make it easier, she thought, not to have to watch what wasn't there. The tea and the rest did her good and when she returned to her post, she felt better. But Rory had gone and so had Sheena. For a moment panic took over and she was looking around with frantic eyes when Sheena came quietly to her side.

'Want me to give you a hand?' she asked. 'You're looking like you've been doing too much.'

'Oh, Sheena!' Jennie was smiling radiantly. 'I thought you'd gone with Rory.'

'No, he told me to tell you he'd to leave with Mr MacGovern and Mr McShane. They're talking to the polis about places for the folk to sleep.'

'Oh, surely they can find somewhere?' Jennie cried, happily serving out apple dumplings and custard. 'There's spoons over there, Sheena.'

'Rory says the Socialists'll no' let them have the Melbourne Hall, can you believe it? At this rate, they'll all be sleeping in the polis station!'

'They've niver got a thousand cells in the polis station?' cried one of the men, and as the laughter spread down the waiting queue, Jennie marvelled at the good humour of these people who had so little and expected even less.

It was late before Jennie and Sheena could leave the ILP hall. Rory had not returned, but some accommodation had been found for the marchers and after they'd left the helpers had to clear away and do the washing-up.

'Och, I'll sleep without rocking tonight,' said Sheena as they went out into the June night. 'But it's been a grand day, eh?'

'A grand day,' Jennie agreed. 'Funny to think of all those people sleeping in the city tonight, isn't it? Poor things. Did you see how haggard they looked? And some of them were in such pain with their feet!'

'Aye, my feet are bad enough, and I only marched from Corstorphine!'

'You did well, Sheena, really well.' Jennie felt she could safely add, 'Rory's really proud of you.'

Sheena smiled. 'Your Rory – he gets so worked up, eh? I think he's like one o' they party balloons. If he wasna tied to you, he'd float right away.'

'He is tied to me,' Jennie said at once.

'Is that no' what I'm saying? You keep his feet on the ground.'

'Oh, yes, I see what you mean. ' Again Jennie was filled with sweet relief. 'Yes, I do that, I have to.'

'Are you going with the marchers tomorrow?' she asked Sheena, when they parted.

'Tomorrow? No, it's Monday tomorrow, I have to go to work.'

'Of course, I'd forgotten. Well, if Ma's willing to take the boys again, I may help with the cooking in Parliament Square. The marchers've got their own cooks, but there's a lot to do.'

'They need all the help they can get, that's for sure. I'll see you soon, Jennie.'

'Yes, and Sheena' – as Sheena paused with her enchanting smile, Jennie said – 'thanks for your help tonight.'

'Nae bother, Jennie. 'Night then.'

'Goodnight, Sheena.'

Jennie watched her walk away, hobbling a little on her sore feet, her blue hat bobbing on the back of her head. Who would have thought lazy Sheena would have done so much? Rachel would never believe it. Jennie turned for home herself, wondering when she would see Rory again, wondering what was happening to the marchers.

When she let herself into the flat, moving quietly so as not to wake the boys, Madge sat up on the couch and looked at her with sleepy blue eyes.

'My goodness, Jennie,' she murmured, 'you look as fresh as a daisy. What it is to be young. I would have been on my knees.'

'I feel fine,' said Jennie.

She never actually heard Rory come to bed, but in the morning when he hastily drank some tea, he told her it had been the small hours before they had found places for all the marchers to sleep. Some had in fact had to sleep at the police station, which made Jennie cry out, 'Oh dear, and we were laughing about that! What about tonight, then? Have you found something for tonight?'

'No, but I havena got time to think of it now. I'm off back to Bonnington Road, they're laying on some breakfast there. Then we'll march to the Ministry of Labour to put the demands.' Rory set down his cup and wiped his lips. 'You mark my words, Jennie, Sir Godfrey'll no' be there, he'll no' even see us.'

'You don't know that for sure, Rory.'

'You just wait and see.' Rory snatched up his cap and briefly kissed Jennie on the cheek. ''Bye, Jennie, expect me when you see me.'

'I might see you in Parliament Square, I said I'd try to help with the cooking there.'

'That's good of you.' Rory gave a quick grin. 'Picture the marchers there, eh? Parliament Square . . . is that no' grand?'

'Grand,' she repeated, smiling, and waved him down the stair.

Parliament Square, at the top of the High Street, was its most solemn and respectable part. St Giles's Cathedral was there, and the Law Courts and the Signet Library, it might be considered the very heart of establishment Edinburgh, yet here the

242

marchers came to sit and lie on the historic stones, and here too came the portable kitchens, manned by the marchers' cooks and women helpers such as Rose and Jennie. As the gallons of tea were brewed, the mountains of bread sliced, the sausage rolls and pies laid out, crowds of Edinburgh people came to wonder and stare at a sight they would probably never see again. The police, however, quickly moved them on.

The day was hot, feeding so many people was exhausting, but none of the helpers flagged. They were doing what they could for a cause that was close to them and the more they saw of the marchers, with their hollow cheeks and shabby clothes, the more they admired the spirit that drove them on. They had endured so much, they had so little hope, but they never gave up.

'Och, it makes your heart bleed,' said Rose to Jennie, 'and the worst of it is they'll likely get nowhere. There's word that Sir Godfrey wouldna even leave London. He'll no' see them.'

'Oh, no!' cried Jennie, shocked. 'Rory said he wouldn't, but I didn't believe it. I didn't see how he could refuse to listen to them.'

'It's all political, hen. Mebbe he wanted to see them, but Ramsay MacDonald said no, it wouldna do, or something o' that sort, eh?'

Ramsay MacDonald was now the leader of a coalition government of Tories and Socialists; they all knew what they thought of him.

As she poured tea and cut bread and butter, Jennie kept looking for Rory but she didn't see him.

'I'd better go home,' she told Rose. 'Ma's had the boys a long time, I should give her a rest.'

'Aye, and give yourself a rest too. The marchers are moving on now, anyway.' Rose, plump and cheerful, gave a loud laugh. 'You'll never guess where – the Queen's Park!'

'Holyrood?' Jennie burst out laughing too, and mopped her damp brow. 'Oh, that's wonderful! Why not, though? Why shouldn't the people rest there?'

'Aye, why not? But it's a bit cheeky, eh? The police'll be having twenty fits, but they canna stop them. The leaders'll be gathering there to tell the marchers what's been happening.'

'Wish they'd better news.' Jennie pulled on her jacket. 'If you see Rory, will you tell him I've gone back?'

'Aye, I will. And thanks, pet, you've done a grand job today.'

'Nae bother,' Jennie answered, echoing Sheena. She wondered if Sheena would come round to see her after work.

Sheena did not come round but Rory came back very briefly, only to have a wash and change his shirt and put his shaving brush and razor in his pocket.

'Looks like we'll be sleeping out tonight,' he told Jennie. 'There's efforts being made to disband the march, but we're no' having any of it. If we canna find a hall, we'll sleep on the streets.'

'Oh, Rory, that's terrible!' cried Jennie. 'I can't believe something can't be found in the whole of Edinburgh!'

'It's all a piece with what's been happening,' Rory said savagely. 'The deputation got nowhere, Sir Godfrey wouldn't come, they had to hand their demands in to some official and God knows what he'll do with 'em. But we're no' giving in, Jennie, we're no' giving in! We'll sleep on Princes Street if we have to. We'll let the so-called quality see just what we're made of! Can you find me a blanket, then?'

'Rory, I don't like to think of you sleeping on the pavement. Couldn't you . . .' Jennie faltered, seeing the look in Rory's eyes. 'No, you wouldn't want to come back here while they were down there, I suppose?'

'No, I wouldn't.' Rory gave Jennie a hasty peck on the cheek and once again was away down the stair, while Jennie, with a heavy heart prepared for her lonely bed.

Chapter Thirty-Four

Abby drove into work as usual on Tuesday morning. It was her last day before her holiday. Tomorrow she would take the train to Southampton where she planned to see their old cottage and visit her father's grave, before embarking on the *Anastasia* cruise ship with Frankie. He was already away on a short trip but would be back in time to join her; she could hardly wait to see him again, to travel with him and come back as his wife. One more day to clear her desk and then . . .! Her heart was singing when she parked her car at the back of Logie's and went in through the staff entrance.

'Oh, Miss Ritchie!' cried Donald Rennie, now one of her senior clerks, 'have you seen Princes Street this morning?'

'Princes Street? No, I came in the back way. What's wrong with Princes Street?'

'I'd go and have a look,' he answered, grinning. 'Bet it'll be the first time you've seen folk sleeping on newspaper, eh? Or shaving in the gardens?'

The marchers, thought Abby. Oh, God, they must have had to sleep on the pavement! She hurried through the stately ground floor of the store to the main swing doors, where Jock MacAndrew was shaking his head.

'Niver in ma whole life, Miss Ritchie, have I seen what's oot there!' he told her. 'Folk dossing doon in Princes Street. Princes Street, the finest street in Europe! I canna believe it!'

'Let me through, please,' said Abby.

The sight the marchers presented was indeed extraordinary. Abby, her car keys still dangling from her fingers, stood transfixed. The scene was like something from a camping holiday, with some men and women folding blankets and newspapers, while others were washing in the fountains of the gardens or even trying to shave. A cheer went up as a tea urn was rattled over the pavement and someone began to sing, then others banged drums and played flutes, and all the while Edinburgh people on their way to work gazed, open-mouthed.

Well, this is something to remember, thought Abby, but it seemed to her disgraceful that the marchers had had to sleep out in the open, that no shelter in the whole of Edinburgh had been found for them. She was wondering where she might make an official complaint and had decided that Rory would know, when she saw Rory himself. He was one of the men trying to shave at the fountain and she crossed the road calling his name. He was laughing and did not hear her and she saw that a girl in blue was holding up a mirror for him. It was Sheena, and she was laughing too.

'Hello, Rory,' Abby said quietly. 'Hello, Sheena.'

They both swung round, their laughter dying. Sheena lowered the mirror. Rory wiped his cheek with a handkerchief.

'Abby, what are you doing here?' he murmured.

'I work at Logie's, remember? I came out to see what was happening. Have you been here all night?'

'Aye, all night. Nowhere else to go, couldna get accommodation anywhere. All a plot, of course, to get the marchers out of the city, but it didna work.'

'You were here, too?' Abby asked Sheena, noting that her flowing dress was crumpled and her hair uncombed, but that she looked as enchanting as usual. Perhaps even more enchanting than usual. With a sinking feeling, Abby saw that Sheena's clear eyes were starry.

'Sheena just came along to see how we were managing,' Rory said quickly, and it seemed to Abby that he too was looking astonishingly handsome, considering that he was wearing no collar and his face was only half shaved. 'So, when she saw me, we got to talking, well, everybody was talking half the night. It's no' easy to sleep on a pavement, you ken?'

'I'm sure it's not,' Abby answered. 'I doubt if I'd have done it myself.'

'I wanted to be with the marchers,' Sheena answered smoothly. 'I was with 'em all day yesterday, you ask Jennie.'

'And we didna see you, Abby,' said Rory. 'Did you no' want to support the march?'

'Good heavens, am I on trial now?' asked Abby with a smile.

'Why, who else is on trial?' countered Rory.

'No one. Actually, I was at the Mound to hear the speeches. If you didn't see me, it was probably because there were about three thousand other people there as well.'

Rory gave an apologetic grin. 'Sorry, Abby. If you'll excuse me, I'd better carry on trying to tidy maself up. The leaders are giving some newspaper interviews this morning and I want to be there.'

'And I'd better get to work,' said Sheena, taking out a comb and running it through her hair. 'Must look a terrible fright, eh?'

'You ken fine what you look like,' Rory told her softly, and at the light in his eyes as they rested on Sheena, Abby's heart grew sick.

Oh, Jennie, she thought, what are we going to do?

Of course, I could be wrong, she told herself as she returned to the desk she had to clear. A few looks, a few words, they needn't mean anything. But she knew she wasn't wrong. Love and a cold could never be hid went the old saying, and there was nothing more true. Those two at the fountain, surrounded by all the noise and distraction of the other marchers, had been people apart, wrapped in the mysterious glow new love could bring. Or old love resurrected.

Nothing must be said, no hint dropped. Jennie must never know. The terrible thing was she couldn't help but know, if she ever saw Rory and Sheena together as Abby had seen them that morning. How would she bear it, if she lost Rory? How would I bear it, Abby groaned, if I were to lose Frankie?

It wouldn't happen. Rory would not be such a fool as to risk breaking up his marriage to Jennie. Think of the two little boys! And as for Frankie and herself, their love was stronger than ever. Wasn't she looking forward now to coming back from the cruise with her wedding ring worn openly on her finger? Abby sighed and as she had always been able to do, put everything from her mind except her work.

*

Jennie waited up for Rory that night and made him a hot drink when he came in late. He was weary but elated. They had found accommodation for the marchers. There would be no more sleeping in Princes Street.

'Aye, we had a good old ding-dong,' he said with satisfaction. 'Went to the Public Assistance Committee and demanded they do something. Wouldna do a thing, so we marched through the city and all the workers joined in, you niver saw such crowds!' He shook his head. 'I've niver felt so proud of Edinburgh folk, Jennie. It's solidarity, you see, and the bosses canna beat it. In the end, the marchers were found places to sleep and tomorrow there'll be food laid on and buses.'

'Buses?' cried Jennie. 'Oh, that's wonderful! I've been thinking all the time of their poor feet!'

'There was talk at one time of folk having to promise not to march to Edinburgh again, but we told 'em what they could do with that idea!' Rory stood up, yawning and stretching. 'I've no idea what'll be done about the things we've asked for, but at least we've put the unemployed back on the map. People all over the country have been told the situation and they're on our side. What's happened here has proved it.' He laughed grimly. 'And the Labour leadership and the TUC have learned a thing or two and all! Now, it's me for ma bed.'

They were lying in the darkness, very near to sleep, when Rory said, 'Sheena came and slept in Princes Street, you ken.'

Jennie lay quite still. 'She didn't have to do that,' she said after a pause.

'No, I thought it was good of her.'

'She stayed all night?'

'Aye, well, we were talking – with the others, I mean. Couldna sleep, really.'

'I suppose there were a lot of you together?'

'Plenty! All lying on the damned pavement!'

'It must have been uncomfortable.'

'Wasna like this.' He drew her towards him. 'You and me in our own soft bed, making love.'

'Why, I thought you were exhausted!' she whispered,

astonished at his passion, and then was lost in wanting him and feeling so very glad that he wanted her.

'Oh, Jennie, I do love you,' he said against her face, when they were staring into the darkness again, breathing hard. 'You ken I love you, eh? I'll always love you.'

'Why, Rory!' She was in rapture. 'What's all this? Why are you talking like this?'

'Do I no' often talk like this?'

'You don't often say you love me.'

'Well, I'm saying it tonight. I love you, Jennie.'

Long after Rory had turned away to sleep, Jennie lay wide-eyed, wrapped in a cocoon of happiness that nothing could pierce, not even those words that still stirred, in her mind, 'Sheena slept in Princes Street, you ken.' For why should she worry about Rory and Sheena in Princes Street when she had Rory safe beside her in their bed?

The next day the marchers went home, riding in state, or at least in buses, having been given no answer to their demands, but content for the time being to have made them. Before they left they burned an effigy of the man who had refused to meet them, the Secretary of State for Scotland.

'Disgraceful!' snorted Malcolm.

'Serves him damned well right!' cried Rory.

Chapter Thirty-Five

Postcards arrived from Abby in Southampton. She had found Will Ritchie's grave. It was very much overgrown but she had tidied it, laid flowers and taken a snap or two with her box camera. For a small fee, the cemetery authorities had agreed to maintain it in the future, so Ma needn't worry about that. As for their old cottage on the outskirts of the city, it was so much changed she wished she hadn't seen it. The quiet country lane she remembered had become a noisy road, the house dilapidated, the lovely apple tree cut down. Her fault for going back. Didn't people say you never should?

'They do,' sighed Madge, sitting with Abby's card in her hand but seeing only Will. 'But I'll never go back now.'

'Poor old Abby,' Jennie said to Rory. 'All these years she's talked about that apple tree and now it's not even there!'

'And now I suppose she'll be off on her cruise,' said Rachel, reading Abby's card at breakfast. 'Isn't it amazing how things always work out for Abby?'

Malcolm looked up from his post. 'You don't think they work out for you? I'd say you hadn't done too badly.'

'I don't notice us going on any cruises, Malcolm.'

Malcolm quietly passed his letters across the table. 'If you'd care to cast your eyes over these bills, Rachel, you might understand why we don't go cruising.'

'You're blaming me for the household expenses? We have to eat.'

'I'm not talking about the grocery bills. I'm talking about art books, gramophone records, dress materials, tickets for concerts I don't even go to, fifteen shillings for a florist's bill when we have flowers in our own garden!'

'It was you who told me to make the house look nice when you invited Mr Abbott!' Rachel cried. 'You seem to forget you're a professional man now, Malcolm, you can't expect to live as though you were still in Catherine's Land!'

'Well, it would certainly be a damn sight cheaper!' As Bobby looked at him with worried eyes, Malcolm tried to smile. 'Look, I'm not unreasonable, Rachel, I know we have to live to a certain standard. But half these bills I have to pay are for things we don't need, that's all I'm saying.'

'Things *you* don't need, you mean.' Rachel's face was dark. 'Why should I do without books and music because you're not interested? It's not as though we were poor.'

'We soon will be, if we go on as we are.' Malcolm gathered up his post and strode to the door. 'Now I suppose I'd better go to work to pay for all your necessities? Your records and your art books and your damned flowers?'

'Please don't swear in front of Bobby,' Rachel replied coolly, and Malcolm, having hastily kissed Bobby's cheek, went out and slammed the door.

'Why is Daddy cross?' Bobby asked, anxiously. 'Is it because we're poor?'

'We're not poor, Bobby.'

'But does Daddy think we are?'

'No, he just doesn't like paying for things, that's all.'

'But you have to pay for things, don't you? I mean, the shops won't let you have them, will they? If you can't pay?'

'Sometimes they let you pay later.' Rachel glanced at the clock and jumped up. 'Come on, Bobby, time for school, we don't want to be late.'

As Rachel hurried Bobby upstairs to clean his teeth, Malcolm stood at the front door, studying the weather. Gillie quietly joined him.

'Your umbrella, sir, doesna look so good today. Will you be back at the same time this evening, sir?'

Malcolm, picking up his briefcase, stared at her.

'I expect so, Gillie. Why do you ask?'

'It's no' for me to say, sir, but do you niver think of coming back a wee bit earlier?'

'What on earth do you mean?'

'Master Bobby has his dancing class this afternoon.' The maid gave a strange, thin-lipped smile. 'Might be worth remembering.'

'I don't know what you're talking about!' Malcolm cried, red spots rising to his cheekbones. 'If you've got something to say, Gillie, say it and stop talking in riddles!'

'I've no' got anything to say, sir,' she answered smoothly, and glided away.

Bloody woman, what was the matter with her? Malcolm walked down the short drive to the front gate. He stopped and looked back at the house. But what had she meant? He felt a sick feeling in the pit of his stomach as he considered Gillie's words. By the time he set off down the street, the red spots had faded from his cheekbones and he was very pale.

'Thank God you came,' Rachel murmured as she let Tim Harley in through the side door. 'I've just about been going crazy here.'

Tim, still slender and youthful, apart from thinning blond hair, stooped to kiss her. 'Don't I usually come on Wednesdays? What's up, then?'

'Oh, it's Malcolm, going on and on about the bills.' Rachel put her finger to her lips as she led Tim up the stairs to her studio. 'Try not to make any noise. I don't want my nosey maid to know you're here.'

'I don't know why you don't leave him,' Tim remarked, watching Rachel shut and lock the studio door. 'Malcolm's done well, but I'm sure you could find some chap who's doing better.'

'You, for instance?' she asked, with a smile.

He laughed uneasily. 'You know I've no money, Rachel.'

Rachel lay back on the studio day bed. 'Don't worry, Tim, I wouldn't dream of looking to you for anything, I know you too well. The thing is, I'm fond of Malcolm, but he doesn't seem to give a damn about any of the things that matter to me. I thought he'd want to make me happy, but he only cares about the bills.'

'Why not leave him, then?'

'Because there's Bobby.'

'Ah.' Tim, beginning to undress, shook his head. 'I've never had any kids myself, but I see your point there.'

'You nearly had one once, didn't you?'

He stood very still, his shirt in his hand. 'What's that supposed to mean?'

'Did you think I didn't know about Sheena?' Rachel smiled, teasingly. 'Oh, don't look so outraged, Tim! You were the one who painted her portrait, I always guessed it was you.'

'I got rid of the portait' he stammered. 'Oh, God, Rachel, why did you never say anything?'

'What was the point. It didn't matter to me.'

'Thank you very much!' he cried angrily. 'That's rich, that is! I come here, I make love to you because you seem to want me to, and now it seems I'm not of the slightest interest to you! If that's how you feel, I might as well go!'

'Oh, come on, I didn't say I didn't enjoy making love with you, Tim!' Rachel drew him towards her. 'There's just no need to pretend it's important to us, that's all.'

'It's all to spite Malcolm, is it?' he asked peevishly, but Rachel again put her finger to her lips.

'No more talking, Tim. We haven't much time.'

Everything was quiet when they opened the studio door, both fully dressed with buttons fastened and hair combed, not a sign to show that they had so recently been in the throes of passion.

'All clear,' Rachel whispered, and they tiptoed down to the first landing. But at the turning to the main staircase, they froze. Malcolm was standing at the foot of the stairs, looking up.

For a moment it was as though they had all been turned to stone. No one spoke, no one moved. Then Tim cleared his throat.

'Hello, Malcolm! We've – I've just been up to Rachel's studio—'

'I know that,' Malcolm replied.

'Tim was looking at my latest work,' Rachel said quickly.

'No, I don't think so, Rachel.'

'Malcolm—'

'Rachel,' Malcolm fixed her with a stony gaze, 'I heard you.'

As a flood of thick bright colour suffused her face, Tim muttered, 'Oh, God.'

'It's lucky I'm no' a violent man,' Malcolm spat out, his Scottish accent returning. 'If I'd been like ma dad, for instance, you two'd no' be standing here wi' your heads still on your shoulders. But I like to think maself civilised, so just get yourself out o' ma house, Tim Harley, before I change ma mind!'

Tim, very white, moved hesitantly down the stairs. As he reached Malcolm, he shrank against the wall and Malcolm laughed.

'Good God, Rachel, what did you iver see in this great jessie?' he cried and giving Tim a shove sent him hurtling down the hall towards the front door. 'Get out!' he roared, 'Get out!' As Tim fumbled with the lock and gladly let himself out, Malcolm turned back to Rachel. The whole structure of his face seemed to change, to sag, to wither, before her eyes.

'I loved you,' he whispered, 'I loved you so much.' He put his hand to his brow. 'You can go in the morning, Rachel. I want you packed and away by the time I come back from work.'

Her world had collapsed around her. Rachel couldn't believe it. In a few short moments, everything she had gained had been taken from her. Her home, her husband, her comfortable life as the wife of a successful professional man. She still had no money of her own, no real means of supporting herself. She would rather die than go back to Catherine's Land. What was she to do? Where could she go? And then, like a knife pain in her heart, she remembered Bobby and the full implications of what Malcolm had said sank in.

Malcolm had moved into the drawing room where he had dropped into a chair and lit a cigarette. Rachel followed, closing the door, although she knew of course that it was far too late now to be worrying about Gillie's overhearing. She went to Malcolm and stood over him.

'You can't mean what you are saying!' she cried passionately. 'I know I've done a terrible thing. I know I've hurt you and I'm sorry for that, I really am, it was stupid and wicked.

But you can't throw me out for it, Malcolm. You can't make me leave Bobby. He's only five years old!'

'Exactly why I want you away from him. I don't want my son brought up by a woman like you.' As he grew calmer, Malcolm's English accent was returning and he was managing to give an impersonation of his usual professional self. But his eyes on Rachel were the eyes of a stranger.

'I'm his mother!' Rachel was now trembling so violently she could hardly stand. 'You can't take him away from me, I won't let you. He needs me. Whatever I've done, Bobby needs me!'

'There isn't a court that wouldn't give me custody, once the facts were known.'

'Court?' Rachel had gone white. 'What are you saying? Are you divorcing me?'

'No, I'm just explaining your position.' Malcolm leaped to his feet and poured himself a drink. 'If you're so fond of Bobby, Rachel, you should have thought of him before you took Tim Harley to your bed. A man you don't love.' He swallowed some whisky, staring at her. 'You don't love him, do you?' As her eyes fell, he nodded drearily. 'No, it was never a love affair, just a bit on the side. You think that makes it better?'

'It's what men do all the time!' she flashed. 'And no one thinks the worse of them!'

'It's not what I do,' he said quietly.

She was silent, sagging against a chair. 'Don't you care at all what will become of me?' she asked at last. 'I've no money, where can I go?'

'As long as you leave Edinburgh, I don't care where you go. I'll give you enough to pay your fare somewhere and a few weeks' rent, until you find yourself a job.' Malcolm drained his glass and set it down. 'There, that's a handsome offer, isn't it? When you think that some men would have given you a beating and thrown you out to starve. Now, go and make up your face, and start putting on your act. Polly will be bringing Bobby back from his class any minute now.'

255

Chapter Thirty-Six

The night was terrible. Though Malcolm slept in the spare room, Rachel would not lie in their bed and sat up all night wrapped in a dressing gown, shivering and weeping angry tears, trying to plan what she would do. Sometimes her mother's tranquil face would come into her mind and at the thought of telling Madge what had happened, Rachel groaned as though in physical pain. How could she have been such a fool, to put herself in this nightmare situation for the sake of sex with a man like Tim Harley? He was a good lover, better in bed than out of it, but he had never been worth the price she was now having to pay, and what made the whole thing worse was that she had no one but herself to blame for her own misery.

But Malcolm was not blameless, either. He had been cruel to her in those early days, making her stay at home, showing her who was master because he had money and she had none, and he was still doing that now. It was true she had betrayed him and she did feel remorse for that now, but that he should be able to cast her out, take away her son, as though they were living in Victorian times, made her grit her teeth with rage. She would not let him get away with it, she would not, for it was Bobby's welfare at stake, not just her own. Somehow she must work out a way of defeating Malcolm and to that end she stayed awake until the dawn broke in the summer sky.

Next morning she went down to breakfast looking calm and poised, as though a volcano of feeling were not shaking in her breast. Malcolm was already at the table, pretending to eat eggs and bacon, while Bobby was in his pyjamas spooning up porridge.

'Tea, ma'am?' asked Gillie, her foxy features blank.

'Thank you,' Rachel answered, resolutely not looking at her. She guessed she had Gillie to thank for Malcolm's presence in the house yesterday afternoon, but would not give her the satisfaction of speaking of it. Nor would she let her see the devastation she had caused by throwing a scene with Malcolm now. But when Gillie had left the dining room, Rachel turned her dark eyes on her husband.

'You're still serious about this, Malcolm?'

'Oh, yes.' He pushed his plate away. 'I'll take Bobby to morning school and you can ring for a taxi.'

'Mummy's not going away?' cried Bobby, who knew taxis usually meant the station and trains and leaving.

'Just for a little while,' Rachel said quickly, her eyes meeting and warning Malcolm over Bobby's head as she kissed him. 'Now you go up and start getting dressed and I'll come up in a minute and help you.'

As soon as Bobby had gone, Rachel and Malcolm faced each other.

'And who is going to look after Bobby when I'm not here?' Rachel asked quietly. 'Polly will not be able to take my place.'

'No, I've thought of that. I'm going to ask your mother to take over.'

'My mother!'

'Yes, why not? She's very good with Bobby and he adores her.'

'But—' Rachel felt stunned. Ma, looking after Bobby? Yes, she could do it and it was true, he loved Madge dearly. But where did that leave her? Unwanted, unneeded? No, she couldn't accept it, she wouldn't accept it.

'But what?' asked Malcolm, scribbling out a cheque. 'You know it's the best solution possible. He'll soon forget you, Rachel. Don't worry about him.'

'Don't worry!'

'Here's your cheque.' He folded it and handed it to her. 'Don't throw it on the floor in a temper, you're going to need it.'

She longed to fling the cheque in his face, but the morning sun streaming in through the open windows suddenly revealed such a look of suffering in his eyes, her own eyes filled with tears.

'Malcolm . . .' She stretched out her hand. 'I know it's no good, saying I'm sorry . . .'

'No, it's no good.' He ignored her hand. 'Goodbye, Rachel.'

'You're really not going to let me see Bobby again?'

'Well, not for some time. We won't want to unsettle him, once he's got used to not seeing you.'

'I'll get him ready for school, then.'

'Please.'

If Malcolm was surprised she didn't cry when she kissed Bobby goodbye, he didn't show it. Perhaps he thought she was being brave for Bobby's sake, which was partly true.

'You be a good boy for Daddy,' she murmured, her face close to her son's. 'And I'll send you lots of letters.'

'But why can't I come with you, Mummy?'

'You have to go to school, remember? But I'll be thinking of you and you must think of me. Promise?'

'Come on, get in the car, Bobby,' Malcolm said shortly. 'We mustn't be late.'

'Goodbye, Malcolm,' Rachel said, as he closed the car door on Bobby and took the driving seat. He made no reply and the car moved away, Bobby waving frantically and Rachel waving too. But still she did not weep. She had things to do.

At twelve o'clock she was in Tim Harley's car outside the large house where Bobby attended private school. Her packed cases were in the boot, a hamper with Bobby's toys on the back seat. While Tim sat smoking and fidgeting, Rachel kept her eyes trained on the closed iron gates of the school.

'The mothers are arriving now,' she whispered, 'see the cars? But Polly will be on foot. She'll be expecting to take Bobby home by bus.'

'This is crazy,' Tim groaned, 'you'll never get away with it. Wherever you go, Malcolm will find you.'

'London's a big place and he won't know where to start looking.'

'He'll hire private detectives, he'll do anything to get Bobby back.'

'And I'll do anything to keep him.' Rachel grasped Tim's

arm. 'They're opening the gates and I see Polly! Drive round the corner, Tim, she mustn't see you. I'm going to get Bobby.'

'But what will you tell her?'

'I'll say the plans have been changed, I'm to take Bobby on a visit. Oh, never mind what I tell her! Just be ready to drive us away!'

'I'm a fool to get involved in this,' Tim muttered as Rachel jumped out of the car. 'I thought you said you'd never expect anything of me?'

'After you ruined my life? You owe me something, Tim!'

'You ruined your own life!' he shouted, but she had already gone.

A few minutes later she was back with a delighted Bobby skipping at her side.

'Quickly, darling, into the car,' she ordered. 'You see, I've brought all your favourite toys.'

'Hello, Bobby,' said Tim, leaning back with a smile, but Bobby was checking through the hamper and scarcely spared him a look. He had never liked 'Uncle Tim'.

'Is everything there?' Rachel asked fondly, as Bobby settled on his teddy bear for a special hug.

'Oh, yes, and I'm glad you changed your mind, Mummy, and said I could go with you. I didn't want you to go away without me.'

'Yes, well, it's a shame that Daddy can't come, but you must promise not to cry if you don't see him for a while.' Rachel closed the car door and took her seat next to Tim. 'Now, Uncle Tim is going to drive us to the station. Isn't that kind of him?' She gave Tim a sharp glance. 'You'll be sure to say nothing if anyone asks?' she said, lowering her voice.

'For God's sake, Rachel, give me credit for some sense!'

'And you'll house my pictures? They should arrive this afternoon. As soon as I can, I'll let you know where to send them.'

'Got it all planned out, haven't you?' Tim said sullenly. 'I hope you realise you're leaving me to face the music?'

'What music?' asked Bobby from the back seat.

'Never mind,' Rachel called. 'It's all right,' she murmured to Tim. 'Malcolm won't want scandal, he won't come near you.'

'I hope you're right,' Tim said with feeling, and they drove in silence to Waverley. A porter was found and Rachel's luggage was taken to the platform. They stood awkwardly together, waiting for the train.

'Rachel—' Tim began.

'Oh, don't,' she said hastily, 'don't say anything.'

'Do you think you'll be all right?'

'Have to be, won't we? Bobby, come here! Don't go near the edge like that!'

'How about your family? I mean, your mother? What's she going to say?'

'I don't know. I'll write to her.' Rachel's face crumpled for a moment, then regained its composure. 'The train's coming. Don't wait, Tim.'

But he did wait, helping the porter to load on her luggage, waving as the London-bound express began to steam away. Neither she nor Bobby waved back.

Chapter Thirty-Seven

The July evening was hot and sultry. Jennie, having opened all the windows in the flat, still felt she couldn't breathe, and when she looked in at the boys saw they had both kicked off their sheets and were snuffling and gasping in their sleep. She straightened their small damp bodies and crept out of their room to sink into her chair, yawning and wishing Rory would come home. He hadn't even been in for his tea, but that was nothing new and at least tonight it was just cold meat and salad, she needn't worry about a meal going to ruin which was so often the case. Perhaps when he did come in, he would be in a better mood than of late, but she doubted it. Ever since the failure of the hunger marchers to achieve anything they wanted he had been very low, the black dog of depression never far away, which meant Jennie was low in spirits too.

Then there was the worry over Rachel. Fanning herself with a knitting pattern, Jennie shook her head over her sister's behaviour. She still hadn't got over the shock of it and neither had Ma. Especially as Malcolm had upset them so much, coming down like a whirlwind that terrible day when he had found Bobby missing. As though they had any idea where Rachel might have gone! The neighbours had certainly enjoyed themselves that evening, Jennie reflected, what with Jessie Rossie hanging out of her sweetie shop to watch Malcolm thundering past, and Marty Finnegan snatching her youngest out of his way and hollering at him to watch where he was going, and Donnie Muir swearing when Malcolm knocked him against the wall as he went rushing up the stair. Jennie herself had come out of her flat because Malcolm had banged on her door in passing, and when she had run up the stair to Ma's, there he was, scarlet in the face and shouting, 'Where is she, where is she?' for everyone to hear. It was so strange, even a bit frightening, for Malcolm was usually so much the gentleman and liked to keep his head and let others have the hysterics. It showed, Rory said, how hard he'd been hit, but it had taken them some time to find out just how hard and what in fact had happened.

Another man, that was it. Malcolm said Rachel had taken up with another man and he had turned her out of the house. Ma had been scandalised, had at first refused to believe it. How could Malcolm be sure about this man, she had tried to ask, but he wasn't interested in giving them the story, only wanted to know where Rachel had gone, because she'd taken Bobby with her and while there was breath in his body he was going to get Bobby back.

'Oh, Malcolm,' Ma had cried 'You didn't try to take Bobby away from her? Oh, that was wrong! No little child should be separated from his mother, whatever she's done!'

'Don't tell me what's right and what's wrong!' Malcolm had stormed. 'Just tell me where Rachel's gone!'

When they had finally made him believe they didn't know where she was, he had gone so white and quiet that Ma had rushed the kettle on to make him some tea, but Rory had gone down to the pub to get him some whisky and that had given him the strength to take himself home. Since then they hadn't seen him, but he had sent word that he was going to employ private detectives to search for Rachel in London, because that was probably where she'd gone. And the letter that Rachel eventually sent did have a London postmark but she said to ignore it, she might well be somewhere else by the time they read it, so if Malcolm came asking, they would know what to say.

'What to say?' Madge repeated blankly. 'There's nothing to say. She tells us nothing!'

'Except that she's all right and Bobby's all right, and that's something,' Jennie said comfortingly.

'Oh, but how could she have been so wicked?' wailed Madge. 'To hurt Malcolm that way, to risk losing her boy!'

'Ma, we don't know the full story.' Jennie had tried to be

loyal to her sister, but in her heart she was sure Rachel had betrayed Malcolm, just for the sake of excitement or some silly reason of that sort. It was all of a piece with her character for her to risk her happiness and other people's for a whim. No doubt she would say it was to do with her artistic temperament. Artists seemed to think they could get away with anything if they pleaded that as an excuse, but in Jennie's eyes it was no excuse at all. There were rules in life and artists should keep them, just like everybody else.

She stirred in her chair, pushing back her damp fair fringe from her brow, then jumped up, smiling with relief. She had heard Rory's step on the stair. For a moment he stood in the doorway and she thought how pale he looked and how thin, his eyes frighteningly large. She ran to him, drawing him to a chair.

'Rory, you're exhausted! What have you been doing with yourself?'

'Just the usual.' He wiped his face with his handkerchief. 'Bit too warm for me today, that's all. Niver did like hot weather.'

'There's some cold supper. Now don't tell me you don't want it.'

'I had a sandwich earlier on. I'll mebbe have it later.'

She shook her head in exasperation. 'Would you like some tea, then? Or lemonade?'

'Aye, a cold drink, that'd be fine.'

As he stood at the open window, drinking the lemonade, trying to find some air, Jennie sat down again. She felt vaguely uneasy, perhaps because there was thunder around. A memory came back to her. Another evening like this one. Her mother and Lily MacLaren at the table, herself in the doorway, knowing what they were talking about. 'Have you heard the news, Jennie? Sheena and Rory are engaged.' Herself, running. Lily's voice coming after her. 'But ha' you seen the ring? A bonnie diamond ...' Jennie leaped up, sending her chair clattering, and Rory swung round.

'I'll put the kettle on,' she gasped. 'I'd like some tea, anyway.'

'Jennie,' said Rory, and there was sweat on his brow, 'can we talk?'

She insisted on making the tea. It gave her something to do.

It put off the talk. For some reason she was sure she knew what he was going to say. At the same time, she didn't believe it. Wouldn't believe it.

When the tea was poured and she could no longer busy herself with cups and milk, she raised her eyes to his.

'All right, then, what do you want to talk to me about?'

He put his hands through his hair. He tried to drink some tea.

'I – I was wondering if you'd heard any more from Rachel?'

'Rachel? You want to talk to me about Rachel?'

'No. I mean, I ken it's worrying you, her going off like that. And Malcolm in such a state—'

'Yes, I feel so sorry for him, Rory. I don't know how Rachel could have done what she did. My own sister!'

'Aye.' Rory looked down at his cup. 'But sometimes, you ken, these things take a hold of you.'

'What things?'

'Well – feelings. They take a hold of you and then you do things you might no' want to do.'

Jennie was very still, very frightened. She seemed to be seeing very clearly, understanding all that was not being said. Rory was not talking about Rachel's feelings, he was talking about his own. He was not trying to explain her actions, he was preparing Jennie for his.

'What is it you don't want to do?' she asked hoarsely, and his head came up sharply and his dark blue eyes flamed in surprise.

'Just tell me, Rory! Don't sit there going round and round it. Tell me so I can be sure.'

'It's Sheena!' he cried. 'I canna live without her. Oh, God, Jennie, you'll have to let me go!'

There it was, then. He had told her. She was sure. She had known, anyway, but to have it put into words made it different. Made it worse. Made it quite unbearable.

'No!' she shrieked. 'No, Rory, no!'

'Jennie, Jennie.' He held her hands as she rocked to and fro in her misery. 'Do you think I want to do this to you? I've been in hell, I'm still in hell. I love you, I love the boys, I dinna want to leave you, but it's like I'm no' ma own man any longer, I've

264

no choice what I do. I have to be with her, because she's in ma blood, the way she was before, and there' s no way I can get her out!'

All the long hours of the evening they sat huddled together in Rory's armchair, Jennie keening like one at a wake, Rory holding her, soothing her, until the night came and they went to bed. Still they lay clasped together, for Jennie couldn't seem to let him go and in any case he didn't want to leave her. She felt no bitterness, only a terrible pain as though she had been shot or stabbed, but the strange thing was she knew she was still precious to him and that he was giving her now all he could. He loved her, but not in the way she loved him. That sort of love he had felt long ago for Sheena and now it was hers again. So there was no hope for Jennie. Rory could no more stop loving Sheena than Jennie could stop loving him. As he said, choice didn't come into it.

But as the first light of morning filtered into their room, Jennie struggled from Rory's arms and fixed him with wild eyes.

'Rory, what about the boys? They're your sons, you can't leave them. What will become of them?'

'I'll send you money, I'll take care of them. I'll take care of you, I promise.'

'How? You've no money. If you leave Edinburgh you'll have no job.'

'I've been offered a job in London, working for one of our MPs.'

'London?' Jennie sank back, filled with despair. 'It's all planned, is it? You'll go with her to London and I'll stay here alone.'

He gave a groan and took her in his arms again. 'Och, I feel so bad, so bad – it's like an illness, it's like going mad. I'm wrecking ma life and I canna seem to stop. I canna eat or sleep or work. Jennie, I tell you I'd give ma soul for her niver to've come back.'

'But she did come back.' Jennie got out of bed and stood looking down at Rory's bent dark head. 'Rory, when will you go?'

'I'm no' sure. Soon. It'll have to be soon.'

'Yes, make it soon.'

Jennie's grief was as strong as ever but it had dulled into a heavy ache around her heart. At that moment she did not know how she was going to live, only knew that she must for the sake of the boys. She could hear them stirring now and while Rory still lay with his head in his pillow, as though he couldn't face the day, she began to get ready. She poured water into her basin, she washed and dressed, she combed her hair. All her moments were slow, she felt there were great weights attached to her arms and legs, but she was keeping going and that was what she had to do.

'I'm going to get the boys up now,' she told Rory, 'then I'll make the breakfast. Will you tell me something first?'

'What?' He lay with his eyes closed.'

'Did she keep the ring? The ring you gave her?'

'For God's sake – I canna tell you. She niver said.'

'She's not wearing it?'

'Of course she's no' wearing it! Jennie, why are you going on about that bloody ring! What's it matter now?'

'I think I must've always thought if she had that ring she'd get you back. But she never needed the ring to do that, did she?'

Somehow they got through breakfast, with the help of the boys behaving just as usual, dropping their bread and butter, wailing over their porridge, wonderfully free of the desolation that was gripping their parents' hearts.

'I'll make arrangements,' Rory said, capturing Hamish who was trying to escape being dressed. 'I'll do all I can, Jennie.'

'Just don't let her come here. I don't want to see her.'

'She won't come.' Rory put on his jacket and cap, keeping his handsome ravaged face turned from her. 'I'll go, then – see to things . . .'

'But you'll be back later?'

'Aye, I'll be back later.'

When the door had closed on him, Jennie stood quite still, listening to his footsteps hurrying away down the stair. The boys were tugging at her skirt and suddenly she gathered them up and ran with them up the stair to her mother's door.

'Ma, are you there?' she cried, hammering with her knuckles.

'Jennie, whatever's wrong?' asked Madge, appearing, white-faced. 'Is it the boys? Has there been an accident?'

'Oh, Ma!' groaned Jennie and fell into her mother's arms.

Chapter Thirty-Eight

In her car parked outside Catherine's Land, Abby was bracing herself for the questions. Had she had a good holiday? What had she seen, what had she done? Where was Frankie? Hadn't he come back with her? She bent her head over the steering wheel, closing her eyes for a moment, then she sighed, picked up her carrier bag of presents and left the car. No point in putting things off any longer. Get it over with, that was the way. Through the familiar door, up the familiar stair, call, 'Jennie, are you there?' But Rory was coming down the stair, Rory, carrying an overcoat and a suitcase, Rory, looking like death.

'Canna stop,' he said at once, sliding his eyes away from Abby's smile of greeting. Her smile froze.

'Rory, what's wrong? Rory, wait!'

But he was away down the stair, head bent, shoulders hunched, and she was left to go up to Jennie's with a terrible fear in her heart.

It was all very quiet. Even Will and Hamish were making no sound, sitting with Madge on the sofa. Jennie, at the table, had dropped her head on her folded arms; she did not look up when Abby came in, but Madge cried out, 'Oh, Abby, you're back! Oh, I'm so glad to see you!'

'Ma, what is it? What's wrong?'

Madge stood up and told the boys in a whisper to go and play in the bedroom, she would come in a moment.

'Wait, I've something for you.' Abby hastily unwrapped the toys she had bought in Portugal. 'See, Will, this is a monkey, if you turn the key he climbs. And Hamish, this is a little horse – look at his lovely soft mane – would you like to stroke it?'

'Abby, that's good of you.' Madge shepherded the boys into the bedroom and slightly closed the door on their delighted cries. 'They'll be all right there for a little while.' She turned a ravaged face. 'He's gone, Abby, Rory's gone.'

Abby wasted no time on expressions of surprise. She sat down by Jennie at the table and made her sister lift her head. 'Tell me about it,' she said quietly.

The telling didn't take long and Abby never said she'd had her own fears ever since seeing Rory and Sheena together in Princes Street. It was Madge who did most of the talking, but Jennie suddenly cried out, her dull eyes catching fire, 'I feel so bitter, Abby! I hate them both! I never want to see them again, never!'

'I don't blame you.' Abby gently held her sister's hands. 'It's only natural.'

'Yes, but to begin with I didn't feel like that. I felt terrible pain, but I wasn't bitter. I sort of accepted it, didn't I, Ma? I felt if it was me wanting to go away with Rory, I'd have to go.'

'Not if you were married to someone else, Jennie, not if you had children.'

'No, I see that now, that's the difference. I couldn't have left my family.' Jennie pulled her hands free and put her hair back from her face, which seemed so pinched and strange it was scarcely the face of the sister Abby knew. 'Maybe I was really thinking all along that when it came to it he wouldn't go, he'd never leave me and the boys. But he came in today and said it was all arranged, he'd a job and a place to go to in London, he'd be sending money every week, and he went into the bedroom and started to pack his things' – Jennie's voice trembled – 'and the boys said, where are you going, Dad? And he couldn't answer' – Jennie covered her face with her hand and let the tears flow through her fingers – 'and I realised he meant to go and he wouldn't be coming back—'

'Except to see the boys,' Madge said flatly. 'The cheek of it, Abby! He expects to see the boys whenever he feels like coming up from London!'

'He might be able to claim that right,' Abby said unwillingly. 'At least, if there's a divorce.'

'There's not going to be any divorce,' Jennie declared harshly.

269

'He will never be able to marry her, I'll never let that happen. And he's not going to see the boys, either. He's forfeited that right, I don't care what anybody says. He's left us and we'll do without him, all of us. That's the way it's going to be.'

'But you must let him pay maintenance,' cried Abby. 'It would be foolish to turn that down for the sake of pride.'

'Yes, I know I need it for the boys, but as soon as I can, I'll do without it.' Jennie stood up. 'I'll go and see what the boys are doing. Ma, you'd better tell Abby about Rachel.'

Abby listened, stunned. She had always thought that Rachel might leave Malcolm, but only when she was ready and when all the conditions were exactly what she wanted. But to be stupid enough to let herself be caught with a lover, to risk losing her son, to have to run away and elude private detectives . . .

'I can't believe it!' Abby cried, 'I can't take it in!'

'Exactly how I feel,' Madge said. 'In fact, I'm reeling. All I've ever wanted was for you girls to find your happiness, and now there's this terrible thing that's happened to Jennie, and Rachel's had to run away we don't know where.' Madge shook her head. 'At least you and Frankie are working things out for yourselves, I can take comfort in that.'

'Ma, would you like to see your present?' Abby asked quickly. 'It's a shawl, I got one for Jennie, too, really pretty, I bought them in Portugal—'

'Oh, Abby,' Madge said tiredly, 'what's wrong?'

Until the very last night there had been no hint that anything was wrong. The cruise to Spain and Portugal had been a tremendous success. Frankie had only had to be on duty in the evenings, so every day and every night they had been free to take delight in being together, had felt they were in the golden glow of honeymoon, from Palma and Alicante, to Cadiz and Portugal. Abby had never been so happy. Then the last night came and Frankie said there was something he must tell her, before they docked next day in Southampton. She had been packing in her cabin, humming to herself, quite unaware until she looked up and saw his eyes that a blow was about to fall. But his eyes were desolate.

'Tell me?' she repeated, still folding clothes. 'Tell me what?'

She had the silly feeling that if she appeared calm, the blow wouldn't land.

'Abby, I've been asked to go to New York.' Frankie was now keeping his eyes down. 'An American guy on the last cruise said he really liked ma style, he said he could get me an opening with a radio band. A radio band in New York! I mean, would I no' be a fool to turn it down?'

Abby closed the lid of her case. 'The pay's good, is it?'

'Terrific. I could earn more in a year there than five at home.'

'So how long would you go for?'

'Well, he's offering a two-year contract. He reckons he could get me that, even though I'm no' an American citizen. They're keen on the Scots, he says—'

'You met this American on the last cruise, not this one,' Abby said slowly. 'So you knew about this offer before I came and you never said?'

'He said he'd give me time to think it over.'

'And you didn't feel you should discuss it?' Abby's eyes were glistening with tears. 'Frankie, I can't believe it! When I was so happy because we'd worked everything out? When we were going home to announce our marriage and you were going to find a job in Edinburgh?'

'I'd niver have found a job in Edinburgh as good as yours,' Frankie said quietly. 'I'd've been playing in some pub and drinking maself stupid and you'd have been ashamed of me. You ken that's the truth.'

'I do not, Frankie! That is not the truth! How can you even say it?'

'Abby, let's be honest, eh? Things'll be better this way.'

'You've accepted the offer?' she asked, trembling.

'Aye, I have.'

'You're not coming back with me to Edinburgh at all?'

'No, I'm sailing for New York next week.'

She turned aside, stricken, and when he tried to put his arms around her she pushed him away. 'What's the next step?' she asked over her shoulder. 'You want a divorce?'

'Abby!' He went white. 'I niver said that, I niver said I wanted to be free!'

'With you in New York and me in Edinburgh, maybe I'd like to be free myself.'

'Abby, Abby, dinna talk like that!' He caught her to him again. 'There's no call to talk about divorce, I'm no' going to be away for ever!'

'And the situation's going to change, is it, while you're in New York? Frankie, it's never going to change. If you want the truth, there it is.'

'Oh, God, Abby, you're tearing me to pieces!'

'And what have you done to me? Letting me come on this cruise, making me feel so happy, and all the time, behind my back, planning to go to America!'

'You could come with me,' he said eagerly, as she jerked herself from his arms and stood with her hands over her face. 'Why not, Abby? Give up Logie's. Come with me and see America, let's enjoy ourselves! I can support you now, we dinna need your money—'

She lowered her hands and stood staring into his face. 'You haven't listened to a word I've ever said, have you? All those times I told you I wanted to work, to have a career of my own? You used to say we wanted different things, but secretly you've been hoping all along I'd still want what you want, haven't you? I think it's your turn to face the truth, Frankie.' She moved to the door of the cabin and twisted down the handle. 'Will you go now, please? I'm tired. I don't want to talk any more tonight.'

Without a word Frankie left her.

'There it is, Ma,' Abby said, after a long silence. 'Frankie's gone to New York. He won't be back for two years.' As Madge caught her breath, Abby added bluntly, 'If at all.'

'Abby, that's awful,' Jennie said from the doorway. She was holding Hamish, who was rapturously cuddling his new horse. 'We'd no idea!'

'Neither had I, Jennie.'

'All three of you,' Madge was whispering. 'I can't believe it. All three of you. On your own!'

'Why not?' cried Jennie. 'I've decided women are better off without men. It's different for you, Ma, because Dad didn't choose to go, but look what happened when you thought of getting married again, how miserable you were, weren't you? We should all steer clear of men.'

272

'For shame, Jennie, think about your Will and Hamish!' Madge exclaimed.

'And it's not only men who betray,' Abby said quietly. 'Malcolm's had a raw deal from Rachel, hasn't he?'

Jennie shrugged, her face dark with pain. 'She's the exception. It's men who are usually to blame, and they should never be forgiven. You may be prepared to forgive Frankie—'

Abby interrupted. 'Forgiveness doesn't come into it, Jennie. I know Frankie never meant to hurt me. He just found it impossible to live the way I wanted him to.'

'But I shall never forgive Rory,' Jennie finished. 'Don't ask me to, I could never do it.'

'Who's asking?' Abby said sadly.

Chapter Thirty-Nine

It felt late when Abby left Catherine's Land, though it was only mid-evening. Exhausted and depressed, she stood with her hand on her car door, considering the lonely drive back to Queensferry, the lonely cottage, the lonely bed. She couldn't face them, at least, not then. Jennie's misery and her own were pressing on her spirit like physical weights, she must find relief, even if it were only temporary.

Maybe she would go to the pictures, or a concert, anything that would fill her mind. She bought an evening paper and saw they were doing Maugham's *Circle* at the King's. She had never cared for W.S. Maugham; all the same, she found herself driving to the theatre and squeezing into a parking place.

'Any tickets left?' she asked at the box office.

'Plenty,' the woman assistant answered. 'It's this hot weather, puts folk off.'

'I'll have a back stall,' said Abby, and with her programme bought chocolates, as though she were a child and could cheer herself with sugar. There was no one well known in the play and, as she looked round the half-empty theatre, doggedly chewing on a caramel, she felt no lift to her depression. Maybe she'd have done as well to go home and read a book, only whatever she read she knew Frankie's dancing eyes would have come between her and the print. As she folded the programme and laid it down, something made her pick it up again. A name was tugging at her subconscious, a name buried deep, not thought of for years. She read the cast list again and there it was. Alan Talbot. Who was Alan Talbot? A young man with spots who had tried for Accounts but who might have been

274

given Carpets, a young man who had wanted to become an actor.

Good Lord, thought Abby, he made it! And she waited with some interest for the curtain to rise.

The set was a stately home drawing room, filled with Georgian props and showing through the usual french windows a fine painted garden. Alan Talbot was first on, playing Arnold Champion-Cheney, MP, and Abby certainly wouldn't have recognised him. No spots now. In fact, he was handsome, his dark hair sleek and well cut, his mouth an actor's mouth, mobile and tender, ready to smile, though for the character he was playing he seemed to have to keep the smiles in check. Abby knew very little about acting, but it seemed to her that he handled his part well in this play about adultery and betrayal that might have been too near the bone for comfort if it hadn't been so frivolously presented. When it was over, she clapped hard to make up for the lack of applause from the people who weren't there, feeling sympathy for the actors, acting still as they took their bows looking brightly round at the sparse audience. When the curtain finally stayed down and people began to trail away, Abby found herself making for the stage door.

She had no idea why, unless it was to postpone again her solitary drive home, but as the cast began to emerge, all looking unrecognisable away from the stage, she suddenly felt a fool. Hardly the thing for a newly promoted partner of Logie's, was it, to hang around with a few young people, waiting for a man she didn't know? She was turning away, relieved not to have gone further with a crazy idea, when she saw Alan Talbot appear and stand in the doorway, taking deep breaths of the night air. He was alone, no other fans seemed to be approaching. Oh, why not? thought Abby, and held out her programme.

'Excuse me – would you care to . . .' She couldn't quite get the words out in her embarrassment, but as he took out his pen to sign her programme he gave such a radiant smile, her heart lightened. Poor chap, he was an actor, he liked appreciation, maybe this wasn't such a crazy idea after all.

'Of course, I'd be delighted,' he murmured, scrawling his name. 'Did you enjoy the play?'

275

'Oh, yes, very much. I thought you played your part very well, and I just wanted to tell you, I'm glad you made it.'

He raised his eyebrows. 'I'm sorry – have we met?'

'Once.' She felt strangely at ease with him, standing outside the theatre in the summer night. 'Remember an interview at Logie's? For a junior job in Accounts?'

'Oh, my God!' His face was breaking into a grin. 'And I thought I might be offered Carpets and you got the job! Have you really remembered, after all these years! Oh, look, this calls for a celebration. Could you come for a drink? I mean, if you've got the time? Or even supper?'

'A drink would be fine.' Abby could scarcely believe she was accepting, but there she was, walking with him to her car and still not finding it strange. They drove down to the North British where over drinks in the cocktail bar, Abby told Alan she was married, her name was Mrs Baxter, and she was still at Logie's.

'Doing what?' he asked. 'Don't tell me – something grand?'

'I don't know about grand. Mr Farrell has just made me a junior partner.'

Alan Talbot laughed, running his hand over his face, shaking his head as his light brown eyes rested on her face.

'No wonder I didn't have a hope in hell at that interview! A junior partner – wow! You know, it doesn't surprise me, doesn't surprise me at all. It's much more surprising that I got to be an actor. Your talent was obvious, mine, let's say somewhat hidden!'

'You've done well,' she told him seriously. 'You wanted to act and you did. I admire you. In fact I sometimes used to wonder if I dared ask your father about you when he came in for meetings, but I never plucked up courage.'

'Then of course he died,' Alan said sombrely. 'I more or less lost contact with Edinburgh after that. My mother moved to St Andrews, my sister married and went south, I'd no reason to come back. Except for something like this play I'm in now.'

'Did you ever marry?' Abby asked.

'Tried it. Didn't last.' He shrugged. 'My wife didn't like my hours, or my pay. Well, it's true, I don't earn much.' He grinned. 'But I don't care about big money or having my name in lights, I've got what I wanted. So, I can tell, have you.'

Abby looked into her glass. 'Not altogether.'

'I'm sorry. Look, I didn't mean to embarrass you—'

'It's all right. I'm just feeling rather low tonight. My husband's gone to America. I'm not sure if he'll come back.'

'I see.' Alan looked as if he didn't know what to say, Abby wondered why she had given him such a confidence, yet didn't regret it. She still felt at ease with him, as though he were an old friend, which was hard to explain but pleasant.

'Another drink?' he asked quietly, but she shook her head.

'Thanks, but I'd better not, I have to drive back to South Queensferry. I've rented a cottage there.'

'I was hoping I could persuade you to have supper with me. No? Well, at least let me see you to your car.'

When she had opened her car door they stood looking at each other for some moments. Alan took her hand.

'It's been wonderful to meet you again, Mrs Baxter—'

'Please, call me Abby. I feel I've known you for years.'

'I feel the same.' He hesitated. 'The play closes here tomorrow night, then it's Perth and Aberdeen and back to London. I wish we could have met again.'

'So do I. You've made me feel so much better.'

'Really?' He gave a pleased smile. 'I'm glad. You made me feel pretty good too, you know. Actors like to be asked for autographs. If they're not famous, like me.'

She laughed. 'Well, I'll keep it and then when you are famous I shall sell it for a lot of money.'

'There speaks the accountant!' He watched her settle herself behind the wheel. 'Listen, if I'm up here again, may I ring you?'

'I'm not on the phone at the cottage but you can always reach me at Logie's.'

'I just ask for the boss?'

They both laughed, then he closed her car door, waved as she drove away and watched her out of sight.

On the drive home she found herself thinking of Gerald Farrell. That first evening when he had taken her to dinner she had thought the worst of him, but he had only wanted somebody to stave off the loneliness. She'd done that for him and now Alan Talbot had done as much for her. But then she and Gerald had fallen in love. At least there was no question of that with Alan.

277

The next day, her first back at Logie's after the cruise, she bit on the bullet and announced that she was married, adding that she would still be known at work as Miss Ritchie. Weathering the storm of interest that this caused, she felt a great relief. She had done what she had said she would do and even if Frankie knew nothing about it, her conscience was clear.

That afternoon when she was catching up on her paperwork, flowers were delivered to her office. 'For Mrs Abby Baxter,' said the messenger and her heart leaped. Frankie? Could Frankie possibly have sent her flowers? He'd known she would be coming back to work that day, but would he have risked using her married name? She tore open the little envelope.

'With thanks again for saving me from Carpets and for joining me for that very pleasant drink, your sincere fan, Alan.'

'Aren't they beautiful?' one of her assistants murmured, and Abby said, yes, the flowers were very beautiful. She was in fact touched and pleased by Alan's thought, but her own thoughts were with a bright-eyed, curly haired man walking the decks of a liner on its way to New York.

Chapter Forty

Madge was walking in Princes Street Gardens, only to get a breath of air and a guilty little break from Jennie's sorrow. Not that she could take a break from her own anxieties, the despair of knowing that all her girls were unhappy, that all their marriages appeared to have been disastrous mistakes. There was nothing she could do about it, of course, but that didn't make things any better; no, made them worse. If you could roll up your sleeves and do something, you could face your life. If you were helpless as she was, you just had to let the tide of misery sweep over you and hope not to drown.

It was a warm afternoon. The gardens were full of summer visitors, exclaiming over the floral clock, sitting listening to the band, buying ices. Madge's thoughts went back to that afternoon long ago when she had sat in these same gardens with her girls and Abby had bought them all cornets. Then Jim Gilbride had appeared, tipping his hat, letting the sun turn his brown hair to burning red. How young she had felt then! Quite a girl, though she'd been nearly middle-aged. And now was nearly fifty. Curiously, she still didn't feel any older, even though she was a grandmother and loaded down with care. Perhaps people didn't ever feel old inside. Perhaps it was always going to be a surprise to look in the mirror and find that the years must have passed, for whose was that stranger's face? Actually, Madge knew that she had aged very little, so perhaps she'd been lucky, but the truth of it was she didn't envy the young. Their troubles were no lighter than her own.

She walked the length of the gardens, smiling at the children playing on the grass, then found a seat to rest a while before going back. She mustn't be out too long, never liked to leave poor Jennie too long on her own.

'Madge,' said a voice and she looked up and caught her breath. She felt she was in a moving picture she'd already seen, for here was Jim Gilbride standing over her again, still tipping his hat, still letting his hair that was now beginning to show grey catch the sun and seem to blaze, as it had done all those years before.

'Jim?' she whispered, shading her eyes from the shock of seeing him as much as the sun. 'Have you been to see Jennie?'

'Aye, come over as soon as I got her letter. She said you'd be down here, didna want to miss you.' Jim glanced at the elderly couple sitting further along the bench and taking Madge's hand brought her to her feet. 'Let's walk a bit, eh?'

Again the film seemed to be rerunning, as they walked together arm in arm, the years collapsing, melting, the past and the present mixing.

'Poor wee lassie,' Jim was muttering, bringing them firmly back to the present. 'If I could get ma hands on that son o' mine! What in God's name was he thinking of, to take up wi' that little hussy and leave his wife and bonnie boys?' Jim turned a stormy gaze on Madge. 'Our grandchildren, Madge!'

'I know, I know. But Rory always did care for Sheena and when she came back . . .' Madge sighed heavily. 'I suppose he lost his head.'

'He'd lose his head if I caught up wi' him. I've a good mind to go down to London and sort him out!'

'It wouldn't do any good trying that, Jim. You've no control over him now. Any more than I have over Rachel.'

'She's just such another. Begging your pardon, Madge, I niver did think she was right for Malcolm. I always said she'd bring him to rue.'

'I feel so ashamed, Jim,' Madge said in a low voice. 'So sad for Malcolm. But what can I do?'

'Nothing, it's no' your fault.' Jim stopped and looked down into her face. 'Och, you've let them wear you out, Madge, all they girls o' yours. Abby, as well. Jennie told me she'd split wi' Frankie.'

'It was Frankie who wanted to go to America,' Madge began, but then her face crumpled in desolation. 'All three of them, Jim, can you believe it? All three of them miserable, and all I ever wanted was their happiness!'

'Aye.' Jim glanced at his watch. 'Madge, time's getting on. Shall we go somewhere for a bite to eat?'

'I can't do that, Jim, I'm sorry. I have to get back to Jennie.'

'I said I might take you somewhere. She's no expecting you.'

Madge hesitated. 'I don't think we should be having meals together,' she said bravely. 'There's Bella.'

Jim's face turned a dusky red. 'You ken fine we've split up, Madge.'

'No, I didn't know that. Not for sure.'

'Aye, well, it's true. Bella's still in Clydebank, I've moved back to Glasgow.'

'Jim, I'm sorry.'

He laughed. 'Och, we should niver have wed in the first place. I only married her because of you. I wanted to show I could do without you, find another woman better than you.' Again he gave a short mirthless laugh. 'Judgment on me, eh? Your turn to laugh, Madge.'

'I'm not laughing. I never wanted you to be unhappy.'

'Just wanted to please your girls, that was what you wanted.'

'You've never forgiven me for that, have you?'

She began to walk on but he caught her by the hand. 'I have, then. I've thought about it for years and I can see now you were right to think o' them. The thing is, have you forgiven me?'

'Jim, it was all years ago, I don't even think about it.'

'Spoiled our lives, Madge.' As she stood silent, her hand still in his, he said, quietly, 'Come on, let's go for our tea. Where's the harm?'

Still she hesitated, feeling the power of his gaze, the strength of his hand holding hers. What was a meal, after all? If he and Bella were separated where, as Jim said, was the harm?

'All right,' she said slowly. 'I'd like to, Jim.'

Immediately he tucked her hand into his arm and marched her fast away before she could change her mind.

They found a little cafe in the West End where they had steak and kidney pie, peas and mashed potatoes, followed by apple tart and a pot of tea.

'Grand,' said Jim. 'Enjoy it, Madge?'

'I did, it was lovely. Thank you very much, Jim, I hope it wasn't too dear.'

'I'd pay a lot more than that to have a meal with you, Madge. Anyway, I'm no' so badly off, now that I'm no' wi' Bella.'

Madge flushed as she drank her tea, wishing he wouldn't talk about his wife, but he seemed unaware of her embarrassment.

'Och, what a spendthrift she was, eh? I couldna keep her going, money went through her fingers like sand. And her cooking' – he shook his head – 'niver had an idea. Threw the stuff in the oven and hoped for the best. I'm no' sure how I'm alive to tell the tale!'

'Oh, Jim!' Madge laughed in spite of herself. 'I think you're exaggerating.'

'Aye, well, mebbe.' Jim leaned forward. 'It's a nice evening, shall we walk a bit?'

'I'd really rather get back, Jim, if you don't mind. Jennie's so low, you see.'

'I'll get the bill, then,' he said without argument, and she breathed a sigh of relief.

All the way back to the Lawnmarket they talked easily without constraint. Madge thought she had never known Jim so honey-sweet. For some reason he seemed to be on his best behaviour, unless he had mellowed and was always like this. Or was he just trying to make up for what Rory had done? Seeing her daughter's expressionless face and dead gaze, Madge knew no one could do that.

'Want any tea?' Jennie asked listlessly, but they told her they'd had some.

'I thought I might have helped getting the boys to bed,' Madge murmured, and Jim chimed in that he'd rather wanted to see his grandsons again before he left.

'I'm sorry, I put them to bed early.' Jennie cleared a pile of ironing from a chair. 'Sit down, then, won't you?'

'Mustn't stay too long,' said Jim, 'I just wanted to see that you were all right.'

'I'm fine, thanks.'

He took out a small envelope and placed it on the table. 'That's for the boys, Jennie.'

'I really don't want—'

'For the boys, I said. You canna refuse me.'

'Thanks, then, thanks very much.'

'And you'll be sure to tell me if you need anything, eh? I want to help.'

'I'll let you know, I promise.'

'Well, I'd better be on ma way. ' Jim stood awkwardly at the door. 'Jennie, there's no' much anybody can say . . .'

'I know. I'm just grateful to you for coming over.' Jennie passed her hand across her brow and tried to smile. 'Think I'll have an early night myself. I've been sewing too long, it's given me a headache. Goodnight, Mr Gilbride, thanks again.' She kissed him briefly on the cheek. 'Goodnight, Ma.'

'Jennie, would you like me to stay?' Madge asked, anxiously. 'Make you a drink, or something?'

Jennie shook her head. 'I'd rather get to bed, Ma, thanks all the same. See you in the morning.' They kissed, affectionately, then Jennie quietly closed her door.

'Oh, dear,' Madge sighed, facing Jim under the same flickering gas jet that had lit their meetings in the old days. 'If I could just wave a magic wand – put the clock back . . .'

'You'd no' be the first to wish that.'

'I know. Are you going back to Malcolm's?'

'He's away to London. Seeking your Rachel.'

'I know she's behaved very badly, Jim, and I'm ashamed of her, but I do wish I knew where she was. You can't blame me for worrying.'

'Aye, when she's got the wean with her and all.' Jim's gaze was as intent on Madge's face as it had always been in that place under that light. 'I'd best be getting away for ma train, then, unless . . .'

'Unless what?' Madge looked at him apprehensively.

'Well, there's plenty trains to Glasgow. I could stay on a bit, if you like.' He took a step towards her. 'I could come up the stair, eh? You could make me some tea.'

'It's not long since we had tea, Jim.'

'We could just have a bit chat, then. It's no' often we get the chance, is it?'

Under his compelling gaze, Madge was like someone hypnotised. She turned and led the way up the stair to her room, conscious all the time of that gaze following her, burning like a flame.

'I remember this room when Rory had it,' Jim murmured, looking round at Madge's things, her rocking chair, her ornaments and vase of flowers, her neatly made bed in the corner. 'Looks better now, I can tell you.'

Madge hung her jacket on a peg behind the door and put her hat in the one cupboard. Her hands were shaking.

'You did well to let Jennie have your place,' Jim remarked from the window, where he had been looking out at the last of the evening light. 'Cut down your own space, though.'

'I didn't mind, I didn't need it.'

'Always were generous.' He turned to look at her. 'You havena changed, Madge, havena changed in any way.'

'That's silly, Jim. I'm forty-nine, of course I've changed.'

'No' to me.' He crossed the floor and took her in his arms. 'I've niver stopped thinking of you, Madge. It was wrong, I was married to Bella, but I couldna help it. Now Bella's no' with me, will you tell me, did you iver think of me?'

'You're still married,' she said uneasily. 'We shouldn't be talking like this.'

'Bella's left me, I'm on ma own, we'll likely get a divorce. Does that no' make any difference?'

'A divorce?' Madge, still circled in his arms was breathing fast. 'You'd never be able to manage it, Jim, you couldn't afford it.'

'I could, I'd save up, I'd sell something . . .' He kept staring down into her face as though his eyes would never be satisfied, and when she would have drawn away, he held her closer. 'I'd do anything to be free, if you'd have me, Madge.' He ran his hand down her cheek. 'You're no' afraid o' me? I couldna bear to think you were still afraid.'

'I'm not, Jim, I'm not,' she said at once, but she was and he knew.

'I'm no' the man I was, you have to believe that. You have to trust me.'

Trust. Yes, there had to be that. And as Jim's eyes, so full of love still searched her face, Madge suddenly let go. All that she had put between them for so many years went down and she gave in to herself and him.

284

'I trust you, Jim,' she whispered.

He gave a long sigh and they clung together, holding fast as though they daren't let go, then began to kiss and kissing as they went moved slowly to Madge's bed. She was afraid now but only of making love. It had been so long, she felt she should be crying, 'No, no, I can't, I can't,' but Jim was so tender, so caring, so unlike his own violent image, she felt a great passion of love for him taking hold of her and so surprised him by her own response, he groaned, 'Oh, Madge, why'd we wait so long? All these years we've let go by!'

'Don't think of it,' she told him, not willing to argue over whose fault it had been that they had lost the years. 'We're together now, let's think of that.'

But the reaction came when they were dressed again and looking at each other with soft sweet glances like a couple of young things, yet devastated because they had to part.

'Why did I ever marry Bella?' Jim muttered, holding his head in his hands. 'Just to spite you, Madge, and look where it's got me!'

'You said you'd try for a divorce? Could you really afford one?'

'I told you, I'd do anything!' He looked at her with sudden fear. 'But if I canna manage it, if it's just no' possible, will you no' see me again?'

'It's all upside down,' she said slowly. 'My world, I mean. I don't know where I am. But I don't want to lose you again, Jim. I know I don't want that.'

'Madge!' He held her hands, his eyes shining. 'Could you no come to Glasgow? I'd niver dare give up ma job to come here, I might niver get another and I need all the money I can get. But you could come to me.'

'I couldn't leave Jennie, Jim. Not just now.'

'No. No, I can see that.' For some moments they sat together in silence, then Jim's face lightened.

'It's like I told you, Madge,' he said, softly, 'there's plenty trains to Glasgow. And back again.'

She went down with him to the street door where they clung together, kissing again, Madge for once not looking round to see if anyone was watching. In fact no one was about and when Jim had finally torn himself away, Madge crept back to her flat, too dazed to think of sleep.

'It's all so upside down,' she had said, and so it was. Once again, Jim Gilbride had turned her whole world into confusion, but the strange sweet thing was that she didn't mind. They had hurt each other badly in the past, she had convinced herself for years that she was better off without him and glad that he had taken on Bella. But now Bella was gone and their feeling for each other had returned, they had slept together and it didn't seem wrong, seemed wonderfully, gloriously right. Though as she rocked herself smiling in her chair, Madge still couldn't believe it. Had she really gone to bed with Jim Gilbride? Had the roof not fallen in, was she still there, herself, in her chair? She had feared and dreaded and secretly wanted it for so long, it didn't seem posssible that it had come at last, but she didn't regret it. Even when she thought of Will, she couldn't wish it undone. For Will, in spite of her love for him, had become more and more shadowy over the years. She was alive and love was for the living. She must take it when she could.

When she finally fell asleep it seemed only a few moments before the light was streaming through her curtains and someone was banging on her door.

'What is it, what is it?' she cried.

'Ma, are you awake?' came Jennie's voice. 'Malcolm's here and he's found Rachel!'

Chapter Forty-One

Two days before, Arthur Bartlett, Malcolm's private detective in London, had telephoned him.

'Miss Kitty Lane, that's the one, sir. She's a lecturer at the Slade School of Fine Art.'

'My wife is with her?'

'In a flat off Russell Square.'

'What about my boy?'

'He's there too, no need to worry. Do I take it you'll be coming down, sir?'

'By the first train tomorrow morning. I'll ring you from King's Cross.'

The house was three-storeyed Victorian, in need of paint but not too run down. Arthur Bartlett, parked at a discreet distance away, pointed out the bay windows of the middle floor.

'That's the flat, Mr Gilbride, and there's my operative in the blue van across the street. I'll just have a word with him, if you'll excuse me.'

Malcolm watched with agonised eyes as the professionally nondescript figure of Mr Bartlett strolled across to the blue van. He appeared to be asking directions, pointing down the street, nodding his head in its grey trilby. Then the blue van moved away and Mr Bartlett returned to his own car.

'Miss Lane's out, sir, probably at work, she went out early this morning. The dark-haired lady and the little boy are out, too. They've been gone about an hour. I'm afraid it's going to mean a wait, sir.'

'I'm prepared.' Malcolm took out his cigarettes. 'If they've been gone an hour they should be back soon. My wife won't keep Bobby out too long.'

He was right. After a half-hour of chat from Mr Bartlett and silence from Malcolm, Malcolm stiffened and caught his breath. Mr Bartlett followed his sharpened gaze.

'You see them, sir? Yes, there's a young lady and a little boy. Looks like they've been shopping.'

Malcolm ran his tongue over his dry lips. 'That's my wife,' he said thickly, 'and that's Bobby'. He began to fumble with the handle of the car door. 'Thanks, Mr Bartlett, you don't need to wait. Just send me your bill—'

'But Mr Gilbride, won't you be needing the car? What are exactly you planning to do, sir?'

'You know what I'm planning to do!' Malcolm answered, over his shoulder. He was already running towards Rachel and Bobby on the doorstep of the house. 'Goodbye, Mr Bartlett!'

'Daddy! Daddy!' shrieked Bobby, hurling himself into Malcolm's arms. 'I knew you'd find me! I knew you would!'

'Oh, God, how did you?' Rachel asked simply.

Over Bobby's head, Malcolm asked, 'Will you please open the door?'

In the upstairs bay-windowed sitting room, filled with abstract canvases and spindly thin furniture, Rachel sat down by the marble fireplace and took off her hat.

'Kitty's out, so you needn't meet her.' She pointed to a chair. 'I suppose you'd better sit down.'

'Thank you.' Malcolm took Bobby on his knee.

'Bobby can go and play with his toys in the bedroom.'

'He's staying here, he wants to be with me.'

'How can he stay when we have to talk?'

'We don't have to talk, we've nothing to say.'

Bobby lying back against Malcolm, smiled and pulled at his father's tie. 'Did you bring me anything, Daddy?'

'I'm sorry, I didn't, Bobby, I didn't have time. We'll get something tomorrow, eh, when we're back in Edinburgh.'

'Are we going home?' cried Bobby. 'Mummy, did you hear what Daddy said? We're going home!'

'How can you?' Rachel whispered, her face flushing scarlet. 'How can you do this to him, Malcolm?'

'Would it be too much to ask for a cup of tea?' Malcolm

swung Bobby from his knee and stood up. 'Then I think we'd better make a start on packing Bobby's things.'

Rachel gave a great sob and covered her face with her hands. 'I was so sure you wouldn't find me!' she wailed. 'I was so sure you wouldn't think of coming here when you'd never met Kitty!'

'Don't give me much credit for intelligence, do you?' Malcolm asked dryly, as Bobby ran to Rachel and put his arms around her. 'All I did was find out from the art college which of your contemporaries had moved down here, then the detectives did the rest. I guessed you'd hole up with somebody you knew.'

'I was planning to move on, I was thinking of going to the West Country, you'd never have found me there!'

'Rachel, this is all a waste of time. I have found you and I'm taking Bobby home. Why not let's get on with packing his things?'

'Because he is not going!' she cried, leaping to her feet. 'I'll never part with him, never! You'll have to divorce me, you'll have to get custody, and even then I'll never let you have him. You can't bring him up, he needs me, he needs his mother. Ma wouldn't be the same, and anyway she'd never agree to it, she'd never let you keep me from my son!'

Malcolm, ashen-faced stood very still, his sandy head bent. 'Bobby,' he said, at last, 'maybe you'd better go and sort out your toys, eh? While Mummy and I have a talk?'

'Mummy, I don't want to stay in London,' Bobby stammered, 'I don't like it here, I want to go home, I want to go home with Daddy.'

'And leave me here alone?' asked Rachel, snatching him to her. 'You wouldn't want to do that, Bobby? You wouldn't want to leave me here alone?'

'No, I want you to come!'

'But if I can't?'

'I want you to, I want you to!'

'Oh, God, Rachel, you'd better come with us,' Malcolm groaned. 'There's nothing else to be done.'

They drank tea from large pottery beakers and ate bread and butter and jam, sitting round the kitchen table, as though they were an ordinary happy family.

'I haven't eaten anything all day,' Malcolm murmured. 'This bread tastes good.'

'It's not a patch on Mackenzie's,' Rachel answered listlessly. 'Malcolm, how can I come back with you?'

Malcolm's gaze flickered to Bobby, but he seemed to have lost interest in his parents and was cutting up his bread and butter into small squares.

'For his sake,' Malcolm said, very low, 'I am prepared to take you back.'

'It wouldn't work, it wouldn't work.' Rachel put her hand to her eyes. 'You know it wouldn't.'

'Obviously, it's not going to be easy—'

'No, it's out of the question.'

'You're not even going to try?'

She stared at him, her face working, then she jumped to her feet and ran out of the kitchen.

'Bobby, into the bedroom for a minute, there's a good boy,' said Malcolm. 'Make a start on packing your toys.'

'Can I take my bread and butter?'

'Yes, yes, take it.' Malcolm ran to the sitting room where he found Rachel at the window, staring down at the traffic winding through the street below. She looked round at his entrance, dabbing at her eyes with her handkerchief.

'I didn't want to go, you know, you threw me out,' she whispered. 'But now that I'm away I know it would be no use going back. You'd always be holding it against me, wouldn't you, what I'd done?'

'Do you blame me?'

'No, but it would be impossible for us to live like that, wouldn't it?'

'I don't think you have any idea what you did to me,' he said heavily. 'The worst of it is, I know you couldn't have done it if you'd loved me.'

'No, that's not true!'

'Why did you, then? Because you were bored?'

'No.' She hesitated. 'I know this sounds silly, but – well, I did it to get even with you.'

'Get even with me?' Malcolm's eyes were outraged. 'That's not silly, it's crazy. What did I ever do to you to make you think of something like that?'

290

'I always resented the way you could rule my life, because you had money and I hadn't.'

'Rule your life? That's a laugh!'

'When it came down to it, Malcolm, you always got your own way.'

'And you thought marriage meant getting your own way?' Malcolm gave a grim smile. 'Well, if it's any comfort to you, you did get even with me, by God you did!'

'I'm sorry, Malcolm, I really am,' Rachel murmured, desolately. 'I never meant you to find out, you see.'

'You mean I wasn't meant to know? Where was the satisfaction then?'

'Well, I knew,' she answered quietly, and Malcolm, shaking his head, dropped into a chair.

'Oh, God, Rachel, what are we going to do? Bobby's the one we really have to think about.'

'I agree.'

He raised his eyes. 'It's funny, but I never knew he meant so much to you. I thought when I told you to go, you'd be quite happy to leave him.'

She gave him a solemn dark stare. 'We've lived together all these years and you could think that? You don't know me at all, do you?'

'Snap.' Malcolm stood up. 'Rachel, whatever it costs us we're going to go back home, the three of us. I'm prepared to admit I was hard on you in the early days, but we'll just have to put everything in the past behind us and get on with our lives. What do you say?'

'You're prepared to do that?'

'For Bobby's sake.' His gaze on her face wavered. 'And because – I suppose I still love you.' Before she could speak he moved away. 'Will you get ready, then? I'd like to catch the sleeper.'

'Malcolm, is it true?' cried Madge. 'Have you found Rachel?

He had been sitting collapsed in a chair in Jennie's flat but stood up and kissed Madge on the cheek. 'Yes, I've found her. And I've brought her back.'

'Oh, thank God for that! Where is she? Where's Bobby?'

'Waiting in the taxi outside. We've just got off the sleeper, came straight here.' Malcolm ran his hand over his badly shaved chin. 'I'm sorry I don't look too spruce—'

'Why doesn't Rachel come up?' asked Jennie coolly. 'Is she afraid to face us, or what?'

'I'm just going to fetch her,' Malcolm said quickly.

'She must have known we'd want to see her,' said Madge, 'and Bobby too!'

Bobby went bounding straight for Madge, but Rachel stood at the door, not looking at anyone.

'Well, Rachel,' Madge said sternly, 'you're back, then?'

'I hope you realise what you've put us all through,' snapped Jennie.

'It wasn't my idea to leave,' Rachel said with a flash of her old defiance.

'Oh, Rachel . . .' Madge rocked Bobby to and fro. 'I don't know what to say to you!'

'It's no good saying anything,' said Jennie. 'Rachel never admits when she's in the wrong.'

'We've decided to put it behind us,'' Malcolm said quietly. 'For Bobby's sake.'

'How very convenient for Rachel.' Jenny put her arms around her two boys who, still in their pyjamas, were staring at Bobby, their amazing cousin, who had travelled all the way up from London on a train with beds! Her voice trembling, Jennie added, 'Not everybody thinks of the children, do they?'

'Jennie, love, you're not helping,' Madge murmured. 'If Malcolm and Rachel have sorted this out for themselves, it's not for us to interfere.'

'All I can say is that Malcolm is more forgiving than I could ever be.'

'It's different for you, Jennie,' Malcolm muttered.

'It's not different at all.'

'Couldn't I make you some breakfast?' asked Madge. 'I'm sure you haven't even had a cup of tea.'

'Thanks, we want to get home, Ma,' Rachel said quickly. 'We'll have breakfast there.'

'Made by dear Gillie, I suppose?' asked Jennie.

'No, Gillie has gone,' Malcolm told her. 'Asked if she could leave without notice. She'd had another offer of employment.'

'Why, I thought she'd still want to work for you, Malcolm!' Madge cried, at which he gave a wry grin.

'No, I'm afraid she never approved of me. Not a real gentleman, you see.'

'I always knew she was a fool,' said Jennie, and Rachel, biting her lip, suddenly reached for her mother's hand.

'I'm sorry I upset you, Ma,' she whispered, 'I never meant to do that.'

Madge glanced at Jennie's stubborn face and smoothed her dress with a trembling hand. 'It's as I say, Rachel, this is between you and Malcolm. The main thing is you're back together and Bobby will be home again. That's all that matters.'

'You know, Jennie used to be so sweet at one time,' Rachel murmured in the taxi, 'but now she's quite bitter. I don't feel she's the sister I used to know at all.'

'Not hard to understand, is it?' Malcolm asked, looking at her with expressionless eyes.

'Here's our house!' cried Bobby. 'Look, it's still here!'

'I should hope it is,' Malcolm said with a laugh and, as he paid the driver, Rachel followed Bobby's skipping steps to the front door.

'Maybe it would be a good idea to move,' she said, when Malcolm joined them. 'Make a fresh start in some other house.'

'Can't do that,' Malcolm answered, taking out his keys.

'Why not?'

'Bobby likes it here, it's his home.' Malcolm gave Rachel another of his expressionless glances. 'And we've agreed, haven't we, Bobby comes first?'

Hand in hand with Bobby, Rachel slowly made her return.

In her flat, Jennie was preparing breakfast.

'Typical, isn't it?' she said to Madge. 'The way things always work out for Rachel?'

'That's the sort of thing she says about other people,' Madge replied.

'But it's true about her. Can you believe that Malcolm has

taken her back? After what she did? Supposed to be for Bobby, but I think it's for himself.'

'Maybe he still loves her. Sometimes people are willing to forgive, you know, no matter what others have done.'

'If you're asking me to forgive Rory, Ma, it's not possible.'

'No, Jennie, I'm not asking that.'

They sat down at the table, the boys in bibs making havoc with their porridge, Madge pouring the tea.

'There's something I want to ask you,' said Jennie. 'You know Archie Shields is thinking of retiring? He's saying I should take on the lease.'

'A tailor's?' cried Madge. 'You could never do men's tailoring, Jennie!'

'Obviously, I'd change it to ladies' dressmaking.' Jennie spread jam on Hamish's bread and cut it into fingers. 'But what do you think, Ma? Would you help me?'

'Look after the boys? Of course I would.'

'I was thinking we could run the shop together. I wouldn't expect you to look after the boys all the time. It all depends on whether I could afford the rent.'

'We'll manage it somehow,' Madge said, with decision. 'I think it's a grand idea, Jennie, I'll help you all I can.'

'Thanks, Ma.' Jennie pressed Madge's hand. 'I don't know what I'd do without you. I just wish there was something I could do for you.'

'Oh, there's no need to worry about me,' Madge said, swiftly, and turned away her head so that her poor daughter should not see the guilty flush of happiness rising to her cheek.

But two days later a letter arrived for her from Jim, the first she had ever received. It spoke of his love, of how they should never give up hope, but the fact of the matter was that Bella had refused outright even to think about giving him a divorce.

Part Four
1939–1945

Chapter Forty-Two

The children of Catherine's Land were lining up for evacuation. They carried spare clothes wrapped in brown paper, packets of sandwiches and their gas masks in cardboard cases. Some were giggling or scuffling, others tearful, while their mothers who were to accompany them on the train stood about with reddened eyes and their fathers shouted orders to 'Behave!' from the front door. All over Edinburgh on that fine September morning, streams of children were getting ready to march to the various stations of the city, to be taken to the safety of the Borders or the Lothians or Fife. It was an operation that had been planned for months, part of the national scheme to spare the country's youth the bombing that would surely follow the declaration of war.

Of the thirty or so children from Catherine's Land, only Jennie's Will and Hamish were not joining the evacuation.

Madge, whose fair hair was now mixed with silver and whose pretty face was lined with worry, had tried to persuade Jennie to think again.

'Supposing the air raids do come, Jennie, you'd wish the boys were somewhere safe.'

'They're all I've got and I'm not letting them go to strangers,' Jennie answered obstinately. 'It's a voluntary scheme, I don't have to send them.

'But if it's for their good, Jennie?'

'Rachel's not sending Bobby.'

Madge only sighed. Everybody knew that Rachel and Malcolm would never let Bobby be sent away. They could scarcely bear to let him out of their sight even to go to George

Heriot's school, and though he was eleven years old Rachel still met him every day at the school gates.

It was 6.30 am. The children and their mothers had to be at Waverley Station for seven. Only the Finnegans were missing. Five of Marty's children were already grown up and away and Terry was fifteen and working in Fountainbridge, but Nancy and Kenny were young enough to be evacuated and should have been at the door.

'Gi' them a shout!' cried Bessie Craig, who had taken the O'Hanlon's flat. 'We're no' waiting for they kids for iver!'

Obediently, one of her sons darted back in from the street and hammered on the Finnegans' door 'Are you no' coming?' he called in a high, piping voice.

The door burst open and Nancy and Kenny appeared, followed by Marty in a thin dress and large straw hat. Now forty-five, but looking older because she had lost her teeth, Marty strolled along, smoking a cigarette and ignoring with queenly disdain the calls for her to get a move on. But when the children began to jeer at Kenny whose head had been shaved, her eyes flashed.

'Kenny, put your cap on,' she lisped sharply. 'Are you wanting everybody to see what that nurse did to your head, then? It's a disgrace, so it is, when a woman calls herself a nurse and cuts all a bairn's hair off!'

'Och, we ken why she cut it off, Marty,' Sadie Pringle from Lily's old flat told her. 'They folk he's going to will no' want what was in his hair, eh?'

'As if there's not plenty got the same!' Marty fired back, aiming a blow at Joanie Muir's grandson who leaped smartly away. 'You leave my kids alone or you'll feel the back of my hand!'

'Let them be, Marty,' ordered Tam Finnegan, coming out of his door. 'I'm away to work. You be back soon as you can, eh?'

'Come on, come on,' ordered Jamie Kemp, now a father of three who lived with his wife and widowed mother in the Kemp's top flat. 'We ha' to get these bairns to the station, so let's get going and stop the argy-bargy, eh?'

'I'm no' sitting next to Kenny Finnegan in the train,' sobbed seven-year-old Ruthie Kemp, at which Kenny himself began to cry and had to be comforted by Madge and given a humbug by Jessie Rossie. By the time all the other children had been given sweets from Jessie's stock, Jamie was agitating that they must get moving and in a straggling line, chewing their sweets and waving, the Catherine's Land contingent at last set off down the Lawnmarket. When they had turned the corner and were out of sight, the adults who were left looked at one another with fear in their hearts. The departure of the children seemed to have brought the war one step nearer. There had been plans, now there was reality.

'What's it going to be like without the bairns?' Madge murmured. 'Catherine's Land will be a ghost house.'

'I wish we could've gone,' said Will, ten years old and a fair handsome boy, like his younger brother, Hamish. Jennie gazed at him in anguish.

'And left me, Will?'

'Well, it'd have been exciting.'

'To live with strangers? You wouldn't have liked it, Will, you'd have wanted to come straight back home.'

'But who are we going to play with, Ma?'

'Not all the children have gone from Edinburgh.'

'They've all gone from here.' He gave her a mutinous blue stare. ''Cept Hamish and me.'

'Let's go up and have our breakfast,' Madge said comfortingly. 'We'll all feel better when we've had something to eat. Think of the poor children on the train, Will! They won't be having any breakfast.'

'They've all got things to eat,' Hamish told her quickly. 'They've got their pieces, samwiches and pies. I wish I could have a pie.'

'Up the stair with you for your porridge!' Jennie cried. 'And think yourselves lucky!'

'Can you believe that Will would want to go away?' Jennie asked her mother later. 'It's true, isn't it, he'd want to come home tomorrow?'

'Of course he would,' Madge answered easily. 'Why, I should think they'd all want to come home tomorrow. It's going to be very difficult for them, among strangers.'

'And did you see the list of things they were supposed to take?' Jennie laughed harshly. 'Those organisers haven't an idea how the poor live! Dressing gowns, slippers, warm coats, soap, toothpaste! Imagine Marty's bairns with dressing gowns and slippers!'

Madge sighed. 'You've been lucky, Jennie, you've been able to provide for your boys.'

'Shouldn't be a matter of luck, should it? Everybody should have a decent standard of living.'

'Well, maybe some good will come out of it all,' said Madge. 'I mean, people might realise now just how bad things are.'

'Why does it have to take a war to do that?' Jennie began to clear the breakfast dishes. 'Tell you something else, though. There'll be an end to unemployment. Everybody'll be needed now for the war effort.'

'Full employment making munitions and aircraft to drop bombs?' Madge shook her head. 'I don't like to think of it.'

'Well, I might have to get that kind of work myself,' Jennie told her. 'I don't see me making a living out of dressmaking while there's a war on. For a start, there won't be the materials.'

As Jennie began to wash the dishes, Madge moved into the living room and sat down, stunned. It had never occurred to her that the dressmaking business they had begun six years ago in Archie Shields' old premises might have to go under. Jennie had done so well, even taking on Miss Watson's clients when she had retired. Was all her work to go for nothing? With air raids and invasion to worry about, Madge supposed she shouldn't even be thinking about the loss of a business. But air raids and invasion were the stuff of nightmare, she could hardly visualise them, whereas Jennie's going out of business, that was something close to her heart and very easily understood.

'Don't look like that, Ma,' Jennie said, as cheerfully as she could. 'It'll only be until the war is over.'

'War hasn't even been declared yet.' Madge tried to brighten. 'Maybe Hitler will back down.'

'Not a chance.'

'You don't think so? Oh, I still can't believe it, Jennie! I remember the last one. They said it was the war to end wars, that was what we all believed. And here we are going to war again. How could it have happened?'

'Dunno.' Jennie's brow was furrowed. 'I suppose you get somebody like Hitler and you have to stop him.'

'Yes, but why did we let him get started? Jim says the Germans were so bitter after the last war, they were just waiting for a man like Hitler to make it up to them.'

'I daresay.' Jennie glanced at the clock. 'I'd better open up, while I've still got something to open. Are you coming to me for Sunday dinner as usual?'

'Oh, yes.' Madge's eyes flickered. 'Jim'll be here.'

'I'll get the joint tomorrow then.' Jennie took her keys from a hook, suddenly frowning. 'I've just thought, the boys'll have to amuse themselves today. There's no school.'

'No school?' cried Madge.

'Well, of course there isn't. Most of the children are away.'

'They'll have to do something for the ones who are left, won't they?'

'I suppose they will, but there won't be many.' Jennie's eyes flashed. 'I still haven't changed my mind, though. I'm not going to send the boys away.'

'You're their mother, it's for you to say.'

'That's right. I make the decisions, there's no one else.'

In the years since Rory had left her, Jennie had never once allowed herself to see him, though she had relaxed her ban on letting him see the boys. Twice a year she had taken them over to Jim's flat in Glasgow, so that Rory could come up and visit them there. The arrangement had worked well, the boys had got to know their father, Rory had been grateful. Last Christmas, however, Rory had sent word he could not come, though he had still sent presents. It was the same in the summer. Payments for maintenance had regularly arrived, but no explanation of his failure to visit. Jennie had put the money into post office savings accounts for the boys and set her face grimly when they asked about their father. 'Out of sight, out of mind,' she said to Madge, but it seemed to Madge that what Rory did couldn't hurt Jennie any more. She had grown her own shell over her feelings and was so well protected she appeared to be almost happy.

Later that day it was announced on the wireless that Hitler had sent troops into Poland and bombed Warsaw. It seemed that the capital of Poland had already been collapsing, even while the children were assembling at Waverley station. Then Madge and everyone else knew that peace was past praying for. Great Britain and France were committed to guaranteeing the safety of the Polish border. Now there must be an ultimatum to Hitler and when he ignored it, as he would, war would be officially declared.

Chapter Forty-Three

Saturday, September 2nd, was a strange day. People moved about as usual, going to work, going shopping, watching football, but to many it seemed as though they were standing still, frozen in time as they waited for the last hours of peace to tick away. Even so, Jennie had a rush of customers to the shop, anxious to order clothes while there was still material to be had, and people battled through the late summer heat at Logie's, to buy whatever they could.

'I suppose I should be pleased,' Gerald Farrell said morosely, as he and Abby watched the crowds in the store. 'But I can't help wondering what these people think when they look at the air-raid shelters in Princes Street Gardens. Does it cross their minds all this shopping might be a waste of time?'

'Yes, I think it does,' Abby answered quietly. 'They know why the shelters are there.'

'Of course,' he said after a pause. 'Sorry. It's not for me to criticise what people do before the bombers come.'

'Maybe they won't. We really don't know what will happen.'

'Well, we know what's happened elsewhere. It's not likely that Hitler's going to spare us, is it?' Gerald ran a hand through his grey hair, then smoothed it again; even at this time of fear and stress, he liked to present his usual elegant self to the world. But he had lost weight and was looking Abby thought, rather older. 'God, it makes me sick to think of my brother!' he suddenly burst out. 'What did he die for at Mons? What did any of them die for in the last war?'

'They did what they were called on to do, Gerald. It was right at the time.'

'So it all has to be done again twenty years later?' Gerald shook his head, his eyes dark with bitterness. 'Only this time it's not going to be just the soldiers who will suffer.'

They moved to Gerald's office where he had called a meeting of his senior staff, most of whom were men. Those under forty knew they would be eligible for conscription; some had already made it known that they planned to volunteer. Whatever happened, Gerald said, he wanted to make it clear that their jobs would be kept open for their return, they need have no worries on that score.

'Aye, if we return at all,' Donald Rennie said in a low voice, and the men shifted and stared at their polished shoes.

Gerald cleared his throat and went on. 'In the meantime, the rest of us will have to do what we can to keep this place going, selling blackout material, or gas mask cases or fire extinguishers, or whatever we have to do.'

He gave a tight smile and glanced from the two older partners, Mr Fox and Mr Maddox, both over fifty, to Miss Naylor, Chief Accounts Clerk, in her forties, and finally to Abby. 'I have no idea what the future holds for us, but we'll do our best to make sure there's a Logie's here for you to come back to. I think that's all I have to say for the moment. When we come in on Monday morning we should have' – he hesitated – 'more definite news.'

As Abby turned to go, the last to leave, Gerald touched her arm.

'I wanted to ask you, Abby, have your sisters sent their boys away from Edinburgh?'

'No, they wouldn't agree to it.'

'Same with Monica. Can't bear to let the girls go, though she's got friends at Berwick who'd take them any time.' Gerald gave a long sigh. 'First bomb and they'll be off, of course, but it might be too late by then.'

'We must just try to look on the bright side, Gerald.'

'That's not so easy when you've been through one war and have to face another.'

'Well, we did win the last one, didn't we?' she asked reasonably, and Gerald's face at last split into a grin.

'Oh, Abby, I don't know what I'd do without you. You're

not thinking of volunteering, are you? Not planning to rush off to be with Alan Talbot, or anything?'

She laughed, flushing a little. Gerald was one of the few people who knew about her relationship with Alan Talbot.

'Alan's thinking of trying for the Argyll and Sutherland Highlanders. I don't think I'd be too popular following them around at the moment!'

'And Frankie?' Gerald asked softly. 'He's still in the States?'

'As you know I haven't seen Frankie since nineteen thirty-five,' she answered shortly. 'And if war's declared tomorrow, I don't know that I shall ever see him again.'

Sunday, September 3, was a fine golden day with everywhere the continued feeling of calm before storm. People went to church, promenaded the streets, or stayed at home and peeled the vegetables for lunch, but everyone had their eye on the time, everyone knew when it was eleven o'clock, the deadline for Germany's reply to Great Britain's ultimatum.

In Jennie's flat her boys sat on the floor, looking from one grown-up's face to another, while Jennie, Madge and Jim kept sombre eyes on the wireless. At fifteen minutes past the hour the Prime Minister, Neville Chamberlain, who only a year before had brought back promises of peace from Hitler, began to speak to the nation. There was nothing unexpected in what he had to say, yet as his measured tones filled the room, the hearts of the grown ups sank. It was one thing to expect something, another to have it confirmed. It was definite now, there was no going back. Germany had been asked to agree to immediate withdrawal of troops from Poland, but 'I have to tell you now,' came the quiet voice, 'no such undertaking has been received . . . consequently, this country is now at war with Germany.'

There they were, the words they had prayed would never be said. It was the end of hope.

'Now may God bless you all,' the Prime Minister finished. 'May He defend the right. It is evil things that we shall be fighting against, brute force, bad faith, injustice, oppression, and persecution, and against them I am certain that right will prevail.'

There was more, of course, government contingency plans, exhortations to the people to carry on, to make every effort, but Jim got up, strode over to the wireless and switched it off. He stood for some moments staring at the set, a still strong-looking man in his late fifties, his brown hair now mixed with grey but his gaze as powerful as ever.

'That's it, then,' he said, turning to the others. 'At war again. At bloody war, after all we went through twenty years ago. I canna believe it.'

'No one can believe it,' Madge answered. She opened the oven door and looked in at the joint that was cooking inside. As though sleepwalking, she slowly picked up a spoon, basted the joint, then closed the oven door and sat down.

'Shall I put the tatties round the meat yet?' Jennie asked tonelessly.

'I suppose so, I suppose it's time.' Madge swung round to look at the clock over the range, but Jim gave a loud laugh.

'Time, is it? We'll be lucky if we've any time left, that's all I can say. We'll be lucky if we're not all blown to bits!'

'Dad,' Jennie said, quietly, 'remember the boys.'

He sat down, holding his head in his hands, then shot to his feet again.

'Well, I'll tell you one thing,' he said, savagely, 'this time I'm going to look out for maself and ma family. I'm no' going to lose ma job and ma house and iverything I have, I'm going to stay in Glasgow and get maself into making munitions or aeroplanes or anything they want, so I can make some money and come out of this war with something behind me. Now that's a promise!'

As Madge and Jennie stared at him and the boys giggled nervously at Granddad's loud voice and burning eyes, Jim put on his coat and said he was going out for a breath of air. 'No more heroics for ME!' he declared from the door. 'Not this time!'

'I thought you'd want to come back to Edinburgh,' Madge said quickly. 'I thought you'd want to find a place nearer me.'

Though it was never mentioned, it was no secret that Jim came over from Glasgow to spend the weekends with Madge. Bella had refused to budge on the question of divorce, so what were they to do? Madge wasn't happy about the arrangement, she had never wished to go against the wishes of her church, yet she couldn't feel that she and Jim were wrong to express their love for one another. At the same time, it had seemed a good compromise for her to remain in Edinburgh and Jim to be in Glasgow. Until now. Now the war had changed everything. Now, with the future so uncertain, Madge was beginning to think that she and Jim should be together, married or not. Staying in Glasgow to make money was not something she wanted Jim even to consider.

'It's bound to be more dangerous in Glasgow,' she told him. 'There's the shipyards and all the industry, the city'll be more of a target.'

'I'll take ma chance,' he said, more quietly. 'It'll no' be for long anyway. If I work the hours, I can soon make enough to put by for our future.'

'How do you know we'll even have a future?' she asked, desperately, but he only kissed her cheek and said he'd soon be back for his dinner.

He was as good as his word and they all sat down to the Sunday joint and Madge's Yorkshire puddings just as they always did, but after the meal was over and the washing-up finished, they didn't know what to do. Somehow it didn't seem right just to go for a walk, or play with the boys. The problem was solved by the arrival of Abby, followed by Rachel with Malcom and Bobby, and Madge was in her element, putting Jennie's kettle on, running up to her own flat for a cake she'd made and some boiled ham for sandwiches.

'Oh, Lord, Ma, don't bother,' sighed Rachel, 'nobody wants to eat.'

'People always want to eat,' Madge answered firmly, and when the sandwiches were made and the cake cut, was proved right; no one refused.

'Boys, you can go and play on the back green,' Jennie told her sons. 'Take Bobby with you.'

Bobby, who had the strained air of a child who knows his parents' happiness depends on him, jumped up with alacrity, but Rachel shook her head. What about that new air-raid shelter down there? There might still be building rubbish around, it might not be safe.

'Get away wi' you, Rachel!' Jim bellowed. 'Dinna mollycoddle the lad! Bobby, you go with the others and dinna worry your head over nothing.'

As the boys raced away, Rachel tossed her head and set her lips in a hard line, but she knew better than to say anything to Jim. It was true he had mellowed over the years, especially where Madge was concerned, but he was still not a man to take kindly to having his views questioned.

Rachel herself in recent years had taken on more of what her family called an 'arty' look, using no make-up, wearing her hair in a roughly cut fringe, affecting dresses that looked like artists' smocks. This had coincided with her greater success as a professional. She had had several one-woman shows, was making quite a name for herself and also an income. Perhaps this compensated her, Abby thought, for a rather shaky marriage, but then who really knew the truth about other people's marriages? Neither Rachel nor Malcolm, now thirty-eight, portly and with receding hair, ever gave anything away.

Jim lit his pipe and looked across at Malcolm.

'What d'you make of it, then?' he asked. 'This damned war?'

'I know it won't be over by Christmas, Dad. I think we can look ahead to a long hard struggle.'

'If we survive, you mean.'

Malcom nodded. 'If we get through the raids.'

'You're no' going to volunteer, are you?'

'I'll be called up anyway. They're taking fellows up to forty-one. Shouldn't be surprised if they make it fifty, before they've finished.'

'Just as long as I dinna have to go,' Jim said grimly. 'I've done ma bit once for King and Country and I'm no' doing it again.'

'I've been thinking, I might paint war pictures,' said Rachel, and frowned at the expressions on the faces turned towards her. 'Don't look like that, they needn't be abstracts! And if you're thinking that's not useful enough, Ma, I'm going to do voluntary work with the WVS. They're opening a canteen for servicemen at Waverley Station.'

'Rachel, I never said a word,' Madge protested. 'All I care about is that we're going to be here to do anything at all.'

As if on cue for these ominous words, the air was suddenly rent by the banshee wailing of a siren.

'Air-raid warning!' shouted Jim, jumping to his feet. 'By God, that was quick!'

'I don't believe it,' Abby gasped, 'not so soon – surely—'

'The boys!' shrieked Rachel. 'They're down at the shelter!'

'Best place for them,' cried Malcom, 'come on!'

Jim took Madge's hand, Malcolm took Rachel and Jennie, and they went hurtling out of the flat, mixing with a flood of people already flowing down the stair, all waxen-faced and panting, as they made for the shelter at the back of the tenements.

'I still don't believe it,' said Abby. 'It must be a practice.'

'You'll be saying that when the bombs start to fall,' Jim grunted. 'Into the shelter wi' you!'

'Where's Bobby?' cried Rachel. 'Oh my God, where is he?'

'Where's Will?' cried Jennie. 'Where's Hamish?'

'There they are!' cried Malcolm, and the boys ran to their parents' arms.

'Oh, Jennie, Jennie,' Madge murmured, as Jennie burst into tears.

'Oh, Ma, I should have sent the boys away. It's a judgment on me, because I wanted to keep them!'

'I still say it's a false alarm,' said Abby, 'you'll see.'

She was right. Some time later, after they had been pressed together in the dank twilight of the shelter which still smelled of earth and mould, the all clear sounded and, one by one, they trailed out into the September evening, blinking, feeling relieved and not a little foolish.

'Thank God, thank God,' Madge murmured, 'it was a false alarm.'

Would the next one be real? thought Abby.

Chapter Forty-Four

It was Monday, October 16th. Abby, back from a snatched lunch, hung her jacket and gas mask on the back of the office door and sat down at her desk. The time was two o'clock.

Outside Logie's, Edinburgh was enjoying a pleasant autumn day. Apart from the air-raid shelters in Princes Street Gardens, there was little sign of war. In fact, people were beginning to wonder when something would happen. There had been disasters at sea, the U-boats had torpedoed the liner *Athenia* and a battleship, *The Royal Oak*, everyone was grieving for the terrible loss of life, but where were the air-raids, where were the clouds of poison gas they had all been expecting? The newspapers were calling the time the 'Phoney War'. Abby, working on policy plans to be presented to the trustees, felt as uneasy as everyone else. This lull could surely not last much longer.

At 2.40 pm she crossed to her filing cabinet to check some figures and heard what sounded like thunder. A dull crack-crack-crack that made her hand on the cabinet drawer shake. Thunder in October? She knew it wasn't thunder. The noise came again and then her telephone rang. She dived to answer it.

'Abby?' came Gerald Farrell's voice. 'That was gunfire. Get down to the main door, fast as you can.'

She took the stairs, not the lift, whirling down, round and round, her heels tap-tap-tapping, her breath coming in short painful gasps. When she reached the ground floor she saw people crowding to the doors and Gerald Farrell standing with Ian Fox and Bernard Maddox appealing for calm.

'It's probably only a practice, no need to worry, let's all stay in the store, let's all keep calm, please!'

'Who says it's only a practice?' quavering voices were asking. 'Why've we had no air-raid warning? We should complain to the Chief Constable, it's a disgrace, it's a downright disgrace!'

Jock MacAndrew, the commissionaire recalled from retirement when his replacement volunteered for the Black Watch, was preventing customers from trapping themselves in the swing doors and calling to Gerald Farrell that shells had been seen bursting over roof tops.

'Aye and some funny looking planes and all! Are you sure it's a practice, sir?'

'Of course I'm not sure!' Gerald gritted, manoeuvering himself through the doors and out into the street. 'Just keep quiet, will you, Jock, until we find out what's going on?'

'Is it an air-raid, Miss Ritchie?' the sales girls were asking as they clustered round Abby. 'Should we no' be going to the shelters? Why've we had no warning?'

'I don't think it's an air-raid, probably some sort of practice,' Abby told them, expressing a confidence she did not feel. 'That'll be why we've heard no sirens. The best thing we can do is to stay put until we're told officially what to do.'

Customers were returning from the street, some looking pale and asking for chairs and sal volatile, and Abby gave orders to the staff to look after the shoppers and keep themselves busy. She herself followed Ian Fox and Bernard Maddox outside, where they found Gerald raking the skies with narrowed eyes.

'See those white puffs of smoke in the distance? They're bursting shells, all right, but I don't see any planes. Jock says there've been reports of enemy bombers being chased by Spitfires.'

'So it could be an air raid!' Ian Fox asked sharply.

'If it is, why have we had no warning? Somebody's going to have to do some explaining. I'm going to ring up about it now. What's happening in the shop?'

'I think they're calming down a bit,' Abby told him. 'They're staying inside, they think it's safer.'

'Very wise.' Gerald grabbed Abby's arm. 'Listen, a fellow's

311

just told us, there's been shrapnel falling in St Andrew Square and Hanover Street. We'd better get indoors ourselves.'

Inside the store, tea was being organised for staff and customers and with the familiar sound of clinking teacups, peace was gradually being restored. Couldn't be much wrong if Logie's was serving tea, could there? No doubt all that activity out there was just a practice, after all.

'Let's get up to my office,' Gerald said, dabbing at his brow. 'See if we can find out something from that ARP contact of mine.'

In the lift the four of them leaned against the walls, each thinking how white the others looked and how they could do with a good stiff drink.

'All right, Miss Ritchie?' Gerald asked.

'I'm fine, just a bit worried about my mother and my sisters, with all this shrapnel flying about.'

'Give your sister a ring. Rachel's on the phone, isn't she? I'll bet my wife's already been on the phone to me. You'd better ring home too,' Gerald added to the men, 'soon as we get some news.'

As he waved them to chairs in his office, Miss Wright, his secretary, came running in to say Mrs Farrell had telephoned and would Mr Farrell call back immediately? And would anybody like tea? 'Whisky, please, Miss Wright,' Gerald ordered, dialling his contact's number. 'We can have tea later.'

'You won't forget to ring Mrs Farrell? She sounded most anxious.'

'I won't forget. Ah, MacDonald, – look, what can you tell me? Yes, I know you are – everybody's on your back – can't be helped. Will you just tell me what in hell is going on?'

The call was a long one. Ian Fox, exceptionally tall and bony with a dome of a bald head and intelligent grey eyes, looked down into his whisky. Bernard Maddox, short, chubby and good-natured, drank his off in a gulp and grinned across at Abby.

'Better than tea in an emergency, Miss Ritchie?'

'Too right, Mr Maddox.'

Gerald put down the receiver and gratefully swallowed some whisky. He raised his eyes to his watching staff. 'Got some news but it's not too clear. Seems there's suddenly been activity all over the skies today. Enemy planes over Rosyth and Threipmuir reservoir. Junkers over the Forth. Spitfires from Edinburgh and Glasgow chasing the lot of them, which explains the gunfire and the shrapnel, but there've been no bombs dropped except on the ships in the Forth. My chap's not sure if they were hit or not.'

'So it's not been a proper air-raid?' Ian asked. 'We should still have had some sort of warning, shouldn't we?'

'Well, that's where the hazy bit comes in. Nobody seems sure why the RAF didn't give one. They control the sirens but they may not have had much warning themselves. There's one hell of a row going on about it.'

'I should damn well think so,' said Bernard Maddox. 'I mean, with all these reports of shrapnel whizzing around!'

'And bullets and shellcases,' said Gerald.

'Any casualties?' Abby asked quickly.

'Some local people hit, but not fatally.' Gerald gave a grim smile. 'But you can be sure there'll be a full enquiry – one of the houses hit was the Lord Provost's.' He glanced at his watch. 'Oh, God, Monica! I'd better give her a ring.'

It was early evening before the activity ceased. While Logie's staff cleared away teacups and cigarette ends and began to put up the blackouts, Abby got through to Rachel. All was well, she'd been down to Catherine's Land to check. Jennie was wailing again that she might send the boys away, but Rachel had no intention of changing her mind about Bobby.

'After all,' she told Abby, 'it's been so quiet, lots of children are already coming home.'

'It hasn't been quiet today,' Abby pointed out.

'No, well, I know it's a risk, but Bobby would suffer so much if I sent him to strangers. I simply couldn't do it.'

'Monica Farrell is sending the girls to Berwick. Gerald is driving them tonight.'

'I don't care,' Rachel said obstinately. 'Bobby is staying at home.'

Poor Bobby, thought Abby. It might have done him good to escape for a while from the overheated atmosphere of his parents' attention, but it was not for her to advise Rachel. She made a round of the departments, checking that everything was back to normal on this extraordinary day, finishing with Accounts where she told the unflappable Miss Naylor and her depleted staff to get off home, they'd all had enough.

'You too, Miss Ritchie,' said Clara Naylor, rising to put on her coat. 'You look exhausted.'

'I feel it,' Abby answered. 'Not that I've done very much, it's just been the strain of wondering what might be coming next.'

'Maybe this was just a one-off?'

'Ah, it's nice to talk to you!' Abby said with a grin. 'You're an optimist!'

Gerald was waiting in her office when she returned, wearing a belted overcoat and smoking a cigarette.

'Any more news?' asked Abby.

'Reports of casualties from a destroyer in the Forth. Some men killed.'

Abby lowered her eyes.

'On the bright side, the Spitfires are claiming hits. And our chaps have picked up three German pilots from the sea.' Gerald ground out his cigarette in Abby's ashtray. 'No more reports of civilian injuries. I'd say we got off lightly.'

'Do we know yet why we didn't get a warning?'

'As we thought, the authorities didn't get enough warning themselves. They weren't to blame.'

'And it's really all over now?'

'It's over now. And I'm off to Berwick. Thank God there's still some petrol to be had. Not for much longer, there'll probably be no private cars on the road by the end of the year.'

'Good job I moved from South Queensferry, then.' Though she had been saddened at the time, Abby was relieved now that she had moved some months before into a small New Town flat.

'Especially if German bombers are going to make a habit of bombing the Forth. Can't do without you, Abby. I keep telling you that, don't I? The thing is, there's a rumour that they're going to extend conscription to fifty-year olds. That would mean me.'

'Gerald, you surely wouldn't be expected to fight again?'

He shrugged. 'Who knows? In the meantime I'm going to have to be more involved with firefighting and civil defence. So are Ian Fox and Bernard Maddox. With so many chaps away

I'm afraid it means that more and more is going to fall on your shoulders. I can count on you, can't I?'

'You know you can.'

He smiled and rested his hand briefly on her shoulder. 'I'd better get off. You too, Abby, don't spend hours at your desk tonight.'

'I'm already on my way. Goodnight Gerald, safe journey.'

'Goodnight, Abby.'

She sat alone at her desk, listening to the sounds of the store closing down for the night. Doors slamming, footsteps clattering down corridors, voices calling. 'There's a light, I can still see a light, pull that curtain over!' 'Wait for me, wait for me.' 'Have you locked that door, Maggie?' 'Och, I'm so tired, I canna put one foot in front of the other.' 'What a day, eh?' Everyone was excited, buzzing over the day's events, their first taste of war. They were all right, they had come through, but would there be more to come? Uncertainty waited to hold them in fear when the excitement waned.

Oh, well, thought Abby, rising from her desk, at least the Spitfire pilots probably enjoyed it.

There was a knock on her door and an assistant wearing her hat and coat looked in.

'Oh, Miss Ritchie, you're still here – that's good – there's someone to see you.'

'I'm just leaving. Who is it?'

The young woman gave a knowing smile. 'It's Mr Baxter, Miss Ritchie. Shall I tell him to come up?'

Chapter Forty-Five

Four years. It was four years since she'd seen him. She'd made a special trip to New York where she'd found him overweight and drinking heavily but making money as a pianist with a radio band. That was not the reason, he explained, that he didn't want to return to her. He loved her just as much as ever, there was no other woman in his life, but her sort of marriage was not for him, he was happier with his piano.

'And your drinking,'' she said bitterly.

'Sure,' he agreed easily, 'my drinking helps, I'm not denying it. Gets me through the days. Why don't you go home and leave me alone?'

'I don't understand you!' she cried. 'It's all different now, our marriage isn't a secret any more, I've done everything you wanted!'

'Except let me wear the pants.'

It seemed there was nothing more to say. She asked him if he was really happy to stay on in America? She'd noticed that he'd dropped his Scottish accent.

'Had to. Nobody could understand me. I didn't understand them, either, so I learned American like it was French. Yes, I'm happy. As happy as I'll be anywhere, I guess.'

'Aren't you at all glad to see me?' she asked, despising herself for scratching for crumbs of consolation.

'Sure, I'm glad. I appreciate you coming, don't think I don't. But it only makes it harder for me if you're around. I think you should go back and do what I told you to do before. Find some guy who's right for you. Because I'm not and I guess I never was.'

'You want a divorce, then?'

He had looked a little shaken. 'Abby, I'll leave that to you.'

She had sailed home, putting the Atlantic between them again which was what Frankie seemed to want, but there had been no divorce. When Alan Talbot had made it clear he wanted a relationship, she'd found she wanted it too, relieved that there would be no strings. This man seemed happy to accept that she wanted a life of her own, that they would just meet when they could and enjoy being together. Maybe neither of them was in love, but each had a deep understanding of the other's needs. It seemed to Abby that that was as good as love. In a week's time, Alan was coming up to Scotland for his board with the Argylls. They would be together again for a little while and she'd been looking forward to it. Now here was Frankie.

He looked thinner and seemed subdued, his blue eyes shadowed, his dark curly hair cut short to his skull. She thought him a stranger.

'Don't you recognise me, Abby?' Somewhere beneath the New York twang his old Scottish voice was just discernible.

'Of course I do,' she answered uncertainly. 'But what are you doing here?'

'I wanted to see you.'

'I do have a telephone at home.'

'Guess I lost the number.' He shrugged. 'But I knew you'd be here. I asked for Miss Ritchie. Seems that was right.'

'I use my maiden name at work but everyone knows I'm married.' Abby held out a slightly trembling hand. 'See, I wear my wedding ring.'

'So you do.' Frankie looked in a lost way around her office. 'I'm sorry – it's been too long – I shouldn't have come.'

'You needn't say that. I'm glad to see you.'

'I seem to remember I gave you a pretty hard time when we last met.'

'As you say, a long time ago.' She looked at her watch. 'I'm afraid we'll have to go, they'll be wanting to lock up. Would you – would you like to go for a drink?'

He shook his head. 'I'm on the wagon. That's why I look like I do. Had to go for a drying out, wasn't pleasant, but it did the trick.'

317

'I'm relieved. I thought you were ill.'

'Never been fitter in my life. Think they'll take me?'

'Who?'

'The navy.'

'Frankie, you haven't come back to join up?'

'Why else?'

Abby's face went blank. She put on her coat without speaking, pulled on her brimmed hat, picked up her briefcase and strode to the door. Frankie followed.

'Abby, I'm sorry. I didn't mean that to sound like it did.'

'That's all right, I know you didn't come back from America for me. Will you excuse me? I have to put off the lights and lock the door.'

'Abby, please will you let me buy you dinner?'

'The restaurants won't be what you're used to in New York.' Abby banged her door shut and locked it. 'We've already got shortages, they're saying we soon won't be able to pay more than five bob for a meal, anyway. Still want to take me to dinner?'

'Abby, I've said I'm sorry. I've come all the way from London to see you. Came straight off the boat, left my bags and took off. Don't punish me.'

As though you haven't been punishing me for years, she thought, but let him take her arm and walk with her to the lift.

'You don't know what you've missed,' she told him. 'Edinburgh's been having an air battle. Spitfires chasing enemy planes all over the city, shrapnel and bullets flying about, oh, we've been having a great time!'

'Knew I should have tried for that earlier train,' he said with a laugh, and for the first time looked like the old Frankie.

Outside the store he exclaimed over the blackout.

'Hell, Abby, how d'you get around in this? No lights in Princes Street, no lights in the Castle! You're going to have to take my hand, I can't see a thing.'

'You'll soon get used to it.' She took his hand and felt his fingers close eagerly round hers. 'Where do you want to eat, then?'

'Anywhere with Scottish food. If I never see another hamburger again, it'll be too soon.'

318

His eyes lit up when he scanned the menu in the small restaurant she found for him.

'Shortages, did you say? They've still got Cockaleekie soup and Cullen Skink – hey, and Chicken Howtowdie! Och, I think I'll soon be sounding like a Scot again!'

'Not that we were used to Chicken Howtowdie when we were young,' Abby remarked. 'Though we lived a lot better than some.'

'Aye, remember the jelly pieces we used to take to school? And how the other kids used to think I was the lucky one because my mother kept the sweetie shop?'

'I remember the humbugs you used to keep for me,' Abby said, laughing, and Frankie laughed too, loooking again like his old self.

'But your mother was a damned good cook, Abby, wasn't she? Sunday tea at Mrs Ritchie's – wow, you'd give your soul for that! How is she, then?'

Abby's mouth twitched a little. 'She's very well.'

'Why the funny look?'

'I have a funny look?'

'Come on, tell me what your ma's been up to!'

'Nothing! Well, its just that Jim Gilbride's back in the picture. Lives in Glasgow but comes over to see Ma every weekend. He's separated from Bella but she won't give him a divorce.'

'Tough.' Frankie played with his soup spoon. 'Are you saying your mother and Jim have a relationship?'

'I'm sure they have.'

'And you're not happy?'

'Oh, I'm happy if she is. It just seems out of character, that's all.'

'I don't see why they shouldn't be happy if they can,' Frankie said slowly. 'If you find the right person, maybe you shouldn't let them go.'

Abby looked down at the tablecloth, relieved when the waiter brought them their soup.

As the meal progressed, she talked of her sisters and Malcolm, of Rory's continued absence, of the changes in Catherine's Land – electricity, imagine! Frankie asked about his mother's shop and Abby told him that Jessie Rossie was thinking she would have to close it for the duration, it would scarcely be worth her while to keep it going. Sweets were already in short supply and would eventually be rationed.

'Like everything else,' Abby sighed. 'Though after today and the gunfire, I'm sure rationing is the least of our worries.'

'Don't like to think of you in danger, Abby.'

'We're all in danger, Frankie. That's what's different about this war.'

'Where are you staying?' she asked him when they had left the restaurant and were stumbling through the blackout again.

'Nowhere as yet. I came straight off the train to Logie's. Thought I'd find a hotel later.'

'Some have closed. The rest are pretty full.'

'I'll get in somewhere. It's only for one night, I'm going back south tomorrow.' Frankie was holding Abby's arm, trying to look into her face. 'Don't think I'm trying to cadge a bed at your place, I wouldn't expect that.'

Abby was silent, wondering if he did expect it.

'I take it you're not still out at South Queensferry?' he asked, awkwardly.

'No, I left last January.'

'So where are you now?'

'I did send you a card, Frankie. I have a flat in Great King Street.'

'Couldn't we have coffee there? I seem to remember going back to your flat for coffee once before.'

'Only you had whisky,' she said tartly.

'Happy days, eh? Come on, show me where it is.'

'Very nice,' he commented, taking off his overcoat and looking round Abby's large sitting room, with its high decorative ceiling and long black-curtained windows. 'I see you've still got the old sofa and chairs.'

'Fancy your remembering.' As Abby put a match to her gas fire, Frankie winced a little at her tone.

'I remember everything about our life together, Abby.'

She made no reply but went out to the kitchen to make the coffee. When she returned with the tray, she found him standing in front of her little bureau staring at a photograph of Alan Talbot.

320

'Who's this?' he asked at once.

'A friend.'

'And you keep his picture on your bureau?'

'It's not always there. Sometimes it's by my bed.'

'I see.' As Alan's eyes gazed innocently out from the photograph, Frankie turned white. 'Is this the guy?' he asked, hoarsely. 'Is he the guy I told you to find?'

'For God's sake, Frankie, are you surprised? You tell me you don't want my kind of marriage, you say you won't come back from America, you say find another man. What did you expect me to do?'

He sat down heavily. 'I don't know. I'm a fool, I guess. I thought you might still be waiting.'

'Still be waiting?' Abby's face turned dusky red. 'I never thought you could be so arrogant. How dare you think I'd still be waiting for you?'

'Because you never asked for a divorce.' He went to her, taking her hands in his. 'Abby, you know I still love you. I've never stopped loving you. As soon as the war came, I knew I had to find you, tell you that. I do want to join the navy, if they'll have me, but I'd have crossed the Atlantic anyway to be with you again.'

'It's too late,' she said quietly, freeing her hands. 'Much too late, Frankie. You told me what to do and I did it. I've found someone else.'

'So now you do want a divorce?'

'I don't know. I might.'

Frankie turned away, to stare again at Alan's photograph.

'Handsome, isn't he? I'll bet he went to a good school, too. What's he do? What's his job?'

'He's an actor, but he's hoping to get into the Argylls.'

'An actor!'

'What's so amazing?' she asked coldly.

'I dunno. Just always thought you'd finish up with some Edinburgh lawyer or an accountant, some guy like that.' He laughed. 'Oh, well, I daresay the Argylls'll want an actor as much as the navy'll want a piano player. Have to take what they can get, eh? Guess I'll skip the coffee, Abby. Go find me a place to sleep.'

As he took his coat and moved slowly towards the door, his

shoulders hunched, she said, sharply, 'Oh, all right, Frankie, you can stay here. I've a spare room, the bed's made up, you might as well have it.'

'Abby, are you sure?'

'I can't bear to think of you falling around in the blackout and not finding anywhere for the night. Come on, I'll show you the room.'

'Maybe I'll turn in now,' he said, standing by the single bed in Abby's narrow guest room. 'Been a pretty tiring day. For you, too.'

'You're right about that.' She shivered, remembering the gunfire, the bursting shells. 'I'm exhausted, to tell you the truth.'

'You still look good, Abby. Still look beautiful.'

'I never looked beautiful. Goodnight, Frankie. The bathroom's just next door and I've put out towels. You won't mind an early start in the morning?'

'No, I want to catch the eight o'clock train.'

They exchanged quick awkward glances, then Abby went out and Frankie, flinging himself on the bed, lay there for some time, quite motionless.

Oh, God, why did I let him stay? Abby asked herself, lying stiffly in her bed, which had been her marriage bed. 'It's too much, it's too much!' Supposing he came to her in the night? Well, she wouldn't sleep with him, she couldn't. He might still be her husband but in name only now. His choice, wasn't it? He'd managed without her all these years, why should he think he could come back and just find her waiting? All right, she hadn't asked for a divorce. Maybe she should have done, but deep in her heart she knew she hadn't wanted one. A 'plane droned overhead and she sat up in bed with a start, then – one of ours, she decided – and lay down again. No sound came from Frankie's room. He must be asleep. He wasn't asleep, she knew it. He was lying awake just as she was, remembering the old days, remembering making love. Don't let him come to me, she prayed, not really expecting any God to be listening. It wouldn't be fair to Alan, it wouldn't be fair to me. Don't let him come, please. But when he didn't, she couldn't sleep for wanting him. Next morning she felt ill and drained, as though she had cried all night, but her eyes were dry.

322

'I'll go with you to the station,' she told Frankie, as she made toast and tea. 'We can walk, I don't drive my car now if I can help it. Suppose it'll soon have to be put up on blocks, for the duration.'

He looked at her with heavy eyes. 'I don't want you to come to the station. I hate goodbyes.'

'All right, I won't come.'

They drank the tea, crumbled the toast.

'You will write to me, Frankie? You'll tell me what you're doing?'

'You care?'

'Of course I care! We've known each other since we were children. Do you think I don't want to know what happens to you?'

'You'll know what happens to me, Abby.' His blue eyes suddenly flashed. 'I'm making you my next of kin.'

Chapter Forty-Six

After that strange day of air battle, Edinburgh settled into a wartime routine. There was never any real blitz over the city, though some bombs and incendiaries were dropped, but there were the changes to get used to, the shortages, the rationing, the queues. There were the unfamiliar foods, dried eggs, dried milk and spam; there were the identity cards and things going under the counter; there were the friends and relatives disappearing into the forces, the favourite businesses closing down.

'Sometimes I dinna feel I'm in ma own country,' Peggie Kemp confided to Madge, and Madge said she felt the same. Except that there was now a rather wonderful atmosphere in Catherine's Land, the feeling that they were all in this together, that everyone had to help everyone else, whatever the cost. This atmosphere was generated by the women, of course, for most of the men were away to the war, with even Tam Finnegan having the time of his life it was said, driving a tank in the Middle East. Only Donnie Muir, who had married Sally, Mr Kay's niece, and taken over the grocery store, had been left because of his asthma. But it was good to have Donnie around, he being such a kind-hearted fellow who did his best for his customers. Madge worried a lot about finding food for the boys, now that Jennie was out all day at a factory making aircraft mouldings. But then, as her family always said, Madge worried about everything: Jennie's long hours, Rachel drawing bomb sites, Malcolm in the army, Abbie's Frankie in the navy (even if Abby did say he wasn't her Frankie any more). Most of all, she worried about Jim, still in Glasgow.

It was true that he was making money because everyone was making money now, but every night he was at risk and every night Madge was at her window, wondering if there was a 'bomber's moon', if the planes would be coming over again, if Jim would be safe. Glasgow and Clydeside were prime targets for the Luftwaffe.

'Aye, I ken you worry, and I'm sorry,' he told her, 'but this is ma chance to put something by for you and me and I'm no' giving it up.'

'You could come back to Catherine's Land, Jim. You could come back to me.'

'Dinna tempt me, Madge But you know you'd always be worrying what folk'd say.'

'Well, I do wish we could be married,' she admitted. 'You'd think after all these years Bella would give way.'

'I'd no' think it,' said Jim. 'I know Bella.'

Though people had money in their pockets and could enjoy themselves when work was over, going to the pictures to see Betty Grable or John Wayne, going dancing or to the pub, singing all the wartime songs, anxiety was always with them. Spirits were low enough after the evacuation of Dunkirk, but when the Germans entered Paris in June, 1940, after conquering Holland and Belgium, hope almost died. Invasion seemed a certainty. Britain stood alone.

'Och, what the hell,' said Jim, when his old flat in Catherine's Land became vacant. 'You're right, Madge, what's money, after all? If the Boche are coming over, I want to be with you. I'll live down the stair, you can live up the stair, so no one can point the finger.' As though it mattered!

Things worked out well. The expected invasion never happened because the Battle of Britain happened instead. With the defeat of his fighter planes by the RAF, Hitler made no move to take Great Britain. It was a victory to cherish, even though the night attacks on British cities did not stop. 1941 brought even more intensive bombing to London, Coventry, Hull, Plymouth, Southampton, Glasgow and Clydeside.

Jim, who had found work in Leith making pipelayer vessels, often thanked God he had removed himself from Glasgow, yet confessed himself still worried over Bella.

'She was a devil to live with and that's a fact, but I canna help wondering how she's managing in Clydebank,' he told Madge, who said of course she understood his worry, it was only natural. Privately, however, she thought if anyone could take care of herself it would be Bella. But early on the morning of March 14th she was shaken from her sleep by Jim.

'I'm away to Clydeside, Madge. There's been a terrible blitz, nearly all Clydebank destroyed. Donnie Muir's just been up and told me, he's had a 'phone call at the shop.'

'Clydebank?' cried Madge, scrambling out of bed. 'Oh, God, that's Bella!'

'Aye, she's in our old house. Donnie says they're saying it's hell on earth over there, I'll have to go.'

'Wait, I'll come with you—'

'No, I dinna want you involved, Madge. Donnie's going over in his van, see if he can find out what's happened to old Kirk's sister. He'll give me a lift. I'll see you tonight, if I can.'

'If you can? Jim, you must come back here, there might be another raid – Jim, wait!'

Madge still in her nightgown, ran down the stair after him, but the street door was already banging shut.

'What's up?' asked Jennie, looking sleepily out of her door. 'Ma, you'll catch your death!'

'Jim's gone to Clydebank, there's been a dreadful raid and he wants to see if Bella's all right.'

'I suppose he's got friends there, too. Ma, you ought to go and put something on.'

'Jennie, listen. Can you get someone else to see the boys in after school? I've decided to go to Clydebank myself.'

'Ma, that's crazy! You know what it's like getting on trains these days and it'll be like a nightmare over there, you'll only be in the way.'

'I've made up my mind, don't try to stop me. I'm going over by the first train I can catch.'

Nothing had prepared Madge for what she saw in Clydebank. She had read about bomb damage, she had seen pictures in the newspapers, she knew all about flattened houses, people searching rubble, survivors with shocked faces. But to see it at first hand, to smell it, to feel the awesome presence of death on such a scale as this – she wanted to run away. Everywhere around her tenements were down, some still cascading into piles of bricks and clouds of dust, as workers from the Civil Defence services battled against the chaos. No one took any notice of her and she saw there were plenty of others there on the same errand as herself, looking for loved ones, some scrabbling in the ruins with their bare hands, others just standing, too dazed to know what to do. Could Bella have survived this horror? Someone said it had started in the evening, with small bombs, then incendiaries. A distillery had been hit, followed by a timber yard, then the shipyard, then a factory. The sky had been a mass of flame and light long before the searchlights began to play; the bombers sending down the bigger bombs had had an easy task, picking out what they wanted. Now as the terrible job of clearing up began, the fear in everyone's heart was plain. Would nightfall bring another raid?

Madge moved slowly round on trembling legs, looking at the scattered possessions of people who might be dead. Sticks of furniture, a kettle, a bicycle, a clock without hands. 'I don't know what to do,' she said aloud. 'I don't know where to look.'

'Who're you looking for, hen?' asked a woman with a scarf tied round her head and hands black and scratched with turning over rubble.

'I'm looking for a woman called Bella Gilbride. She lived here in a tenement.'

'There was a lot of tenements here, hen.'

'I think it was called Saint Anne's.'

'Aye, that was here. No' here now.'

'What happened to the people?'

'Some took to hospital, some took over there.' The woman pointed to a small low building, still intact. 'Try there hen, eh?'

'Thank you very much,' said Madge.

The building, an improvised rest centre, was filled with people in blankets. They had dirty faces empty of all expression. Some were drinking tea. The grown-ups were silent, unable to put into words their feelings at losing everything they had except their lives, but the children were crying, quietly keening as though at a wake for their dead homes.

Bella wasn't there, nor of course was Jim, and a WVS worker

explained that the centre was only for those who could walk or wait for treatment. Urgent casualties had been taken to hospitals in the district, but it wasn't possible to say where Mrs Gilbride had been taken. 'Ask outside, dear, the Civil Defence people will know.'

As Madge thanked her and turned away, a man sitting with a bird in a cage said he knew Bella Gilbride, aye, and Jim Gilbride, too. They'd been neighbours once.

'Oh, have you seen them?' Madge cried 'Do you know where they've gone?'

'I couldna tell you,' he answered, and burst into a strange dry sobbing.

Out in the shattered streets, Madge stood uncertainly, swaying a little in the dust and rubble. She shouldn't have come, she thought, Jennie had been right. She was only in the way and should just go home. But she didn't know if she even had the strength to get herself home.

'Mrs Ritchie?' someone said, and a young man got out of a van and took her arm. 'Mrs Ritchie, whatever are you doing here, then?'

It was Donnie Muir.

'Oh, Donnie!' cried Madge. 'Have you seen Jim?'

'Aye, I have.' Donnie coughed and wiped his lips. 'He's away to Glasgow. Mrs Gilbride's been taken to one of the hospitals. She's awful bad, Mrs Ritchie. We had to help dig her out.'

'Dig her out? Oh, that's terrible!'

'Aye, but get in the van, Mrs Ritchie, you look about all in.'

When she was sitting half collapsed in the seat next to his, he told her he had found Sally's auntie and she wasn't too bad, shocked, but not hurt, and he'd taken her to a friend whose house was still standing. Now he was going home but Jim had gone with Bella in the ambulance after they'd helped to dig her from the ruins of the tenement. 'Went down four floors,' Donnie said sombrely. 'Didna go to the shelter, you ken.'

'Four floors,' Madge whispered, and felt things going vague and cloudy. From a great distance she heard Donnie saying he was going to drive her to the hospital in Glasgow.

'I can hear you wheezing, ' she said faintly. 'You shouldn't have tried to do any digging.'

'Och, it's just the dust. Dinna worry yourself, Mrs Ritchie.

I've got a bit o' petrol left from ma ration for the deliveries, I'll ha' you in Glasgow in no time, then I'll go home, nae bother, nae bother at all.'

He insisted on buying her tea and a cheese roll in the hospital canteen before she went up to see Bella.

'It's very kind of you, Donnie. I'm desperate for the tea, but I don't think I could eat anything.'

'Sure you can,' said Donnie, and she did, and felt fractionally better. Well enough to thank Donnie from the bottom of her heart, well enough to go up herself to Bella's ward, trembling at what she might find.

Poor Bella, poor Dutch doll. Madge felt guilty now that she had never cared for her, had seen her only as an obstacle to her marriage with Jim. If she were to die that obstacle would be removed, but no one should have to die like Bella, blown from her home into terror and darkness. And for Madge to be married to Jim, to take happiness because his wife had suffered, no, no, that wouldn't be right, no, she wouldn't want that.

'Mrs Gilbride?' As Madge made her request to see Bella, the staff nurse looked dubious. 'I'm not sure if you can see her, she's in a side ward. Are you a relative?'

'Yes,' Madge replied, deciding not to go into details. 'I've come over from Edinburgh.'

'Well, her husband's with her at the moment. I suppose I could let you in, if you don't stay too long.' Again the nurse gave Madge a doubtful look. 'Do you know she's been very badly injured?'

'Yes, I've been told.' Madge followed the nurse to a narrow little room where a bandaged figure lay on a bed and Jim was sitting on a chair. As soon as he saw Madge, a light came into his eyes and he leaped to his feet. The nurse gave them both a stern look and said to Madge, 'Only a few minutes, please. You can get another chair from the corridor if you like. Don't sit on the bed whatever you do.'

'Oh, Jim!' Madge stood looking down at Jim's wife. She lay quite still; apart from her dark eyebrows and the dark eyelashes of her closed eyes, she was quite colourless. White face, white bandaged head, white bandaged hands folded over a white sheet. Only her shallow breathing gave any sign that she was alive.

'We'd some good times in the early days,' Jim muttered. 'Niver thought I'd see her like this.'

'Remember the good times, Jim, that's all you can do. Oh, I wish I had some flowers.'

Another nurse appeared and said it would be best if Madge left and perhaps Mr Gilbride could come back later. She was going to give Mrs Gilbride an injection.

'You'd best get off home, Madge,' Jim said wearily in the hospital corridor.

'You think I can just go home and leave you?'

'You have to think of your girls, Madge. There might be another raid,'

She caught her breath. 'Jim, I couldn't —'

'There's Jennie,' he said flatly, 'there's the boys,' and she lowered her eyes.

Once again the wheel had turned. At one time it would have been Madge putting her family before Jim, Now it was Jim reminding her of where her duty lay.

'I'll go back,' she said quietly.

That night there was another bomber's moon. Madge sat up, wrapped in a blanket looking out at the sky. Sometimes she heard 'planes going over but she never knew whose they were.

'That's one of ours,' some people could say, or, 'That's one of theirs,' but Madge just had to wait to find out whether she should be afraid or not. Tonight she was afraid anyway. As soon as it grew light she washed and dressed and put on her wireless for news. Another raid over Glasgow and Clydeside, but much lighter casualties ... the announcer's voice seemed to fade away as Madge sat very still. Another raid. She'd expected it, but was still not prepared for the shuddering fear that possessed her. First Bella, then Jim, that's what she could be facing. Perhaps they had died together, man and wife, and she who had never been Jim's wife would be left alone.

'Ma!' shouted Jennie at her door. 'Ma, it's Sally from the shop!'

'It's all right, Mrs Ritchie!' Sally cried, as Madge flung open her door. 'Mr Gilbride's safe, he's just been on the phone. He's come through the raid!'

For some moments Madge couldn't speak. She clung to

Jennie, letting Jennie make soothing noises as though she were the mother and Madge were the child. Then she raised her head and looked at Sally.

'Did Mr Gilbride say – did he say anything about Mrs Gilbride?'

'Aye.' Sally lowered her voice. 'He said to tell you, Mrs Gilbride died in the night.'

Chapter Forty-Seven

As the weeks passed after the horrific blitz on Clydeside, it gradually became apparent that Jim was not well.

'He's not been himself since Bella died,' Madge told Abby. 'He looks all right, he goes to work, but there's something wrong.'

'Ma, that was a terrible time for him. I mean, there were over twelve hundred people killed in those Clydeside raids. You saw what it was like in Clydebank and that was Jim's old home. Then there was the shock of finding Bella, watching her die, it's no wonder he's taking time to recover.'

'Yes, that's what everybody says. I have nightmares myself about those raids.' Madge shook her head. 'But I'm not like Jim.'

To begin with he had appeared to cope very well. He arranged Bella's funeral and attended with Madge and the girls and what friends were still around. He ordered a stone to be put up later and went back often to visit the grave. If he seemed to be taking things hard, it was quite understandable; he had lost not only the woman who had been his wife, but also friends and neighbours in the most appalling circumstances. As Abby said, it was not surprising he was taking time to recover. But what was worrying to Madge was that as the time went by he seemed not to be recovering at all.

When he came home from work he began to sit alone in his flat and when Madge came down to cook a meal he would say he didn't want anything. It would take endless persuasion to make him eat something, and then he would sit staring at her with that old brooding gaze of his which she had always dreaded and had been so glad not to see in recent years. When she asked him what was wrong he always said nothing, until one evening he grasped her hand and looked long into her face.

'I should've been there, Madge, I should've stayed in Clydebank. Then she'd have gone to the shelter and she'd no' be dead.'

'Jim, you're not blaming yourself for Bella's death?' Madge cried, mystified. 'You know that was nothing to do with you. You and Bella had been separated for years, you couldn't have been expected to stay in Clydebank.'

'It was my fault, Madge, I see that now. But what can I do? I canna undo what happened.'

'No, you can't. You must put it all out of your mind, Jim. You must get on with your life.' Madge hesitated. 'Because it's my life too.'

He made no answer, she doubted if he had even heard what she said. He released her hand and sat staring into space. She knew he needed help, but where to get it? She decided to leave the matter for a while, see how he progressed. He might just suddenly come out of this, fling aside the black dog and be his old self. Hadn't he always gone up and down, swinging from one mood to another?

At first it seemed as though she had done the right thing, for he appeared to brighten a little, even to taking an interest in the war news, which semed to show Germany triumphing again, invading Greece and Yugoslavia, consolidating positions in the Middle East. When Rudolf Hess, Hitler's deputy, parachuted into Scotland in May, Jim was as intrigued as everyone else. Had he really brought a peace plan? What a piece of nonsense! Madge was thrilled, she'd been right not to worry, Jim was on the mend. But the improvement did not last. There had been further raids on Clydeside which Jim had seemed to ignore, but suddenly he began to compare them with Clydebank, to say all over again that he should never have left Bella to face the bombs alone.

'It's finished me,' he said dully. 'I canna get over it.'

'You can, you can!' cried Madge, but the distant look in his eyes told her he wasn't listening.

'I dinna think I'll go to work tomorrow, Madge. I dinna feel

333

up to it, somehow. Ma head doesna feel right. You'll let them know, eh?'

'Yes, Jim, I'll let them know,' said Madge and that same evening went to see Jim's panel doctor.

'Well, I'll have to see him, of course,' said Dr Ogilvy. He was elderly and weary, rushed off his feet because his partner had joined up, but still conscientious and thorough. 'But from what you've told me, Mrs Ritchie, it sounds like neurasthenia. That's to do with the nerves, a nervous debility you might say.'

'Mr Gilbride has never been a nervous man,' Madge told him. 'Even on that day of the raid, he seemed quite in control.'

'But he'd gone through a terrible experience. Not only helping to dig for his wife, but seeing his old home in ruins, finding some of his friends dead. These things take their toll.' The doctor rolled a pen between his fingers. 'How much has he talked of his experiences, do you know?'

'Not very much. Except, as I told you, he seems to be blaming himself now that he wasn't there when the raids came.'

'The classic symptom of guilt. I'll come and see him tomorrow.'

Madge, looking doubtful, thanked the doctor. She wasn't at all sure that Jim would consent to see him.

In fact Jim didn't seem to mind when Dr Ogilvy appeared at the door of his flat the following afternoon.

'Is it ma head you've come about?' he asked. 'Aye, well I could do with something for it. It's good of you to think of me.'

While Madge waited apprehensively across the landing, Jim let the doctor in and closed the door. A short time later Dr Ogilvy came across to talk to Madge.

'Yes, it's as I thought, Mrs Ritchie. Your neighbour is suffering from neurasthenia.'

'Nervous debility, you called it?'

'Yes, almost a sort of shell shock. We used to see a lot of cases like this in the Great War.' Dr Ogilvy sighed. 'Soldiers then, civilians now. Not much progress, eh?'

'But can you help him?' Madge asked quickly.

'I'm afraid there's no miracle cure. The only thing that really helps is rest. Absolute rest. And the best place to rest would be in hospital.'

Madge's eyes widened in horror. 'An asylum?'

'No, no, just a place where he can have complete rest and quiet. Not easy to find in wartime, but such places do exist.'

Madge hesitated. 'How much would it cost? Mr Gilbride couldn't afford a lot.'

'I can get him into one of the homes supported by voluntary contributions, he wouldn't have to pay.' Dr Ogilvy put on his old-fashioned, wide brimmed hat. 'I'll arrange it as soon as possible, Mrs Ritchie. Good afternoon.'

'I'm no' going,' said Jim flatly. 'I'm no' going into any loony bin, and you can tell the doctor that now.'

'It's not a mental hospital, Jim, it's just a place for you to rest,' Madge told him urgently. 'Look, you want to get better, don't you? You know you're not well?'

'It's just ma head, and the doctor's given me some pills for that, so what else do I need?'

'Rest, Jim, rest.'

'Well, I can damned well rest at home. I dinna need to go to hospital.'

'If only we could get Malcolm back,' said Abby, but Malcolm, now commissioned, was with his unit in the Western Desert. As for Rory, no one knew what had happened to him. He had sent Jim cards at Christmas but no news of himself. No doubt he too was in the forces by now.

'Jim wouldn't want to see Rory,' Madge remarked. 'He let him come to Glasgow to see the boys, but he's never forgiven him for leaving them and Jennie.'

'At least Jennie seems to have got over Rory,' said Rachel. 'She's been so much happier lately, hasn't she? I'm glad she didn't send the boys away.'

They all agreed that Jennie was much happier, apart from all the anxiety of the war, of course. But she was making good wages at the factory in Fountainbridge, saving hard for the boys' future and her own. 'Pray God, Rory stays out of her life,' said Madge. 'But tell me now, what do I do about Jim?'

'He'll go to the hospital in the end,' Abby answered. 'Deep down he knows he must if he wants to get better.'

A few days later, Jim went into a hospital for nervous

diseases some miles from Edinburgh. It was a great weight off Madge's mind, though visiting him was difficult and she was herself beginning to feel very tired. But Jim was in good hands, he would get well, that was all that mattered.

The girls visited Jim when they could, but time was scarce for them. Jennie's hours at the factory were long. Rachel was busy organising a small exhibition of her wartime pictures which for the first time showed figures, though so oddly shaped most people thought they were just part of her usual block patterns. Still, the pictures sold, the critics saying they represented the 'essence of war', and 'conveyed in powerful terms the impact of destruction', while Madge and Jennie shook their heads and wondered why anyone would ever want to put them on their walls.

Abby was still doing what she could to keep wartime Logie's functioning, while Gerald, Ian Fox and Bernard Maddox spent more and more time on Civil Defence duties. The work was a challenge, but she didn't mind that and revelled all the more in her rare breaks when Alan came home on leave. They would spend short ecstatic times together, never mentioning Frankie, never discussing the future, just delighting in each other, taking the days as they came.

But Frankie did occasionally write to Abby, short matter-of-fact notes with no word of love. He had been on convoy duty to Malta, after a naval battle with the Italians at Cape Matapan. So far he seemed to have been lucky, had come through without a scratch, but Abby worried about him constantly, sometimes wondering if he cared whether he survived or not. She had begun to feel rather resentfully guilty because she was happy and he was not, but he had surely brought his unhappiness on himself. At one time she had thought he too might come to Edinburgh on leave and hoped he wouldn't, she couldn't face the complexity of her feelings. But he never came, so that was all right.

One evening when Jim had been in hospital for about a week, Jennie came home from work to an empty flat. Rachel had taken the boys off to the pictures with Bobby, Madge was not yet back from visiting Jim. Jennie didn't mind. It was nice to have a quiet time for once, to make herself a snack and put her feet up. The summer evening was warm, Catherine's Land was quiet, even though a number of the evacuated children had returned. She was yawning, wondering whether she should wash her hair, when she heard a step outside her door. There were always steps outside her door, but she found herself suddenly sitting up in her chair and listening hard. After a few moments she got up and went to the door and listened again, but could hear nothing. She looked back at her living room, so peaceful in the evening sunlight that was streaming through the long windows and she began to tremble. She flung open the door and cried, 'Who's there?'

A man was standing outside Jim's flat. The electric stair light, permanently on because the stair was so dark, shone clearly on his face and Jennie swayed. The man was Rory.

Chapter Forty-Eight

He had changed. In the harsh landing light his handsome face was bones and shadows. It had a yellowish tinge. His shabby jacket and flannel trousers hung loosely; he seemed weary, leaning against his father's door as though for support. But his dark blue eyes fixed on Jennie were as beautiful as ever. Though all the bitterness of the years was rushing back to consume her, his looks still stabbed her heart.

He spoke her name. His gaze was full of appeal. All she wanted was to slam her door in his face, but she couldn't seem to do it and bit her lip in frustration. She had so often pondered on what she would do if ever she met him again, what she would say, how she would make him suffer. And here he was before her and she was saying nothing.

'I came to see Dad,' Rory said quietly. 'But there's no answer.'

'He's in hospital,' Jennie said roughly.

'In hospital? He told me he wouldna go.'

'He wrote to you?'

'He asked me to come.'

'I see.' She was trembling with the wildness of her feelings. If she had thought for one crazy moment that Rory had come to see her, had wanted her forgiveness, it seemed she could think again. She was turning away blindly, when he said, catching his breath, 'Jennie, I know I shouldna ask you, but will you let me in? I need to sit down.'

'You want me to let you into my house?'

'Please?'

Her face cold and set, she stood aside so that he could move

338

past her into his old home. He had left his small case on the landing and she picked it up and followed him, watching him closely as he sank into a chair and closed his eyes. In the natural light of the living room, he looked a little better, but not well.

'Can I get you anything?' she asked reluctantly, as she put down his case. His eyes flew open.

'Some water, please.'

'I could make you some tea.'

'Water will do.'

Jennie filled a glass and gave it to him. When he had drunk it, he said,

'I'll go as soon as I can, dinna worry.'

She looked at him for a long moment. 'What's the matter with you?' she asked quietly. 'Are you ill?'

'There's something wrong with ma blood. A form of anaemia.'

'Anaemia? I thought only women got that.'

'Seems not. I've had it for years.'

'Since that Christmas you didn't come to see the boys?'

He nodded. 'I wasna too good then. I'm better now.' He looked round the flat. 'Where are the boys, Jennie?'

'With Bobby. They'll be back soon.'

'Will you let me see them?'

'I thought you said you were leaving.'

He was silent, looking down at his long, bloodless hands.

'Where were you thinking of going?' Jennie pressed him.

'Well, to Dad's. But he's in hospital. How is he?'

'He just has to rest.'

'I gathered it was some sort of breakdown.'

'Came on after Bella died in the raid.'

'Oh, God.' Rory put one of his fragile hands to his brow. 'I'd have come up then, but I wasna sure if he'd want it. Then out of the blue he wrote and asked me to come himself. Said he felt bad, he couldna explain, but he'd like to see me.' Rory's gaze was again fixed on Jennie's face with a look of appeal. 'Jennie, you understand I couldna refuse?'

'Of course I understand, you had to see your dad.'

'But I'll get out of your way now.' Rory stood up, slowly flexing his fingers. 'Thanks for letting me rest.'

As he made his way slowly to the door, Jennie called after him, 'Wait! What are you going to do?'

'Find somewhere for the night.'

'I've got a key to your dad's flat. I could let you in.'

'Could you? That'd be good of you.'

She hesitated. 'Have you had anything to eat? Maybe you'd like a sandwich.'

He shook his head. 'I couldna put you to the trouble.'

'You're exhausted, I can't let you go over to that empty flat without even a bite to eat.' Jennie was keeping her eyes down, embarrassed by her own offer. 'Donnie Muir let me have a ham shank. Would you like a bit of that?'

'I would.' Rory gave a thin smile. 'It'd make a change from liver.'

'Liver?'

'I have to eat liver. Raw, if I can get it down.'

Jennie made a face. 'For the anaemia? I don't think I could do that.' She hesitated. 'Is it serious, what you've got?'

'I've had it since nineteen thirty eight and I'm still here.'

'Oh, well then . . .'

She went to cut the sandwiches, her hands shaking as she buttered the bread and sliced the ham. It didn't seem real, what was happening. Rory back in the living room. But the hurt and the bitterness flowing back were real enough. Her eyes filled with tears she would not let fall.

He did not eat much, but when he sat back in his chair, drinking the tea she had made, it seemed to her that he was looking stronger.

'You're very good,' he said quietly.

'No.' She took away his plate and returned with sheets and a pillowcase. 'I'd better make up a bed for you in your dad's flat, there won't be one ready.'

'I must look terrible,' he said harshly.

'What do you mean?'

'Well, you wouldna be doing all this for me if I was well, would you? Och, I ken you hate me. And you've every right. I hate maself.'

'Why are you talking like this?' she cried, suddenly bursting into the tears she had been trying to conceal. 'There's no point, no point!'

340

'Jennie . . .' He leaped up and put out his hands to her but she knocked them aside. 'Just tell me, have you brought her with you?' she asked chokingly. 'Is she somewhere waiting for you?'

His face was a mask. 'Sheena? I havena seen Sheena for six years.'

'Six years?' Jennie went white. 'I don't understand. Haven't you been living together?'

Rory lowered his eyes. 'It didna work out. Sheena got tired of me. And I . . .' He ran his hand over his lips. 'I realised what I'd done.'

'And you told me you couldn't live without her!' Jennie said contemptuously.

'Aye, I did say that. When I was crazy.'

'Oh, it's easy to say that, isn't it? Crazy people don't have to feel responsible.'

'I'll tell you this, there's never a day goes by that I dinna feel guilty about what I did to you and the boys.'

'But you never thought of coming back?'

'I couldna. I couldna face you. I did try to see the boys because I was their father. I thought they should get to know me, whatever I'd done. But I couldna ask you to take me back.'

'So you wasted all those years?' she said slowly. 'All those years, because of her?'

'Would you have taken me back if I had come?'

'I don't know.' She looked into his desolate eyes. 'You killed something in me when you left me. It's what Rachel did to Malcolm. They're together, but it's never been the same. It would've been like that for us.'

'That's what I knew,' said Rory.

There were voices outside the flat and Jennie turned her head.

'It's the boys. They're back from Bobby's.'

They came rushing in, full of the film they'd seen, *The Big Store*, with the Marx Brothers. 'Och, Ma you should've seen it! There was this big shop like Logie's and they were all swinging across the counters and—' As their eyes found Rory, their voices died away. They stood quite still, Hamish open-mouthed, Will turning brick-red.

'Here's your dad,' Jennie said levelly. 'He's come to see you.'

'Why?' asked Will coldly. 'Why's he come now when he stopped coming before?'

'I was ill,' said Rory quickly. 'I couldna come before, Will.'

Hamish took a step towards him. 'Are you better, then?'

'Yes, I'm a lot better.'

'You don't look better.'

'I'm no' as bad as I look. It's just that my blood is short of something it needs, makes me look pale.'

'Sort of yellow,' Hamish corrected, studying his father's face with interest, then he suddenly flung his arms around him. 'I don't care about your face, Dad. I'm glad you've come back.'

'He hasn't come back,' said Jennie. 'Not to stay.'

'Och, no,' snapped Will, 'he's never wanted to stay, has he?'

'You're wrong there,' Rory retorted, over Hamish's blond head. 'I've always wanted to stay.'

'Let's make up the bed,' Jennie said quickly. 'Say good night to your father, boys. He's sleeping in your Granddad's flat.'

'Why's he not sleeping here?' asked Hamish.

'Because he's come to see Granddad.'

'And you said he'd come to see us!' cried Will.

'I suppose I canna expect Will to want me,' Rory said despondently, as Jennie unlocked Jim's door. 'He thinks I've let him down.'

'And haven't you?'

'I told him I was ill, I couldna come to see him.'

'Has it slipped your mind he knows you left us?'

'Slipped ma mind? Oh, God, Jennie—'

'You'd better sit down while I make the bed.'

Rory dropped into a chair and sat with his head sunk on his chest and his eyes closed, while Jennie swiftly made up a bed for him.

'That's you, then,' she told him. 'It's all ready.'

He sat up and looked around his father's home with vague surprise. It seemed better cared for than he remembered, the range black-leaded and shining, the old chairs polished. And somebody had made new curtains and put plants at the window. Surely not his father?

'Fancy Dad coming back here,' he remarked. 'He's never made it look like this, has he?'

342

'No, that's Ma's doing,' Jennie replied. 'She looks after it for your dad.'

'They're friends again?'

For the first time since meeting Rory again, Jennie smiled. 'Certainly are. They'll probably be getting married soon.'

'Ah, I'm glad, I'm really glad. Dad always thought the world of your Ma.'

'Sometimes had a funny way of showing it.'

'Maybe he's like me.' Rory fixed Jennie with his great eyes. 'Crazy.'

Jennie looked away. 'Think I'd better say goodnight now. Ma can tell you tomorrow how to get to the hospital.'

'Will you no' be going?'

'I'll be at work. I make aircraft mouldings at Fountainbridge.'

'You're working in a factory? Jennie, you dinna have to do that! I've always kept up with ma payments—'

'I like to be independent, I've put your money into savings for the boys. How did you manage to send anything, anyway, if you've been so ill?'

'The MP I work for and the Party have been very good to me. When I was first ill, they let me have sick pay. Then when I got better – went into remission, the doctors call it – I was able to go back to ma job.' Rory's voice was lifeless. 'Canna join up, though. That makes me feel pretty bad.'

'You're working now?'

'When I can. I take it as it comes, I'll probably keep going for years.' With sudden bitterness, he added, 'If you're interested.'

Their eyes met and locked. Jennie was about to speak, was putting out her hand, when Madge's voice called from the door.

'Hello, is anyone there?'

'Only me, Ma!' Jennie called back, her voice shaking.

'I saw Jim's door open, thought I'd better check.'

Madge came in, looking hot and flustered. 'Oh, Jennie, you'd never believe how long I had to wait for those buses!' When she saw Rory struggling up from his chair, she stopped short and turned pale. 'Rory?' she whispered.

'He's come to see Jim,' said Jennie.

'Dad sent for me, Mrs Ritchie.' Rory was keeping his eyes down and his voice low. 'I'm sorry.'

'You don't have to apologise to me,' Madge said coldly. 'What have you been doing, Jennie? Making up a bed?'

'Well, there wasn't one ready. Rory has to sleep somewhere.'

'Perhaps we'd better say good night, then.' Madge's pretty face was strangely severe.

'Yes, I was just going.' Jennie, without looking at Rory, moved to the door. 'Good night, Rory.'

'Good night, Jennie, and thank you. Mrs Ritchie, shall I see you tomorrow?'

'What for?'

'Well, Jennie said you'd tell me how to get to the hospital to see Dad.'

'Oh, I see.' Madge nervously swung her shopping bag. 'I can do that, I suppose.'

'I'd be very grateful.'

Her lip trembling, Madge left Jim's flat, followed by Jennie. On the landing, Madge turned at once to her daughter.

'Now why did Jim have to go and do a thing like that?' she cried. 'Sending for Rory, of all people! I never wanted Rory to come up, never! Upsetting you and the boys just when you've all settled down without him!'

'He's not with Sheena now, Ma.'

'What difference does that make? If she's left him, serve him right, but it doesn't alter what he did to you.'

'Do you think I don't know that, Ma?'

'Jennie, you wouldn't take him back?' Madge asked anxiously.

'He hasn't asked to come back. Let's not talk about it.' Jennie gave a great sigh. 'Listen, Ma, do you think you could try to get me some liver tomorrow? Rory has to have it. He's got anaemia.'

Chapter Forty-Nine

Rory said he would stay a week. Every day he made the long tiring journey into Peeblesshire to see his father, always (after the first time when Madge went with him) travelling alone. When he arrived at the gaunt old house that had been converted into the hospital, he was usually too exhausted even to speak, but Jim never noticed. It seemed to Rory that his father spent most of his time looking at what was no longer there.

Sometimes they would sit outside on the overgrown terrace, from which steps led down to the gardens that were fast returning to the wild. There were no gardeners at the hospital now, and even the medical staff consisted only of elderly doctors brought out of retirement and very young nurses. Rory didn't see that much could be done for his father in the circumstances, except to give him the peace and rest that had been prescribed. Even the peace was occasionally put at risk by the other patients, particularly a thin-faced, red-haired man who liked to put forward his own plans for defeating Hitler while declaiming on Churchill's faults as war leader.

'Now, what would that turncoat know about running a war?' he bellowed one afternoon when Rory was there. 'Did he no' cross the floor and more than once? Used to be a Tory, took up with the Liberals, went back to the Tories – you canna trust a man that changes his mind!'

As Jim shook his head, making no reply, Rory sat with his head bent and self-hatred filling his heart.

In the evenings, Rory would return to Jim's flat and lie down until he found the strength to swallow the liver Madge found for him, then he would go over to talk to the boys and wait for

Jennie to come home from work. Hamish was always perfectly at ease with him and even Will was slowly coming round, especially when Rory handed over the chocolate he had brought from London.

'Had to queue for that,' he remarked, 'but I was lucky to get it. Sweets'll be going on the ration soon.'

'Don't you want a bit?' Will asked him and, when Rory shook his head, gave his father a curious look. 'Is it true you have to eat bits of raw liver?'

'Ugh!' cried Hamish. 'How can you, Dad?'

'It's surprising what you can do when you have to,' Rory replied.

As soon as they heard he was back, Abby and Rachel came over to meet him at Jennie's; Abby as worried as Madge over the damage he might do her sister, Rachel strangely pleased to see him.

'Sounds a terrible thing to say,' she confided, 'but it's nice not to be the only black sheep around here. What people don't realise is that it's just as bad to be the guilty party as the innocent one.'

'I wouldna say that,' Rory answered quietly.

'Yes, it's true, because the innocent ones get everybody's sympathy and the bad folk like you and me have to go around struggling with guilt. It's not pleasant.'

'Deserved, though.'

'You don't mind wearing sackcloth and ashes?' she asked impatiently.

'Doesna put back the years,' he said bleakly. 'The years I took from Jennie and the boys.'

Neither Rachel nor Abby made any comment on Rory's appearance, but they were, he guessed, both secretly shocked. Perhaps it lessened Abby's severity of manner towards him, though the look in her dark eyes was not one he wanted to meet.

'You're not planning to stay, are you?' she asked sharply, drawing him aside.

'No, I only came to see Dad.'

'That's just as well. You may have split up with Sheena, but it's too late for you to come back to Jennie. She's made a life of her own without you and we don't want to see her hurt again.'

'I'm no' going to hurt her,' he said steadily. 'I told you, I'm no' staying.'

She sat back, relaxing a little, and he felt able to tell her he'd been sorry to hear about her and Frankie.

She shrugged. 'One of those things.'

'I saw him, you ken.'

'Saw him? Where?'

'In a pub in London. On leave with some other navy men.' Rory smiled reminiscently. 'Playing the piano.'

'And drinking a lot, I suppose?'

'You canna expect a sailor no' to have a drink, Abby.'

'He'd given it up, that was the thing. Did you speak to him?'

'Aye. He was telling me a bit about the life on the convoys. Pretty hard. I dinna blame him for taking a drink or two and enjoying himself back home.'

'No, he has a right to do what he likes.' Abby turned aside. 'It's really nothing to do with me what he does. We've parted and that's an end to it.'

Later, over the light supper Jennie had made, Rachel asked Rory how he had found his father.

'Pretty strange. Unlike I've ever seen him before.'

'Did he talk about the raids?'

'Didna talk about anything much. When I asked him why he'd asked me to come up, he said he just wanted somebody of his own again. Even me,' Rory added, in a low tone.

'Somebody of his own?' Jennie repeated. 'Why, he's got the boys and Bobby and Ma.'

'He seemed to want somebody from the old days.'

'Because he wants to live in the past,' said Abby, 'before anything happened to Bella and he got caught up in all the horror of the raid. Did you speak to the doctor?'

'Aye, he was quite hopeful. Said he was sure Dad would come out of it eventually, though it would take time.'

'How long?' asked Rachel.

'He couldna say.'

After Rory had gone to his early bed and Rachel had gone home to Bobby, Abby turned to Jennie.

'How are you managing?' she asked gently. 'Not letting this get you down?'

'No, why should I?'

'Come on, you know what I'm talking about.'

'Well, I scarcely see Rory. I'm out all day at work, he's at the hospital. He'll be gone next week.'

'You won't let him stay, will you?'

'Ma keeps asking me that. He doesn't even want to stay.'

'But would you let him, if he did?'

'No, I wouldn't. I told him things could never be the same and he agreed.'

'The thing is, he's not well, is he? He's got this anaemia.'

'He's getting better. He's in what they call remisssion.'

'That's a relief, then.'

But Abby privately thought she would not be happy until Rory was on the London train and moving out of her sister's life for ever.

On Rory's last day Madge said she would go with him to see Jim, in case Jim felt bad about saying goodbye.

'Quite frankly, Mrs Ritchie, I dinna think he'll take much notice, but I'm sure he'd like you to be there anyway.'

'Maybe.' Madge sighed deeply. 'Sometimes I feel like you, he doesn't notice either way.'

It was a beautiful June day when they came to Jim on the terrace. He was alone, a paper full of the news of the German invasion of Russia slipping unread from his knee.

'How are you feeling?' they asked.

'Fine,' he replied, and lay back and closed his eyes.

Madge and Rory exchanged glances.

'You look as though you should rest yourself,' Madge told Rory, for though she knew she would never forgive him for what he had done to Jennie, she could not withhold her natural sympathy when she saw his exhaustion. 'That long walk up from the bus does you no good at all.'

'True.' He took a chair and like his father lay back and closed his eyes.

Madge herself was glad to take the weight off her feet She looked around at their peaceful if neglected surroundings, relieved that the man with the red hair was not in evidence that day to disturb them. How wicked to criticise Mr Churchill! If anyone could get them through this war it would be Winnie. Insects droned through the warm still air, birds at a distance swooped and called, and 'Summer's the time for me,' thought Madge, remembering a poem she had learned at school. 'When every leaf is on the tree ...' How did it go? 'And Robin's not a beggar, and Jennie Wren's a bride, and larks hang singing, singing, over the wheatfields wide ...' It was a long time since Madge had seen any wheatfields. She thought it nice to be in the country again, though not of course for the reason that Jim was ill. Here where it was so quiet and pleasant no one would ever think there was a war on. Her eyelids drooped, she was beginning to nod, then was suddenly frighteningly awake. Jim was sitting upright, staring at Rory with eyes full of horror.

'Will you look at him, Madge?' he whispered. 'He's ma Rona all over again, he's Bella!'

Madge fearfully turned her own eyes on Rory. What was Jim seeing? Rory was only sleeping, yet it was true his face seemed as colourless as Bella's that last time Madge had seen her, his lips as white, his fine nose as pinched. Only the line of his dark eyelashes against his cheeks broke his pallor, as hers had done. With Jim still staring fixedly at his son, a rising fear made Madge shout, 'Rory! Rory!'

The dark lashes trembled and parted, Rory's blue eyes looked sleepily around.

'What's the matter?' He sat up abruptly. 'Is it Dad?'

'No, no, I'm all right,' Jim said through dry lips. 'Dinna worry, son, dinna worry.'

'Mrs Ritchie?'

Madge gave a shaky smile. 'Must've dropped off, woke up too suddenly. Sorry, Rory.'

A nursing assistant came into view, pushing a trolley with thick white cups of tea and some plates of Marie biscuits.

'Tea, Mr Gilbride?'

'Aye, I'm parched, but could you no' give ma guests a cup too?'

'Well, I'm no' sure—'

'Och, come on!' Jim's brown eyes flashed, his smile was broad, and Madge caught her breath. It was as though a curtain had parted and a glimpse of the old Jim was being revealed. 'Don't go back, don't go back!' she wanted to cry, but his smile faded and the light in his eyes died.

'Suit yourself,' he muttered, sitting back, 'it doesna bother me.'

It was time to say goodbye. Rory had gone to the men's cloakroom, while Madge sat holding Jim's hand. If only he would come back again! She searched his face for some sign of animation, but it was a shuttered room, she could not see the Jim she loved. She was loosening her fingers from his when his hand tightened and held her fast.

'Madge,' he said urgently, and her heart leaped, for there was brightness in his eyes.

'Are you feeling better?' she cried.

He wasn't listening to her. 'Madge, let's get wed, eh? Let's no' wait any longer, let's get wed now.'

Her heart sank. The brightness she had seen was something wild, irrational; she didn't know how to respond. Not daring to say that Bella had only been dead three months, she tried to calm him.

'You're not well yet, Jim. We can't get married until you're really well, can we?'

'I am well, I'm better, I just want us to be together.' He flung his arms around her. 'Madge, you have to listen to me, you have to let us get wed, because I need you, you're all I've got, everybody's leaving me, I'm alone and I canna face it!''

'What do you mean, Jim? No one is leaving you!' Madge struggled free from his strong clasp. 'Why do you say you're alone? You have all your family, you have me—'

'I am alone, I am, I feel it. Everybody's going, like ma Rona went and Bella and Rory—'

'Rory's only going to London, he'll soon be back.' Madge looked round desperately and gave a gasp of relief as she saw Rory returning. 'Rory, come quickly, your dad's upset because he won't see you again!'

'Dad, it's all right, it's all right.' Rory flung himself down beside Jim's chair and looked lovingly into his father's face. 'I'll be back before you know it. Come on, now, take it easy, take it easy.'

But Jim was threshing and moaning, and a nurse arrived, then a doctor. Jim was given a sedative and taken to his bed, while Madge and Rory waited in the corridor, Rory's arm around Madge's shoulders, though it wasn't clear if he was able to support her.

'He's sleeping already,' said Dr Ferguson, a quiet capable man in his early sixties. 'Sometimes these upsets happen and it's not always clear why. Did anything happen this afternoon, do you know, to bring this on?'

'No, he seemed fine until we were just about to go,' Madge answered. 'Then he seemed to get upset because his son had to leave.'

The doctor glanced at Rory, who said he had to return to London.

'You couldn't delay your trip for a day or two?'

'Maybe.' Rory hesitated. 'I'm not sure.'

'Well, if you could, it might help your father over a bad patch.' Dr Ferguson spoke cheerfully, but as Madge and Rory walked slowly away he stood for some time thoughtfully watching their retreating figures.

Rory was lying on his bed resting when Jennie came over to say she hadn't been able to find any liver that day.

'But the butcher let me have some shin and I've made a really nice stew, I'm sure it would do you good. Would you like to come and have your tea with us tonight?'

He sat up, smiling. 'How come you're home so early?'

'My weekend off. We always finish early on Fridays when it's a weekend off.' Jennie stood looking down at him, not returning his smile but not looking unfriendly. 'Will you come, then?'

'Yes, I'd like to.'

How polite they were, how stilted. Yet when he was at the table, Madge's old familiar table, it seemed to Rory that the atmosphere round him was warm. Hamish was chattering away, firing questions about London, the Blitz, the number of bombs dropped, had he seen the King and Queen, and so on, while Will looked on indulgently and Jennie, flushed from cooking, served the stew.

'I know it's not the right thing for a hot day, but the boys don't like salad and I thought you should have the beef, Rory. You're looking weary today.'

'Aye, I'm no' too grand. It's been a tiring day. Dad had a bit of a setback.'

'I know, Ma told me. It's so disappointing.' Jennie glanced

351

at Rory's plate. 'But you're not eating anything! Come on, you must keep your strength up.'

'Waste not, want not, Dad,' said Hamish. 'Can I have your stew?'

'Hamish, don't be so greedy!' cried Jennie. 'Your dad has to finish it.'

Rory laughed. He didn't feel at all hungry, didn't in fact feel well, but just for a moment it was as though he was part of the family again, as though the black cloud of guilt had lifted from his brow and all those long years apart had never happened.

'Let him have it, Jennie,' he said easily. 'I'm really not hungry. Maybe I'd better have a bit of a rest again.'

She hesitated. 'Why don't you rest on my bed?' she asked, conscious that her bed had once been theirs. 'You needn't go to your dad's yet.'

'You're sure you don't mind?' He too was conscious that in entering their old room some sort of step was being taken.

'Go on. I'll bring you some tea as soon as I've washed up.'

The room had scarcely changed since he had shared it with Jennie, except that there was a new coverlet on the double bed and the old-fashioned washstand had been replaced by a fitted hand basin. Jennie would be proud of that, Rory thought. There were photographs of the boys by the bed, and one of Rachel with Bobby and Malcolm, showing Malcolm in his officer's uniform. Rory stared at that for a long time, also at the snapshot of his father and Madge sitting on the sands at Portobello.

Portobello. Rory's thoughts went back to the day in 1925 when Sheena had walked with Tim on those same sands and he had walked with Jennie. Och, what a fool he'd been, then and since! When Jennie had been so close to him and he hadn't recognised the gold he'd held or the dross he'd wanted. He moved his head on Jennie's pillow, feeling great unease of mind and body, but then Jennie came in with the tea and he felt better.

'Now you will drink this?' she asked sternly, and he nodded eagerly.

'Aye, I'm thirsty, very thirsty.' While he drank, she sat in the old basket chair and watched him. When she rose to take his cup, he murmured to her not to go and she sat down again. 'I wanted to ask you, would you mind if I stayed on for a day or two? As Dad is no' so good?'

'No, I wouldn't mind. You're not well enough to travel, anyway.'

They sat quietly together, listening to the voices of the boys next door playing some game, the noises of Catherine's Land they both knew so well. Then Will put his head round the door and asked if they could go out for a bit, it was still so light and so warm.

'Yes, but don't go wandering too far,' Jennie warned him. 'And be home before it gets dark.'

'Have the evacuees come back now?' asked Rory. 'Seem to be plenty of children around.'

'Didn't seem much point in keeping them away. Edinburgh's had so few raids.'

'I'm glad you've got the boys. Are you really managing pretty well, Jennie? I mean, in spite of the war and everything? You've got friends and a bit of money, so things are no' too bad?'

'Why are you asking me all this?' she murmured uneasily. 'So you needn't worry about me when you're in London?'

'I wouldna go to London if you wanted me to stay.' Rory's dark blue eyes were steady on Jennie's face. She couldn't meet them.

'Rory, I don't know what to say to you. I told you how it would be if you came back, things wouldn't be the same.'

'I'd settle for what there was.'

'Would you?'

'Aye.'

'Maybe I would to,' she said breathlessly. Slowly she bent her face to his and their lips met. When they drew apart, neither spoke for some time, then Jennie stood up.

'I haven't actually done the washing-up,' she said, laughing a little. 'I wanted to come and talk to you. But I'll do it now and you can have your rest.'

'You'll come back soon?'

'Soon.' She looked back at him from the door and gave him her own sweet smile, the smile he always saw in his mind's eye when he pictured her; then she left him. He wanted to cry after her, the way a child cries who can't bear his mother to say good night, but exhaustion was overtaking him and he knew he must lie still. There was pain somewhere. He couldn't make out whether it was in his head or his chest, and he couldn't seem to focus on the light around him. He closed his eyes. That seemed the easiest thing to do.

'Rory,' whispered Jennie later. 'Rory?'

And then her shriek, echoing through the flat, transfixed her sons coming up the stair and brought all the women of Catherine's Land running.

Chapter Fifty

The day of the funeral was damp and grey; it seemed right to
the mourners that the sun had deserted them. Jennie had asked
that people should not wear black, but Jim, marching like a
soldier up the cemetery path, wore his dark suit and Malcolm
in service dress wore a black band around his arm. There
had been no formal church ceremony – Rory would not
have wanted it Jennie said – but Jim had asked a Church of
Scotland minister to conduct a short service over the grave.

'Mebbe Rory would no' have wanted it, but I do,' he
declared, and Jennie, still stunned by the shock of Rory's
death, had not argued. What did it matter, anyway? If it made
Jim feel better to have prayers said to a God Rory had never
believed in, why not have them said? Funerals were for the
living. The dead could take no comfort.

Oh, but it was hard to think of Rory as one of the dead! His
doctor in London had told Dr Ogilvy that his heart was
already damaged, that in those last days in Edinburgh he had
been living on borrowed time. But if he had come back to
Jennie when he had first fallen ill, if he had told her then that
he had pernicious anaemia, she would have saved him. Yes, she
was sure of it. She would have cared for him, seen that he had
the right food, saved his strength, she would have pulled him
through because she loved him. No matter how she had fought
against it, no matter how she had maintained that things could
never be the same between them, that love was still there, a
part of her, and always would be until she died herself. But her
dying was a long way away. Ahead of her lay empty years she
didn't know how to face.

She was vaguely touched by the number of people who had come to say farewell to Rory. Not only the neighbours from Catherine's Land, but one-time colleagues of Rory's from the local Labour Party (those who were not away in the forces), friends of Jim who remembered him as a boy, even a few fellows who had worked with him at the builder's yard long ago. Then there were the people Rory had known in London, among them a keen-faced man with a limp who introduced himself as John Ward, the MP who had employed Rory as political agent. 'One of the brightest, most enthusiastic workers I've ever known,' he told Jennie. 'I can't tell you what a loss he is going to be. Many of us had him tipped for the Commons himself in the next election.' Rory an MP? Jennie had held her sons close and smiled mistily at the idea.

'Do you hear that, boys? Your dad might have been a Member of Parliament!'

Will, very subdued, nodded, but Hamish burst into tears and Madge came quickly to comfort him.

Madge herself had been reflecting on how death changed things. When people were alive you were free to judge them. When they died, judgment was suspended, at least for a time. Rory had betrayed Jennie, no one could forget that, but now that he had gone they would remember the good things of his life and that was how it should be. 'Speak no ill of the dead', the old saying went and Madge thought it right, for the dead could not answer back.

As the minister and the men carrying the coffin halted at the grave, Madge's eyes went to Jim and poor Jennie standing together as chief mourners. Jim looked almost his old self. He wasn't, of course, but since that terrible afternoon when he had last seen Rory, he seemed to have found the strength to face his grief. He had been prepared for it, he told Madge, he had seen death in Rory's face and after his brief moments of panic had made himself accept it. In a strange way it had helped him to accept Bella's death too, but it would still be some time before he would be well enough to leave hospital. There had been no more talk of getting wed.

Jennie, leaning on Jim's arm, was wearing an old blue costume which had been one of Rory's favourites. Oh, poor girl, thought Madge, to have kept it all these years! Didn't that alone show she would have taken him back? Madge was sure she had been thinking of it, had maybe thought for a little while her happiness could be returned to her. Now her only comfort must be that she was a widow and no longer a wronged wife. The sorrow of losing Rory would be hard to bear, but not as hard as the pain of rejection.

Rachel, standing with Malcolm and Bobby, was thinking, So Rory's no longer like me, no longer the guilty party. He was dead and had escaped all blame, he was washed white as snow. But she didn't envy him. It was a terrible thing to die before your time, before you had finished your work. Work was really all that mattered to Rachel, apart from her family, and she supposed she must include Malcolm there. He had lost weight since joining up, really looked quite smart in his service dress and hadn't lost any more hair, Had he minded that he had never been as handsome as Rory? Probably not because he had his own compensations, his brains, his material success, he need never live in Catherine's Land, nor any place like it. Rory, of course, was different there, he would never have left Catherine's Land if it hadn't been for Sheena. And at the thought of Sheena, Rachel looked up and blinked in disbelief. Was it possible? She turned to catch Abby's eye and saw that her sister was already quietly leaving the graveside, making her way towards two figures standing together in the distance.

It had begun to rain. The two women had put up umbrellas and as the water dripped and slid around them, their water-clear eyes fixed on Abby were totally innocent.

'How dare you?' whispered Abby, shaking with anger. 'How dare you come here today, intruding on my sister's grief? How dare you?'

'Hen, we only came to pay our last respects,' Lily MacLaren said gently. 'No need to speak to us like that, eh?'

'How did you even know about Rory? Who told you?'

'Saw it in *The Scotsman*, didn' we, Sheena?' Lily, unchanged by the years except that her dark hair was greying, looked at Sheena, who nodded calmly.

'You can say what you like, Abby, but I've got ma rights. That feller being buried today would've been married to me, only your sister wanted to hang on to him. She shouldna forget that.'

357

'And you shouldn't forget that you left him, Sheena. You'd tired of him, but he'd already tired of you. He wanted to come back to Jennie, she was his wife. You have no rights at all.'

'You canna stop us staying if we want to.'

'No, but I'm asking you to go, to leave before Jennie sees you. Please, will you do that?'

'Abby, can I no' speak to your ma?' pleaded Lily. 'The sweetest woman in the world and ma greatest friend. Is her and Jim wed yet? Och, I canna tell you how I've missed her all these years!'

'If you really care about my mother, you'll go, Mrs MacLaren, and take Sheena with you.' Abby, breathing hard, glanced back desperately at the people round Rory's grave, listening now to the minister's words. 'Oh, for God's sake,' she burst out, 'will you go?'

Slowly the umbrellas were turned and the two slender figures picked their way across the uneven path to the cemetery gate. Abby, still shaking, watched them go then, stumbling a little, returned to the mourners.

Rachel had wanted to provide refreshments at her house, which was more suitable than Catherine's Land, she told Madge, with more space and cloakrooms and everything.

'If it's fine we can go in the garden,' she added, 'and I'll get my daily to hand things round.' (Rachel had long ago dispensed with a full-time maid, you couldn't get them anyway, now that there was a war.)

'It's not a party,' Madge had replied. 'Jennie's flat was Rory's home, it was where they were happy. She wants people to go back there.'

'And you'll get something from Mackenzie's, I suppose?'

'Well, they're very good, letting me have things when they can. Annie's back there now, you know, working part-time. Did you know her girls had left school? Yes, both making aircraft parts with Jennie, I can't believe it!'

'Time goes by. All right, Ma, if it's what Jennie wants, let them all come back to Catherine's Land.'

The London contingent made their apologies, they had to catch an evening train, but everyone else went back to Jennie's, squashed in somehow, and ate the fish paste sandwiches,

Mackenzie's teacakes, rock buns and fruit cake made with dried egg and currants left over from the Christmas ration. Abby had managed to bring sherry from Logie's and people were cheerful as they are at funerals, even though Jessie Rossie began to talk about telegrams and how she never slept a wink at nights for worrying about her boys. But Archie Shields said soldiers themselves saw no point in worrying. If your number was coming up, it would come up, there was nothing you could do, at which the company howled him down and said it was all right for him, his number wouldn't be coming up anyway. At seventy-three, he replied with dignity, his number could come up any time.

Jennie worked hard all afternoon, making tea, passing sandwiches, showing no sign of her feelings, but she did not join in the talk. Finally, Abby missed her and found her in her room, looking at the bed where Rory had died, not crying, just sitting very still.

'Oh, Abby,' she murmured, and felt for her sister's hand.

'Don't you worry about those people out there,' Abby told her. 'We'll look after them.'

'No, it was good of them to come, I want to see to them, and it's better to keep busy.' Jennie looked into Abby's face. 'Thanks for what you did today,' she said quietly.

'Oh, God, you saw them?'

'I had the feeling she'd be there.'

'The cheek of it! The sheer bone-headed lack of feeling!'

'They don't actually mean any harm, you know. I see that now.'

'Jennie, you used to say you hated Sheena!'

'Well, I did. I suppose I still do in a way, because she took Rory from me, but I don't believe she ever set out to do that. Things just happen for Sheena and Lily. They just go along with them.'

'So if they think of coming to the funeral and upsetting the family, that's all right, then?'

'No.' Jennie shuddered. 'If Sheena had come up and spoken to me, I don't know what I'd have done.'

Madge came in and said people were beginning to leave, did Jennie want to come and say goodbye? Jennie rose at once, but Abby put her hand on her arm.

'Listen, Jennie, I've been thinking, this place is going to be very painful for you, isn't it? So full of memories? Isn't now the time for you to make a fresh start somewhere else?'

'I don't understand you.'

'Well, will you let me help you to find another place to live? A house, maybe, with a garden?'

Madge in the doorway drew in her breath sharply. Jennie gently freed herself from Abby's hand.

'Another place to live? Why would I want that? I'm happy here.'

'We could afford something better, '

'You could.'

'Yes, I could afford it for you. As I say, it's bound to be sad for you here—'

'No, it's not sad. It's my home. It was Rory's home. He came back to me here. I'll never leave it.'

'You say it's full of memories,' Madge put in. 'Jennie wants those memories. How could she start all over again somewhere else?'

Abby shook her head in a gesture of defeat. 'It was only a suggestion. If it's not what you want, that's all right.'

'I appreciate the offer, Abby, I really do,' said Jennie.

'I know, I know. Look, you go and say goodbye. We'll make a start on the washing-up.'

Everyone had left except the family, and now Rachel and Malcolm said they must go too. Rachel, putting on her hat, said, 'Jennie, would you like me to paint a portrait of Rory some time? I don't usually do portraits, but I think I could make a good shot at one if you wanted me to.'

'Rachel, would you?' cried Jennie. 'Oh, I'd like that!'

'A conventional likeness?' Malcolm asked cautiously.

'Of course, of course,' Rachel answered irritably. 'I know what Jennie wants.'

'Would you need a photograph?' asked Jennie. 'Shall I get one for you?'

'No, I'll do it from memory. It'll be my memory of Rory, but as you want him to look.'

'Oh, Rachel, you're special, aren't you? No one else could do that for me.'

As Rachel gave one of her rare smiles, Malcolm came up to kiss Jennie goodbye. He had only a forty-eight hour pass and had to fly back to his unit next day.

'You'll let Rachel know if there's anything we can do? Promise?'

'I promise.'

'It's a funny thing' – Malcolm blew his nose – 'Rory and I were never close, never shared any interests, and I was angry with him when he, you know, went to London. But now he's gone, I feel – I can't describe it – as though half of me's gone too.'

'So, take care of yourself,' Jennie murmured. 'Come back safely, Malcolm.'

'Aye,' muttered Jim, briefly embracing his son, 'for God's sake, come back.'

Abby said regretfully she must just look in at Logie's, there would be letters to sign, a few things to do.

'We'll stay with Jennie,' Madge told her. 'Jim doesn't have to go back to the hospital until tomorrow.'

Abby called her nephews to her. 'Will, I'll come back soon and go over those arithmetic problems with you. Hamish, you help Will to look after your ma.' She turned to Jennie.

'I don't have to tell you, but if you need me, I'll be there. Just take each day as it comes.'

'Each day as it comes,' Jennie repeated, and flung her arms around her sister, unable to say more.

When she had hugged her mother and kissed Jim, Abby went slowly down the stair and out into the Lawnmarket where it was still light, still early, for the day that had seemed so long was not yet over. A little sunlight was filtering through the cloud, it might be a fine evening, but Abby's thoughts were dark. She felt a weight on her spirits, which was not wholly the effect of Jennie's grief; partly it was to do with that earlier talk of telegrams. Who wasn't afraid of them? Such flimsy scraps of paper, such messages of horror. 'Very much regret to inform you . . .' And then the words that changed one's life. Crossing Princes Street, Abby tried to put her fears from her. Think positively, remember the slogan, 'It might never happen', that was the thing. Alan might never be lost in battle, Frankie might never be lost at sea. But as she took the lift to her office, she could not shake off the premonition that something bad awaited her there.

Even from the corridor she could smell the cigarette smoke and guessed she would find Gerald, wanting perhaps to comfort her after the funeral. Sure enough, he was there, stubbing out his cigarette and rising to his feet at her entrance.

'Abby, I thought you might come back here. How did it go?'

'Oh, as funerals do.' She took off her hat and looked at him, wondering if it was her imagination, or did he look particularly strained? Of course, he was usually tired, he worked too hard, he smoked too much . . .

'What's wrong?' she asked quietly.

'I'm afraid I've some bad news.'

She went white, she felt icy cold.

'Is it Frankie?' she whispered.

'No, it's Alan Talbot. He's been badly wounded.'

She bowed her head. Relief, terrible guilty relief, filled her being. Only for a moment. As genuine fear for Alan replaced that other feeling for Frankie, she began to tremble and reaching out to support herself on her desk, found Gerald at her side, helping her to a chair.

'His mother's been trying to reach you all day,' he told her quietly.

'Poor woman. It was good of her to do that. She doesn't like me, you know, doesn't approve—'

'Abby, dear—'

'Gerald, please tell me the truth. Is he dead?'

'He's not dead. He's being flown home from Eritrea to a military hospital in England.'

'Will you let me go to him?'

'You don't need to ask that. Here, let me get you something.' Gerald unscrewed the pocket flask he always carried and poured her a little brandy. 'Drink this, you'll feel better.'

She swallowed the brandy obediently, feeling its fire begin to melt the numbness that held her. 'Thank you for telling me, Gerald, it was better from a friend. I was thinking that I couldn't have faced a telegram. Not that they'd have sent me one.'

'Wouldn't they? Why not?'

'You forget, I'm not Alan's next of kin.' Abby's voice shook a little. 'Only Frankie's.'

Chapter Fifty-One

Alan had been lucky. When the Italian landmine exploded outside the town of Asmara where the Argylls were garrisoned, two soldiers lost their lives. Alan only lost an arm.

'What's an arm?' he asked Abby when he could speak. 'A left one, at that? I'm still alive and I've got you, haven't I?'

'Oh, yes!' she cried, putting her lips to his cheek which was criss-crossed with surgical plasters. Oh, God, she thought.

It had been a nightmare, visiting him in the Aldershot military hospital; making the journeys on crowded, ill-lit trains; meeting his elegant, cold-faced mother at his bedside; worst of all, seeing Alan himself, a mass of bandages, tubes and wires, surrounded by grave medics who would never say if he was going to recover or not. In fact, he had made an astonishingly good recovery, even if it had been very slow. Apart from a few facial scars, there was really very little to show how near he had come to death. Except for the loss of his arm, of course.

'But that doesn't matter at all, darling,' Mrs Talbot told him. 'They can make such wonderful artificial limbs today, you know.'

'That's true,' said Abby, sitting at the other side of Alan's bed. 'There's been terrific progress.'

'So I needn't be another Captain Hook?' he asked, with a grim smile. 'Maybe so, but the army's not impressed. I'm to be medically discharged as soon as possible.'

'Well, I'm not sorry!' his mother cried. 'You've done your duty, you're out of it now!"

'So is Corporal Henderson, so is Private Wray.'

'I know, I know. ' Mrs Talbot patted Alan's hand. 'My heart

goes out to those boys' families. But you must think of yourself now, you must put it all behind you and try to get back to health.' She glanced across to Abby. 'Shall you and I go for a cup of coffee, Mrs Baxter? I think Alan ought to rest now.'

In the canteen, surrounded by convalescent soldiers in their blue hospital uniforms, Mrs Talbot wiped the rim of her thick white cup with her handkerchief.

'Lipstick stains,' she said in a whisper, 'you have to be so careful.' She sipped her coffee and fixed Abby with a cool pale stare.

'Mrs Baxter—'

'Please call me Abby.'

'Abby,' Mrs Talbot repeated with conscious effort. 'I hope you won't mind if I speak freely?'

'Not at all.' Abby stirred her coffee.

'I know we don't know each other very well, so perhaps you will regard this as an impertinence . . .'

Abby sighed and shook her head.

'But I'm naturally concerned for my son's happiness, especially now. I need to be sure about his future. You understand, don't you?'

'Of course. Any mother would want to know her son's plans. The thing is' – Abby drank her coffee – 'we haven't any.'

Mrs Talbot's features sharpened and a little nerve throbbed in her temple beneath her dark felt hat. 'I know it's difficult, you haven't obtained your divorce yet. Is that the problem?'

'I haven't actually filed for divorce, Mrs Talbot. My husband is in the navy, I don't feel that I can—'

'Of course, of course. But a divorce is planned, isn't it?'

'I can't even tell you that. You may find this hard to believe, but Alan and I haven't actually discussed the future. It never seemed to come up, somehow.'

'He is very attached to you, you know.'

'We've always had a wonderful relationship.' Abby paused. 'But completely without strings. That's what we both wanted.'

'I see.' Mrs Talbot lowered her eyes. 'Well, you may find he has a different outlook now. He may want to marry and settle down, start a family. Do you mind if I ask your age?'

'I'm not too old to have a family, but I've no plans for

365

that, either.' Abby tried to smile. 'I'm sorry, I'm not very satisfactory to you, am I?'

Mrs Talbot sat back in her hard canteen chair. She said stiffly, 'We are discussing Alan's happiness here. I'll tell you frankly, that's all that matters to me.'

'And to me, Mrs Talbot.'

'Is that true? Will you promise me then that you won't do anything to hurt him? He has been hurt enough already, hasn't he?"

'I won't do anything to hurt him,' Abby said steadily. 'I promise you.'

On December 7th, 1941, the day the Japanese attacked the American base of Pearl Harbor, Alan was transferred to an orthopaedic hospital in Edinburgh for the fitting of his artificial arm and rehabilitation. Things became easier then for Abby, except for the weight pressing on her mind and on her heart.

How can I tell him? she asked herself after every visit to the hospital. I can't. That's all there is to it.

They still never disussed the future, always carefully avoided any discussion of divorce for Abby and marriage for themselves, but she only had to look into Alan's eyes to know that he would have liked to discuss them. It had been true once that their relationship was without strings, as she had told his mother, but it was true no longer. Alan had moved on. He wanted commitment. And Abby? She wanted Frankie.

'You don't look well, Abby,' Jennie told her. 'Are you worried about Alan?'

In common with Madge and Rachel, Jennie had now met Alan and liked him. She liked Frankie too, but he was temperamental. Alan might be an actor, but he was steady and dependable. Abby would always know where she was with Alan.

'No, I'm not worried about Alan,' Abby answered. 'He's fine, learning to manage the new arm quite well.' She tried to lighten her expression. 'I expect I'm just tired. Things at work don't get any easier.'

'I'll bet they don't.'

'It's all these government restrictions on manufacturers, we can hardly find any suppliers. Do you know, we can't even get combs at the moment?' Abby shook her head. 'I ask you – combs! As for lipsticks, they're gold dust!'

'And we do need our lipsticks,' Jennie said with a smile, and for a fleeting moment, she was the old Jennie. But it was too soon for her to keep that look, too soon for her to put aside her grief. She found solace in hard work at the factory, in her sons, and in the portrait of Rory painted by Rachel. Everyone in the family thought it the best thing Rachel had ever done, and though it was quite outside her usual range, she herself was pleased that she had caught Rory's solemn good looks so well.

'Hen, d'you no' think it's too lifelike?' Jessie Rossie asked Madge. 'Jennie'll niver get over Rory when he looks like he'll just walk oot o' that frame!'

'She doesn't want to get over him,' Madge answered. 'I used to feel the same about my Will.'

'And now you've got your Jim!' cried Jessie. She added, slyly, 'Even though you're no' married yet.'

'It's too soon after Rory's death,' Madge answered, flushing. 'And then we had to get Jim better.'

'Aye, it's grand he is, eh?' Jessie put her hand on Madge's shoulder. 'Dinna worry about your Jennie, Madge, she'll find somebody else one o' these days.'

'Maybe.' Madge privately didn't think so, but she only said she must go, she had to give Jennie's boys their tea, they would soon be back from Heriot's.

It had been Abby's idea that Jennie should try to get Will and Hamish into the merchant school where places were still provided for poor fatherless boys, following George Heriot's original foundation. At first Jennie had hesitated, Rory had not approved of private education, which was one reason why Abby hadn't suggested paying fees for the boys herself. But both boys were bright, particularly Will, who had Abby's own feeling for numbers. It seemed only right that they should be given their chance. Jennie had given way and when both boys were accepted, admitted that she was pleased and proud that her sons should be going to the same school as Rachel's Bobby. Only the boys themselves complained. It was no fun having to wear a uniform and run the gauntlet of all the jeers and catcalls of the other kids when they came home from school.

'I'm sure they don't mean any harm,' said Madge. 'And they're not as lucky as you, you know. Just pretend to take no notice. It's probably the same for Bobby.'

'Bobby? He's all right, he lives in Morningside.' Will's fair face was set hard with discontent. 'Wish we lived in Morningside 'stead of Catherine's Land.'

'Your ma can't afford to live in Morningside, you know that, Will,' Madge said uncomfortably.

'Aunt Abby said she'd help us to move, only Ma said no. Now why'd she say that?'

'She likes Catherine's Land,' said Hamish, 'and so do I. Anyway, Bobby says when he grows up he's going to leave Morningside fast as he can.'

'He said that?' asked Madge.

'Aye, said he was tired of living with his ma.'

'Hamish, that's enough!' Madge hurriedly began to serve up her shepherd's pie. 'We don't want to hear any more about Bobby.'

'Said he was sick of his ma painting all the time, said he'd never want to be an artist.' Hamish forked up his pie with relish. 'I wouldn't mind being an artist, or else a tailor.'

'A tailor!' echoed Will contemptuously. 'What d'you want to be a tailor for? There's no money in that!'

'I like to watch Ma with her scissors – clip, clip' – Hamish ran his hand through the air, whistling and clicking his tongue – 'and then there's the cloth all cut out and just right. Aye, I'd like to do that.'

'I'm going to be an accountant like Uncle Malcolm,' said Will. 'Or else I might run a big store like Auntie Abby.' His blue eyes shone. 'You should see her adding up – columns this long' – he too lifted his hand in the air – 'and all in her head and always right.' He lowered his hand. 'Bobby says he just wants to do nothing. I said he was a loony. Everybody has to do something.'

'Why?' asked Hamish.

'They need to make money, stupid!'

'Will, don't talk to Hamish like that,' said Madge.

368

'Folks shouldn't need money,' Hamish declared. 'They should be able to do just what they like.'

'Och, listen to him, Gramma!' jeered Will, cleaning up his plate with a piece of bread. 'It's only when you've got money that you can do what you like, Hamish. Isn't that right, Gramma?'

'I suppose it is,' Madge said with a sigh. 'But that's enough talk about money.'

While Hamish carried away their plates, Will rested his cheek on his hand and looked into space. 'When I see Auntie Abby again,' he said thoughtfully, 'I'm going to ask her if she'd still like to buy us a house. I've had enough of Catherine's Land.'

Everyone was depressed by the war news. When the United States had entered the war after the Japanese attack on Pearl Harbor, spirits had risen. America, by sheer weight of numbers could surely crush any opposition. But the small figures of the Japanese had begun to assume giant proportions. They swept through the Philippines, they captured Hong Kong, they captured Singapore, they moved into Burma, they even threatened Australia. It seemed the whole world was in peril from the Axis forces, and though Germany was struggling in Russia, the outlook for the Allies was bleak.

Alan had left hospital in January to recuperate at his mother's home in St Andrews. Once a week he came to Edinburgh to see Abby and they would go out for a meal, paying their permitted five shillings for rabbit pie or anonymous rissoles, and Alan would try not to be self-conscious about his artificial limb and Abby would work so hard at being bright she sometimes thought she should have been on the stage herself. But when Singapore fell in February, Alan could not be cheered.

'There were men of the Second Argylls out there,' he told Abby. He looked unseeingly round the crowded restaurant. 'God knows what's happened to them.'

'Taken prisoner,' she said, desolately. 'We've already heard that Sammie Muir's in Japanese hands. His brother keeps the little shop at Catherine's Land.'

'Oh, God.' Alan looked down at his plate. 'The thing is,

what the hell am I going to do? I feel so useless, so bloody useless!'

'There's no need for you to feel like that,' she said urgently. 'Your mother's, right, you've done your bit.'

'My bit,' he said disgustedly.

'Well, it's true. You've done all you can, now you must leave it to others.'

'And what are they going to do? Singapore was our main base in the Far East and it's gone. As I see it, things are about as bad as they can be.'

'May as well eat our dinner,' Abby said quietly. 'Such as it is.'

'I know you won't like this idea,' she said later, when they were trying to tackle a strange cardboard-looking tart, 'but you could always consider going back to acting.'

'You're right, I don't like it,' Alan retorted. 'You really think I could go back to that at a time like this?'

'There are still theatres, people still need entertainment. If most of the actors have joined up, they're going to need you, aren't they?'

'Even if I wanted to go back, do you think anybody'd take me?' He glanced down at his left arm. 'With this?'

'Who's going to notice? Anyway, if you didn't have that they'd ask why you weren't in the forces. When they see that, they'll know.'

Alan was silent for a moment, then suddenly grinned. 'Abby, you really are the most down-to-earth person I've ever met! Actually, it's not a bad idea. I could get on to my old agent and see what there was going.' He sighed. 'To be honest, anything'd be better than being cosseted by Mum. She tries to make me happy and only succeeds in driving me up the wall.'

'She's going to miss you, if you take off again.'

'How about you? Will you miss me?'

'I'm not even going to answer that.'

'You've been very good to me,' he said in a low voice. 'And you've had your own troubles, I know.'

'Everyone has troubles these days.'

He moved the salt cellar round the pepper pot. 'Ever hear from Frankie?' he asked casually.

Abby's dark eyes flickered. 'What's made you think of him?'

370

'I'm sensitive to what other chaps are up to. Wondered what he might be doing.'

'He's still on convoys. Going to Russia now.'

'Russia? With the Lend Lease aid?' Alan whistled under his breath. 'Poor devil, that'll be no picnic.'

'No.' Abby looked for a waitress. 'Shall we try the coffee, or play safe and order tea?'

'Hate to say it, but it's nearly time for my train.'

She took a deep breath. 'Why don't you come back with me?'

A dark flush rose to Alan's cheeks and his tiny scars showed white. 'Maybe that wouldn't be such a good idea.'

'Why not? You're not thinking about your arm, are you? You know that doesn't matter to me.'

'It matters to me.'

Abby glanced round at the neighbouring tables, then leaned across the table. 'Are you saying that you're never going to have sex with anyone because you've lost your left arm?'

'Anyone?'

'Well, me.'

'Abby, we haven't made love since I came back. You don't know how I'm feeling.'

'Tell me, then.'

He raised his eyes to her face. 'I'm terrified.'

With a sinking heart, she took his good right hand. 'Alan, you're better. Why should you be terrified of making love to me?

'Because of how you might feel.'

'I keep telling you, I shan't mind.'

'You would. In fact, you do. I can see it in your eyes. You've put on a very good show, darling, you've been very brave, you've been wonderful, but things aren't the same, are they? They're never going to be the same between you and me.' He glanced away from her stricken gaze and got to his feet. 'For God's sake, Abby, let's get out of here!'

They stood together in the blackness of the night, and she was reminded of the time she and Frankie had stood like that, trying to see each other's faces. But she would not think of Frankie.

'I'm not letting you go back to St Andrews tonight,' she told Alan. 'Please don't argue.'

He shrugged. 'All right, I won't argue. Let's go.'

She had no coffee but she did have a bottle of wine, one of the few left in her little store. They drank it in her sitting room, Alan slumped in an armchair, Abby at his feet. Suddenly she swung round to look up into his face and he smiled, a gentle, rueful smile.

'I'm sorry, I've messed things up, haven't I? Getting possessive just at the wrong time.'

'Don't say that.'

'We never used to make demands, did we? That was what was so special.'

'You've a right to make demands. After what you've been through.'

His face changed. He leaped to his feet. 'After what I've been through? You sound like my mother. Have some more of this, have some more of that, enjoy yourself, you deserve it! Why should I deserve anything at all when other chaps are six feet under?'

'I'm sorry, I'm sorry, I didn't mean to upset you!' Abby cried.

'So why do you talk as though you were some sort of treat I should expect to have because I've only got one arm? If I can't be loved on equal terms, I don't want to be loved at all.'

She stood up and faced him with a dark, pleading gaze. 'Alan, let's not talk any more now, let's just go to bed.'

'Bed won't solve anything. That's just another treat for a good boy, isn't it?'

'I wish I could get it through to you that I really don't care about your arm!'

For a long time he stared into her face. 'Then what's wrong, Abby? What's happened to us?' With his good hand he drew her close, and she saw a sudden intelligence, a sudden fear, swim into his eyes. 'Is it Frankie?' he whispered.

Is it Frankie? The words pierced her heart.

'No!' she cried. 'No, of course not!'

But she was a fraction of a second too late. Alan let her go and stepped away, his face wiped of all expression.

'Why didn't you tell me? Did you think I wouldn't have known?'

'There's nothing between Frankie and me now, Alan, there hasn't been for years!'

'But you still love him. Don't look like that, Abby. You've nothing to reproach yourself with. You never actually said you loved me.'

'I thought I did, I thought I did! Oh, Alan, I'm so sorry. I never wanted to hurt you like this!'

'I think I always knew, deep down, that what we had wasn't going to last.' Alan took up his overcoat and began painfully sliding his artificial arm into a sleeve, while Abby, her hand to her mouth, dared only watch.

'You're leaving?' she asked, at last. 'Oh, God, Alan, what are we going to do? I promised your mother—'

'Never mind what you promised my mother. I told you, she thinks I should have the moon if I want it.' He laughed. 'But I don't expect the moon.'

He walked to the door and she ran after him, offering to go with him to the station, to call a taxi. 'Alan, will you please wait?'

'I don't want you to come to the station and I don't want a taxi. I may have only one arm, but I do have two feet and I can walk. Don't worry about me, there's no need.'

She flung her arms around him and kissed him on the mouth. 'Alan, you'll write? You'll keep in touch?'

'I'll write, I'll keep in touch.' He loosened her arms from his neck and opened her front door. 'Goodbye, Abby.'

She was crying too hard to answer him. She felt as though something very dear were being torn away from her and would never be replaced. Even as she saw him disappearing into the blackout, swinging his artificial arm, she wanted to run after him, crying it was all a mistake, she loved him, they could be married. But after a long chill moment she closed her door. Two men she had sent away from her, two men who loved her. She moved into her sitting room and stood looking down at the two empty wineglasses on the table. She had never felt more alone.

Chapter Fifty-Two

The dark days passed, became weeks, months, years. There were defeats, some victories. There were telegrams.

'It's always darkest before the dawn,' Madge would murmur.

'What dawn?' Jim would wonder.

He was grateful that he had recovered from his own personal nightmare and was able to work again, though every night when he came home there was a knot in his stomach for fear of bad news waiting. Once, the fears were realised and he found Rachel sobbing on Madge's shoulder: Malcolm had been wounded at El Alamein. Turned out it was only superficial, a shoulder wound that could be treated at a field hospital, but Tam Finnegan, injured in the same battle, had to be sent back to Aldershot and afterwards was posted to light duties in the UK. Lucky Tam, everyone said, and lucky Malcolm, for there were worse telegrams to come. Jamie Kemp reported missing in Sicily. Billy Rossie reported dead at Monte Cassino. Sammie Muir reported dead in Japanese captivity.

'I canna believe there'll be any dawn,' said Jim.

But Frankie miraculously survived. News filtered through of appalling losses to merchant ships and their escorts; Abby lived on a knife edge. Then gradually the battle against the U-boats was won and the sea lanes were made if not safe, at least safer. Frankie was able to write his laconic letters home saying he was OK, hoped Abbie was the same, and she always replied telling him that she was. Not for worlds would she mention the break-up with Alan. Where was the point? There could be no future for her with Frankie. Until the war was over, none

374

of them knew in fact if they had any future at all. Even Alan, working for ENSA, the services' entertainments organisation, was not necessarily safe. He was abroad, precise location unknown, but certainly in some war zone. 'Can't sing, can't dance, but I'm an entertainer,' he wrote cheerfully. 'Not on a par with Rita Hayworth, exactly, but we give the chaps something to watch and take their minds off Jerry. Take care.'

Abby treasured his few letters, was certain he would continue to keep in touch, was equally certain they would not meet again.

By 1944, there was much talk of invading Europe. The Russians, after horrific fighting and the siege of Leningrad that lasted for 900 days, were gradually clearing the Germans out of their country. The RAF was bombing Berlin. The tide in the Far East was slowly turning the Allies' way. It was time to defeat the Germans on their own territory.

People were not too surprised, therefore, when one June morning they got up to hear the wireless announcer triumphantly declaring,

'This is D-Day! This is D-Day!'

'There's your dawn,' Jim told Madge, but she shook her head.

'I'm thinking of all the lives that are going to be lost before it comes,' she murmured.

'Aye, more names on the cenotaph,' muttered Jim. 'What a bloody daft world we live in, eh?'

All the same he came in one day with a marriage licence in his pocket.

'Bella's been gone three years, Madge. So's Rory. I reckon we could think of ourselves now.'

'Oh, I don't know, Jim.' Madge gave a long sigh. 'It doesn't seem the right time somehow.'

'Mebbe not. We'll leave it, then. Come on, let's go to the pictures.'

They went to the pictures a lot. Everyone did. Sitting uncritically through the war films, the musicals, the costume dramas, the comedies, leaving their cares behind for an hour or two until the news reels brought them back to reality. But by the spring of 1945, the newsreels were showing more and more good news. There was no doubt then of Allied victory; the only question was when would it come?

As the Russians advanced upon Berlin, Hitler committed suicide in his bunker. His forces had already collapsed and were surrendering to Field Marshals Alexander and Montgomery. Mussolini had been executed. All that remained was for the final unconditional surrender to be made to General Eisenhower, Supreme Commander in Europe. It came on May 7th. The documents were signed. The war in Europe was officially over.

But when was VE Day? On Tuesday, May 8th, Edinburgh like the rest of the UK, waited. Did they celebrate, or didn't they? The streets were busy, flags were appearing on shops and public buildings, but people weren't sure what was happening. Then the news came. At three o'clock, the Prime Minister would make the announcement. This was VE Day. It was official.

'Thank God for that,' said Gerald.

'A public holiday,' said Ian Fox.

'Tomorrow, too,' said Bernard Maddox.

'So we close the store?' asked Abby.

'We close the store.' Gerald gave a long contented sigh. 'Everybody home to celebrate, except you three and Clara Naylor.'

'We don't go home?' asked Bernard.

'You come to my office for a drink. I've a bottle of champagne I've been saving for this very day.'

'You were confident it would come?' asked Ian Fox, his long face breaking into a grin.

'No, I wasn't. I kept it all the same.'

Outside in Princes Street, the crowds were beginning to increase, spilling up the Mound and into the Gardens, sending the sound of their singing and laughter up to the windows of Gerald's office, The feeling of joy was almost palpable. Victory had come at last and not just victory, but peace; at least, in Europe. After tomorrow people would have to begin counting the cost, remembering that there was still another enemy to defeat. But today they were going to savour the moment and enjoy themselves. And that was official, too. Hadn't they been given a holiday?

'Looking back, what was your worst moment?' Clara asked, sneezing as the champagne tickled her nose. 'I'd say, Dunkirk.'

'When France fell,' said Bernard. 'The Germans were just across the Channel, we were quite alone.'

'The fall of Singapore depressed me most,' said Ian. 'But that war's not over yet, so maybe I shouldn't mention it.'

Abby sipped her champagne and thought of Alan. The night they had talked of the fall of Singapore was the last time she had seen him. He hadn't written for some time and wasn't likely to write again; she had seen the notice in *The Scotsman* of his engagement to a Miss Selina Lulworth from Guildford. So, goodbye dear Alan. Her eyes grew a little misty. She was glad he was happy. She felt she could never have made him as happy as he deserved. All the same, it was strange to think of his engagement. When it might have been to herself.

The others had moved on to discussing demobilisation. How soon could they expect the chaps back at Logie's?

Not for some time, was Gerald's opinion. 'Takes far longer than you think to get everyone out. I'm afraid we'll just have to carry on as we are for the forseeable future. But at least we haven't got to worry now about firewatching or ARP duties.' He looked across to Abby. 'Mr Fox, Mr Maddox, I say we should drink a special toast to Miss Ritchie here, for holding the fort so well, and to Miss Naylor for all her help and support.'

'Oh, please!' Abby and Clara Naylor lowered their eyes, blushing, but the men drank the toast anyway, then Gerald said they should all get off home and enjoy themselves.

'And don't forget, it's a holiday tomorrow!' he cried, and Clara, now rather merry after the champagne which she told Abby always went straight to her head, laughed and said they wouldn't come to work by mistake. When she had left with Ian and Bernard, Gerald turned to Abby.

'You, too, Abby. No lingering to solve one last problem.'

'I'm on my way.'

But she hesitated, searching his narrow features which seemed to her to be suddenly more marked by fatigue than she remembered.

'You've been overworking,' she said quietly. 'Why don't you take a holiday?'

'A holiday? You must be joking. Life's going to be busier

than ever, now that the war's over. It's not going to be any bed of roses here just because the Germans have surrendered.'

'You haven't had a rest in five years, have you?'

'Nor have you.' He touched her hand. 'Abby, I meant that toast just now. I couldn't have got through without you. Logie's couldn't. You realise that, don't you?'

'I'm going,' she told him, laughing. 'This is getting embarrassing. Give my best to Monica. Have a good celebration.'

'And you. Oh, and Abby – mind if I ask – any news of Frankie?'

'No news. Would you say that was good?'

'I'd say so.'

They exchanged long affectionate looks, then Abby left him, hurrying to join the crowds in Princes Street and share their joy.

She had never seen so many people. Everybody seemed to have left their homes to join hands with strangers, some in uniform, some out of uniform; to sing and dance, hang on the fountain in the Gardens, sit on benches, breathe in the wonderful scent of victory. The Mound, of course, was a solid mass, but Abby managed to progress towards the Lawnmarket, looking out for her mother and Jim who might be on their way down, seeing instead her nephews. So tall now, they seemed like young men, even Hamish who was only fourteen. And how handsome they were! Will and Hamish so like Jenny, though Hamish could still at times remind people of his father, and Bobby with Rachel's dark eyes, but a droop to his mouth that was also hers and a flat bored expression that Abby found disquieting.

'Hello, Auntie Abby!' they cried, circling her. 'You off to join the dancing?'

'No, I'm on my way to see your Gramma.'

'Gramma's out with Granddad and Auntie Rachel,' said Will. 'You'll never find them in all this crush.'

'How about your ma?'

'She's at home. Said she was going to see Mrs Rossie.'

Abby nodded. Poor Jessie. 'I'll go up and see your ma, maybe celebrate later.' She took some coins from her purse. 'Here you are, boys, you might want something to spend.'

Their eyes lit up, and Hamish clasped her hand. 'Oh, thanks, Auntie Abby! Know where we're going now? The

American Services Club! They say they're throwing out chewing gum and chocolate and all kinds of stuff and all you have to do is catch it!'

'Well you just be careful,' Abby warned. 'If there are any fights or any drinking, you stay out of it!'

'Don't worry,' groaned Bobby, 'I've practically had to put that in writing to please Mum already.'

He melted away into the crowd, Will and Hamish following, and Abby moved on, skilfully avoiding soldiers dancing reels in the Lawnmarket, feeling her heart lurch as she saw sailors rolling a barrel up from the High Street, but guessing Frankie wouldn't be one of them. (He wasn't.) Donnie Muir's shop was still open and she decided to look in, say hello, and pick up one or two things.

'Aye, it's grand news, VE Day,' Donnie told her, wheezingly, 'but it's VJ Day we want to see, you ken.'

'I know,' Abby said sympathetically. 'We're all thinking of Sammie. Is your ma feeling any better these days?'

'She's managing, thanks. Like the rest of us.' Donnie wrapped up Abby's cheese and found a jar for Sally's home-made potted beef. 'Any news of Frankie?'

'Not lately.'

'But he's all right, eh? That's the main thing.'

'Yes, that's the main thing.'

Abby, carefully not looking at Mrs Baxter's old sweetie shop long since closed by Jessie Rossie, opened the door to Catherine's Land and stood looking up the stair. It looked rather worse than usual. No one cleaned it except Ma and Ma was often tired these days. How often had she stood there, thought Abby, wishing Ma and Jennie were away? How many times had she offered to find them somewhere else and how many times had they turned her down? Maybe she would look for something for Ma and Jim anyway. Jennie, so attached to her memories of Rory, would probably never move, but Ma should have her little garden before she got too old for it. As soon as the holidays were over, Abby decided she would go househunting.

She was about to climb to the Rossies' flat when Jennie came round the corner of the stair. Her solemn, pretty face broke into a smile when she saw her sister and she hurried down.

'Abby, I'm glad to see you! Come on in, we'll put the kettle on.'

'You've been with poor Jessie? I met the boys on the Mound, they said you weren't going out.'

'No, I didn't feel like it. Neither did Jessie. It's hard, you know, for people like her, when everyone else is so happy.'

'I know.' Abby took off her hat and sank down into a chair. Suddenly she felt very weary.

'Haven't got much to offer you,' Jennie murmured, setting out cups and saucers. 'The boys seem to have eaten everything.'

'Don't worry, I got some potted meat and a loaf at Donnie's. I'm not hungry, anyway.'

The sisters made a sandwich and drank their tea. It was peaceful, sitting together, just the two of them. Didn't often happen that the house was so quiet.

'You know what somebody told me the other day?' asked Jennie, breaking the silence. 'The doctors have found something to cure what Rory had. Just an injection – puts back what was missing. Fancy' – her voice shook – 'that's all it would have taken.'

'You can't be sure, Jennie. Rory's case might not have been so simple.'

'No, mebbe not.' Jennie leaned her cheek on her hand. 'I suppose I'd feel better if he hadn't – you know – wasted all those years we might have had.'

Abby stirred her tea. 'I've wasted years, too.'

'You mean you and Frankie? You can still do something about that.'

'No. We did our best and it didn't work out. Now we have to go our separate ways.'

There were voices at the door and Madge and Jim came in, followed by Rachel. They looked flushed and happy and Madge carried a flag which she said she was going to put at her window.

'Ah, you should have come out!' she cried. 'It was wonderful just being there. Better than Armistice Night, even. Everybody so happy, singing and dancing and shaking hands!'

'Shoulda seen those American guys on the Duke o'

Wellington's statue!' exclaimed Jim, flinging himself into a chair. 'Riding the horse and singing "Roll out the Barrel"!'

'I just hope Bobby's all right,' Rachel murmured. 'There'll be a lot of drinking going on, I don't want him involved.'

'I let Will and Hamish go,' said Jennie.

'Aye, and they'll be fine,' said Jim easily. 'Canna keep them in on a night like this!'

Madge, shaking Jennie's teapot, said maybe they should put the kettle on again. 'Did you hear we were planning a street party?' she asked Abby. 'I'm going to get everyone together and work out what we need. Can you sweetheart Logie's into giving us anything?'

'Might be able to get a few eggs. Strictly on the qt.'

'I've plenty of sugar,' said Rachel. 'Bobby and I don't take it, I just keep on saving it up.' She frowned a little. 'Oh, what a difficult boy he's turning out to be! I never thought he'd be so cold and hard when he grew up. Sometimes I think he really doesn't like me.'

'Och, dinna be so daft,' Jim muttered, taking one of the potted meat sandwiches. 'What lad doesna like his mother?'

'I just get the feeling that he's only waiting to leave school to be off, and then we shall never see him again.'

'It'll all be different when Malcolm comes home,' Madge said comfortingly. 'There'll be a change in Bobby then, you'll see.'

'Maybe.' Rachel sat for some moments looking darkly into space, then brightened. 'Listen, I haven't told Abby my good news!'

'What good news?' asked Abby, relieved that Rachel had some.

'You remember my picture of Catherine's Land?'

Jennie and Madge exchanged glances

'Of course,' said Abby, 'what about it?'

'It's been bought by the Scottish National Gallery, for their contemporary art collection! Can you believe it? Me, in the National?'

'Rachel, that's marvellous!' cried Abby.

'Bloody miraculous,' Jim muttered.

'I really do congratulate you,' Abby went on. 'I feel so proud. My own sister, in the National!'

'Does it have to be that picture?' asked Jennie, pouring more tea.

'Why, what's wrong with that one?' fired Rachel.

'Nothing. It's just that, well, will people know what it is?'

'I've called it Tenement,' Rachel retorted. 'That should give them a clue.'

'I'm sorry, Rachel. Of course I'm just as thrilled as Abby. We're all thrilled, honestly.'

'Except Bobby. He says he can't see why anyone should pay good money for my work.'

'I'll speak to him!' cried Madge. 'There's no call for him to be rude to you like that. After all you've done for him, too!'

'Maybe I've done too much,' Rachel said quietly, but no one answered that.

The clock was striking six when Madge cried, 'Listen!' and they heard the sound of church bells.

'Victory bells?' asked Rachel.

'And for peace,' Madge answered, softly. 'Do you remember when we used to think we'd hear them for invasion?'

'We've been lucky,' said Jim. 'Haven't we?'

Again, no one spoke. They looked from face to face, listening to the bells, thinking of those who could not.

Chapter Fifty-Three

'What sort of place was it you were wanting, Miss Ritchie?' asked Miss Pritchard, who ran Logie's property department.

'Something small, with a garden. It's for my mother, not for me.'

Miss Pritchard bent her pale blue gaze on a spread of leaflets on her desk. 'There's one in the Colonies in Stockbridge. Would that be any good?'

'Might be.'

The Colonies was the name given to a number of small streets of terraced houses, built for artisans and clerks and those who aspired to something better than tenement living.

'Is it for rent?' asked Abby.

'No, for sale. I've several lettings, if that's what you'd prefer.' As Miss Pritchard shuffled through her papers, Abby's eye was caught by a familiar name.

'What's that one?' She leaned forward and tweaked up the sheet.

'Glenluce Place? That's a conversion. Big house made into two flats. The upper one's sold.'

'So, what's going? The ground floor and basement?'

'Double basement. But they're huge rooms, Miss Ritchie.'

'Yes, I know.'

Abby looked down at the particulars. She read the number. Somehow she had already guessed what it would be. The house was the Ramsays' house, where she had been a housemaid twenty-five years before. She was aware of Miss Pritchard staring at her.

'I might be interested in this for myself,' she said lightly. 'When's viewing?'

'By appointment only.'

'Could you make one for tomorrow? Say about two o'clock? I could take a late lunch.'

'Certainly, Miss Ritchie. What about the other properties?'

'I'll come in again later.' At the door, Abby looked back.

'What's the name of the person selling Glenluce?' she asked casually.

'Ramsay. A Mr Lennox Ramsay.'

At a few minutes before two o'clock on the following day, Abby strode through the West End and turned into Glenluce Place. She was wearing a square-shouldered dark blue jacket and matching box-pleated skirt, with her only pair of silk stockings and highly polished pre-war shoes. A large crowned hat was tilted over her brow, showing her rich dark hair to be still without grey, and though there were little lines at her eyes and mouth, she thought she looked not too unlike that young housemaid who had been thrown out of the Ramsays' house in 1920. Not too unlike, yet totally different. Would Lennox Ramsay recognise her? Would she recognise him? She stopped and looked up at the façade of the great stone terraced house she remembered so well. There were the steps she and Tilda had swept and scrubbed, the brass bell-push and letterbox they had polished, the long windows they had cleaned. The brass was not so well polished today, the steps had not been scrubbed for quite some time. Didn't look as if the Ramsays had any housemaids now.

She rang the bell. At one time it would have been answered by Sarah Givan, long since retired to Aberdeen. Mrs Moffat must be dead now, Abby supposed, and Tilda had heard Edna was married and away to the west coast. All scattered, then, that below-stairs household. And a good thing too!

The massive front door was suddenly thrown open by a stout, middle-aged man in a dark suit. His fair hair was receding, his eyes surrounded by puffy flesh had become smaller, but Abby had no difficulty in recognising Lennox Ramsay.

'Mr Ramsay?' She waited to see if he would recognise her.

'Mrs Baxter?' No spark of recognition lit his eyes. The smile

384

he gave her was the polite welcome he would have given any prospective buyer. 'Do come in.'

She was at first disconcerted by the fact that beyond the vestibule the large and impressive hall appeared to have vanished. Then she realised that it had been divided by a partition.

'The vestibule is shared,' Lennox Ramsay was explaining. 'But each flat has it own inner door and its own hallway, as you can see.'

'And the stairs to the upper flat are on the other side of this partition?'

'That's right. Of course, the hallways are on the narrow side, but who wants a great big hall these days?'

'Who indeed?' Abby glanced down at her particulars. 'Now on this floor there's a drawing room, dining room, double bedroom and bathroom? And the kitchen is in the basement?'

'The upper basement. There are three further bedrooms on that floor, with storage on the floor below. Masses of space, Mrs Baxter!'

Abby made no reply. Her eyes were darting everywhere. Standing with this man in the house where he had humiliated her so long ago, she was possessed of a suffocating excitement. At the same time she wasn't quite sure why she had come.

'This is the drawing room,' Lennox was saying, throwing open the door of what had been the morning room. Abby, trembling, seemed to see again the figures of Mr and Mrs Ramsay, sitting on either side of the plaster chimneypiece.

'*I'm sorry to disturb you, ma'am,*' a youthful voice echoed in her brain. '*I wondered if I might speak to you for a moment?*'

'*Very well, Abby . . . what is it you wish to say?*'

'Splendid room, isn't it?' asked Lennox Ramsay, walking about the echoing, empty room. 'Wasn't the drawing room in the old days, of course. That's upstairs in the other flat. But we used to sit here a lot when I was a boy.'

'This is your old home, Mr Ramsay?'

'Yes. My brother and I were born here.'

'Really?'

'Came to us when my father died at the beginning of the war. Far too big for either of us, so we decided to convert. Everyone's doing that these days, you know. Can't get the staff to keep these great barns going.'

'No, I suppose not.'

What's happened to his mother? Abby wondered. Was that bad-tempered, pretty-faced tyrant dead, too? But Lennox was moving on.

'This is the dining room, Mrs Baxter. Quite adequate, I think you'll agree.'

She didn't recognise it. A slice of a room with a window squashed into one corner. What could it have been?

'This was the library,' Lennox Ramsay told her, answering her thought. 'We had to chop it in two to make the master bedroom. We were advised that most people prefer that to be at ground level.' He looked around, smiling. 'But imagine anyone's wanting a library these days! As I remember, no one read the damned books anyway!'

Suddenly Abby grew tired of the charade she had devised for herself. She moved into the centre of the room, she looked at the walls once lined with the books she had risked so much to read, and she swung round to face Lennox Ramsay.

'I used to read them,' she said, quietly.

His narrow eyes snapped, his heavy mouth dropped open. 'My God,' he whispered, 'I know you. You're – you're—'

'Abby Ritchie, upper housemaid.'

'Abby Ritchie . . .' He took out a handkerchief and touched his brow. 'Well, well, after all these years . . .' His slack lips tightened. 'So what are you doing here?'

'Not buying, I'm afraid. In fact, I suppose I owe you an apology. I've taken up your time to no purpose.'

'And I haven't got much. I'm due back in Aldershot to-morrow. I made a special effort to be here today to show you round.'

'You're in the army?'

'Major, Royal Artillery. Look, I don't know why you came here, but—'

Abby shrugged. 'When I saw the old house on the market, I couldn't resist coming back to look at it. It was wrong, I apologise.' She walked into the hall, Lennox following.

'No, wait – Mrs Baxter . . .'

She turned and fixed him with the dark eyes he was beginning to remember very well.

'Forgive me, I'm curious – now we've met again, may I ask

386

what you've been doing all these past years?' He gave a tight little smile. 'I hope you don't mind my saying so, but you look rather prosperous.'

'I don't mind. I'm a partner with Logie's.' As she saw his jaw drop and his eyes widen, the moment was very sweet. 'Seems I did know which way up to read the arithmetic book, after all, Mr Ramsay.'

'A partner with Logie's. Good God.' Suddenly Lennox laughed. 'Oh, Abby – I can't help calling you that, do you mind? I think I did know all along that you were going to go places. Mama knew it too, that's why she was so peeved.' He shook his head. 'My poor mother . . .'

'What's happened to her?' asked Abby.

'In a nursing home, I'm afraid. That's partly why John and I are selling. We need a bit of cash.'

'Aren't you both lawyers?'

'I am, but I haven't had a chance to make much money of late.' Lennox's face grew bleak. 'And John was badly injured in Normandy. He won't be doing anything for some time to come.'

'I'm sorry.' Abby lowered her eyes. 'Look, I'm sorry to have bothered you – please excuse me . . .'

'Listen. Won't you come downstairs, have a drink with me? I've still got some furniture down there, made a temporary sitting room, and I've managed to find some whisky, don't ask me where.'

'I don't think so. Thanks all the same.'

Abby didn't want to see any more ghosts that day. Mrs Moffat in the old kitchen which would no doubt be unrecognisable now. Herself and Tilda in that little room they'd shared, where she'd taken her candle to light her books on those black, cold mornings. Edna, failing to get the range going, having her ears boxed and howling. And Millie Robinson, leaving with her ten pounds bonus because she was pregnant with Lennox Ramsay's child. Good old days, thought Abby, her lip twisting. What am I doing being polite to this man? I don't suppose he's changed.

'Abby, I'm sorry,' he said, quietly. 'I daresay I was a pretty poisonous fellow when I was young. You have to try to understand, it was—'

387

'Don't tell me.' She held up her hand. 'The way of the world, right?'

'Well, it was. But I'm not proud of the way I behaved and I want you to know that. And I never wanted you to get the sack.' He gave a rueful smile. 'Though I suppose it was the best thing for you in the end, wasn't it?'

'Yes, it was.' At the front door, she looked back at him. 'Well, thanks for showing me round.'

'My pleasure. Wish you could have met my wife, but she's down south with her parents. She's really taken me in hand, you know.'

'Nice for you. My husband's in the navy.'

'And he's come through? That's good.' He held out his hand. 'No hard feelings, Abby? It was all a long time ago.'

After a slight hesitation, she shook his hand. 'A very long time ago. Goodbye, Major Ramsay.'

She knew that as she walked away down Glenluce Place, he was still at the door watching her.

Had she made a fool of herself, going back? As she returned to Logie's, Abby felt uneasy. The chance to see the old house again, to show Lennox Ramsay what she had become, had proved too much for her to resist. But had it been childish? Wouldn't it have been better not to get involved in paying off old scores?

No! As she reached the swing doors of Logie's front entrance, her spirit flared. It had been good to go back, to teach Lennox something of a lesson. It had taken away the sting from that remembered humiliation which had haunted her all the years, however well she had done. She was sorry about John Ramsay's wounds, she was even sorry that Mrs Ramsay was ending her days in a nursing home, but she was not sorry that she had gone back to Glenluce Place.

'I'd do it again!' she declared to herself, smiling at Jock at the doors, but Jock's look was strange.

'Miss Ritchie, we've been waiting for you!' he cried. 'Mr Fox has got a taxi for you at the back. Hurry now!'

Her hand went to her lips.

'Has there been an accident? Is it my family?'

But Ian Fox was rushing towards her, his long face white.

'Miss Ritchie – Abby – thank God you're back! I've a taxi waiting—'

'But what's happened? Will you tell me what's happened?'

'It's Mr Farrell.' Ian's eyes were filled with compassion. 'He's in the Royal. He's had a heart attack.'

Chapter Fifty-Four

Abby was running through the store, oblivious of the stares of the customers and the frightened looks of the staff; running, running, as though movement would help, would stop the pain that was like a heart attack in her own chest.

'He might be all right,' Ian tried to tell her, as she found the taxi and threw herself into the back seat. 'It might not be a bad one – he just came back from lunch . . .'

Her eyes looked at him unseeingly. 'Thanks, Ian. I'll get to the hospital.'

He nodded, his lip trembling, and closed the taxi's door. 'Driver, the Royal Infirmary!'

Streets, traffic, she saw none of them, but here was the hospital and she was shovelling coins into the driver's hand and running again. Reception, where was Reception? Mr Farrell? Off again, running down corridors, passing nurses, doctors, people in dressing gowns. And then she saw Monica and the running stopped.

Gerald's wife was in a small waiting room attached to a private ward, sitting with her adopted daughters, Lindsay and Sara, terrified, white-faced schoolgirls. Standing near Monica's chair, as though ready to give instant support, was a distinguished, elderly man Abby recognised mistily as Hector Armitage, Chairman of the Trustees. Still cool and golden-haired, Monica looked for a moment exactly the same as always, but she was someone coming apart. As soon as she saw Abby she ran to her and held her close, shaking uncontrollably.

An icy despair descended on Abby. Nothing could have

390

brought home more clearly the horror of the situation than this sudden show of dependence by Monica. Though there had been surface friendliness over the years, there had always been constraint. Understandably on Abby's side; she had her guilt to remember, but Monica knew nothing of their affair. Abby had always assumed Gerald's wife simply did not like her. That she should turn to her now with such abandon filled Abby with foreboding.

'How is he?' she whispered.

Monica raised drenched eyes. 'Holding his own. They say it's not a massive attack, only mild.' She gave a hysterical laugh. 'Mild! Can you imagine it?'

'Mrs Farrell – Monica – don't distress yourself,' Hector Armitage murmured. 'That means there's every chance Gerald's going to be all right.'

'May I see him?' Abby asked fearfully.

'I'm afraid not, he's having treatment.' Monica shook her head. 'Drugs, I suppose. There's not much they can do, is there?'

'There's plenty!' cried Mr Armitage. 'He's in excellent hands!'

'Abby,' Monica said in a low voice, 'they say it's a warning.'

'Warning?'

'That he'll have to slow down. If he lives.' She gave a sob and her daughters sobbed with her.

'He'll live,' said Abby. 'He's strong, he'll pull through. And as Mr Armitage says, it's encouraging that they say the attack was a mild one.'

'But he could have another, couldn't he? He could have another attack any time!'

'Well, he'll have to follow the doctors' instructions. Slow down, have more rest. I told him myself' – Abby's voice shook – 'I told him on VE Day, he should take a holiday.'

'Holiday? He doesn't know the meaning of the word!' Monica put her handkerchief to her eyes. She sat down, taking her daughters' hands. 'Oh, if only I'd been firmer! Insisted!'

'You mustn't blame yourself. People do what they want to do.'

'Abby, everyone wants to live.'

They were silent, wrapped in their own fears, until a doctor came in, white coat flapping, and they jerked to attention.

'He's going to be all right,' he said gently, adding after a pause, 'this time.'

'Thank God!' cried Monica and her daughters threw their arms around her.

'Any chance of seeing him?' asked Mr Armitage, and Abby drew in her breath.

'I'm sorry, we'd like it to be just Mrs Farrell for today. Mr Farrell is comfortable now, but it's vital he should rest.' The doctor smiled encouragingly. 'We'll see how he is tomorrow.'

As Monica rose to follow the doctor, Abby swallowing her disappointment, told her she would take the girls to the canteen for a cup of coffee. They would wait for her there.

'I'll come with you,' said Hector Armitage. He took out a silk handkerchief and wiped his brow. 'Don't mind telling you, Miss Ritchie, this has all been a bit of a strain.

She gave a painful smile. 'A bit of a strain? Yes, I'd say so.'

Colour came back into the girls' cheeks as they drank thin coffee and ate digestive biscuits in the hospital canteen, while Abby bravely made conversation, asking them about school, what were their plans. Lindsay was doing Highers that summer, she was hoping for a place at university. Did she want to work at Logie's? She had discussed it with Daddy but hadn't made any decision. Sara was only fifteen, she had no idea what she might do.

'All I want is for Daddy to be well again,' she cried, her voice quavering. 'He will get better, won't he, Miss Ritchie?'

'Yes, he will. The doctor sounded very hopeful.'

'If that attack is a warning, what does that mean exactly?' asked Lindsay. 'Will Daddy have to give up work?'

Abby exchanged glances with Hector Armitage. 'I don't know. Maybe not. Maybe he'll just cut down his hours.'

'Yes,' Mr Armitage agreed heartily. 'That's what he could do.'

Monica joined them, still pale and shaken, but a little more cheerful. Gerald was looking better.

'Oh, my God, when I first saw him' – she shuddered – 'he had just arrived at the hospital. They were deciding what to do

– he'd collapsed in his office, you know, after lunch. Miss Wright said he'd been running up the stairs – what was I saying? Oh, yes, he looked so terrible, so colourless, I thought—'

'Monica, don't dwell on it, ' said Mr Armitage. 'Have some coffee.'

'Coffee?' She looked round distractedly. 'What am I doing, drinking coffee?'

'Gerald's looking better, he's going to be all right. You must try to relax, my dear, save your own strength.'

'I suppose so.' Monica drank some coffee. 'Thank you, Mr Armitage – Abby – you've both been so kind.'

'Would you like me to take the girls home?' asked Abby. 'If you're staying on at the hospital?'

'They've told me to not to stay. There's nothing I can do and they just want Gerald to rest. I'll come back first thing in the morning.'

'Mummy, could we see Daddy tomorrow?' asked Lindsay.

'Could I?' asked Abby softly.

'Yes,' Monica answered firmly. 'You must all see him tomorrow.'

Hector Armitage and Abby shared a taxi back to Logie's. Abby was astonished to find that the time was only five o'clock.

'Time seems to stand still in the Royal,' she said, wearily.

'Yes, hospitals have their own timescale.' Mr Armitage fixed Abby with a speculative grey eye. 'Miss Ritchie, may I have a word?'

'Of course. Come up to my office.'

'I'm sure you've already thought of the consequences of Gerald's heart attack,' he began without preamble. 'I mean, for Logie's.'

She looked at him blankly. 'I'm afraid I've given it no thought at all, Mr Armitage.'

'Well, of course I know concern for poor Gerald must come first, that would be your natural reaction—'

'Yes.'

'But the fact of the matter is that things have to go on. However much we care about a person, a firm like Logie's has to be kept running. It has to be managed.'

Abby sat back in her chair. 'I suppose I've been doing that unofficially for quite some time.'

'That's my point,' he said readily. 'I want you to do it officially. I want you to take over from Gerald. On a temporary basis, of course, because we don't know yet what's going to happen. I say if he has any sense he won't come back.' Mr Armitage shook his head. 'I remember his uncle. Fine man, Miss Ritchie. Years of achievement ahead of him. But' – he waved his hand – 'ended up dead on the golf course. We don't want that to happen to Gerald.'

Abby shivered. 'This is all a little premature,' she said quietly. 'I don't want to do anything without Mr Farrell's agreement.'

'You shall have it. My suggestion will be what he wants, I'm sure of it. He thinks so highly of you, Miss Ritchie, we all do.'

'This store has been his life,' she murmured. 'I can't imagine Logie's without him.'

'Nor I. Except, as I say, I had to watch him follow his uncle. Logie's was Stephen's life too. What Gerald will want is to know the store is in safe hands. And that means you, Miss Ritchie.'

She sat without speaking, staring into space, thinking of how under any other circumstances this moment would have been one of triumph. To take over from Gerald. In her wildest dreams, she would never have thought of it. Yet now it meant so little.

'Miss Ritchie, what do you say?'

She raised her eyes. 'A temporary measure, you said?'

'Until we know the situation.'

'Very well, Mr Armitage, I'll do my best.'

He gave a sigh of relief. 'I'll arrange a board meeting as soon as possible, to give you authority.'

'When you've seen Mr Farrell,' she said pointedly.

'When I've seen him. Don't worry, it will all be done as he wants it.'

'As he wants it,' Abby repeated.

Rachel telephoned her at home that evening.

'Abby, weren't you supposed to be getting Ma some eggs?'

'Eggs?'

'For the cakes for the victory party. You haven't forgotten, have you?'

Abby felt a thousand miles away. 'Rachel, there's been bad news. Gerald Farrell has had a heart attack.'

'Oh, no! My God, is he going to be all right?'

'We hope so. But you'll know I haven't had time to think of the victory party. When is it?'

'Tomorrow. Look, don't worry about the eggs. I'll ask Donnie again. But try to come to the do, won't you? Ma'll be so disappointed if you don't.'

'I really can't promise.'

'Well, there's something else. My picture's going on exhibition next week. You must try to see that. I mean,' Rachel added hastily, 'if Gerald's all right.'

'I'm afraid that's all I can think of,' Abby answered.

She slept fitfully that night, dreaming of a victory party on a golf course. Ma was cross with her, she hadn't brought any eggs. 'Now what shall we do?' cried Ma, but Abby was looking at someone lying at her feet, and when she turned the figure over the face was Frankie's. She was glad to wake up, though the nightmare of Gerald's illness was still with her. Relief did not come until she saw him later that day, looking very white, his face seeming smaller against his pillows, but still recognisably Gerald, still very much alive.

'Oh, Gerald,' she whispered, and he tried for a smile.

'Don't tell me – I look a fraud.'

'If you knew the fright you gave us!'

'Won't happen again.'

Please God, she thought, putting some fruit and magazines on his locker and looking around his room filled with flowers. 'Now, I've had my orders. I'm not to stay too long, I'm not to tire you, I'm not to let you talk.'

'Except to let me tell you I've seen Hector Armitage.'

'Oh, no, Gerald you are not going to be allowed to talk about work!'

'You don't want me to be worrying?'

'There's no need for you to worry.'

His shadowed eyes sought hers. 'If you'll do what Armitage wants.'

'I've said I will. Please, Gerald, just relax.'

'I want it too, you see, that's the point.'

'As long as you do,'' she said uncertainly.

'Abby, I do. I trust you.'

She covered his hand with hers. 'Gerald, if I know that, I can do anything.'

'Always could,' he murmured sleepily, and closed his eyes. 'Always could.'

Monica was waiting outside his room. She was herself again, composed and beautiful, her gaze on Abby guarded.

'I thought you'd like to have some time with Gerald on your own,' she said quietly. 'I know what this has been like for you.'

Abby's eyes widened, she very slightly caught her breath. 'Thank you,' she answered. 'That was good of you. I – I hope I didn't tire him.'

'You couldn't do that.'

For a long strained moment, the two women looked into each other's faces, then Monica smiled slightly and went in to see her husband. Abby stood very still, watching her.

Was it possible that Monica did know about that very brief affair with Gerald? In all these years she had never said a word. Perhaps she had understood how little it had meant. Perhaps she had not felt blameless herself. Whatever the truth, she had behaved well. Abby, leaving the hospital, felt ashamed. She prided herself on her intelligence and her understanding, but she had failed completely, it seemed, to understand or appreciate Gerald's wife.

It was still difficult for her to realise that she was officially running Logie's. In practice, she had been doing that for years but Gerald's had been the ultimate responsibility, even if he was mostly out of the store on Emergency duties. Now there was no Gerald. There was the Board of Trustees, but they depended on her to act as the chief executive, it was not for her to depend on them. If she had not been so worried about Gerald, she might have been awed by her position. As it was, she decided she could only do her best. For Gerald, for Logie's. For herself.

The staff had been told of the new arrangement and had accepted it, but of course it had been stressed that it was only temporary. If Gerald did not come back, Mr Armitage had told Abby that the position would be reviewed. The other partners would be returning from the forces. Perhaps a new decision would be made. And perhaps not.

Abby, her thoughts still with Gerald and Monica, went through Logie's swing doors, nodded to Jock who touched his cap, and went up in the lift to her office. She had made it clear that she would not be using Gerald's office, would not be sitting at his desk, though she had agreed to borrow his secretary. Now she sat down at her own desk, sighed over her piled in-tray, and took up her pen.

The door opened and Miss Wright appeared. She asked about Gerald, gave a relieved smile when Abby reported that he was much better.

'Oh, that's wonderful. Has he had our flowers?'

'They were beautiful. I'm sure he'll be writing as soon as he's able.'

'You're looking much better yourself, Miss Ritchie.'

'I think we're all feeling better.' Abby smiled and the secretary turned to go.

'Oh, Miss Ritchie, I almost forgot – your sister rang.'

'Oh, God,' said Abby, bending her head to her desk blotter. 'The victory party! Miss Wright, will you order me a taxi?'

Chapter Fifty-Five

Early on the morning of the victory party, Madge dressed carefully in a pale blue patterned dress and matching jacket, which she had made out of an old pre-war outfit. She took a pink rose from a glass on her chest of drawers and pinned it to her lapel. Then she combed her silvery fair hair and put on her new hat. She had only bought it the day before and wasn't used to it, wasn't sure it suited her, though the girl in the shop said she looked lovely, just like Queen Elizabeth, and had she seen the pictures of the Queen on the palace balcony on VE night, with the King and the two princesses? Folk were saying the girls had been allowed to go out and mingle with the crowds, and why not, eh? Poor lassies, they didna get much chance to have a good time like ordinary people. Meanwhile, Madge had been studying the pale blue hat with its halo brim and had said recklessly she would take it. But now she had to wear it she wished she'd found one with a bit of veiling, that would have been just the thing to hide all her little lines. Too late now. She picked up her bag and her pre-war gloves and moved to the door of her flat. For some moments she stood looking round, remembering Rory, remembering Gramma. It had come to mean a lot to her, that little flat. She sighed and went out.

'Are you there, Jessie?' she called, knocking quietly on Jessie Rossie's door, and a moment later Jessie's ravaged face appeared. She too was wearing a patterned dress and jacket, both made long ago by Madge, and a large hat with cotton flowers.

'I'm ready, hen,' she said throatily. 'Just wait till I pin on ma rose.'

Joanie Muir was ready too, wearing a dark blue outfit and a white hat, but she had forgotten her flower and had to run back for it.

'Now for Jim,' said Jessie, smiling. 'Och, is this no' grand, eh?'

He was waiting outside his door, straight and tall in his best suit.

'Madge!' he whispered, and tried to take her hand, but she was fussing with his buttonhole, trying to hide a sudden fit of nerves.

'Come away, then,' said Jessie. 'You'll no' want to be late, eh?'

And the four of them went lightly down the stair and out into the fresh May morning.

It was still early when they returned, hurrying up to Jim's flat where a bottle of port stood waiting.

'Port!' cried Joanie. 'Where'd you get that, Jim?'

'Been keeping it.' He filled their glasses. 'You'll no' mind drinking this early?'

'Are you joking?' Joanie seized her glass and glanced at Jessie.

'To Mr and Mrs Gilbride!' cried Jessie. 'Drink up, Joanie!'

'To our witnesses!' Jim replied, and he and Madge drank, too.

'Och, I canna believe it,' Jessie said with satisfaction. 'You two married at last.'

'Aye, you'll be Darby and Joan before you've even had a honeymoon,' Joanie told them and Jim laughed.

'What of it? From what I've heard, this Darby and Joan were happy, eh?'

'We're not having a honeymoon,' Madge put in. 'After the party we're just going up to Loch Lomond for a couple of days.'

'But why did you no' want the girls at the weddin'?' asked Jessie. 'What'll they say when they find out?'

'To be quite honest, we'd waited so long, I felt a bit silly about it,' Madge confessed. 'We decided we'd make it all as quiet as possible, just have you two for witnesses and then announce it at the party. The girls won't mind. I think they'll be relieved.'

'Aye, and Malcolm couldna be here anyway,' Jim murmured, and though he didn't say his name, they knew he was also thinking of Rory. Jessie and Joanie shed a few tears, remembering their own lost sons, then said this should be a happy time and kissed the bride and groom.

'Yes, I've baking to do,' said Madge, taking off the halo hat which in fact suited her very well. 'Thank goodness Rachel managed to get me a few eggs!'

By the middle of the afternoon the tables were set up on the green at the back of the tenement, and bunting had been draped around the old air-raid shelter and its entrance fastened so that the children couldn't get inside.

'Remember that first night of the war when we all came down here?' asked Sally Muir. 'I was so terrified, ma teeth were chattering.'

'I can't bear to think about that time,' said Madge, pinning a paper tablecloth over one of the tables. 'Looking ahead and wondering what was going to happen.'

Jennie's eyes on her mother were thoughtful. 'You're looking very nice, Ma. Have you had your hair done?'

Madge, who had changed out of her blue outfit, said quickly, 'Oh, a couple of days ago, not today.'

'And Jim's looking smart too. He's wearing a buttonhole.'

'Well, it's a special day, isn't it? Jennie, will you give me a hand putting out these little jellies?'

The women busied themselves setting out the sandwiches, buns and scones, while the men put up the decorations, red and white streamers and flags.

'No' too many union jacks,' called Archie Shields who had come over to join them. 'Let's have our own flags, eh?'

'Aye, next thing we ought to try for is home rule,' said Robbie Kemp, 'now that the war is over.'

'Can you no' remember the war's not over?' Donnie Muir asked fiercely. 'This is no' VJ Day!'

'Sorry,' said Robbie, lowering his eyes. The Kemps had had good news. Jamie, reported missing, had been found alive in a field hospital and had returned to active service in Germany. Robbie, like the the rest of the families of the men who had come through, felt uneasy in the presence of the Muirs and the

Rossies. 'Why us, not them?' they knew the bereaved ones must be thinking, but that was a question no one could answer.

'Will you look at this spread?' asked Marty Finnegan, arriving with her contribution, which was a large tin of peaches Tam had just happened to find when he was home on leave. Tam was always good at finding things, no questions asked, and Madge just said, how lovely, would someone find the tin opener?

People were beginning to arrive. Rachel brought Bobby looking bored. Will and Hamish carried out chairs. Mr Kay came round, walking with a stick. There were Pringle children and Craig children, there were Rossie grandchildren, Finnegan grandchildren, Kemps, Muirs, and some children mysteriously not known to anyone who had been accepted anyway. All were opening packets of crisps, spooning up jellies, scuffling and scrapping and being brought to order by Jim, as the women carried round pitchers of lemonade and fussed over the food.

'Now where is Abby?' asked Madge fretfully. 'She promised she'd be here.'

'You know Gerald Farrell had a heart attack,' Jennie reminded her. 'She may not have been able to get away. Why does she have to be here, anyway? What's so important?'

'Nothing, nothing.' Madge hurried off and Jennie and Rachel exchanged glances.

'I'll give Abby a ring,' said Rachel, 'she ought to be here. I can call from the 'phone box on the corner.'

It was hot and stuffy in the telephone box and when she had left a message for Abby, Rachel was glad to push open the heavy door and get some air. Suddenly a man appeared and took the door from her, holding it for her.

'Thank you,' she said, sidling past him, but he lightly touched her arm.

'Rachel, don't you know me?'

It was Frankie.

'Oh, my God!' cried Rachel. 'Where did you come from?'

He was very thin, dressed in civilian clothes, his dark hair mixed with silver curls that shone in the sunlight, and he looked older. But his blue eyes were very bright on Rachel's face and she thought him more attractive than she had remembered.

'Frankie, it's so wonderful to see you!' She flung her arms around him and kissed his hard cheek. 'We didn't know what had happened to you. Are you out of the navy, or what?'

'Only on leave, don't know when I'll get demobbed.' His eyes were dancing, he seemed pleased with her welcome. 'Is Malcolm back?'

'No, I wish he was. But, Frankie, have you seen Abby?'

His eyes stopped dancing. 'No, not yet. Thought I'd come up and see your ma first.'

'You're just in time, we're having a victory party on the back green – come on!'

As she led him back to Catherine's Land like some sort of prize captive, he asked hesitantly if Abby was at the party.

'No, but she's supposed to be coming, I've just been 'phoning. The thing is, poor Gerald Farrell's just had a heart attack, Logie's is in a bit of a state.'

'Guess Abby's very upset.'

'Yes, but he's going to be all right. Don't worry, I'm sure you'll see her.'

Frankie looked apprehensive.

'Look who's here!' cried Rachel, as they came up the basement steps on to the green, and those who remembered Frankie ran to greet him.

'Frankie, this is wonderful!' Madge exclaimed. 'Why, we never thought to see you today. Abby said she hadn't heard from you for weeks.'

'I'm sorry, I should've written. Mrs Ritchie, you're looking terrific.' Frankie kissed Madge and Jennie and shook Jim's hand. He looked around at the watching children, the tables spread with the debris of party food, the waving flags and bunting, and he gave a long sigh. 'Can't tell you what it's like to be back here at last.'

'After all those years at sea,' Jennie said softly. 'Frankie, how did you ever get through it?'

'Guess you have to.' He took her hand and held it. 'Jennie, I'm sorry.'

'About Rory? Thank you, Frankie.'

'How did you get through that?'

'Like you say, you have to. I'm over it, as much as I ever will be.'

'And are these your boys?' He looked wonderingly at Will and Hamish. 'And is this Bobby?'

'Hello, Uncle Frankie,' Bobby said eagerly. 'Do you still play the piano?'

'Whenever I can. Hey, but you've all grown so much, you know, I'd never have recognised you!'

'You look the same but you sound like an American,' said Bobby. 'You're not going back to America, are you?'

'I'm not sure. I'm not even out of the navy yet.'

'Will you tell us about it?' cried Hamish. 'Will you tell us about the convoys? Did you see the Tirpitz go down? Did you see the Scharnhorst?'

'Boys, boys, let Uncle Frankie have some tea!' cried Madge. 'Oh, I do wish Abby would come.'

'She's here,' shouted Will. 'Auntie Abby's here!'

A silence fell on the party as Abby came up from the basement and stood at the top of the steps. She looked pale and not her best – the hours of strain had taken their toll – but to the people of Catherine's Land she still had the air of belonging to another world. She was Madge Ritchie's clever daughter, she was a senior person at Logie's, she was from Catherine's Land but no longer of it. Like Rachel she had spread her wings and flown, but Rachel was arty and nobody in Catherine's Land reckoned much to artists. It was Abby they held in awe. Such a view of herself was the last thing she would have wanted. These people were her mother's friends, she believed they were hers too, and it was true they wished her well and smiled as she came forward to join them. But their smiles were for a stranger.

At first she didn't see Frankie. She was looking curiously at her mother who was hovering nervously at her side, and it was Madge herself who said, 'Abby, don't you see Frankie?'

Abby slowly turned her head. A deep colour rose to her brow, her dark eyes shone. Then a shutter came down, the glow faded.

'Frankie?' Her lip trembled, but she was trying hard to appear composed. 'I never expected to see you.'

'Hello, Abby.' Frankie's face was empty of feeling. 'Sorry I didn't say I was coming.'

'You're on leave?'

'Got ten days.' He added quickly, 'I've booked myself a hotel room.'

Abby said nothing. After a desperate pause, Frankie said, 'I was sorry to hear about Gerald Farrell.'

'Yes, it was a terrible shock. He's getting over it, though.'

'Coming back to work?'

'I don't know about that.'

'Things won't be the same.'

'No.'

He cleared his throat. 'Means promotion for you?'

'As a temporary measure.'

'But you're really running Logie's?' He gave a wry smile. 'I'd better take on the sweetie shop, eh?'

'I don't know what you mean.'

'Don't you remember when I said—' He shrugged. 'Oh, skip it.'

'Excuse me, Abby,' Madge intervened tremulously. 'I'd just like to speak to you for a moment. You and Rachel and Jennie. Oh, yes, Frankie, you too. I – I've something to tell you.'

'Tell us?' repeated Rachel. 'Tell us what?'

'Can you no' guess?' asked Jim, coming up and putting his arm around Madge. 'Show 'em your ring, Madge.'

She held out her left hand and their eyes went to her wedding ring.

'Ma, that's not Dad's ring!'' cried Jennie.

'No, it's mine,' said Jim. 'We were married this morning at St John's.'

There was a stunned silence. Frankie in embarrassment moved a little away.

'I'm still wearing your dad's ring,' Madge said hastily. 'It's on my right hand, that's all.'

'It doesna mean your ma's forgotten your dad,' said Jim, 'but she's going to let me make her happy now. Come on, it's no surprise, is it? Were you no' expecting us to get wed?'

'I'm very happy for you both,' Abby said at once, and took her mother into her arms. 'Congratulations! It's wonderful news!'

'Wonderful!' echoed Rachel, leaning forward to kiss Madge's cheek.

'I said you should have done it long ago,' Jennie whispered. 'But why didn't you tell us? Why didn't you let us come?'

'Jessie said that. She was a witness.' Madge wiped tears from her eyes. 'We just felt we'd waited so long we'd like to creep off by ourselves, just the two of us, but we had to have witnesses, so we asked Jessie and Joanie. We fixed it up for today before we knew about the party, but then we thought it would all work out well because everyone's here and I suppose that's all there is to say, really.' She smiled up at Jim. 'We're married.'

'Listen, everybody!' cried Jessie, banging on the table. 'I've an announcement to make. Jim and Madge were married today. There's some drink going round, so get yourself a glass and drink a toast, eh? To the happy couple!'

'It's only beer or lemonade,' Madge whispered to Abby. 'All we could get, apart from some port we had this morning.'

'I might have been able to get you some wine,' Abby whispered back. 'Oh, Ma, you should have said.'

Everyone was crowding round, drinking the toast, slapping Jim on the back, kissing Madge, and the three sisters stood back, watching the scene.

'Well, married at last,' Rachel said, with a smile. 'I never thought Ma'd do it.'

'I must admit I'd given up thinking she might,' said Abby.

'I'm glad she did,' Jennie said stoutly. 'Jim really adores her, all he wants is to make her happy.'

'As long as that's true,' Abby murmured. 'Oh, but I'm sure you're right. They'll be happy.'

'For goodness' sake, they're old enough to know their own minds anyway,' laughed Rachel. 'Why should we sit in judgment?'

Abby laughed with her. 'Good for you, Rachel. I'll get them some champagne tomorrow. We ought to celebrate.'

'Aren't they going on honeymoon?' asked Jennie.

'Aye to Loch Lomond,' said Joanie Muir, joining them. 'Is that no' romantic? Och, I think it's beautiful. Your ma deserves to be happy, eh?'

'We all deserve that,' said Rachel.

'May I see you this evening?' Frankie asked, drawing Abby aside.

'I'd like to,' she answered slowly. 'But there's all the party to clear up.'

'There's plenty folk here to do that.'

'Yes, but why shouldn't I?'

'Because I want to see you.'

'All right, then,' she said, unsmilingly. 'We'll try to find somewhere to have a meal.'

'All you people out to the Lawnmarket, Madge and Jim are away!' cried Jessie, but Madge shook her head at her, laughingly.

'Heavens, all this fuss, we're only going for two days!'

Rachel, glancing at Jennie standing on the steps of Catherine's Land, saw that her eyes were filled with tears and knew she was remembering that time the two of them had been young brides, running the gauntlet of the well-wishers as Madge and Jim were running it now. She moved closer to her sister and pressed her hand, and Jennie, understanding, hugged her close. Jim flung out the usual coins, the children scrabbled, everyone waved and cried good luck!

'Just as though we were young things starting out,' Madge commented, still embarrassed. She was wearing her blue outfit again, with the Queen Elizabeth hat, and was still wishing she had a bit of veiling to hide behind.

'We're no' young things,' Jim answered, holding her hand fast, 'but we're starting out. Being married, it's different, eh?'

'From not being married?' asked Madge. 'It certainly is.'

As the taxi moved away, Madge took a last look at her daughters, Jennie standing with Rachel, Abby standing alone. Where was Frankie? Not far away. Madge could see him moving to Abby's side. Oh, she did hope those two would get together again. Hadn't they wasted enough years? Like me, she thought, looking down at her new wedding ring and then the thick gold band Will had put on her finger all those years ago.

'It'll be all right, Madge,' Jim whispered. 'You'll see.'

'Yes,' she answered, smiling. 'I know.'

Chapter Fifty-Six

'What's on the menu, then?' asked Frankie, with determined cheerfulness, as he and Abby settled themselves at the restaurant table. 'Whale meat?'

'Don't ask,' Abby answered. 'You never know these days.'

'Whatever it is, it'll be better than the stuff I've been having lately.'

She looked at him sombrely. 'You've had quite a war, haven't you?'

'Wasn't the only one.' Frankie turned his blue eyes on the waitress who came to take their order. 'What can we have?'

'There's fish,' she said pertly, 'or spam and salad.'

'What sort of fish?'

'Couldna tell you.' She looked around, tapping her pencil on her notepad. 'It's white, that's all.'

Frankie looked at Abby. She said she'd have the spam.

'Make that two spams. Got any wine?'

The waitress laughed. 'Don't you know there's been a war on?'

'I had noticed.' As the waitress flounced off, Frankie grinned. 'That's what you call the big welcome home, eh?'

Abby said, quietly, 'There is a welcome home for you, all the same.'

'There is? I wasn't sure.'

'Why did you never come home on leave before?" she asked abruptly.

'I wrote to you, I kept in touch. I didn't think you wanted more than that.'

'So why now? Why come back now?'

He hesitated, then took from his wallet a small newspaper cutting. He laid it on the table.

'That's why.'

Abby picked the cutting up. It was from the *Times*, the notice of Alan Talbot's engagement. She laid it down.

'I never thought you'd see that,' she said levelly. 'When did you get to read the newspapers?'

'Oh, from time to time. Somebody had this old copy and the name kinda jumped out at me.' Frankie dropped the cutting into the ashtray on their table, put a match to it and watched it burn. 'Abby, I'm sorry. He didn't look the sort of guy who'd do that.'

'Do what? I was the one who broke things off.'

'You were? I thought you told me—'

'I know what I told you. And I really did think he was the one. The one you told me to find, if you remember.'

Frankie lowered his eyes. 'So, what went wrong?'

'Well, he was badly injured in Africa, he lost an arm—'

'I didn't know that.'

'Yes, it was terrible. He came up to Edinburgh to get better, have the new arm fitted. He really needed me. And I let him down.' Abby's eyes filled with tears she quickly brushed away. 'It wasn't because of his arm, Frankie.'

'You don't have to tell me that.' As she seemed unable to continue, he asked gently, 'But what was it, then? If you'd decided he was the one?'

Abby hesitated. 'I realised he wasn't. I wanted him to be, I wanted it more than anything, because—'

'Because of his arm?'

She nodded. 'And I'd made up my mind I wouldn't tell him the truth. Whatever happened, I wouldn't tell him. But somehow he seemed to know, anyway.'

'Poor guy,' Frankie muttered, 'I know how he felt.'

'No,' said Abby wearily, 'you don't know. Or, else you needn't.'

'Needn't?'

'Your spam,' announced the waitress, clashing down their plates. 'Everything OK?'

'Fine, thank you, just fine.' They couldn't wait for her to go.

'Oh, God, Abby,' Frankie whispered, urgently, 'what are you trying to tell me?'

She sighed. 'You know what I'm trying to tell you.' She lowered her voice. 'I still love you.'

'I'm supposed to know that? Last time we met you sent me away.'

'Only because you wanted to go.' Abby stared down at her plate. 'You made it pretty plain over the years that we couldn't make marriage work. I came round to agreeing with you.'

'You still think that?'

'I don't know. Nothing's changed. I'm still at Logie's.'

'Running Logie's.'

'All right, running Logie's. How do you feel about that?'

'Maybe not the way you think.'

'Go on,' she said softly.

'Well, for a start, it's not true to say that nothing's changed. I've changed.'

'Have you, Frankie?'

He nodded. 'Guess the war's changed us all. All the guys like me, anyway.'

'How has it changed you?'

He shrugged. 'Made me see what matters. That guy who said you're a long time dead – he knew what he was talking about.'

'It terrifies me,' Abby murmured, 'to think of what you must have seen.'

'I'm not going to talk about it.' He fixed her with his blue gaze. 'I only know I'm alive, I've been lucky, and I'm not going to waste what I've got.'

'What does that mean?'

'It means,' he said deliberately, 'whatever it takes to make our marriage work I'll do it.'

She caught her breath, her dark eyes shone with emotion.

'Say something,' he urged, but she shook her head.

'I don't know what to say. You make me feel ashamed.'

'Oh, come one—'

'No, you've survived, you're safe, and I'm so grateful, I'm ready to thank God on my knees, but I've done nothing for you.'

'Abby, I don't want you to do anything.'

'Yes, but I've changed too.' She leaned forward. 'I keep thinking of Gerald, you know. Logie's was his life, but now he's letting it go. He came close to death and he's found out there are more important things for him. There should be for me.' She stretched out her hand to take Frankie's. 'If you want me to go to America with you, I'll go.'

He pressed her hand. He tried to smile. 'You'd only end up running Macy's. Och, Abby, I'm not asking you to do anything like that. There's no need for you to give up what you've worked for all these years. I had success in the States, I'll try for the same here.'

'On the wireless?'

'Why not? I've met a guy who plays saxophone, he's the best. And there's another who plays clarinet, he's good too. Our idea is to form our own band, play the hotels, get into radio. As soon as we get demobbed, we'll be on our way.'

'You'd be based in London?'

'Yes, guess we would, but there are trains, right? I'd have my life, you'd have yours, but—'

'We'd have a marriage. Oh, Frankie, I can't believe it. are we really going to be able to work this thing out?'

'If we want to, I guess we can.'

Their eyes met above their untouched plates. They were both very serious, unwilling almost to breathe, in case their new chance of happiness burst like a bubble in their faces.

'Do you want this stuff?' Frankie whispered.

'No, I don't want it.'

'Shall we go, then?' He looked round for the waitress.

'Back to my flat?'

'I guess you don't want to go to my hotel.'

'I'd forgotten you were booked in there.'

'I could unbook myself.'

'Why don't you?'

Again their eyes met. Frankie put some money on the table. He grasped Abby's hand.

'Come on, quick – let's go before you change your mind.'

'Remember that night when you made me sleep in the spare room?' Frankie asked, when they had made love in their old double bed and all the long arid years of separation had faded.

'God, I don't know how I managed to stay there! You must admit you were cruel to me, Abby.'

'Cruel to myself, too. I lay awake all night wanting you to come.' She caught his hard lean body to hers. 'Oh, what fools we were, weren't we?'

'You can say that again.'

'We've been lucky. I keep remembering Jennie and Rory.'

'Aye, Rory made his mistakes.'

'And never got a second chance.'

'Well, we're taking ours.' He began to cover her face with kisses. 'No more talking, Mrs Baxter.'

'Mrs Baxter ... I've been thinking, things are going to be different after the war, women are not going to give up their chance to work this time. Why shouldn't I make it plain at Logie's that I'm married? Be Mrs Baxter instead of Miss Ritchie?'

'You're in charge, you can make the rules.'

'Only temporarily in charge. There won't be a permanent decision made until the men come back from the war.'

'Come on, who's going to beat you in an interview?'

'If it goes to one of the chaps who's been fighting for his country, I don't think I should complain.'

'No, let the best man win, I say,' said Frankie. 'Even if it turns out to be a woman.'

In the morning she told him of her plans to move her mother and Jim out of Catherine's Land. Frankie, making toast, looked dubious.

'I dunno, Abby. They've lived there so long, they seem quite happy. Why uproot 'em?'

'Frankie, Ma has spent all those years there and never had a garden. Hasn't even got a bathroom. She and Jennie go to Rachel's for baths these days. It's ridiculous!'

'Maybe Catherine's Land'll be modernised, now that the war's over.'

'It'll be years before that can happen. I shouldn't be surprised if there are building restrictions in force till the fifties or sixties. And sometimes I wonder just how safe the building is. There haven't been any repairs for years. If the rents rocket because of huge roof bills, Ma and Jim might as well go.'

'How about Jennie?'

'She'll never go. She associates the place with Rory and that's all that matters.'

'She really forgave him, didn't she?'

'Yes, she'd have taken him back.'

'Anybody hear what happened to Sheena?'

Abby shuddered. 'No, but I expect she and Lily are still creating havoc somewhere or other. Just as long as they don't create it here.' She spread her toast with margarine. 'But I'm serious, Frankie. I'm going to have another go at Ma as soon as she comes back from her honeymoon.'

'Her honeymoon,' Frankie repeated. 'Isn't that something? Say, why don't we go for a second honeymoon?'

'You don't mean a cruise?' she asked, wickedly.

'I certainly don't. If I never had to see the sea again, it'd suit me fine.'

Chapter Fifty-Seven

There was a family gathering at Jennie's when Madge and Jim came home, looking so well and happy Frankie whispered to Abby they looked as though they'd been at the cream.

'How about that, then? Great to think you can still be in love at their age, eh?'

'Ssh, I'm going to speak to them now,' Abby replied. She raised her voice. 'Ma, I don't know if this is the right time to tell you, but I've been looking at properties for you and Jim.'

Jennie's head jerked up, her eyes sparkled. 'What do you mean, properties?'

'Houses with gardens. For Ma and Jim.' Abby's own eyes flashed. 'Why not?'

'Yes, why not?' asked Will.

'Abby, I don't see why you have to interfere,' Jennie said, her voice shaking. 'Anyway, we don't know what's happening – we've had letters—'

'What letters?'

Jim took an envelope from his pocket. 'We've all had one of these, Abby. From Drew's.'

Drew's was the property firm which owned Catherine's Land and a number of other tenement buildings in the Old Town.

'They've been doing surveys on all their houses,' Jim went on. 'Seems some passed and others didna. Catherine's Land didna.'

'What does that mean?' asked Frankie.

'Means they're no' prepared to spend the money on what has to be done.'

'So what are they going to do?'

413

'They're going to put the place on the market.'

'Sell Catherine's Land?' Abby cried.

'Aye. You'd better read the letter.'

It didn't take long for Abby to cast her eye down the typed pages. Then she looked up. 'It's worse than I thought,' she declared. 'Everything needs doing, the roof, the floors, the timbers, the windows. The chimneys need to be rebuilt, the pipes need replacing, there's extensive dry rot . . .' She shook her head. 'I had my suspicions but I'd no idea the position was as bad as this. I suppose I can understand why Drew's don't want to keep it on.'

'But who'll buy it?' asked Frankie.

Jim shrugged. 'I went down to see Drew's. Seems there's plenty of interest. The university thinks it'd make a students' hostel. The Church of Scotland's got the same idea.'

'Then everyone would have to leave?' Abby turned to look at Jennie.

'It's what you want, isn't it?' Jennie snapped. 'Everyone out of Catherine's Land?'

'I never said everyone.'

'Only Ma and me? Well, I don't want to go. And neither does Ma!'

'You won't have any choice,' said Rachel. 'You can hardly live with the students.'

'There's other firms interested,' said Jim. 'One's willing to try to get a grant from the government for complete modernisation. They say they'll get it, if they stick to residential use.'

'So why couldn't Drew's do that?' asked Jennie quickly.

'Because they say the rents would have to go sky high, they dinna want to get involved.'

There was a silence. 'A Labour government would control the rents,' said Frankie. 'And they say Attlee'll get in at the next election.'

'What, and beat Mr Churchill?' cried Madge. 'Oh, I don't believe it!'

Frankie smiled. 'You haven't heard the lads talking, Mrs Ritchie. They don't want to go back to the old days, they want a change.'

'Change is coming anyway,' muttered Jim.

'Ma,' said Abby, 'what do you want to do?'

Madge's gaze went to Jennie. 'I suppose' – she hesitated – 'I suppose we should stay on here. Until we see what happens.'

Jennie gave a little sigh. 'I say that, too. I say we should stay until we have to go.'

Abby and Frankie exchanged glances. 'Fair enough,' said Abby, briskly. 'Let's say no more about it.'

'Abby—' Madge began, but Abby cut her short.

'It's what you want, Ma, not what I want. Let's leave it.'

'Listen,' said Rachel brightly, 'my picture's on display at the National. Who wants to come and see it?'

'Not me,' muttered Bobby. 'I've seen it and I don't want to see it again.'

'You mind your cheek!' cried Jim. 'Your ma's a very clever woman and dinna you forget it!'

'I should think you'd be proud of her,' put in Abby. 'I am.'

'All right, I'm proud,' rapped Bobby. 'I just don't like art galleries.'

'Nor me,' said Hamish.

'We thought we'd go out,' said Will.

'Out where?' asked Rachel.

'Oh, anywhere.' The three boys looked down at their feet.

'Go on, then,' said Jennie. 'If you want to go, go.'

'Take care!' cried Rachel, but they were already out of the flat and rattling down the stair.

'Remember the Kemps and the Rossies?' asked Abby, smiling. 'Hurtling down the stair like that?'

'Don't get sentimental,' said Rachel. 'Used to drive you mad.'

'Come on.' Jim flung open Jennie's door. 'If we've got to see this picture, let's away.'

There was quite a crowd round Rachel's picture in the National Gallery's exhibition of contemporary art. People came up to congratulate her as she ushered in her family, and Madge was scarlet with pride, though Jim was uneasy and Jennie overawed. She still wished another of Rachel's pictures had been selected for this honour but coming here, seeing it on display, she couldn't help but feel that it was rather wonderful after all.

'This is it,' Abby told Frankie, guiding him to the sinister dark oblong glowering from its canvas. 'What do you make of it?'

'Gee, I'm not sure.'

'It's called Tenement,' someone said helpfully.

'Catherine's Land,' Abby whispered. 'Do you get the feeling of the people inside?'

Frankie stood back, screwing up his sailor's eyes. 'Yes, it's funny, but I guess I do. They're not there, yet you feel 'em.'

Abby looked at the signature at the bottom of the painting. Rachel Ritchie. She felt a glow of pride.

'Rachel got there,' she said softly. 'Rachel got where she wanted to go.'

'Guess you did, too,' said Frankie.

They all walked slowly back from the gallery at the foot of the Mound to Catherine's Land. The evening was fine, the children were out playing peevers on the pavements, sending their tiles into the chalked squares, squealing with laughter. At an upstairs window, next to a fluttering victory flag, Jessie Rossie's washing was dancing in the breeze.

'I was going to open up the shop,' Jennie said falteringly. 'I was going to start my dressmaking again.'

'You can still do that,' Madge told her. 'Wherever you live.'

Jennie glanced back at Abby and Rachel. 'It's not all bad living here, you know,' she said defiantly. 'Maybe it's not the New Town or Morningside, but it's warm and friendly. Everyone wants to help, everyone sticks together.'

'That's true,' Abby answered. 'And if you really want to stay here, Jennie, I hope you can. I mean that.'

Jennie said no more but when they saw Marty Finnegan at her door, she paused.

'Did you get one of those letters from Drew's today, Marty?'

'Piece o' nonsense.' Marty laughed, showing her new false teeth. 'Put it in the bucket.'

'We may have to move out, you know, if they turn it into a place for students.'

'Who says they will?'

'Well, we just don't know, do we?'

'Wait and see, then. I'm staying put.'

'Me, too,' said Jennie, and smiled.

Madge, up the stair, was looking at Jennie's door which had once been hers, and at the electric light which had once been gas. Her eyes met Jim's and he took her arm and turned her towards his door.

'Home, Mrs Gilbride,' he murmured. 'Good night, all.'

'Good night,' said Madge. She kissed Jennie and Rachel, then hugged Abby and Frankie. 'Oh, you two – oh, I'm so happy for you!'

'And we're happy for you, Ma.'

'Come on,' said Jim, and Madge, with one last wave, followed him into his flat and closed the door.

'Want to come in for a bit?' Jennie asked her sisters.

Rachel said she would, but Abby said she and Frankie were going up to the hospital to visit Gerald. They exchanged kisses.

'I suppose you think I'm stubborn?' Jennie asked Abby. 'Stubborn and selfish? I know Will wants to go.'

'Don't worry about Will. He'll go himself when he's ready.' Abby's gaze softened. 'You do what you want to do. We understand.'

'And Ma's been here too long, you know, to want to move.'

'I'm beginning to realise that. Look, all I want is for people to have a better way of life. It has to come, Jennie. One day.'

'Do you think I don't want that? I do. I just want it here, that's all.'

'Imagine Catherine's Land modernised,' Rachel said, thoughtfully. 'Baths and showers. Maybe central heating. Maybe a lift!'

'No climbing the stair?' Frankie said with a smile.

But they all knew they wanted more than baths and showers and a lift for the people of Catherine's Land.

When they came out into the street again, Abby stood watching the children.

'This is where change has to start,' she murmured. 'With the children.'

'It'll take time.'

'But change is coming, Frankie. People won't live the way they used to.'

'Just hope it all works out.' He looked at her, a little ruefully. 'Hope is the word, eh?'

'Hope is the word.'

Abby took some pennies from her purse and put them into the children's hands, smiling at their cries, then she turned to look back at the old house. Matthew Kerr's house that he had built so long ago and named after his Catherine. She thought of all the long line of people who had lived and struggled here. What did the future hold for Matthew Kerr's house now?

'I remember the day we arrived,' she said softly. 'Ma was so young, though of course I didn't think so at the time. She was so worried, watching the men bump the piano up the stair. 'Oh, be careful, be careful!' she kept saying, and all the other tenants were looking on and Gramma Ritchie was buzzing round shouting orders. Then Lily MacLaren came drifting down and said did we want a cup of tea, but we ended up making one for her. Oh, Frankie – I feel so sad. Maybe it's true, I'm getting sentimental in my old age!'

'Come on,' he whispered. 'Let's go.'

Still she lingered, looking up at the high windows with their suspect frames, the roof that was no longer sound. But the house had been rescued before. It could be rescued again.

'I remember Rachel saying to Gramma, "Why is this place called a land? I thought a land was a country." And Gramma said, 'It's no' a country, pet, it's just a house.'

'Just a house? Guess it was always more than that.'

'A way of life.'

'That'll soon be gone.'

'Maybe.' But Rachel's picture came into Abby's mind. Her tenement. Humanity one had to feel behind a dark surface. Strong, vibrant, courageous. It came to her that not everything need be changed.

She took Frankie's arm and they turned away, walking slowly, then more quickly, as behind them the evening sunshine lingered over Catherine's Land and the children played.

Also by Anne Douglas available from Piatkus:

AS THE YEARS GO BY

Forced by the post-war boom to leave their shabby
Edinburgh tenement for a new bungalow on the outskirts
of the city, Madge Gilbride is comforted by the fact that
at least she has her family near her. And when her
grandsons, Will and Hamish, fall in love with local girls
she is delighted.

But life is not plain sailing – especially for Will. In love
with the fiery Kate Rossie, he discovers she wants both a
husband and a political career. Conventional Will makes a
choice he will regret for years – a sensible marriage of
convenience to the suitable Sara.

As she watches her grandchildren with their own families'
joys and troubles, Madge can't help but remember her old
tenement home and hope that the new generation of
Gilbrides never forget their roots . . .

978-0-7499-3125-4

BRIDGE OF HOPE

Josie Morrow and Lina Braid are best friends. But although Josie has an understanding with Angus, Lina's brother, her mother has far more grandiose plans than for her to marry a local boy. She sees civil engineer Duncan Guthrie, a lodger in their Queensferry boarding house, as a much better catch. However, it is Lina who Duncan falls for, forcing her to break her promise to her childhood sweetheart in order to marry him.

Josie believes she could never hurt Angus in that way . . . until she meets Firth of Forth bridge worker Matt MacLeod. But there are more barriers to her relationship with Matt than the fact that she is already spoken for. Matt is an atheist and unacceptable to her staunch Presbyterian father. Josie is torn between her family and her love for Matt. Does she have the courage to follow her heart and accept the consequences?

978-0-7499-3232-9

BUTTERFLY GIRLS

Rose Burnett, Martie Stewart and Alex Kelsie grew up in
the Colonies, a housing development by the Water of
Leith. Only Rose, a lawyer's daughter, did not belong.
Still, when Alex and Martie both decide to train as nurses
in Edinburgh, they're relieved to see Rose's friendly face –
even if she is now Staff Burnett.

Whilst Martie is determined to escape the misery of her
childhood and find a rich husband, Alex has more
romantic dreams. She's had a crush on Rose's brother
since they were children and is secretly excited when he's
admitted to hospital with a mild case of TB. But, though
Tim Burnett finally seems to notice her, nurses in the 1950s
are strictly forbidden from any personal involvement with
their patients.

They all laugh when one of the patients nicknames them
the 'Butterfly Girls' after the Butterfly wards they work on,
but, as Rose points out, nursing is for keeping your feet on
the ground, not flying. Alex is risking more than her heart
in pursuing a relationship with Tim . . .

978-0-7499-3308-1

GINGER STREET

The Millar family live next door to the Riettis on Ginger Street, a row of Victorian tenements on Edinburgh's south side but their circumstances couldn't be more different. Ruth Millar would like to stay on at school but her father's salary as a grocer's assistant is barely enough to put food on the table, let alone such luxuries as an education. By contrast the Riettis own the local corner shop and a little cafe at the end of Ginger Street.

Ruth's father dreams of one day owning his own business. Meanwhile Ruth secretly dreams of Nicco Rietti. But not only is Nicco older, he is Italian and Catholic, three things which make him out of bounds for Ruth, especially with the threat of war on the horizon . . .

978-0-7499-3383-8